MW01534602

By Kris Tualla:

A Woman of Choice

A Prince of Norway

and

A PRIMER FOR
BEGINNING AUTHORS

A Prince

of Norway

Kris Tualla

Goodnight Publishing
http://www.GoodnightPublishing.com

A Prince of Norway is a work of fiction. Names, characters, places and incidents are products of the author's imagination or are used fictitiously and are not to be construed as real. Any resemblance to actual events, locales, organizations, or persons, living or dead, is entirely coincidental.

Published in the United States of America through:

Goodnight Publishing
www.GoodnightPublishing.com

info@GoodnightPublishing.com

© 2010 by Kris Tualla

All rights reserved. No part of this book may be used or reproduced in any form or by any means without the prior written consent of the Publisher, except for brief quotations used in critical articles or reviews.

Goodnight Publishing and its Logo are Registered Trademarks.

ISBN-10: 1451503326
EAN-13: 9781451503326

For my precious husband,
who supports me with
endless love and care.

With love to Tanita, Seana, Jon-Paul
and Marisa. Thanks for being such wonderful people.
To Ashley and Mason who bring me joy.

And to my Friday Coffee friends
for sharing my journey.

Chapter One

*Y*ou're a *what?*" Sydney blurted.

Nicolas Hansen's wife of four months gaped at him and her dark brows plunged dangerously. He stroked a forefinger across his upper lip, calluses rasping his stubble.

"A prince."

Nicolas lowered himself onto the leather ottoman in the event his feisty spouse's shocked response involved fists. His gaze flickered around his dark, mannish study, and landed back on her.

He cleared his throat. "It's on my mother's side. Her grandfather was King Christian the Sixth of Norway and Denmark."

Sydney's wide, gray-green eyes did not leave his, though her hand flailed to the side in search of a seat. Nicolas shoved his favorite leather chair toward her with his foot.

She submerged between the worn, over-stuffed arms as if she hoped their bulk could block out the bizarre reality he had just doused her with. "So those portraits in the stairwell…"

"…look royal for a reason," Nicolas finished the sentence.

Her stunned expression didn't shift. "*Skitt.*"

Surprised at her imitation of his scatological Norse, Nicolas laughed.

Sydney—decidedly *not* laughing—pressed palms against her violently flushed cheeks. "Why didn't you tell me?"

"To be truthful, I forgot. It's not as though we live in Norway." Nicolas scraped his fingers through his hair and shrugged. If he acted unconcerned, perhaps she would take his next words well.

"Nor am I in any danger of becoming king, I don't believe."

"You don't *believe?*" she shouted. Her dilated pupils obliterated any trace of color in her eyes. "Nicolas! You're an *American!*"

As if he were unaware.

He dragged his gaze away from hers and hefted the package of letters which—after an eighteen month, multi-continental sojourn—had arrived at his estate that day. The missives very strongly demanded his immediate appearance at the royal court in Christiania, Norway or he would suffer the penalties of his disobedience.

"Nicolas?" she squeaked. Her cheeks hollowed and lost their bloom. "What is this all about?"

He exhaled, resigned. There was no point in delaying the telling; it would only anger her and postpone his preparations for departure. He fixed his gaze on hers and arranged his features in a deliberately calm set.

"After Denmark's unfortunate alliance with Napoleon, Norway fell to Sweden in 1814; an act completely disregarding the previous five centuries or so that Norway happily spent under Denmark's sovereignty. So what remains of Norway's royal family has decided to pull together their various members and test the viability of finally gaining the country for themselves."

"And choose a king of their *own*, not a Danish one?" It was an accusation more than a question. In spite of his attempt to downplay the summons, Sydney looked desperate as a drowning cat. She leaned back and away from him. "Is there any wine?"

Nicolas pushed up from his perch and poured her a glass. Her hand trembled as she reached for the crystal goblet. He knelt beside her chair while she gulped the burgundy liquid in a very un-ladylike manner. He stroked his fingers through her straight, dark hair; that particular action usually soothed her mood.

"Don't worry, *min presang.*" Ever since the day he confessed he loved her, Nicolas had called her *my gift*. He kissed her temple and inhaled the warm, rosy scent of her. "Other than my trip to Norway and back, nothing about our lives will change."

Sydney wagged her head and fixed her intense gaze on his. Mossy pewter shards pierced his fantasy and it shattered with irrevocable finality.

"I love you, Nicolas. You are sensible of that. But you are so very, *very* wrong."

₨₧

Nicolas stirred and stretched in his sturdy cherrywood bed, glad as always that it was built for his substantial six-foot-four frame. He reached for Sydney in the dark, but she wasn't beside him. Kirstie must be hungry. He resettled and waited for her to return.

Sydney had been quiet during dinner, and afterward busied herself upstairs with his six-year-old son, Stefan, and their three-month-old daughter, Kirstie. For the first evening since their wedding, she didn't sit with him in his study. He didn't know why she avoided him—well, that was not entirely true. The revelation of his royal blood was an obvious shock to his new wife. But he sorely missed her company nonetheless.

Now he ached to feel her soothing warmth against him. The unsettling letters had his gut twisted, and his dozing dreams were filled with grasping images of Norway. But king? The idea was ludicrous. Impossible. Unwanted.

And yet it coiled seductively in his core.

After a pace, Nicolas rolled over to look for light coming from the nursery door. That portal was dark; but faint candlelight seeped under their bedroom door. Unable to fall asleep without her, he threw the covers back, pulled on his drawstring drawers, and went in search of his missing wife.

One step out of the bedroom and he saw her. Sydney sat on the polished staircase, staring at the display of gilt-framed portraits by the light of a single candle. The groan of wood under his bare feet announced him. She looked up at him as he descended the stairs.

He was surprised by her red-rimmed eyes and wet cheeks. "Sydney? What's amiss?"

She sniffed and ran her hand under her nose. "You're royalty."

His sardonic grin showed how much stock he put in that. He

waved a dismissive hand.

"I'm the same man I was this morning. I'm the same man you married. Please don't trouble yourself over this." He lowered himself to the stairstep above her and encased her with his legs. He began to massage her shoulders through the wide neckline of her cotton and lace nightgown.

Though he wasn't certain Sydney would give him any purchase, she leaned into him. A faint purr of appreciation encouraged his ministrations, yet she continued to wipe her cheeks.

"Can you tell me why, exactly, these people insist that my new husband travel halfway around the world?" she ventured, her soft voice ringing clear in the night-shrouded manor.

Nicolas coughed sleep from his voice. "My grandmother's brother Frederick became king in 1746. He had two wives, a mistress, and seventeen children."

Sydney glanced at him, her brow crinkled and her mouth slanted sideways. Clearly she was not favorably impressed thus far. But she was listening.

"His eldest son Christian became king after him. He died in 1808 and *his* son, Frederick took over. Are you with me thus far?"

"Yes, I think so," she murmured.

"*This* particular Frederick was defeated in Napoleon's war, and in 1814 my cousin Christian the Eighth became king."

Sydney snorted softly. "They weren't much for changing names, were they?"

Nicolas chuckled, glad to see her mood lifting a bit. "No. At any rate, when Sweden made their move on Norway, Christian abdicated."

"And that is how, in 1814, Sweden gained control of Norway?"

"Yes."

"And now these seventeen descendents of Frederick want to take the throne back?"

"Yes."

Sydney's shoulders tensed, bunching under his hands. "What do they expect of you?" she asked at length.

"They wish to know if I'm with them or against them." He pushed his thumbs into the tightening knots at the base of her neck. She groaned and her shoulders slanted downward. "And they want my land."

"Mm. There," she grunted and tilted her head. "How much land are we talking about?"

"Fifteen thousand acres."

Sydney turned and stared up at Nicolas from her nest between his thighs. In the dim candlelight her eyes were wide, dark pools fringed in stiff black foliage. "Fifteen thousand acres! Nicolas! Your estate here is only five hundred—and Rickard leases two hundred of those!"

He nodded; when she compared his holdings that way, the one was considerably more impressive. He felt his face grow warm, glad she most likely couldn't discern his blush in the dim light.

"*Skitt*," she huffed.

Nicolas smiled. "You've adopted my favorite word."

Sydney shrugged a little under his fingers. "It's a good word. And it suits the situation."

"It does that, I suppose."

Sydney leaned against him again and he resumed his massage; he felt her relax a little. Her voice was soft, but her words were hard.

"What happens if you don't go?"

Much as he hoped she wouldn't, he expected she would ask him that. Since the letters arrived, he had asked himself the same thing several times. He pulled a deep breath; there was no way around answering her.

"I lose my land with no recompense. And I lose all of my hereditary claims," he said.

"Are those important to you?"

Nicolas hesitated, wrestling with his response.

His first journey to Christiania had been thrust upon him, but he met it with as much panache as a nineteen-year-old from the wilds of Missouri could muster. Though the landscape and customs were unfamiliar, and the language demanded his undivided concentration, he couldn't deny that something in the center of his being recognized Norway as home. Once summoned, that distant memory bubbled up from his belly and nested behind his heart.

Yet alone in his study earlier tonight, he tried to convince himself that he really didn't need to go. He was quite well situated on his estate in Cheltenham. His financial status was such that he could still manage if he were to relinquish his holdings, cut his ties with Christiania and gave up his royal hereditary claims. He tried to convince himself none of that was important because he lived here. On his estate, in the Missouri Territory, in America.

But he failed. Miserably.

"Nicolas?" Sydney looked at him over her shoulder.

Facing her trusting gaze, he wasn't capable of hiding anything from her. "Yes," he admitted. "They are."

Sydney drew a deep breath and let it out slowly. "All right, then. You'll do what you must."

"*Jeg elsker deg, min presang.*" I love you, my gift.

"*Jeg elsker deg også,*" she replied.

Nicolas slid his hands off her shoulders and inside the front of her soft cotton nightgown. He smiled as he cupped her breasts, pliant and warm. He leaned over and nuzzled her ear, inhaling the scent of her hair. His desire for her solidified and tightened in his groin. He needed her in so many ways.

"Now, my wife, will you please come back to my bed?" he whispered.

April 2, 1820

Nicolas rummaged through the recesses of the stable storeroom and dragged out his dusty travel trunk. He brushed it off, wiped it down, and opened it up.

A cloud of memories wafted out on the musty odor of neglect. The first time he packed this trunk he had been excited. And—if he were honest—scared. Norway was distant and unreal, existing only in his grandparent's memories and his mother's descriptions.

Now he would pack again, but this time with diminished enthusiasm. He wished he could simply give up the land and the hereditary ties, and remain here with Sydney and his children. But the arrival of the letters made it clear that those things were more a part of him than he ever realized.

And then, of course, there was the possibility of becoming king of Norway.

Nicolas had no idea what to do with that startling twist. Though of direct royal lineage, he was born and raised as an American. Kings—or princes—of any country met suspicion in this young land, less than fifty years from claiming her independence from an oppressive British lunatic. It never crossed his mind that he might be tapped for a throne.

He had to confess, though, he was quite intrigued by the prospect.

Who wouldn't be?

Nicolas set the open trunk on the lawn to freshen in the sun. He tested the lock; with a good oiling it should do. Then he headed to his study to draft the letter informing his cousins that he did intend to come to Christiania and should arrive in late June.

At dinner, Sydney's manner was cool and succinct. She waited for him at the formal dining room table, linen napkin resting across her lap and hands folded in front of her empty china dinner plate. Before their maid Maribeth carried in the first platter of food, she asked, "How will you get to Norway?"

Her query caught him off his guard; he hadn't yet thought his journey through. "I sailed from Baltimore the last time. That seems reasonable to do again, I suppose," he said.

Her calm tone betrayed no emotion. "And how will you get to Baltimore?"

Nicolas accepted the roasted lamb from a wordless Maribeth with an appreciative sniff and an absent-minded smile. A sudden idea brightened his answer. "I believe I'll try one of those new steam paddleboats down the Mississippi, and then up the Ohio into Pennsylvania. That should ease the journey."

"And then?"

He looked at the ceiling and tried to imagine a map on its recently re-plastered surface. "I believe going by river it's about seven hundred miles to western Pennsylvania. I understand that might be accomplished in as little as two weeks."

"How long will it take from there?" Sydney pressed.

Nicolas squinted to see his mind's map more clearly. "It's about two hundred and fifty miles across Pennsylvania to Philadelphia. Land travel is about forty miles a day in good weather."

He turned his attention back to the meal, forked a slab of the savory meat onto his plate, and handed the platter to Sydney. She handed him the bowl of green beans in exchange. Her expression was still flat, she gave nothing away. Unable to discern her mood, he spoke to fill her silence.

"And if I'm going to Philadelphia, I should take the opportunity to check on my mother's estate."

"That's three weeks of travel," she said, ignoring his last statement. She meticulously buttered a roll. "How far is Philadelphia from Baltimore?"

"Only eighty miles, give or take," he said and tossed her an unconcerned shrug for good measure. He was under some sort of inquisition and hoped to deflect her intensity until he could figure out why. She didn't appear angry and that fact was oddly worrisome.

The pair ate in unexplained quiet for a course. Nicolas generously refilled their wine. Sydney was clearly pondering hard on something; her countenance was somber, pensive. Her darkening eyes moved over the room's inanimate inhabitants, but Nicolas doubted she saw any of them. He was afraid to guess what she was considering. Certainly she wouldn't leave him because of this.

Would she?

The possibility stumbled his heartbeat.

Finally her soft voice slid through the clatter of silver on china. "How long does it take to sail to Norway?"

Nicolas swallowed his food and cleared his throat. "Four weeks to sail from Baltimore to London, and another week to sail to Christiania."

"Five weeks, then. And coming back is the same?"

"No, it's a bit longer—ten days, maybe two weeks more since we sail against the current."

"So the sailing there and back would take twelve weeks. Three months," Sydney calculated.

"Yes, I suppose it would."

Sydney chewed her last bite of lamb for a long time before accepting another helping of green beans. Her brow wrinkled. "Add the six weeks to get from St. Louis to Philadelphia and back. That's eighteen weeks so far."

"It's only two days, Philadelphia to Baltimore," Nicolas quickly pointed out. As though *that* was in any manner helpful.

"Nineteen. Two months going and two-and-a-half on the return?"

"That's about right." Nicolas considered Sydney. She was definitely working up to some point, but whatever it was still eluded him. But her brow puckered attractively and half of her coral-colored lower lip was caught in her teeth. He smiled; his wife was so beautiful.

Maribeth set a warm slice of apple-raisin pie in front of each of them. Nicolas smelled cinnamon and nutmeg steaming from the pastry and his mouth watered in spite of the large meal. He picked off a chunk of crust. It flaked deliciously in his fingers.

Maribeth returned with two cups of strong black coffee. Sydney added cream to hers. "When is the latest you can sail from Norway to come back?"

"The end of September, to be safe," Nicolas answered through a tasty bite of pie. He sipped the aromatic coffee to wash it down.

Sydney stared directly at him then. Her intense expression pinned him like a hunting dirk. "That's six months from now. Allowing a month to prepare for the journey, and four-and-a-half months of travel, that means you would have but six or seven weeks in Christiania to complete your business."

Nicolas gasped and nearly choked on a chunk of hot apple. He coughed it free but his gut twisted, threatening to expel his supper. He now knew her point—and he had walked headlong into it.

No part of her countenance eased, screwing the dirk deeper. "Can you guarantee that's possible?"

He waved one hand to push the imagined knife from his chest. He tried to sound offhand, confident. "I shall certainly try, of course."

"And if you're not successful?" Her words punctured him as effectively as the phantom dirk's blade. Nicolas tried to concoct a parry to deflect her, but couldn't. She had him.

"Nicolas?" Her voice was still soft. Like the underbelly of a wolf.

His shoulders sagged, pressed down by truth. "Then I'm there 'til spring."

Sydney jerked a nod and leaned back in her chair. "That settles it."

"What?"

"I'm going with you."

"What!" he exploded.

She leaned forward and spoke slowly, distinctly. "I am going with you."

Nicolas scoffed. "What about Kirstie? She can't be weaned so young!"

"She's coming as well. And before you ask, so is Stefan."

"*Helvetet med det!* That's absurd!" he shouted.

"Why?"

Nicolas planted his elbows on the table and spoke over tightly clenched hands. His knuckles blanched. "You want to take an infant and a six-year-old halfway around the world? For what purpose?"

Sydney pushed back her carved maple armchair and stood. She rested fists on the table and her glare cannon-balled across it. "You want me to spend the first year of our marriage alone? For what purpose?"

"The journey's too arduous!" he bellowed.

"Being apart from you would be too arduous! Our full marital relationship has only one month's maturity!" she retorted, her voice rising in pitch.

Nicolas threw his hands wide, barely missing the wine bottle. "There's no certainty that I'd be gone a full year!"

"There's no guarantee that you won't!" Sydney declaimed. "And I don't care to spend our first anniversary with you living on another continent!"

Nicolas rose and faced his angry wife across the table. Her stubborn nature and refusal to accept his decrees without argument were in full infuriating force. He attempted to sound calm, using irrefutable male logic in the face of her feminine fury.

"Sydney. Be reasonable. It's simply too dangerous!"

She glowered at him. "Oh? Might you die?"

Nicolas stepped back with that direct hit, but his wife didn't flinch.

"Please do me the honor of answering my inquiry, Nicolas." She hissed his name.

He narrowed his eyes and ground out his words. "There's always a chance, with ocean travel, that something might go amiss."

Sydney stood straight; righteous anger made her taller than her five-and-a-half feet. Her eyes burned into his, green flames under thick black smoke. "Do you truly expect me to sit here alone, waiting and wondering for a year, armed with that knowledge?"

Nicolas slammed his fist on the table and the silverware scattered for cover. "Madam! I expect you to obey my wishes!" he shouted.

Sydney crossed her arms. Fierce and defiant, she stared at him with lips pursed so tightly that they lost color.

"Fine," she spat.

That was unexpected. "What?"

"I said fine." Her thunderous expression didn't match her words.

Nicolas cocked his head, wary. "We're in agreement, then?"

"We're in agreement. You want me to remain here, with your children, while you go off to Norway. Alone."

"Yes…" Nicolas felt he was walking into a trap. Ridiculous. As her husband and head of the household he merely asserted his authority. After all, it was the sensible path to take.

"It's your wish to be separated from me," she added.

"No! That's not my wish, Sydney, not at all." Nicolas relaxed a little and injected a hint of sympathy into his tone. "But it's for the best. You must know that."

"I see."

Sydney sat down to finish her pie and Nicolas followed suit. But she didn't meet his eyes, nor could he engage her in conversation. She set her napkin by her half-finished dessert. Then she gripped her garnet and filigreed wedding ring and spun it on her finger.

"Our separation shall begin now."

Nicolas scowled. "What do you mean by that?"

"It's your belief that you'll be better off without my company on this 'arduous' journey. If that's true, you should begin your preparation in all aspects. I shall sleep in the nursery."

"Sydney!" Nicolas barked.

One eyebrow lifted. "What?"

"That's not at all necessary!"

Sydney stood and, with a very sweet smile, defied him. "Yes, Nicolas, it very much is."

Chapter Two

April 3, 1820

*N*icolas stood in his bedroom staring into his wardrobe. He was washed for dinner and still half-naked, when Sydney came looking for him.

"I need clothes," he stated.

The carved cherry wardrobe held a few work shirts. Even fewer dress shirts hung next to his navy blue velvet frock coat and brocade waistcoat. Three pair of nankeen breeches lay folded on a shelf next to the calfskin pair. The aromas of camphor and cedar wafted out.

"And a new greatcoat." He looked down at his wife. "I can't appear at court wrapped in furs! I'll go to St. Louis tomorrow and order a suitable wardrobe."

Sydney plucked a single long blond hair from that dark blue velvet.

"I love the way this color matches your eyes, even if your loosed hairs do stand out against it like chalk on slate."

She wiggled her fingers and the abandoned strand floated out of sight. "Will you be gone overnight?"

"I see no reason, if I leave early enough and the weather holds."

"Might I go with you then?"

Nicolas welcomed the idea of her company on the twenty-mile round trip. Perhaps—after sleeping only one night in the nursery—

she was already softening toward him.

He smiled down at her. "Even so. Do you have a purpose?"

Sydney nodded. "I want to show Kirstie to Rosie. She hasn't seen her since she was born."

"Oh."

Nicolas wasn't accustomed to the notion that his new wife and his ex-whore had become friends. Their daughter's untimely January birth—away from his estate and in St. Louis—had required Rosie's help. For her efforts, though, he would remain forever grateful.

"And books," Sydney added. "Deeply romantic ones. If you intend to abandon me for such a long time, I'll need some type of suitable diversion in my bed."

Nicolas clenched his jaw, irritated at the reminder of her mutiny.

"Fine," he acquiesced. "We'll leave at dawn."

Sydney slid her hands over his chest and kissed him very, very well. He pulled her close and tangled his tongue with hers. She moaned a little and pressed her hips against him.

Her hands dropped to his arse and her fingernails raked over his breeches causing his muscles to tense and quiver. He could feel her pulse quicken when his lips dropped to her neck. His need pooled in his groin.

"*Min presang?*" he whispered.

"Supper's ready," she whispered back, and slipped from his grip.

That night she slept in the nursery again.

Forbannet sta kvinne! Damned stubborn woman!

Naked as was his habit, Nicolas tossed in his lonely bed and kicked the cloying covers to the floor. He was completely unable to reason with her because she would not *listen* to reason!

How could he, in good conscience, take her and the children on such a long expedition? What about the estate? What about Stefan's schooling? How could infant Kirstie's needs be adequately seen to?

"*Skitt!*" he grunted and pummeled his pillow into lumpy submission. "*Skitt! Skitt! SKITT!*"

He swore he heard a giggle through the nursery door.

Skitt.

April 4, 1820
St. Louis

The morning dawned gray and heavy as the slate and stone that comprised the Hansen manor. Sydney was worried they might be rained on, but by the time Nicolas drove the carriage into St. Louis, the sky had transformed into polished turquoise striated by mere remnants of silver vapor.

Nicolas drove them straight to the tailor shop and hired a boy to carry a message to Rosie for Sydney. Then they got down to the business of creating his Norway-worthy wardrobe.

"Is this the woman who needed the breeches?" The tailor Ibram Mosel eyed her over a pair of wired spectacles. "Did they fit?"

She smiled. "Like a glove, sir! And if they were indicative of your skills, then my husband will be the envy of Christiania!"

"Husband, you say?" Ibram turned to Nicolas, eyebrows echoing the upper curve of his glasses.

"We were married, um, last winter. Year," Nicolas sputtered.

Sydney felt her cheeks bloom. Their marriage, after all, was only a month older than their daughter.

Ibram winked at the healthy three-month-old in Sydney's arms. "In plenty of time, eh?" He chuckled and pushed Nicolas toward the mirror. "Let's see if marriage has changed you in other ways, shall we?"

While Ibram measured her husband, Sydney moved around the small shop, fingering fabrics and examining buttons. She turned and caught Nicolas watching her in the tailor's tall mirror. His intense navy stare shot straight to her belly. How could she hold on to her resolve to stay away from his bed when his sensual gaze warmed her womb so easily?

Ibram's voice doused them both. "Stop thinking about her, Mister Hansen. I need an accurate inseam." Nicolas blushed and his gaze skittered away from hers.

The shop door blew open.

Rosie entered in a whoosh of taffeta and flowery perfume. "Where's that baby girl?"

Sydney laughed her relief at the raucous distraction and hurried to place Kirstie in Rosie's eager arms.

"Oh! She's the spit of Nicky, the poor thing!" Rosie teased. She winked at her erstwhile customer and jerked her head toward Sydney. "Even with a woman this beautiful, you big blond Norwegians still win out!"

"It's a curse," Nicolas teased back over Ibram's head. "Ask the English. Or the Scots. Or the French. Shall I go on?"

"Pah!" Rosie waved her free hand at him.

"Do you have time for coffee?" Sydney asked.

Rosie grinned. "As long as you let me hold this little princess, I have lotsa time!"

The women walked a couple blocks to a café. Silver wisps now burned away, the turquoise sky was unblemished.

"Coffee. Strong and black," Rosie said to the serving girl. She turned to Sydney. "I'm not always up this time of day."

Sydney laughed. "I'll have mine with cream, please."

Rosie held Kirstie on her lap. "Your marriage is going well?" Rosie probed. "No ghosts?"

"No ghosts. We are in the midst of a minor disagreement, however." Sydney explained the letter from Christiania, and her desire to go to Norway.

Rosie cocked her head. "Are you sure about that? It's a long way and a helluva lot of work!"

"I know, Rosie. But I would rather that, than to live without him." Sydney sipped her coffee before giving her nightmare a voice. "And if something happened to him…"

"Now don't go thinkin' such as that! After all you been through, the both of ya? And to find each other and all? Nothing'll keep you apart."

A smile tugged one corner of Sydney's mouth. "I've begun a campaign to convince him I should go."

"Oh?" Rosie leaned forward.

"I'm sleeping in the nursery."

Rosie rocked back and hooted. "Ha! That'll win him for sure! I swear, that man's got the strongest—" Embarrassed horror defined her abruptly silent features.

Sydney rescued her, firmly capping her erupting jealousy. "Yes, Rosie. He does."

The fancy woman blushed right through her rouge. "I'm so sorry, Sydney."

"It was before he knew me. Don't think a thing of it."

Rosie nodded and petted Kirstie's hair. The girl squirmed and whimpered.

Sydney stood and lifted the infant from Rosie's lap. "It seems I need to go to the carriage and feed her."

Rosie stood as well. Her expression was pensive and a little sad. "Thanks for gettin' me so's I could see her. She's a beauty, and there's no doubt."

"I'm glad I saw you, Rosie." Sydney's hug crackled Rosie's abundant taffeta sleeves.

Rosie held her longer than Sydney expected, and then leaned away and winked at her. "Best of luck on your trip to Norway."

April 9, 1820
Cheltenham

Nicolas and Sydney sat on the front porch after dinner, listening to the forest whisper in the dark. A quarter moon cast weak shadows on the newly greening lawn. There was no breeze to relieve the spring humidity that condensed on his night-cooled skin.

Nicolas sipped brandy as was his habit, but Sydney had already finished her second glass of port wine. Sleeping away from his wife made him jumpy and the brandy did help soothe his nerves. Perhaps she grew tired of their nightly separation and was using the port for the same reason? Perhaps she would open her door soon.

Even though the brandy calmed his nerves, it did nothing to assuage his mounting yearning. He hardened just watching her fingers trail across her throat. Slide along the neckline of her gown. Brush over her bosom. Curl in her lap.

Skitt.

Indignant protests from disgruntled chickens jarred the night. Nicolas grabbed Sydney's arm and she almost yelped before he pushed his forefinger against her lips and jerked his head toward the front door. He pulled her into the house.

"Stay here," he commanded. She nodded, wide-eyed.

He trotted down the hall and retrieved his rifle from its nest by the kitchen. Then he slipped out the back door. With an experienced predator's stealth, he hurried silently toward the chicken coop as his eyes swept the yard, seeking any movement.

The door to the chicken coop opened and Nicolas froze. A man stepped out and carefully closed the door, slipping the latch into place with an almost imperceptible click. He carried a dead chicken by its feet.

"I would suggest you move no further," Nicolas warned.

The man's head jerked in Nick's direction before he bolted toward the woods. Nicolas fired the rifle in his direction.

"Stop or I won't miss the next time!" he bellowed. The man whirled to face him. The dead chicken bounced off his leg.

Nicolas trotted closer. When he was a few yards away, he realized the man was a Negro. Discarding the chicken, he charged at Nicolas, fists swinging in wild arcs.

Nicolas had the man by half-a-foot, fifty pounds, and ten years of experience. With an economy of movement he grabbed the Negro by the neck and dragged him toward the house, ripping his shirt as the desperate man resisted his capture. When Nicolas reached the back porch, he planted his sizable fist in the Negro's belly and then flung him onto the floor. Sydney waited with an oil lamp. Her eyes and mouth rounded when she saw the thief.

"We had a weasel in the coop. He got one of the hens." Nicolas nudged the man hard with his boot. "Stand up!"

The Negro climbed to his feet and straightened with difficulty. He lifted his chin and turned to face Nicolas. Sydney gasped.

"What?" Nicolas frowned at her.

She pointed and her hand shook. "His back."

"Turn around!" Nicolas barked.

The black man's back was a web of pink scars and fresh red weals. Nicolas's stomach clenched. "*Hva i Gud's navn*—are you a runaway?"

"I'll die before I go back. So if that's what you have in mind, I'll ask that you show me mercy and be quick about it." His educated accent was a surprise.

Nicolas looked at Sydney, but her gaze went behind him. He twisted to look over his shoulder. Standing in the outer light of the lamp was a beautiful Negress with skin the color of lightly creamed tea. She couldn't be more than eighteen years old. And she was very pregnant.

"Sarah, no-o-o!" the man moaned. "Why didn't you stay hidden?"

Sarah looked from the man to Nicolas, then to Sydney. For a

tense moment, no one moved. Then Sydney stepped forward and held up the lantern.

"You may have the chicken," she said.

"It's not your business, Sydney!" Nicolas countered. His harsh tone reflected his concern; helping slaves escape was a serious situation. "Stay out of this."

Sydney faced him, her jaw set in warning. She glared at him for a moment and he felt chastised to his marrow by her righteous determination. Then she set the lantern on the porch and disappeared into the house.

"Please, sir. I beg you to let her go," the man pleaded. "I'm the one who stole the hen. She's innocent."

"Jaqriel…" Sarah's voice was Cajun spiced. "I cannot go on without you."

Jack rolled his eyes and shook his head. His shoulders rounded and he curved inward with a soft sob.

Nicolas narrowed his eyes at Jack. "How far have you come?"

"I—I don't rightly know." He straightened again and met Nicolas's eyes. "How far is it to St. Louis?"

"About ten miles."

Jack's uneasy look jumped to Sarah. "I reckon eighty miles, give or take."

"In how many days?"

"Five."

And she's far gone with the babe. Nicolas frowned at one then the other, pondering his course of action.

Sydney reappeared carrying a quilt, her old work shirt, and a small cast iron skillet. She knocked past Nicolas and handed the items to Sarah.

"These things are mine to give." Her stance and her tone challenged Nicolas to disagree. "The shirt should fit your man."

Sarah accepted the gifts with a small curtsy. "Bless you, Ma'am."

"And take a second chicken."

All eyes turned at Nicolas's words; surprise at his sudden transition was displayed on every face. He ignored his own wife's apparent lack of faith in him and continued, "Do you need a place to sleep?"

"No, we travel at night," Jack answered.

"Let's get the bird." Nicolas turned toward the coop. "You can be on your way, then."

April 10, 1820

Nicolas awoke at dawn with the immediate need to relieve his bladder. It took him a moment to realize where he was.

After yester eve's episode with the escaped slaves, he and Sydney walked through the house in stone-like silence. He retreated to his study and she stomped upstairs. Nicolas finished yet another glass of brandy in his study and knew that his banishment from his wife's bed needed to end.

And it needed to end now.

He shoved open the door between his bedroom and the nursery and stepped in, decided and determined. Moonlight filtered through the clouds and grayed the room, so he had no trouble crossing to his wife's narrow bed. He dropped to his knees beside it, and rested his face in the crook of her neck. She was warm and soft and smelled of rose oil.

"I need you, wife," he declared. "I love you. I miss you. *Gud forbanner det*, I burn for you."

She turned toward him. "Nicolas—"

"Hush, *min presang*."

He dug through the bedclothes in search of her. When his hand found what he desired, he climbed onto the small bed and kneeled between her legs. He pushed his breeches down to his knees and lowered himself to her. Entering her sent heat—and indescribable relief—coursing outward from his groin until his entire body tingled with it. He stroked urgently, satisfying his need with single-minded resolve, and sweeping her to a sobbing, shuddering release in the process. The last thing he remembered was her lying trembling in his arms.

Now his head felt too heavy for his neck, so he used the chamber pot rather than venture out to the privy. Then he tucked himself back on the narrow cot alongside his wife.

"You couldn't bide eight days without me in your bed," she whispered, startling him. He didn't know she was awake. He grunted, not able to conjure words to refute her.

She twisted toward him. "What makes you believe you could

last eight months or more?"

Nicolas rubbed his hand over his aching forehead. "It's different when I see you daily and you sleep under my roof," he objected.

"You're a very passionate man, Nicolas. We both know that well. What happens when your hand no longer suffices? Will you seek comfort from a more substantial source?" she pressed.

Nicolas leaned up on an elbow and faced her; his unbelieving shock sculpted his countenance. "Are you daring to suggest that I would break my marital vows?"

"No..."

"Then what?" he growled.

"I'm suggesting that you don't put yourself directly in the path of that temptation." Sydney rested a cool hand on his cheek. Her eyes were seductively dark in the pinking light. "But if you don't care for your own needs husband, then I beg you to please have a care for mine. For without your presence I will most assuredly die of loneliness."

Chapter Three

*N*icolas had been at the ancient oak desk in his study for two hours later that morning when Sydney came in and set a mug of coffee and a still-warm oat muffin at his elbow.

"What are you working at so diligently?" She leaned on the desk and looked over his scribbles while Nicolas bit into the muffin.

"How far is Shelbyville from Louisville?" he mumbled through the pastry.

"Twelve miles. Why?"

Nicolas washed down the muffin with a long swallow of the strong black coffee. "If we plan to winter in Christiania, then we might take our time getting there."

Sydney slammed upright. "We?"

"We could get off the paddle boat in Louisville and spend some time with your parents."

Sydney's hands flew to her face and her eyes welled, gratifying him deeply. Why had it taken him so long to see this was absolutely the right thing to do?

"Oh, Nicolas!" She threw her arms around his neck and very nearly choked him. "It's been so long since I last saw my mother! Do you truly mean this?"

Warmth, thick as winter syrup, suffused his chest and he pulled Sydney into his lap. "I do, *min presang*. I don't know what I was thinking. I could never leave you for so long."

Sydney relaxed into him and her joy lit the room. "I love you, husband."

Nicolas chuckled. "And I hope you still do when this questionable odyssey is completed!"

ℰℭ

"…the four passages."

"Five."

Nicolas raised his brows in question over the bowl of buttered carrots. "Five?"

His wife nodded. "I'll need assistance on the journey. I'll not be able to handle all of the cooking, the laundry, a young boy who needs schooling *and* a suckling infant on my own."

Nicolas pondered the situation. "I see."

"Might I go?"

Both Nicolas and Sydney swiveled in search of the source of the question. Only Maribeth, their elder housekeeper Addie's young assistant, was in the room. Sydney looked at Nicolas, her surprise evident. Quiet and shy by nature, Maribeth rarely said anything at all.

The reticent maid continued, "Please, Sir. I've never been anywhere. In my twenty-three years, I've never been beyond St. Louis."

Surprised by the shy girl's sudden and completely unexpected interjection, Nicolas didn't respond right off. Maribeth shifted her supplication to Sydney.

"I'm a hard worker, Ma'am, and I don't complain. And Stefan and I are fast friends."

Maribeth's brown eyes widened and her cheeks flushed with the effort of speaking up. Nicolas realized with a start, that the girl could actually be quite pretty. "I can cook, too. Addie taught me."

Nicolas threw his hands up and laughed.

"*Ved, Gud!*" he wheezed. "In six years as your employer I've not heard you put two sentences together!"

Maribeth's color deepened to an astonishing shade of crimson. She dropped her gaze to her rough, twisting hands.

"But," he continued between chuckles, "I've no objection. It's up to Mrs. Hansen."

Maribeth turned to his wife, who then turned to him and said, "You'll need to hire help for the estate while we're gone. It's too much for Addie and John alone."

Nicolas nodded his agreement. "I'm sensible of that. The necessity became quite clear after the incident with the 'chickens' the other night. So it's apparent I'll need to hire help in either case."

"Well, then." Sydney smiled at Maribeth. "You had better see to your winter wardrobe. I understand it's quite cold in the north Atlantic."

If their status had been different, Maribeth might have hugged Sydney. As it was, her cheeks spread wide in the biggest grin Nicolas had ever seen on the girl. She bounced in a brief curtsy to each of them.

"Thank you, Ma'am! Thank you, Sir! I'll not give you cause to regret this! You have my word!" Maribeth flew from the room.

"We may have just had all of her words," Nicolas quipped.

"Either that," Sydney laughed, "or her words have only now been unleashed!"

ഇൻൽ

Nicolas lay in bed and traced the landscape of Sydney's back with his fingertips; four months into their marriage he still couldn't keep his hands off her. She was so warm, so passionate, and so responsive. He no longer felt complete without her close by his side. Very, very close.

"Mm. That feels good," Sydney purred and snuggled into him.

"I ran into Rickard this afternoon when I went for Stefan. He was waiting for school to let out. Said he was taking Miss Price on a picnic for supper."

"He's smitten and he has it bad. He was never like that with me," Sydney spoke from under her arm, her disheveled hair muffling her words. "But I do wonder if his notorious past with women will dissuade the fair Bronwyn."

Nicolas chose to ignore her reference to Rickard's courting her. After all, that was four months and one marriage ago. "I doubt that she knows about it," he said.

Sydney shifted, tossed her hair back with one hand and faced him. "Was Lara your first?"

"My first what?"

Sydney raised one expressive eyebrow. Nicolas startled at the intrusively intimate memories summoned by her query. He slid his gaze to the waning fire.

"Why do you ask me such a question?"

"So she was not."

Nicolas frowned. "The question remains."

"I want to know everything about you. It shaped the man I fell in love with."

He was not at all convinced. "I still don't see the need."

Sydney pulled away from him. She retrieved her nightgown from the foot of the bed, where he had tossed it before making deliberate, sensual and shattering love to her. She slipped it over her head, and sat cross-legged on the mattress next to him. Nicolas could smell the warm musky scent of their lovemaking on her. Her eyes were forest green in the firelight and her dark hair tumbled around her shoulders. *Helvete* she was beautiful.

"I know about Rosie. And of course there was Lara." She brushed her hair back from her face. "I just want to know who else."

"But why, Sydney?"

"I don't know for sure. But it feels important." She reached out and touched his cheek. "Please, Nick?"

Nicolas placed his calloused hand over her smaller, softer one and moved his lips to her palm. He kissed it and tickled it with his tongue as he pondered her question. Sydney only called him 'Nick' when what she asked of him was serious. He lowered her hand from his lips.

"How much do you wish to know?"

"Everything. And everyone."

He still wasn't sure. What sort of woman asked such a question? His stubborn new wife, apparently.

Nicolas sat up and leaned back against the headboard. Sydney scooted closer and held on to his hand. Her fingers were cool, but her palm was warm. He scratched his chest absently.

"When I went to Norway to meet my extended family, one of my cousins was a beautiful woman named Sigrid. She was twenty-seven, and had been married at the age of eighteen to a nobleman more than twice her age. She wasn't happy with her marriage, that much was clear. And seeing the obese, hairy thing she was wed to, I could understand."

Nicolas shifted his weight and raked his free hand through his hair. "Now, I don't mean to boast, but I was the height I am now and I had a decent beard. I looked older than nineteen. Sigrid pursued me, and when she learned that I was still a virgin she doubled her efforts."

"What did she do?" Sydney whispered.

"She began walking me to my room after dinner. At first she pulled me into the window casements in the halls and she used her hand on me while we kissed behind the drapery. Then one night, after she had more than her usual amount of wine, she took me in her mouth."

"Oh." Sydney's glance dropped to that part of him.

"*Å min Gud!* I didn't know women did such things! But the effect was swift, for sure. And not the least bit unpleasant. Soon she was walking all the way to my room and coming inside."

Nicolas's mouth curved into a mischievous half smile. "And not long after, I was coming inside as well."

Sydney slapped Nicolas's chest in mock consternation. "How long did this go on?"

Nicolas held up his two pointer fingers about ten inches apart. "About yea long." Sydney smacked him again, but she chuckled.

Nicolas rubbed his chin. He hadn't thought of Sigrid in years. The memory was now distant enough to be polished by nostalgia. "We consorted for seven or eight months, as I recall. We started with the window casings and moved to culmination a few weeks after that."

Sydney nodded slowly.

"But I knew I was coming home with the intent of marrying Lara when I finished my university career. And while Sigrid was very beautiful and talented in bedsport, she wasn't..." He paused and searched for the right words. "She couldn't divorce, so she took one lover after another. And she drank too heavily for my taste."

"How sad," Sydney murmured.

"It was a sad situation, true." Nicolas leaned toward his wife. Recollection stirred his arousal once again. "But she was a *forbannet* fine teacher!"

"Sigrid was one of the names you suggested for me."

Nicolas sat back, for the moment distracted from his purpose.

"Was it? How can you remember that?"

"It struck me as an odd name. I hadn't heard it before."

"It's a common Nordic name." Nicolas's hand slid under Sydney's nightgown and hit its target. His arrow stiffened. "Shall I show you some more of my lessons?"

Sydney scooted closer and wrapped her legs around him, opening to him. "Did Lara know about Sigrid?"

"No," Nicolas grunted. Then he added, "She never asked."

He brushed his lips over Sydney's. Her eyes softened and she pulled her nightgown over her head. It landed at the foot of the bed once more.

April 21, 1820

Nicolas's advertisement in the *St. Louis Enquirer* described the position of "Short Term Employment" as "Assistant to the Housekeeper and Foreman" and indicated "Room, Board and Stipend" for compensation. Prospective employees began to arrive, appearing at his doorstep every other day or so. Most were victims of the country's depression of 1819, desperate for work of any kind.

The first candidate to appear was a woman whom Nicolas judged to be a bit older than himself. She appeared at the door and looked around nervously. He led her into the study and indicated a seat.

"Thank you, sir."

Nicolas sat in his favorite stuffed-leather chair and faced the woman. "The position isn't permanent," he began. "It's just while my family and I are away on an extended journey."

"I see."

"Have you experience in running a household?"

"Oh yes, sir. I have three boys of my own."

Nicolas frowned at that. "Do you? And how old might they be?"

"They are ten, seven and five." The woman shifted in her seat. "But they aren't a bother."

Nicolas cleared his throat as he considered how to respond to her revelation. "You do understand that this is a live-in position?"

"Yes, sir. That's why I am applying."

"I don't understand."

The woman leaned toward Nicolas, her haggard eyes begged for his compassion. "My husband, he likes the drink. Likes it so much in fact, that he gets worked up when someone gets between him and the whiskey."

Nicolas's shoulders sagged as he realized what was facing him.

"My boys, well, they don't always understand how to stay out of the way."

Nicolas shook his head. "I'm sorry. I've only the one room."

"They can share with me. It's no matter."

Nicolas considered the woman and her situation. A woman with three young children of her own wouldn't be a help to Addie and John. On the contrary, she'd bring extra work along with her.

Correctly reading Nicolas's silence, the woman added one last qualification. "I'm strong and able, Sir. I'm but twenty-seven."

That fact shocked Nicolas. He attempted to hide it by standing and circling around behind his chair, while he struggled for ideas. Facing the woman, he dragged his fingers through his hair.

"With regret, Madam, I feel your situation makes you unsuitable for this particular position."

The woman's shoulders and gaze plummeted in defeat.

"However—" Nicolas sat at his massive oak desk and reached for his quill and ink. "I can give you a letter of introduction if you're willing to go to St. Louis."

The woman frowned at him. "Why?"

"My lawyer is there. He's a bit older and never married. I believe he might be in need of a housekeeper." Nicolas spoke as he penned a quick note to Nelson Ivarsen explaining the situation. As he waited for the ink to dry, he turned back to the woman. "And if he doesn't, he'll put you up for a week, at my expense, while you search for other positions there."

"Thank you, sir." Her voice wavered on the edge of tears.

Nicolas handed the letter to the woman. When she reached for it, he didn't let go until she looked him in the eye. "Mr. Ivarsen is a good lawyer, should you need an advocate."

"Thank you again, sir," she whispered.

When the woman was gone, Nicolas opened the drawer with the heavy pewter flask and downed a swallow of brandy. He sighed and considered how blessed his life had become.

The next candidate was a young man in his late twenties. As he fidgeted in the entryway of the manor, his eyes skittered around the space, taking in every detail. Nicolas watched him, unseen behind the door of his study, and didn't like what he saw. He had a strong feeling this particular person was not as he seemed. Or more likely was *exactly* as he seemed.

"Best of luck to you!" Nicolas gently pushed the man out the door as their brief interview ended. If his instincts were right, there was no way that snake would be let loose in his garden.

The third prospect was too old, older than his foreman John and half as robust. The fourth was an obese woman in her thirties whose knees were so bad she couldn't manage to walk up the stairs to the spare bedroom. The fifth smelled so bad, Nicolas told her the position had been filled and didn't let her in the house. Frustrated by the continuing parade of unsuitable applicants, he contemplated changing their travel plans, though he couldn't puzzle out how to make that work.

Then candidate number eleven or twelve—Nicolas had lost count—knocked at the door, and introduced himself as Jeremy McCain. Nicolas led the young man into his study. Tired of wasting time, he went straight to the heart of the matter and fired questions at the boy.

"How old are you?"

"Twenty-two."

"Have you experience running an estate?"

"No, sir. But I am a fast learner and hard worker."

"What was your last position?"

"I was assistant to the owner of a dry goods store in Oakville."

"Why did you leave?"

The young man stared straight into Nicolas's eyes. "My wife was treated poorly by some women in the town."

That statement piqued Nicolas's curiosity. "You're married?"

"Yes, Sir."

"How long?"

"Almost a year."

"And how, exactly, was your wife treated poorly?"

Jeremy McCain leaned his lanky form back in the chair and directed his own question at Nicolas. "Do you own slaves?"

Surprised by Jeremy's forthrightness, Nicolas answered without thinking. "No. Neither did my father before me."

Jeremy nodded. "All right then."

"Your wife?" Nicolas prompted.

"My wife's mother was Sauk Indian. Her father was a French fur trader." Jeremy watched Nicolas intently. "Her mother left the tribe to follow the trader and Anne—Anehka—was born a year later."

"How old is Anne?" Nicolas was startled into wondering if any of his visits to the Sauk had resulted in half-breed offspring.

"Twenty."

Nicolas considered the intense young man. "Why did you ask me about slaves?"

Jeremy's voice was controlled, though one foot wiggled and his cheeks were splotched with angry scarlet. "If you owned slaves, then you would consider one race superior to another. My wife's parentage could be a problem and I wouldn't work for you."

Nicolas was impressed, and that was not an easy thing to accomplish. Jeremy radiated confidence and strength of character. And lurking beneath his businesslike surface, there was something quite likeable about the young man. Nicolas stood and offered his hand. "I like what I see, Mr. McCain. Can we agree to terms?"

Jeremy stood as well, but didn't take Nicolas's hand. "Please, Sir, call me Jeremy. I do have one request."

Nicolas waved his proffered hand in curious invitation. The boy surely had grit. Nicolas respected grit.

"Could my wife be allowed to work here as well?"

Nicolas's brow puckered in consideration. "Perhaps."

"She wouldn't need the stipend, only board. She would share my room, of course." Admittedly a young husband, Jeremy blushed at his own words.

Nicolas forced his grin not to appear. "I believe that to be reasonable. Her assistance to Addie, my housekeeper, would be appreciated I'm sure."

"Then I accept." This time Jeremy held out his hand. Nicolas took it. Jeremy's firm handshake was a little moist.

"Well, Jeremy. Shall we take a look around the property?"

For the first time that day, a smile split Jeremy's face. With a deep sigh and a wag of his head, Nicolas saw the weight of the world lift from the younger man's broad, thin shoulders. "Yes, sir, Mr. Hansen!"

Chapter Four

May 9, 1820

*T*he wagon was piled with traveling trunks and rolled bedding. Nicolas drove; his foreman John Spencer sat beside him. Sydney, with Kirstie on her lap, nested amidst the luggage with Stefan and Maribeth. Gray-haired and teary-eyed, Addie Spencer waved them off, wiping her eyes with her ever-present white apron. Jeremy and Anne McCain stood beside her on the porch.

"The place is in good hands, Nick," John opined with a backward glance. "You done well with those two."

Rickard Atherton rode up alongside the wagon. His auburn hair was tied with a leather thong, though wavy strands mutinied repeatedly and curled around his ears. He was almost as tall as Nicolas but not as broad. He narrowed his beautiful hazel eyes and shaded them with one hand.

"If you've no objections, I should like to accompany you to St. Louis."

"Happy to have your company, Rick. But what's your purpose?" Nicolas asked.

Rickard blushed adorably—Sydney had thought him stunningly handsome since the first day she met the two friends—and pushed a wide-brimmed hat lower on his brow. "It's Bronnie, actually. She has a taste for a certain kind of chocolate and I can't get it in

Cheltenham. Thought I might surprise her tomorrow at dinner."

"You mean Miss Price, *Onkel* Rick? My teacher?" Stefan's bright blue gaze considered his uncle from under one flat palm.

He grinned at his nephew. "As a matter of fact, I do."

Sydney poked Nicolas from behind. *See?* He cast her a sly sideways glance and shifted on the bench in amused acknowledgement.

Nicolas was the more beautiful male of the pair in her estimation. The dark, changeable blue sky of his eyes captivated her, and his thick blond hair was a fitting golden crown as it turned out.

Conversation between Nicolas, John and Rickard about what needed attention on the estate during Nicolas's absence helped pass time. The bumpy two-hour journey to the docks of St. Louis was otherwise uneventful, except for Stefan's frequently repeated queries as to how much farther was it? Finally Nicolas stopped the horses and whirled to face his son.

"Stefan. Today's the shortest of all of our days. If you ask that question one more time, I'll be forced to tie a rag over your mouth!"

Stefan's eyes widened and he leaned against Sydney's leg as Nicolas ranted on. "We're going to a great lot of places and we'll be gone a very long time. You're forbidden to ask that question again! Do you understand my words?"

Stefan nodded and pressed against Sydney, seeking protection from his father's irritation. She squeezed his shoulder, sent Nicolas a chastising glare, and hit upon an idea.

"Stefan, let's make a map of our journey! Then each day, you can mark down where we are and where we're going. Would you like that?"

"Yes, *Mamma*." He ventured a small smile and glanced up at Nicolas.

"You can even keep a list of how long it takes us to get from one place to another, so you can guess how long the next part will take," she continued. Nicolas relaxed some and tousled his son's hair in a non-verbal apology. Then he winked at her.

Nick's still learning new habits, she reminded herself.

"Can I draw on the map?" Stefan asked her.

"Certainly!"

"Can I make sea monsters on the water part?"

Nicolas quirked his brows. "Where did you learn of such things?"

Stefan squinted up at Nicolas. "From Alex McAvoy's *pappa*. He said there's a sea monster in a locked mess in Scotland."

Rickard laughed, and then turned it into a cough when Stefan appeared offended.

"Ah, of course." Nicolas turned, hiding his twitching grin. He slapped the reins and the horses strained forward.

"Can we make the map tonight, *Mamma?*"

"Let's do." Sydney smoothed Stefan's perpetually unruly auburn locks. They were wavy like his uncle Rickard's. Like his mother Lara's must have been.

Sydney hugged her stepson. It was a shame Stefan never knew her.

May 10, 1820
St. Louis

Steam-powered paddleboats still caught attention at the docks, being a recent addition to Mississippi River travel. This particular paddleboat had the name *Missy O* prominently painted on her bow. She looked clean and bright and sturdy.

The boat's purser herded the Hansen party to a pair of rooms out of the eight tucked in the upper deck. Their two whitewashed cabins were spacious, about nine feet square, and had shuttered windows. Both were furnished with a built-in platform bed on top of a bank of drawers, a small table and two little wooden chairs.

Nicolas eyed the bunk, which Sydney doubted reached six feet in length. He shrugged.

"I expected as much. The floor will do." Then he tossed her a mischievous grin. "But I'll come visiting."

His words sent a pleasant shiver of anticipation up her thighs.

She tugged on his arm until she could reach him with a solid kiss. "See that you do, husband."

Sydney helped Maribeth and Stefan settle into one cabin; Kirstie would share her bed—and Nicolas her floor—in the other. The boat shuddered and belched. They all scrambled outside to watch the marvelous new vessel propel itself.

White steam clouds above them danced an airy reel with black billows of coal smoke. Accompanied by a loud creaking groan, and the ch--ch-chant of the steam engine, the huge paddles aft-ship began to rotate. Water drops sluiced off them and scattered like sparkling gems in the sun.

Stefan jumped up and down on the deck, his excitement uncontainable. Maribeth stood gripping the rails, rooted to the boards, eyes darting and cheeks flushed. Sydney slipped her hand into Nicolas's and squeezed. He squeezed in return. The St. Louis shoreline backed off and they were on their way.

"This is it, *min presang*," he said, gazing down at her with impossibly blue eyes. "Our adventure has begun."

At the end of the day, with Stefan finally tucked in bed, Sydney sat in one little cabin chair and nursed Kirstie to sleep. The baby's blue-gray eyes turned violet in the fading pink sunlight retreating through the small window.

After losing two sons during her first marriage, this beautiful daughter was such a blessing that it made Sydney's heart ache. She laid the slumbering Kirstie on the bed, kissed her hair and the back of her neck, and surrounded her with pillows to keep the four month-old infant from rolling off the mattress. After refastening her bodice and smoothing her hair, she went in search of her husband.

Nicolas stood on the foredeck in the waning sunlight, legs braced wide and hands clasped behind him. Chin pointed into the wind, his nostrils flared and his long blond hair danced around his jaw.

The brushed cotton shirt Sydney made him for Christmas was pressed against his broad chest by the breeze. He was so magnificent, he took her breath away.

"Hello, husband." Sydney slipped her arms around his waist.

"Hello, wife."

"Is the world under control?"

Nicolas's laugh vibrated deep in his chest. "That it is. Are the children asleep?"

"Kirstie is. Stefan's in bed, though my guess would be he's wide awake."

"I'll go see him before we retire."

They remained entwined on the deck until stars surrounded the waning half-moon. The steady chug of the coal-powered engine and the mesmerizing splash of water off the rotating wooden paddles offered a unique harmony.

"This is quite a journey," Sydney whispered. "Never could I have guessed my life would take such a turn."

"And I never expected to return to Norway." Nicolas rested his chin on Sydney's head; they were silent for a pace.

"But I'm glad to go," he added, his deep voice nearly swallowed. "And I'm so very glad to have you with me."

May 21, 1820
Louisville

"*Mamma?* Are you coming?" Stefan squirmed outside her cabin door. "*Pappa* said we're almost there!"

When Sydney and Kirstie appeared on the deck, Nicolas held Stefan on his shoulders like a god and his progeny, limned in late morning gilt. The farms that flanked Louisville were already in view.

"What time are we expected to dock?" Sydney's heart was trying to climb up her ribs and look out her mouth, so eager it was to reach her childhood home—and her long-missed mother.

Nicolas peered down at her. "In less than an hour, so says the boatswain."

The Louisville dock was crowded. Landlocked necks craned for glimpses of familiar faces onboard as the *Missy O* nudged toward the pier. She teased the wooden abutment twice before tucking herself against its side.

Ropes flew through the air and dockhands looped them around iron grappling hooks to secure the steamboat to the dock. The engine belched a snow cloud of steam and the paddle wheel stilled.

"Siobhan! Hansen!" Robert Bell's Scots-tinged baritone carried over the din of the day.

"Da!" Sydney stood on tiptoe and waved to her father. She smiled so widely her face hurt.

A jumble of introductions and re-introductions bubbled through the Hansen party as they gathered beyond the gangplank. Sydney cried her joy in deep gulping sobs, and Nicolas assured Stefan that such a thing as happy tears truly did exist.

Robert laughed and draped his arm around his only daughter. "Aye, it's so good to see you again, girlie!"

It required a full, maddening hour to get their trunks off the paddleboat and loaded into Robert's wagon. Once on their way, Sydney wondered if the horses were actually slowing down as they neared her parents' home. She handed Kirstie to Maribeth and stood in the wagon to get a better look.

"Sit down then, girlie," her father chided, grinning. "We'll get there and soon enough!"

Nicolas looked over his shoulder at his wife and smiled. Sydney's breath caught as she considered him. She saw the man her mother would see, so completely different now from the man Sydney met last spring. And so diametrically different from her first husband. The one who betrayed her. And then tried to kill her.

"*De er slik vakker,*" she whispered. You are so beautiful.

Nicolas laughed. "Just because you know how to say it, doesn't mean it fits every occasion!"

"It fits this one well. Trust me, husband."

The wagon rounded the last bend and Sydney saw the white two-story clapboard house nestled in a quilt of horse pasture. A figure on the porch stood up and shaded its eyes against the low angle of the sun.

"Mother!" Sydney jumped from the side of the moving wagon. She caught her balance and ran toward the house, skirts hiked well above her knees. "Mother!"

The figure descended the porch steps and ran forward, skirts hiked in the same manner. "Siobhan! My darling girl!"

By the time Sydney reached her mother, she was sobbing wildly. Until this moment, she couldn't admit how much she had ached for her mother's calm and nurturing presence during the horrific turbulence of the past year.

And to be called 'Siobhan' again—after living for more than a year as 'Sydney'—reached a part of her that she thought had died.

"So many times I needed to talk to you!" she croaked through her sobs.

"My poor child, your Da told me everything!" Ciara Bell was four inches shorter than her thirty-one year-old 'poor child' but that didn't prevent her from encasing her in a sturdy maternal hug.

The wagon stopped and everyone dismounted. Sydney turned and reached out with one hand as she wiped tears with the other. "Mother, this is my husband, Nicolas Reidar Hansen."

Nicolas extended his right hand. "It's my pleasure to meet you, madam." -

Sydney watched her mother's eyes travel up Nicolas's solid six-foot-four-inch frame and land in his navy blue orbs. Slowly she laid her hand in his.

"Mr. Hansen. I believe you are even more than I was expecting."

Nicolas blushed. "Please call me Nicolas, madam."

"And you must call me Ciara." Her fingers began to wiggle as her eyes dropped to the baby resting over Nicolas's shoulder. "And this must be my granddaughter?"

Nicolas deftly laid Kirstie in Ciara's arms. She pulled the babe close and pressed her against her bosom.

"I never thought... I mean, it seemed as though..."

"I know," Sydney beamed at her mother. "I feel the same."

Ciara's smiling gaze fell to Stefan. "And who are you?"

"Stefan Atherton Hansen. I'm six-and-a-half." He pointed to Sydney. "She's my *mamma*."

"And so she is!" Ciara's voice choked a bit. "And I'm your grandmother."

"*Pappa* and *Mamma* told me already."

Ciara gazed at the bright-eyed, baby in her arms who was gnawing industriously on her fist and drooling everywhere. "Your sister is beautiful, Stefan."

"She can't talk yet."

"No, I don't imagine that she can. But I can see that you're ready to teach her when the time comes, are you not?"

Stefan nodded emphatically, his auburn hair flopping into his eyes as usual.

"And this is Maribeth, our maid and my other right hand on the journey." Sydney pulled the shy girl forward. She dipped and nodded in a brief curtsy, blushing.

"Welcome to you as well, dear."

Sydney looked to the front door. "Where is Andrew?"

"Courting. Across the river in Jeffersonville."

"Finally!" Sydney laughed. "Do you like her?"

"I do. She's a fine young woman. So, is anyone hungry?" Ciara's eyes twinkled at their unanimous acknowledgement. "I believe supper is almost ready. Robert, will you show them to their rooms to freshen up?"

"I can take Kirstie," Sydney offered.

"Over my dead body," her mother cooed.

❦

Sydney sat on the top step of the staircase to nurse Kirstie away from Nicolas's distracting snore. She wanted her daughter to sleep, though that state eluded her this first night. Too many childhood memories jostled their way into her thoughts, each one demanding her full attention. Sleep just was not that interesting in comparison.

"I thought I heard you," her mother whispered, lowering herself quietly next to Sydney. She held a single candle in a brass holder.

"I'm sorry we woke you," Sydney whispered back.

Ciara stroked Kirstie's curls. "I'm not! I was hoping."

Sydney smiled and leaned against her mother. "What do you think of him?" she murmured conspiratorially.

"Nicolas?" Ciara shook her head slowly. "He's such a big man, and exceedingly handsome, and so… so…"

"Different from Devin?"

"In every way I can imagine," she concurred. "And he is good to you?"

"In every way *I* can imagine," Sydney giggled.

Her mother's blush was visible even in the candlelight. "You have been blessed, Siobhan. God has seen you through your trials, and blessed you richly."

Sydney looked down at the healthy nursing babe in her arms. "He has, Mother. He truly has."

Kirstie closed her eyes and sighed contentedly as if to agree.

The days in Shelbyville flew far too quickly in Sydney's mind. Though she knew Nicolas was anxious to move on, gentleman that he was, he never let it show.

And, after Sydney repeatedly hugged her mother goodbye, and Robert Bell drove the Hansen family back to the port at Louisville, Nicolas held Sydney in his lap while she cried.

Not once did he complain that she soiled three of his freshly-laundered handkerchiefs in the process.

Chapter Five

Eastern Pennsylvania
June 17, 1820

*T*he wind had shifted.

Cool gusts from the northwest replaced the mild southerly breezes that had accompanied the Hansen's canvas-covered Conestoga wagon across Pennsylvania for the last week. Dawn was nebulous; nothing more than a gradual graying of the night sky.

The heavy, hugging air smelled waterlogged. Insects buzzed, frantically searching for a haven. Even the blue jays and squirrels ceased their arguments. Nicolas drove the horses hard in hopes of beating the coming storm.

"We'll have warm, dry beds tonight," he promised over his shoulder. "We should reach Philadelphia by candlelighting!"

The ashy afternoon aged slowly as an old man. Then the first rumbles of thunder nudged toward them from the north. Once again, Sydney experienced the terror that always made her feel like a foolish child. She didn't know why she feared thunderstorms; she only knew that she did. And, as ashamed as she was, she couldn't make her fears disappear.

"How are you doing back there?" Nicolas twisted to look at her.

"We're tired, cramped and hungry. So I suppose we're fine!" she attempted to joke. The sky grumbled again, louder and closer. Her heart grumbled louder as well.

"*Mamma!* That's thunder! Can I sit with *Pappa* and watch the lightning?" Stefan looked eagerly to his father.

Nicolas patted the seat next to him and Stefan scrambled into it. "Sydney?" he asked.

She clenched her jaw. "I'll be fine."

"I'll get us there as quickly as I'm able."

"I know."

The storm had stalked them all day and now had them in its trap. Clouds above them were cut open by daggers of light and they bellowed their displeasure. Ripped repeatedly, they couldn't hold the rain. They poured out their contents on the lone wagon slogging along the road in the deepening gloom. Sydney curled around her baby daughter and prayed for the storm to die.

A few eternities later, Nicolas stopped the wagon under the large portico that extended from the front of a darkened house. It provided welcome relief from the rain that had pounded the wagon's canvas covering for hours.

Nicolas climbed down from the wagon and Sydney eagerly followed his lead. The front door was locked, so Nicolas reached above the tall doorjamb and retrieved a key hidden there. With a reassuring smile, he unlocked the door and pushed it open. Then he re-hid the key.

"I'll take the horses to the barn. See if you can find a lamp."

Sydney nodded and held Kirstie close to her bosom as she stepped through the door. Maribeth followed with Stefan's hand gripped in hers and closed the door behind them. The house was black inside.

Sydney wondered how she was supposed to find anything in the unfamiliar darkness, when a quick succession of blinding flashes outlined everything in pale blue light. She could not help herself; she shrieked at the immediate punch of thunder and dropped to her knees.

In the quiet aftermath, a man's voice sent the lightning through her veins and thundered in her gut.

"Ladies, I recommend that you stay right where you are."

Sydney heard the terrifying click of a rifle hammer. Shaking, she reached for Stefan and pulled him behind her. Kirstie squirmed against Sydney's crushing grasp. A brief flash of sparks ignited a lamp at the top of the stairs. The man held the lamp so that Sydney couldn't see his face. But she could see the gun.

"Who are you?" he demanded.

"S-sydney Hansen."

"Hansen?" The voice sounded skeptical.

"Yes. My husband owns this property."

"You're lying."

Sydney's mouth popped open. She shook her head, but before she could speak, another flash-boom combination caused her to flinch and cry out.

"Who are you?" the man demanded again. He slowly descended the stairs.

Between the man with the gun and the terrifying storm, Sydney fought the urge to burst into hysterical tears. She mustn't; Maribeth and the children were in her charge. She looked up at the threat again, and he held the lamp slightly to the side. Now she could see that he wore a distorted version of her husband's face.

"G-gunnar?" she stammered.

He stopped. "Tell me who you are!" he bellowed. Stefan pressed against her back and Kirstie began to fuss. Maribeth stood still as a statuette, and just as silent.

Certain that she now knew who addressed her, Sydney struggled to her feet. She tried her best to sound confident, friendly.

"My name is Sydney Bell Hansen. I am married to Nicolas Hansen. This is our daughter, and his son."

The lamp swung in lieu of a pointed hand. "What's your name, boy?"

Sydney pulled Stefan from behind her. "Tell your Uncle Gunnar your name."

Squinting at the lamp, he obeyed. "Stefan."

"How old are you?"

"Six-and-a-half."

The door behind them jerked open and Nicolas blew in with a gust of wet air. He pushed the door shut and looked toward the lamp on the staircase.

"*Hva helvetet er De gjøre her?*" he blurted. What the hell are you doing here?

"*Og hva helvetet er De gjøre her?*" Gunnar responded.

For a moment, no one moved.

Then the brothers rushed each other. They punched, hugged and slapped in a physical expression of pure male joy. Their booming laughs echoed as they shouted in a garbled mixture of Norse and

English. Finally, Nicolas pulled Gunnar toward Sydney.

"This is my wife, Sydney. And this is our daughter, Kirsten. And you know Stefan, of course. This is our maid Maribeth. Was she at the manor when you visited last?" Nicolas beamed at his brother.

Sydney looked up at Gunnar. Though not as broad, he was a good two inches taller than Nicolas, whose arm angled up as he draped it over his younger brother's shoulders.

"Maybe she was." Gunnar's eyes were on Sydney, not Maribeth. "But when did you get married again, Nick? I never thought that would happen."

"It's a long story. One that plays well over dinner," Sydney demurred. "Perhaps tomorrow we might satisfy your curiosity?"

Gunnar ogled the traveling troupe as if seeing them for the first time. "You're all wet!"

"And tired and hungry!" Nicolas added. "Might you give us a hand with the horses? And could we find a bite to eat before we retire?"

෨෬

Sydney fell onto the mattress and didn't move. It took them over an hour to unload the wagon, dress everyone in dry nightclothes, and serve up soup and bread from Gunnar's pantry. Another hour was required to settle the children into bed while Maribeth washed the dishes and Nicolas and Gunnar tended the horses.

The bedroom door creaked open and clicked shut. A whisper floated toward her. "Sydney?"

"Mm."

"Are you asleep?"

"Mm-hmm."

Nicolas chuckled. She heard his boots drop to the floor before he slipped out of his nankeens. He grunted a little as he pulled the shirt over his head. Then he slid against her. His skin was icy and damp.

"Oh, my Lord!" Sydney squealed and jerked aside.

"Warm me, wife!" Nicolas pulled her back against him. It was their first night alone—and in a real bed—for a week and a half. Though his torso was chilled, one stiff part of him was quite warm already.

"Warm me," he breathed into her ear and bit her earlobe. "Warm me, *min presang*." He put her hand around his firm flesh.

Sydney turned to face him and pulled her nightgown up to her waist. She eagerly wrapped her legs around Nicolas as he lowered himself into her. She shuddered as his cold body and heated groin pressed her into the mattress. Moving slowly at first, Nicolas groaned his pleasure and Sydney purred in response. She ran her hand through his damp hair and twisted her fingers in it. She bit his lip and played with his tongue. She lightly scratched his buttocks with the nails of her free hand.

Nicolas responded with swift, powerful strokes that carried her outside of herself. She arched her back and squirmed beneath his massive bulk as everything faded from her awareness but the clenching pulse that radiated from their joining. Nicolas shook and gasped, his face screwed tightly into the expression that mimicked pain, but signaled exquisite pleasure. He collapsed, panting, beside her. They lay in a tangle of hot and cold, hard and soft, wakeful and drowsy.

His culminating kiss was deep, soft, perfect.

"I like Philadelphia already," Sydney whispered.

June 18, 1820
Philadelphia

The sun grew tired of playing hide-and-seek, so she burned away the remnants of the storm. Then she pushed her beams through the curtains and spilled them across the bedroom floor. Sydney rolled out of bed and spread the drapes for her first look at Nicolas's land. Mist rose from the wet ground and it water-colored the landscape under an aquamarine sky.

Tilled fields extended from the house, neatly furrowed and sprouting bright green. A bank of deciduous trees outlined each field and pasture. Cows grazed to the north. Small white houses sprouted here and there.

The drive below emerged from the portico and curved back toward the road. Squinting through the haze, Sydney could make out tall, brownstone townhouses, white church spires, and red brick buildings which comprised the center of Philadelphia.

"What do you think?" Nicolas had one eye open, the other buried in his pillow.

"It's beautiful! And very impressive, to be sure. How much of what I see is yours?"

The eye closed. "All of it."

Downstairs, Sydney asked Maribeth to help her raid the pantry. Together they pulled together a late breakfast of pancakes, eggs, steak and fried potatoes. Sydney set the table, then sat with Kirstie on her lap. Maribeth poured coffee for everyone while Gunnar retrieved a bottle of cream from the cool bottom of the well.

"Can I have coffee, *Pappa*?" Stefan was acting very grown-up since he took his meals with the adults.

Nicolas grinned at his son. "You may. But be careful, it's hot."

"Add some cream and sugar," Sydney suggested. "I believe you'll find that more to your liking."

Stefan nodded, pushed his hair out of his eyes, and put four spoons of sugar into his cup.

"That'll do." Nicolas stopped him from adding a fifth. "Now the cream."

Stefan added cream until his cup brimmed. The color of the beverage closely resembled oatmeal. He leaned over the cup and slurped it without lifting it from the saucer.

The door to the kitchen opened with its spring twanging. Then it slapped shut.

"I'm sorry I'm late, Gunn, but the pastor was so long-winded this morn! I swear, sometimes—Oh!"

Mouth wide and brown eyes wider, a woman in her mid-twenties stopped smack in the doorway. She wore a burgundy skirt and peasant-style blouse. A white crocheted shawl draped over her arms and looped behind her. Her outrageously red hair was tied up on the sides and hung down her back in a riot of ringlets.

"Bridge... Um, Brigid. Flaherty. This is my brother, Nicolas." Gunnar blushed from chest to scalp. "His wife, Sydney. Their children Stefan and Kirstie. And their maid, Maribeth."

"His wife?" Brigid's brows dipped. "But you said she was—"

"His second wife," Gunnar interrupted.

"Oh." Brigid dipped in an awkward curtsy. "Pleased to make your acquaintances."

"I know you." Nicolas squinted. "Don't I?"

"My mother was the housekeeper here, and her mother before her." Brigid's glance shifted to Gunnar and back to Nicolas. "Now I'm, um…"

"Brigid keeps the house for me," Gunnar jumped in.

"Of course!" Nicolas smacked the table. "When I was here as a youth! You must have been only, what, ten or eleven years old? I do remember you!"

Brigid stepped into the dining room and pointed at Nicolas. "Nicky, right? That's what they called you? You used to play awful tricks on me! Scared me half out of my wits!"

Nicolas threw his head back; his booming laughter filled the room. "My, but you were a gawky little thing!"

"Yes. Well." Brigid flushed and cleared her throat. "Gunn—um, Mr. Hansen. I'll clean the kitchen. Please inform me when your guests are finished and I'll take care of the dishes." With an awkward curtsy, Brigid quit the room.

Sydney looked at Nicolas, fully expecting him to address the electricity that snapped between Gunnar and Brigid. But before he could speak, Gunnar clapped his huge hands together and faced his older brother.

"So. Tell me how this marriage came to be," Gunnar suggested. He did not acknowledge the beautiful redhead's arrival.

"I'm going to feed Kirstie in another room," she demurred, rising from the table. "You go ahead, Nicolas."

Nicolas smiled at her, eyes twinkling, and turned his attention to Gunnar. "Are you ready for a good story?"

80CB

Nicolas stood in the back yard of the huge house and lifted his chin. The sun warmed his skin and he inhaled the fertile bouquet of wet soil. Green foliage under a sapphire sky filled his field of vision. Suffused by a sense of peace, he walked the property with Gunnar at a leisurely pace.

"I didn't expect you to be here, Gunn. When do you go back to the navy?" he asked.

Gunnar stepped ahead of him and picked up a branch blown down by yesterday's storm. His hunched stance foreshadowed his words. "I don't."

That stopped Nicolas. "What?"

Gunnar turned, his expression clenched. "I'm not going back. I resigned my commission."

Nicolas stared stupidly at his younger brother. "When?"

"Last October."

"You've been here since then?"

"I have."

Gunnar stalked off, peeling leaves from the branch. Nicolas followed in cool silence. Several minutes passed without any offered explanations before he asked, "Will you tell me why, Gunn?"

"It's complicated," he clipped.

Nicolas waited. Their pace dwindled in contrast to his growing frustration. "Complicated? Is that all you have to tell me?"

Gunnar whipped the denuded branch in whistling arcs. "Since I was a boy, the navy was all I wanted to do. But when I approached thirty years of age, things began to change."

"What sort of things?" he prodded. His brother was not making this an easy conversation and he wondered why.

"I began to think I might want a wife. Children." Gunnar's tone hardened. "Like you."

Nicolas considered his sibling, puzzled at the rising anger coloring his cheeks and darkening his eyes. His chin jutted in a manner that was distinctly Hansen.

"So I pondered my opportunities for a year or so, and decided to resign."

"What did you need to ponder?" Nicolas frowned his confusion. They stood in the speckled shade of a large elm tree. Cheerful lozenges of sunlight chased over their tense forms.

The branch arcs grew faster, wilder. "How to live for one. And where."

"And you chose here, then?" Nicolas pressed.

Gunnar stopped swinging the branch and rounded on him. Nicolas prepared for the strike, but it didn't come in spite of Gunnar's fisted hand.

"How can I 'choose' here, Nick?" he sneered.

Nicolas shook his head and spread his hands in question. What on earth was Gunn's point? He was a naval officer—a ship's *captain*—and he had an entire country to choose from. Why not choose Philadelphia?

Gunnar narrowed his eyes and spoke slowly, as if speaking to an idiot. "This isn't my estate, Nick. It's yours."

Before Nicolas could respond, he slammed the branch hard against the tree, frightening a flock of doves.

"Everything is yours!" he shouted. The branch launched; like an unbalanced javelin it tumbled end-over through the air before Gunnar's stride chewed the space between them. He threw his arms wide and growled, "Every damned thing we can see is *yours!*"

Nicolas was stunned. Gunnar was furious, and that anger was directed squarely at him.

But he hadn't done anything—other than be born first over three decades ago. That wasn't his fault. Their current circumstance was common here, and in Europe, and had been for centuries. Why had this suddenly become a problem?

Gunnar planted his feet and crossed his arms. "Tell me this, Nick. Why are you here now?"

Nicolas shrugged, trying to discern the underlying question. "I told you. We're on our way to Norway."

"It was the letter, then, wasn't it?"

"You know about the letter?" That was yet another surprise; he hoped no more were on their way.

Gunnar shook his head at his oblivious older brother. "Who do you think sent it on to you?"

"I hadn't thought about it," Nicolas admitted.

Gunnar snorted. "When I arrived here in October, there was a mountain of correspondence that Brigid's mother had set aside. I took the liberty of going through it." He glanced a challenge.

Nicolas nodded. Even if his brother's actions *did* irk him, he wasn't about to argue the point now. He knew better than to pour oil on a fire.

Gunnar pried a rock from the dirt with the toe of his boot. "When I finally found it, I knew it was important. I knew you needed to have it." He picked up the rock and threw it accurately at a nearby tree trunk. Bits of bark scattered. "So what do they want of you?"

Nicolas cleared his throat. "It seems that the descendents of King Frederick the Fifth are considering a bid for the throne of Norway.

"Are they, then?" Another rock hit the beleaguered trunk. "Take it back from Sweden?"

"Yes."

"And why are you their concern?"

Nicolas shrugged and tried to downplay the summons. "They merely want to know where I stand. They want my support is all."

Gunnar waited until Nicolas looked him in the eye. "And are you a candidate for that throne?"

Nicolas pulled a face. "No. No! I have no such aspirations."

Gunnar set his jaw and narrowed his eyes at his older brother. Nicolas raised one brow and waited.

"So, Nick. Why exactly *are* you going to Norway, then?" he pressed.

Nicolas waved his hand dismissively. "There's property to be checked on, decisions to be made concerning tenants."

"Hmph!" Gunnar kicked the ground, exposing more pebbles.

"Hmph what?"

Gunnar called him out. "You don't pack up your wife, your children, and your maid, and travel halfway around the world, over land and sea, simply to 'check on property'!"

"You would go, too, if they asked!" Nicolas snapped.

Gunnar threw another stone. And another. And another. Then he crossed his arms over his chest, his gimlet stare jabbing Nicolas. "Well, they've not asked for *me*, then, have they?"

Nicolas jammed his hands onto his hips. "Be fair, Gunnar. They've never met you. You joined the navy and didn't go to Christiania!"

Gunnar shook his head slowly. "That particular option was never offered to me, Nick. I did what I had to do." This rock went the farthest.

"*Å min Gud,*" Nicolas muttered.

For the first time in his life, Nicolas began to realize that he had been treated not only differently, but preferentially by their parents. Or maybe it was their grandmother, Frederick's sister Marit Christiansen, who controlled his opportunities. Ultimately the distinction was unimportant; it had happened. Repeatedly. After all, the estate in Missouri was his as well, wasn't it.

He sat down hard on a log and squinted up at Gunnar. "Did you wish to go?"

Gunnar shrugged in an offhand manner. "Does it matter now?"

He sat on the log next to Nicolas. The brothers were silent. Nicolas pushed damp dirt around with the toe of his boot while Gunnar stripped bark from fallen sticks, releasing the sweet smell of the green wood beneath.

Nicolas swallowed, his mouth suddenly dry. "I never intended to take everything from you."

Gunnar sighed heavily. He peeled more bark. "I know."

"I never considered that you might care." Nicolas now understood how completely selfish that view was. Why had he never thought of it before? It was suddenly quite obvious.

Gunnar looked unexpectedly contrite. "It was simply the firstborn prerogative. Don't concern yourself overly, Nick. I understood my place from early on. It's not your commission to change the way of the world."

That was an interesting way to phrase it, considering the royal summons. Kings *could* change the way of the world.

Nicolas made a swift decision. He knew what he wanted to say, but he struggled to find words that wouldn't offend. His voice was carefully flat. "Gunn, you're aware of the 'Panic of 1819' are you not?"

"I am. What of it?"

"Well, land prices dropped all over the country. Here, in Pennsylvania, they dropped quite a lot. About eighty percent or so."

"So your point is that this land is worthless? Come on, Nick!" Gunnar whipped his boot with the bark-less sticks. "Whatever you think of me, I'm not a fool!"

"That's not my point at all!"

"Then what?"

"Gunnar, I didn't *panic* in the Panic." The corner of Nicolas's mouth curved. "I bought land."

Stunned realization stole over Gunnar's face. "How much land?"

"Seven hundred acres."

"Seven hundred?" Gunnar jumped to his feet. "Seven hundred acres? Where?"

"Over there." Nicolas pointed north. "And some over there." His arm swung to the west.

Gunnar took a step back. "Nick! That's—that's—what are your

plans?" he stammered.

"Well, I didn't have any specific plans, as such. That was one reason we stopped here. I needed to set up some tenancies, appoint an overseer, that sort of thing."

Gunnar stiffened, his jutted chin lifting. "Are you suggesting that I work for you?"

"No, I'm not." Nicolas shook his head and considered his brother. "Not at all. But I am wondering if you might like to buy it from me."

Gunnar scoffed, his face gone ruddy. "I resigned my commission, Nick! I haven't had an income for months and little chance to save on my naval salary before that! How in God's name do you expect me to pay you?"

"I haven't had time to think through the details, Gunn. But I'm sure there's an arrangement that would benefit us both."

Gunnar began to pace in random circles, laced fingers resting on his head. He stopped and examined the clear morning sky, then dropped his hands to his hips. He spoke over his shoulder.

"Such as?"

"Such as…" Nicolas figured quickly. "Let's say I give you control of everything here in Pennsylvania. You pay me a percentage each year as compensation for the land."

Gunnar turned to face him. "In perpetuity?"

"No. Only until the land is paid for. One hundred percent of the seven hundred acres. And at thirty dollars an acre that shouldn't take too long!"

Gunnar's jaw dropped. "That's all you paid?"

Nicolas grinned. "I told you the price dropped."

Gunnar looked more than a bit stunned. "I suppose I might agree to that. What about this estate? Will you keep it?"

Nicolas gazed across the land. He thought of his home in Missouri and his holdings in Norway. "I love this land, Gunnar. I truly do."

"Well, it's easy to love." Gunnar sank back onto the log. "I understand, Nick."

"Understand what?"

"Why you want to keep it, of course!"

Nicolas folded his legs under him and pushed up from the log. He brushed away bits of bark, which clung doggedly to his nankeens. Arms resting across his chest, he strode, slowly, away from Gunnar. After a pace, he returned.

"I'm thinking of letting you buy twenty-five percent of it from me."

"Are you?" Gunnar's eyebrows nearly disappeared into his scalp.

"I am." Nicolas grinned. "Then another twenty-five percent could be my wedding gift to you." He waved his hand in an offhand manner and sat back on the log. "I would keep fifty percent interest for Stefan and Kirstie, of course."

Gunnar paled. "W-wedding gift?"

"For you and the lovely Brigid Flaherty."

"How—I mean, she—we—" Gunnar flushed scarlet.

Nicolas slapped his brother on the back. "Spit it out man! Is it her or not?"

Gunnar nodded spastically, his pale cheeks suddenly maroon.

"Has it been going on long?" Nicolas prodded.

"I met her when I came here in October. She's quite accomplished, and interesting to converse with. I knew straight away that she could make me happy."

"Have you asked for her hand?"

Gunnar shook his head. "I had no prospects, Nick. Nothing to offer her."

"Well, now you do. Seven hundred acres to lease and fifty percent of this estate, with rights of occupancy." Nicolas peeled a long stem of grass and stuck the end in his mouth. "I would say that makes you a fine catch."

Gunnar's smile began slowly, but soon commanded his entire countenance. "It does, doesn't it? Ha, ha! It sure as *helvete* does!"

Nicolas punched Gunnar in the arm. Hard.

Chapter *Six*

June 30, 1820
Baltimore

*S*ydney had never seen an ocean-going vessel. She stood on the dock and stared in awe at the fat masts towering overhead and the legion of men who clambered over them. Webs of rope strung mast to mast, and mast to deck. Rows of thick, round windows rode high above the water line. Nicolas told her that when the ship was fully loaded, they would be just above the waves.

"And don't call it a boat, whatever you do!" he chided. "This is a seafaring ship and her captain wouldn't take kindly to the slur!"

Sydney glanced at him to see if he was serious. He was. They walked up the plank and asked for the purser. A narrow Irishman with cropped orange hair edged in white answered.

"Aye, then! Welcome aboard, mates! Are you in for a fair journey?" He tousled Stefan's hair. "Where'd ya get that red hair, son? Air ye Irish?"

Stefan shook his head. "I'm Norse," he answered, unaware his dead mother was as English as the King.

"Are ye then?" He squinted up at the blond blue-eyed tower that was Nicolas. "Well, let's get you to your quarters, shall we?"

The cabins were a bit smaller and a lot darker than on the paddleboats, but they were furnished in a similar manner. While

Sydney and Maribeth tried to find places for all of their things, Nicolas took Stefan on deck and showed him around the ship.

"Will we manage in these rooms for a month, Maribeth?" Sydney's fists rested on her hips.

"It'll be close, that's sure." The maid grunted and pushed a small trunk against the wall. "But think how joyous our arrival will be."

Sydney laughed out loud, startling Kirstie who dozed on the bed. Nearing six months of age, crawling was on her near horizon and Sydney was already devising methods to corral her safely without stifling her need to explore.

The ship began to move backwards, easing away from the dock. Sydney collected her sleepy daughter, and she and Maribeth climbed to the deck. Heavy midday sun pressed down on them. Sydney felt rivulets of perspiration trickle down the groove of her back and the backs of her legs.

Flocks of seamen hung in the rigging. They unfurled sails, tossed ropes and shouted to each other, their voices challenging raucous gulls for dominance. Sails were lashed in place and the ship rotated so her bowsprit pointed into Chesapeake Bay. Gliding south, past Fort McHenry, she gradually picked up speed. Sailing through the bay was like sailing on glass.

Not so when they reached the ocean. The ship rolled and pitched in a slow, steady, relentless rhythm as she skimmed over the deep blue waves.

The water matches Nicolas's eyes, Sydney thought as she leaned, white-knuckled, over the railing. Her stomach had emptied and the last of the spasms seemed to have passed. Nicolas assured her she would grow accustomed to the movement soon. She hoped he was right.

Sydney wiped her face with a damp cloth and considered the endless water around her. Land disappeared before supper the first day, and she experienced a moment of unexpected panic. The ocean was so huge and the boat—*ship*—so small! How could the captain possibly know where they were? And if they were lost, how could they ever be found?

Nicolas had assured her that with compasses and star charts, the captain knew their position and direction very well. He even took her to the bridge to see for herself. But what calmed her most was observing the sailors who made a living sailing back and forth across this endless blue prairie. They went about their duties, relaxed and joking, confident in the outcome of the voyage.

Sydney wiped her mouth again and breathed deeply. Only she and Maribeth seemed affected by the ship's gallop. Stefan ran all over the vessel with such abandon that Sydney feared for his safety. She insisted he be accompanied by an adult whenever he was on deck.

Meals on the ship were served in an open, well-ventilated space at the stern of the ship. The captain's chief cook was quite creative, so food on the journey was an unexpected pleasure; to say nothing of the casks of French and Italian wines stored below deck, and tapped liberally at every meal. Sydney wondered aloud to Nicolas if it truly was only the ship's motion that caused her to lurch to their cabin in the evenings.

The days of endless blue water fell into a comfortable pattern. Sydney and Nicolas agreed that mornings should be spent with Stefan's lessons. In the afternoons Nicolas taught them all Norse at Sydney's request. The lessons were more entertaining than anyone expected, especially when a mispronounced word gave a phrase an entirely unintended meaning. There were moments when Nicolas laughed so hard, he could barely breathe.

ഇരുഗ്ര

Sydney slept with Kirstie safely tucked between her and the wall in the narrow bunk. Nicolas slept on the wool mattress on the floor of their cabin; as on the paddleboats, the bed was far too short for him. He sorely missed the feel of his wife beside him. Curled against him.

And bucking under him.

Early in the second week, when he woke to Kirstie's hungry whimpers, he waited until the babe was diapered and fed and settled back to sleep. Then he rose to his knees and slid his hand under Sydney's blankets. She opened her thighs with a soft hum of surprise. Nicolas stood to kiss her. His lips trailed down her neck to her breasts and her breathing quickened. Grasping her knees, he turned her sideways pulled her to him.

Entering her was like stepping into heaven.

Nicolas stood beside the bed and rocked forward and back, his hands pressing down on Sydney's hips. Sydney fumbled for his arms and grasped his wrists for answering leverage. The motion of the ship added a dreamlike dimension to their dark coupling. Nicolas held back, unwilling for the increasingly pleasurable sensations to end. Sydney squirmed and stiffened under him. Her thighs tensed and her body shook. He watched her hungrily in the dim moonlight that snuck through the tiny porthole. She was so beautiful, so sensual, so exciting.

Nicolas let go, then. Pulsating gratification clutched his gut and spiraled throughout his body, tingling his fingers and toes. It left him limp, satiated, and deeply content.

For one night.

The next night Nicolas sipped his brandy alone on the ship's aft deck. As was his habit at home when he wasn't able to sleep, he sat outside in the night air and enjoyed the amber liquor. Only here, he sat on a coil of rope, not a wood bench. And instead of listening to the forest, he heard the soft rhythmic swish of the ship's wake in the endless Atlantic waves. Innumerable stars filled the infinite black sky, more than he ever saw in Missouri.

Gunnar's question still tugged at him; why *was* he going to Norway?

Nicolas told himself it was because he simply wished to return. The trip was important for Stefan to see his heritage. Christiania was a romantic city he wished to share with Sydney. And he really did need to deal with his holdings there.

But he wasn't able to convince himself. He knew the truth.

Nicolas gulped the brandy and poured more from the pewter flagon he brought from home. Leaning back, he considered the eternal expanse of twinkling ink above him. He drew a deep breath, held it, and let it out slowly.

It was because he was intrigued by the idea that he could be a king.

Norway and Denmark shared a king for centuries. In fact, his great-grandfather, Christian VI, was actually Danish. But now the displaced royal family was searching for a kingly candidate who was Norwegian. Nicolas's father was pure Norse. And his grandmother, Frederick's sister, married a Norseman. That made his mother half-Danish and half-Norwegian.

Nicolas was as full-blooded as any prospect. And a direct descendant of King Christian VI. That made him a very likely prospect.

And, incongruent as the idea was, that was why this American was going to Norway.

To see about becoming a king.

℘⃝℃

Days lengthened and the wind cooled as they sailed north. Clouds inflated and deflated, adorning the sky with curved shapes of alabaster, amethyst and pewter. Occasionally they blessed the ship, baptizing it with gentle sprinkles. A school of porpoises played alongside one day, prompting Stefan to draw several on his journey map.

Sydney and Nicolas perfected the art of silent lovemaking in a sardine tin. Then one morning, she woke with sensations she had not experienced for fifteen months. She told Nicolas that she felt like her head was in a vise and her insides were trying to crawl out.

"Willowbark tea," she pleaded. "And a diaper."

"Should I bring your breakfast?" Nicolas offered, rubbing her shoulder.

Sydney gagged and shook her head slightly. "Tea," she whispered.

Worried, Nicolas summoned Maribeth and turned Sydney over to the maid's care. He paced the ship and waited for Sydney to feel well enough to talk to him. He hadn't ever seen a woman in such pain and looking so ill who wasn't in danger of dying. Unable to withstand it any longer, he went below deck to find out for himself. After a soft knock, he let himself into the cabin.

"*Min presang?*"

Sydney had a wet cloth over her eyes, but she flopped a hand in his direction. He closed the cabin door and pulled the tiny chair next to the bed. A bloody rag on the floor suddenly made sense to him. He had been married before; he knew of such things. It just caught him by surprise.

"Is it your course?" he asked quietly.

"Mm-hmm."

Intense relief they had not made another child tingled down

Nicolas' spine and circled to his belly. He wasn't even aware it had been on his mind, but now he realized the fear had never left him. Pulling a deep sigh, he tried to look concerned, not happy.

"Is it always like this for you?" he asked, stroking her arm.

"Mm-hmm."

His elderly housekeeper, Addie, did indeed know what she was talking about. She told him that Sydney experienced a cycle soon after he found her—contrary to Lily Atherton's accusations about the timing of Sydney's pregnancy. Understanding flitted through Nicolas's mind and prompted an uncharitable *ødelagt liten bitch*. Now that he knew what it was like for her, these symptoms were unmistakable.

"So every month you'll have it like this?" he probed.

"Uh-uh." The shake of her head was almost imperceptible. "My cycle is never regular. Only five or six times a year."

"Thank the Lord," Nicolas commented. Fewer chances for another baby.

"I do…"

Embarrassed at her misinterpretation of his words, Nicolas grimaced.

"…but that's probably why I only conceived twice in eleven years with Devin."

His complacence disappeared. Sydney conceived Kirstie the one and only time they lay together before their daughter was born. "You and I—"

"Were unlucky." Sydney lifted the cloth and looked at Nicolas with one gray-green orb. Her skin was pale. Purple circled under the eye he could see. "Or, as it turned out, quite blessed."

Nicolas brushed his lips over hers. "Do you ever feel like someone else was in control?" he whispered.

She dropped the cloth back in place. "All the time."

Sydney took her meals in bed that day and did not hold any lessons. She got out of bed for lunch the next day and by the afternoon was feeling well enough to help Maribeth with the additional laundry. Buckets of seawater were hauled onboard and the women scrubbed the diapers and menstrual cloths by hand. They rinsed them in a second bucket of seawater, and hung everything on a line to dry. As thanks to the crew for stringing the line and hauling the water, the women washed a few items for them as well.

Nicolas asked Sydney to take a walk with him that night. Iridescent foam from the ship's wake glowed pale blue-green in the bright August moonlight. Flat-topped thunderclouds towered over the southern horizon. Outlined in silver by the moon, their internal lightning glowed in bursts of orange and pink.

Sydney leaned back against Nicolas's chest and he held her there. "How amazingly beautiful!" she murmured. "I've never seen such a sight."

Nicolas rested his chin on her hair, his arms looped under her breasts. His pulse began to race as he considered what he wanted—needed—to say to her. He couldn't imagine her being pleased with him. He felt like a complete ass, but there was no help for it. The likelihood must be addressed.

"What's on your mind, husband?"

Her words surprised him. He hadn't quite gotten up his grit just yet. "How did you know?" he stalled.

Sydney pressed against him. "While you're a romantic man, your romance usually requires a locked door, not an open deck. Not that I'm complaining, mind you! I'm very well satisfied with your romancing."

Nicolas kissed the top of her head in response and corralled his courage.

"So what is it, Nicolas?"

He pulled a deep breath, and then his words came out in a rush. "Children. Babies, rather. I don't want you to have any more."

There. He said it. His feelings were sharp as crystal and he wondered if they cut her.

"I know," Sydney whispered. She was very still.

Nicolas's arms tightened around her and he leaned down, pressing his cheek against hers. He couldn't read her cryptic reply, but he made an assumption. "Are you very angry with me?"

She paused. "No."

His brow rippled. He expected a different answer. "Are you sad?"

"Yes." She sniffed and wiped her nose with the heel of her hand. "Kirstie is such a beautiful child."

"She is that," Nicolas conceded softly. "I'm so sorry, *min presang*. But you understand my fears. I can't lose you and continue to live."

Sydney jerked a small nod, her tear-dampened cheek slippery against his. They were silent a while. The swish and slap of the ship's wake filled Nicolas's awareness. He wished he could feel differently. He wished his first wife hadn't died birthing Stefan and his stillborn twin. He wished he might fill Sydney's belly with a houseful of children, if that's what she wished.

But the very idea caused his heart to pummel his ribs, his skin to sheen with sweat, and pinpoints of light to dance in his vision.

Sydney's soft voice pulled him back to the ship's deck. "Truthfully, we may not need to be concerned."

"Oh? Why? Because of your past difficulties?" he posited, relieved but curious.

"Well, there's that," Sydney conceded. "And your injury."

Nicolas inhaled quickly. The possibility hadn't ever occurred to him. He assumed that because he was able to perform sexually that all else was in order. He felt Sydney's damp cheek warming against his.

"I'm not sure of this, Nicolas, but it seems that your... emission... is different now than it was a year ago. It's thinner in consistency. And there's less of it."

Nicolas stood stunned. Could it be? Might that brutal kick to his groin last January actually be a blessing? He was painfully swollen for a fortnight, and it was longer than that before he experienced an erection. Nicolas contemplated the odds, finding the idea unexpectedly pleasant.

He whispered, "I hope you're right, *min presang*. Because bedding you is one of the greatest pleasures of my life."

Sydney turned in his arms, quirking a brow. "One?"

Thoroughly relieved, Nicolas smiled broadly at her teasing. "My life is full of pleasures since you fell into it. That one does happen to be my favorite, however."

"That's a very diplomatic answer, husband." Sydney lifted her chin. Moonlight caught in her eyes and sparkled them with lightning of a different sort. "Perhaps you should consider politics after all."

Chapter Seven

August 2, 1820
London

A surge of rare English sunshine invaded the room.

"Must you do that?" Sydney moaned. She rolled over and pulled a pillow over her face. Her muffled voice escaped from under it. "Kirstie was up twice last night! And your lusty actions have worn me out."

Nicolas laughed and abandoned the window to bounce back into bed, dislodging her makeshift blinder. "Do you know what a temptation you are? To be able to share your bed all night for the first time in nearly five weeks?" His hands explored under the bedclothes, searching for her. "I can't get enough of you!"

She threw the pillow aside. "Husband! You don't intend to—"

"And why not?"

"I shan't be able to walk!" she protested.

Kirstie whimpered in her cradle and lifted her head, changing the course of the early morning. With a half-serious moan, Sydney surfaced from under the bedclothes. It was time to begin their first full day in London.

"There are so many people here," she marveled later as the Hansen party strolled across the crowded Tower Bridge while Londoners in all manner of dress flowed around them.

Sydney pointed at a multi-turreted stone fortress. "What's that?"

"That is the Tower of London," Nicolas informed.

Maribeth spoke up. "William the Conqueror started it in 1066."

"Really?" Sydney was surprised by the quiet maid's interjection. She turned to Nicolas. "That's over seven hundred years ago!"

"And every English monarch has had their coronation at Westminster Abbey since William in 1066."

Her eyes widened. "Really?"

"Even crazy King George whom we rebelled against. By the by, did you know that his youngest sister, Caroline Mathilda, was married to Norway and Denmark's *also* insane Christian the seventh?"

"Who was king when you were in Norway?"

"The insane Christian the seventh. I left in 1807, and he died in 1808."

"You must tell me more about that sometime," Sydney stated. "In case that information becomes important once we're there."

"I will." Nicolas grinned. "Of course, King William the Conqueror was of Norwegian descent."

Sydney's look was skeptical. "And how is that?

"It's God's truth!" Nicolas lifted Stefan and pointed at the castle. "William was Norman, or 'Norseman.' Vikings settled in the north of France. The area was called Normandy as a result."

Sydney shook her head. "I've never seen anything so old."

"I'm hungry, *Pappa.*" Stefan tugged at his hand. "Can we have lunch?"

"I believe that's a fine idea!" Nicolas looked around. "How about that tavern over there? Next to the bookstore?"

"Ooh! A bookstore! Might we stop there after we eat?" Sydney shifted Kirstie on her hip.

"Let's do. Maribeth, might you enjoy a book as well?" Nicolas asked. "It appears you have finished reading your others."

A shy smile spread across her face. "*Ja herr. Jeg ville like det.*" Yes, sir. I would like that.

Nicolas threw his head back and laughed. "*Godt gjort!* Well done!"

Sydney wandered through the aisles of books and inhaled the

essences of ink, leather and paper. She selected two books for Stefan, then found Nicolas in a section of newly printed books.

"Look at this." He held out a book. "It's called the 'Sketchbook of Geoffrey Crayon, Gent.' And the author is Washington Irving, an American. Seems to be a collection of essays."

"Will you buy it?"

"Yes, I believe so." Nicolas looked up from the book. "Have you found aught?"

Sydney shrugged. "I don't know. Have you any suggestions?"

One corner of Nicolas's mouth lifted. "Are there any romantic novels?"

Sydney laughed. "I'll see."

Maribeth selected two books about Norway. She counted out coins in the palm of her hand and accepted the wrapped package with a beatific smile. Sydney nudged Nicolas.

"We did a good thing, bringing her."

"That we did," Nicolas agreed. "She is truly blossoming."

ঙা৪

The ship to Christiania was very much like the ship to London, and so were the sleeping arrangements. After nursing Kirstie the first night, Sydney lay abed and listened to Nicolas. He wasn't breathing like a man asleep, and there was no hint of a snore.

"Are you awake?" she whispered.

Nicolas answered in kind. "I am."

She slid off the bunk and joined him on the floor. She curled against him and rested her head on his shoulder. "What's weighing so heavily on your mind?"

Nicolas sighed and stretched as far as he could. He turned toward the tiny porthole. Moonlight haloed his strong, Nordic profile. "When I was at the dock this morning seeing to our passage, an argument occurred. A dandy shot a longshoreman and didn't appear to care. As though the man's life meant nothing."

Sydney shuddered. "Oh."

"Taking a human life is…" Nicolas drew a shaky breath. "Well, it must never be taken lightly."

Sydney laid her hand against Nicolas's cheek. "How many men have you killed?" She felt his jaw tense. "I know of Edward, and you were right to act the way you did."

Nicolas nodded, then swallowed. Sydney felt his throat work as though it were too dry to complete the task.

"Three," he rasped. "The first one happened in Christiania. You may hear of it, so it's best I tell you now." Nicolas pushed himself to sitting on the mattress, so Sydney sat up as well. His eyes were black in the dim light.

"When I went to Norway, I had need to learn sword fighting, so I was trained by Christian's best swordsman. It was difficult, but I worked hard at it. And I did well.

"This swordsman, his name was Einar Borgsen, had a wife by the name of Disa. She watched us train on the odd occasion, but I didn't think anything of it. Then one day, Einar came to me in such a fury as I'd never seen. He was shouting at me, and Disa was crying and screaming at him.

"It was hard for me to follow their Norse because they were arguing with each other, but Einar said something to the effect of, 'You fucking cuckhold, I'll cut off your cock and then cut out your heart'!"

Sydney's jaw dropped. "Nicolas! Were you?"

"No! Later I discovered that Disa kept a diary where she wrote out imaginary scenarios. She apparently liked to describe various sexual acts, in great detail, and had chosen me as one of her characters."

"And Einar found the diary, I'm guessing."

"That he did. And no amount of denial or explanation could sway his misguided conviction that I was performing a very impressive array of nearly impossible conjugal acts with his wife."

"Oh, Nicolas. What happened?"

"He went after me with the sword. At first I only defended myself while I tried to figure out what was happening. I knew he thought I was bedding his wife, but I didn't know why! I just kept telling him that I was not. And Disa kept telling him I was not.

"With all the shouting, it didn't take long for a crowd to gather. Einar was berserk! He kept after me." Nicolas ran his hand through his hair. "He laid open my cheek."

"That's where the scar came from," she whispered.

"Finally, he yelled at me to 'stop being such a coward!' and was I 'no more than a weak American fop?' Then he cut me—"

Nicolas touched the scar over his heart, "—and I knew he would kill me if I let him. I fought in earnest then. In a couple of strokes I got him in the neck. He bled to death."

Nicolas turned to the tiny window again. "I sat down hard on the ground. My arm was shaking and burning. And I started to cry."

He faced Sydney, then. Embarrassment sunk his cheeks and twisted his brow. "Imagine that? Here I was this tall, strong, bearded buck, blubbering on the ground like a child. I couldn't stop for a very long time."

Nicolas looked down and pleated the blanket between his fingers. "I didn't go to dinner that night. I sent word to Sigrid that I was in my room. As I hoped, she came to me. I was so hard, I hurt."

Straighten the blanket, and pleat it again. "I used her violently that night. I don't know why it was like that, but Gunnar told me about war and battles and the need to fuck afterwards."

Nicolas lifted his eyes to Sydney. "I'm sorry about the language, but the act in that case has nothing to do with love. It's not at all gentle and is very one-sided."

Sydney touched his cheek, tracing the scar. "That explains why whores do such good business around battlefields."

One side of Nicolas's mouth curved up. "That it does."

"I assume you were not held responsible for Einar's death?"

"No. There were enough witnesses to uphold the fact that I tried not to hurt him, and then acted in my own defense when he pressed."

"What happened to Disa?"

Sydney watched his brow twitch. "I don't know."

"Thank you for telling me, Nicolas."

Nicolas nodded. "As I said, you may hear of it."

"Was the other in Christiania as well?"

Nicolas shook his head. "I prefer not to talk about it." He slid down and patted the mattress. "Come warm me. I need you."

∽∾

The wind on this trip was colder and blew harder. As they drew closer to Norway, a change came over Nicolas. He seemed to stand taller, hold his head higher. He was more formal with the crew on this ship than he had been on the crossing. And in turn, they were more respectful of him. They called him 'sir' all the time, and one surprised deck hand even titled him 'your lordship.' Nicolas merely smiled and didn't bother to correct him.

"*Mamma?*"

Sydney was tucking Stefan into bed. "Yes?"

"Is *Pappa* a king?"

Sydney started; Nicolas had resolved not to tell Stefan the true nature of their journey. He believed them to be walking into a politically charged situation and didn't want Stefan inadvertently used as a pawn. If he knew nothing, he was of no help to any side.

"Why do you ask me that?"

Stefan shrugged. "He looks like a king."

Sydney smiled. "That he does."

"Is he, *Mamma?*"

"No, he's not."

Stefan thought a minute. "I bet he could be. If he wanted."

You are more right than you know, little man. Sydney pushed back the perpetual auburn tangle and kissed her stepson on his forehead. "Go to sleep now."

Once the children were settled, Sydney ferreted out a bottle of wine and two glasses. She found Nicolas on the deck, reading his new book by lamplight.

"Is it a good book?" She handed Nicolas the bottle of wine.

His inquisitive look was tempered by a crooked grin. "Yes it is."

He uncorked the bottle and poured into the glasses Sydney held in front of him. "What's on your mind this evening, *min presang?*"

"I believe it's time for you to tell me about the royal family."

"Ah!" Nicolas took a sip of his wine. He lifted the glass into the moonlight. "This is quite good."

"Yes. Delicious. Now tell me about Christian the seventh and why he was insane."

Nicolas considered her over the rim of the glass. "Christian had some peculiar habits. He used to prowl the streets with a medieval spiked club and use it on strangers he passed by."

"That's horrible!" Sydney exclaimed.

"He was a short man, and fairly slender. That may be why he developed such an obsession with being tough." Nicolas leaned closer. "It was said that he masturbated so obsessively, his doctors feared for his health!"

Sydney snorted. "I will not comment on that particular habit in your presence."

Nicolas laughed and refilled his wineglass. "He was crowned King at sixteen. But even afterward he still stormed through the streets, smashing up shops and brothels."

"That's lovely. Not exactly a benevolent ruler."

"Ha! No. Within a year he married Caroline Mathilda, King George's sister. But he misliked her and continued to 'engage' with whores. And with other young men, apparently."

Nicolas shook his head. "Caroline died at twenty-four years of age. And by the time I met him, Christian was in a very bad state. His valet would find him sitting in the corner of his room, staring and distressed. Sometimes, he beat his own head against the wall until he was bloody."

Sydney shuddered. "But, even so, Caroline birthed an heir?"

"Frederick the sixth, who became king when Christian died in 1808. He was already forty, but he had assumed responsibilities for his incapacitated father years before that."

She frowned. "Do your cousins have titles? Like in England?"

"My cousins all use the royal prerogative and are called Dukes and Duchesses of various land holdings. I also have a title," he added, looking at her from the edge of his eye. "As do you."

Sydney smacked her palm loudly against her chest. "*I* have a title? What is it?"

"I'm Lord Hansen, Greve of Rollag. As my wife, you are the Lady Hansen, Grevinne of Rollag. It's because of the land I own."

"Greve and Grevinne?" Sydney asked.

"Count and Countess. Rollag is where my land is."

Sydney emptied the last of the bottled wine into her glass. "Do you have any more surprises I should be aware of?" she asked sharply.

"Most likely," Nicolas confessed. "But they've not come to mind at the moment."

Sydney gulped the burgundy liquid. "Which of your cousins will be in Christiania?"

"I don't know. Anders Fredericksen and his half-brother Erling sent the letter. They're my mother's first cousins."

He slipped his arm around Sydney and she gradually softened, leaning into his shoulder. Illuminated by the moon, the sails glowed overhead and the North Sea glittered around them.

"I have mixed feelings about arriving tomorrow," Sydney admitted. "On the one hand, I'm tired of traveling and look forward to sleeping in a regular bed, and selecting my dress from a wardrobe, not a trunk!"

Nicolas chuckled. "And the other hand?"

"I can't help but feel that we're walking into a very tenuous situation."

Without comment, Nicolas lifted his wine and drained the glass.

A Prince of Norway

The Patriarchs:

Anders and Erling

The Candidates:

Karl, Espen and Nicolas

The Pawns:

Sigrid, Dagmar and Sydney

Chapter Eight

June 12, 1806
Christiania, Norway

*N*ineteen year-old Nicolas Hansen squared his shoulders, jutted a jaw already lengthened by his thick journey's beard, and marched down the gangplank with completely fabricated confidence. His eyes darted from mouth to mouth as the crowd at the Christiania pier shouted in rapid, slang-filled Norse. Though able to understand most of their words, his mind struggled to string them into coherent thoughts.

"*Vil De liker leie en vogn?*"

The voice at his elbow startled Nicolas and he stared down at its source. A pudgy man in a knit cap repeated his question, "*Vil De liker leie en vogn?*" Would you like to hire a carriage?

"Yes. Er... *ja,*" Nicolas nodded. "*Behager.*" Please.

Nicolas followed the man to an open carriage hitched to a large, shaggy beast. The horse swung his huge head toward the sound of their boots on the cobblestones.

"W'ere you go?" the man spoke in broken English having correctly assessed Nicolas's native tongue.

"Akershus *Slott.*" Akershus Castle. The man lifted an eyebrow and his eyes passed over Nicolas's tall frame and well-tailored clothing. He nodded and climbed into the driver's seat. Nicolas scrambled into the back and the carriage jerked forward.

Akershus Castle and fortress were built on a hill overlooking the harbor. Towering more than six stories, the castle's plain sides were surrounded by stone walls that belied the opulence within. When Nicolas introduced himself to the soldier at the gate, he was escorted to the castle's main entrance and handed off to a uniformed butler, who in turn led him up a grand staircase and instructed him to wait.

Nicolas stood straight, feet planted and body swaying out of habit with the rise and fall of the ocean. Soon the butler returned and ushered him through another doorway into a richly appointed drawing room. A tall man in expensive clothing strode towards him.

"Lord Nicolas Christiansen! *Søskenbarn!*" Cousin!

Frederick VI looked younger than his thirty-eight years, his blond hair and blue eyes a reflection of Nicolas's. He grasped Nicolas's hand in his and pulled him into an embrace. The men pounded each other's backs in filial affection.

"Or maybe I use English, eh?" Frederick grinned at Nicolas.

Nicolas shook his head and answered in Norse. "My mother would be ashamed if her diligent tutoring came to naught. I must use Norse and grow comfortable with it."

"Wonderful!" Frederick laughed and continued in that language. "Come, sit and tell me of your journey. Are you hungry?" Without waiting for a reply, he waved a hand at the butler who disappeared and returned shortly with trays of delicacies.

Thus began Nicolas Hansen's year of education in the ways of Norway, and his deceptively calm introduction to her turbulent royal family.

August 13, 1820
Christiania, Norway

Those memories pushed against Nicolas with all the strength of the insistent North Sea wind. He stood on the bow of the ship, one foot propped on the railing, as the ship slid into the Christiania harbor. His pale gold hair—a color common on the bare heads bustling around the port and a reminder that he himself was of this race—flew around his head and cast the prescient shadow of an airy crown. He squinted up at Akershus Festning; the fortress towered over the docks.

"Is that the castle?" Sydney stood beside him with Kirstie on her hip. Maribeth followed Stefan all over the deck, trying to keep him from getting in the crew's way.

"The walls you see are the fortress. The castle is the large building inside. And over there, see that pitched roof? That's the Great Hall." Nicolas leaned toward Sydney and pointed. "Are you able to see the church spires on the other side? The royal mausoleum is in there."

"When was this castle built?" Sydney shaded her eyes and looked up.

"1299. But it was rebuilt in the mid-1600's to make it more Renaissance in style."

Sydney dropped her hand. "Does it appear anything has changed since you were last here?"

Nicolas chuckled. "Eight-hundred-year-old cities don't usually change much."

೮ාᲝ

"*Pappa*? Is this castle yours?" Stefan held his father's hand for balance, his head tilted so far back he could barely walk.

"It's where my family lives." Nicolas clarified. He introduced himself to the gate guards and their arrival was an echo of his first visit. A tall white-haired man entered the room and walked purposefully toward the Hansens.

"*Og her han er! Mottakelse,* Lord Nicolas, *Greve of Rollag! Og mottakelse til din vakker familie!*" And here he is! Welcome, Lord Nicolas, Count of Rollag! And welcome to your beautiful family!

Nicolas answered in Norse. "Thank you, Your Grace. I trust you're well?"

"Indeed! I'm in good health for a man of sixty-four. Is this your wife?"

Sydney appeared to follow the pleasantries and she smiled at his cousin.

"Prince Anders Fredericksen, I present my wife, the Lady Siobhan Sydney Bell Hansen, Grevinne of Rollag."

"It's a pleasure," Anders said in English.

She answered: "*Det er min fornøyelse også.*" It is my pleasure as well.

Anders laughed, surprised. "*Du taler Norse?*"

"*Bare litt.*" A little.

Anders ginned broadly, his blue eyes sparkling. "How delightful!"

Nicolas introduced Stefan, Kirstie and Maribeth.

Anders continued in Norse, "Have you other staff with you?"

"No, I'm afraid my estate in Missouri required their continued presence," Nicolas demurred.

"That's not a problem. I shall assign you a valet, and Lady Hansen a maid, for the duration of your stay here." Anders waved his hands and whispered to the butler.

Nicolas bowed at the waist. "Thank you. That's very considerate of you."

"Peder will show you to your rooms. Please take your time to settle in. Dinner is at eight." Anders lifted Sydney's hand. "I look forward to seeing you then, Lady Hansen."

"*Takk du,*" she replied.

ഇൗങ

Sigrid remembered well the first time she saw Nicolas; tall, bearded and terrified. His lean body rested against the wall of the Great Hall as his eyes darted around the room. At nineteen, Nicolas did not yet have his man-weight, that thickening of bone and muscle that heralds physical maturity. But he was more than adequate, nonetheless. And so heartbreakingly beautiful. Sigrid's heart ached at the memory of his navy blue eyes and easy, sensual smile.

Sigrid closed her eyes and slowly pressed her hands along her body. It had been a simple task to get him into bed. She giggled at the memory.

He stood still as she undressed him, his jaw set, and his eyes huge and dark. She rubbed scented oil on him, and then unrolled the sheep's intestine over his exigent member.

"This is to ensure we don't make a baby," she explained. Then she lay back on his bed and lifted her skirts. She held her hands out in invitation and he stepped to the bed. He kneeled between her thighs and she pulled him in.

Nicolas shook off his virginity the way a dog shakes off water. What he lacked in experience, he made up for in enthusiasm. And as time passed, Sigrid was able to teach him the intricacies of pleasing a woman. He was an eager student and he learned well. Very well.

But when the time neared for him to leave Christiania, Nicolas stopped following her from the Great Hall. She pressed him for an explanation.

"I'm sorry Sigrid. I'll be leaving soon and I've a bride waiting for me in Missouri. I can't continue our play. But I have enjoyed it immensely and will remember you always. Thank you." He kissed her hand and walked away.

Sigrid was devastated. She spent the next several days—was it a week?—in her room steeped in an alcohol haze. But she always sobered and felt the loss afresh.

After all this time she could hardly believe that the widower Nicolas was back in the castle right now. That he would be at dinner tonight. She drew a deep, steadying breath. What would he think of her, thirteen years later? Was there any chance he would be willing to rekindle that spark? Sigrid looked in her mirror and convinced herself that she was every bit as beautiful at forty-one as she had been at twenty-eight.

She wondered how Nicolas looked. Older, surely. More mature. More manly, no doubt. Was it possible he might be even more beautiful? His life in America as he described it was very physical. He worked hard with his body. Her fingers stroked down an imaginary muscled chest and tangled delightfully in the nest of hair far below.

She poured herself a third glass of akevitt and dug through her wardrobe for the perfect dress.

೫つC೫

"Has he arrived?" Erling asked his half-brother.

"Yes," Anders sank into a chair.

"How does he look?"

"He looks magnificent."

"Excellent. How long is he staying?" Erling handed Anders a

glass of akevitt.

"We didn't get that far in the conversation." Anders downed the liquor and winced. "I sent them to their rooms to settle in. As we anticipated, he didn't bring a full staff. Peder will assign Haldis as Mrs. Hansen's maid and Tomas as Nicolas's valet."

"Perfect choices!" Erling nodded his satisfaction.

☙❧

Sydney noticed her first. The woman descending the stairs had a tight grip on the railing and an intent stare fixed on Nicolas. Her hair was faded blond, her eyes faded blue. She wore a tight gown with a precariously low décolletage. Her step was just a bit unsteady.

"Nicolas?"

He turned toward the voice. "Duchess! How are you?"

"Dearest cousin! It has been forever! You look wonderful." Sigrid kissed him hard on the mouth and slipped her arm in his. "Why did you never write to me? I so missed your friendship."

"Did I never? I don't recall." Nicolas unwound Sigrid's arm. "May I present my wife? The Lady Siobhan Sydney Bell Hansen, Grevinne of Rollag."

"What?" the woman blurted. Her brows drew together. "No! You're wife died!"

"I remarried, Duchess." He took Sydney's elbow, turned, and spoke slowly to his wife. "This is Her Grace, Sigrid Andersen Haugen, Duchess of Harstad, my second cousin and daughter of Anders Fredericksen, Duke of Stavanger, whom you met earlier."

Sydney—who had followed all but a word or two of the exchange—curtsied without taking her eyes from Sigrid's. She responded in Norse, "It's my pleasure, Your Grace."

"You speak Norse?" Sigrid looked straight through her. She appeared to be more than a little stunned by the introduction.

"A little, yes." Sydney slipped her hand into Nicolas's and squeezed. He squeezed back.

"We have a daughter who is six months old," he added.

"Seven months." Sydney smiled extra sweetly.

"Nicolas, your letter didn't indicate that you had family accompanying you." Sigrid fanned herself frantically. Urgent spots of red blurred over her cheeks. Her eyes darkened and her brow wavered.

"The first letter didn't, no. When I decided to bring them, I sent a second letter."

"Father?" Sigrid's arm shot out and grasped Anders. "Did you receive a second letter from Nicolas?"

"Why, yes, I believe so. You look lovely this evening, Lady Hansen." Anders smiled. "I trust your rooms are *tilfredsstillende?*"

"*Tilfredsstillende?*" Sydney looked to Nicolas.

"Satisfactory."

"Ah! Yes, thank you." Sydney returned Anders' smile.

"And here is my half-brother, Erling Fredericksen, Duke of Trondheim." Anders waved Erling over.

"It's good to see you again, Lord Hansen! You look quite well!" Erling offered Nicolas his hand.

"As do you, Your Grace."

"And this must be your beautiful wife?" Erling swept Sydney with an appreciative gaze.

"May I present the Lady Siobhan Sydney Bell Hansen, Grevinne of Rollag."

"Pleased to meet you, Your Grace." Sydney curtsied.

"I assure you, Lady, the pleasure is entirely mine." He kissed her hand.

"Siobhan? Is that not an Irish name?" Sigrid's injected query was an undisguised slur.

"Yes, it is, Your Grace."

"And Bell?"

"Scots." Sydney spoke confidently and wondered what Sigrid's point might be.

Sigrid turned to her father, smiling tightly. "I believe our Vikings invaded both countries, did they not, Father? And on innumerable occasions?"

"Sigrid!" Anders chided, looking distraught.

"Sydney, at the least, is a Norman name. Have you Norman blood after all?" Sigrid lifted one eyebrow.

Sydney looked to Nicolas; she did not understand the question in Norse. He answered for her.

"It's only a name, Duchess; given because it suited her."

Sigrid lifted Sydney's left hand. "Is this your wedding ring? A simple garnet?" She blinked slowly at Nicolas. "Could you not have done better?"

"I chose it because of the color. It goes well with her eyes."

Sigrid's gaze flicked to Sydney's eyes and back to the ring.

"How very—colonial." She dropped Sydney's hand and walked stiffly away.

Even though Sydney did not understand every word, she understood what was being discussed. Her jaw clenched as she ran through a satisfying list of completely inappropriate responses in two languages.

Nicolas took her arm and leaned down to whisper in her ear, "Would you like me to purchase you a more suitable ring?"

"Don't trouble yourself." Sydney stared straight ahead. "I wouldn't wear it."

The doors to the Hall opened and the dinner crowd wandered into the room. Sydney didn't wish to appear unsophisticated, but her jaw dropped at the size of the space. A raised table in the front held eight chairs. Two long tables, with two dozen seats on either side, extended from the raised table in an enormous U. Overhead, carved wooden struts, darkened by centuries of smoke, towered three stories above them. She held tight to Nicolas's arm. He led her toward the front and took a seat to the right of the head table. It was a seat of honor, and he took it with confidence.

Sigrid sat at the opposite table, facing them. An obese older man, shuffling with a cane and panting with the effort, dropped into the chair next to hers. His skin was pasty but for splotches of red on his cheeks, and his enlarged scarlet nose betrayed a life of debauchery.

That must be the 'fat hairy beast' Sigrid was married to. In spite of the way the woman glared at her, Sydney felt a moment of pity for the much younger wife.

Then her stomach growled; she was hungry and the food smelled wonderful. Uniformed servants hurried around the room, pouring wine, beer and akevitt at each place. Sydney pointed at the unfamiliar liquor.

"What is that?" she asked Nicolas in English.

"Akevitt. It's Scandinavia's answer to Russia's vodka. It's distilled from potatoes then flavored with anise, dill or fennel." Nicolas lifted his glass and sniffed. "This appears to be anise."

Sydney sniffed hers and recognized the scent. "Why is it so yellow?"

"The darker color either means it's been aged longer." Nicolas's eyes twinkled and he whispered in her ear, "Or, to save money, the use of young casks!"

Sydney observed others at the table. Most were on their second or third glass. "Should I drink it now?"

Nicolas nodded. "Give it a try."

Sydney downed the alcohol and regretted it immediately. Her chest burned all the way to her stomach, and that recepticle clenched in violent protest at being set on fire. Her eyes watered. She grabbed her beer glass and gulped the cooling liquid.

"Perhaps I should have warned you. It's quite strong."

Sydney's voice pinched. "That would have been helpful!"

"Most do follow akevitt with beer, that's why both are poured. Purists, however, claim beer ruins the delicate flavor and aftertaste," Nicolas explained.

Sydney rolled her eyes. "Who can tell that when one's gullet has been stripped?"

"Here." Nicolas speared her appetizer and lifted it from her plate. "Taste this."

Sydney sampled the pink smoked fish. It was good, and did seem to complement the akevitt, now that her taste buds were beginning to recover. "What was that? I liked it."

"Smoked salmon."

"And what is that?" She pointed at another dish.

"Lutefisk. Don't try that tonight." Nicolas spooned it onto his plate. "Even more than akevitt, this is an acquired taste, to be sure!"

The appetizer course was completed and soup was brought out. The server at their table turned suddenly and dropped a bowl of soup right in Nicolas's lap.

"Gud forbanner det all til helvete! De uvitende suckling av en fatherlass plugg! Hellig dritt!" he bellowed. He blotted his breeches and continued with a paragraph of curses so intense that even Sydney understood his point.

Guests within earshot responded with stunned silence. Mouths gaping and eyes wide, they stared, horrified, at Nicolas. He looked at Sydney as realization dawned, and he bloomed scarlet. Unlike their family and friends in Missouri, these people understood his words.

Every single one of them.

Sydney slapped her hand over her mouth. Nicolas's eyes rounded and his lips moved silently for a long moment. Then he stammered the Norse words of his apology.

"I—I'm so very sorry! Please forgive my rude outburst and accept my truly humble apology."

"Hmm." Anders, at the head table, considered his younger cousin. He quirked one brow. "You ignorant suckling of a fatherless pig? I must confess that's one I have not yet heard."

Someone snickered, then coughed to cover it.

Anders moved his gaze around the room. "Perhaps we can learn from our American cousin after all, eh?"

The next snicker was not disguised. Nicolas blew a slow breath in relief.

A maid used the disruption to slide next to Nicolas and whisper urgently. Her eyes darted to Sydney. She spoke so rapidly, Sydney couldn't follow. Nicolas put up his hand to stop the maid, and turned to face her.

"It seems, Madam, that your services are required."

Sydney was confused. "Mine? How?"

"As best I can make out, my cousin Eirik's wife Linnet is confined with birth pains. She is English and speaks no Norse. The midwife speaks no English."

"But I don't speak enough Norse!" Sydney objected.

Nicolas spoke deliberately to the maid but she would not be dissuaded. She reached over and grabbed Sydney's arm.

"*Behag Madam. Vær så snill og komm.*" Please, Madam. Please come.

Nicolas shrugged, but his eyes implored her to comply. Sydney sighed and pushed back her chair.

"*Ja, jeg kommer,*" she said to the maid.

Then she addressed Nicolas, "If I don't return presently, please send a dinner tray. And Maribeth, when Kirstie is hungry."

Nicolas squeezed her hand. "Thank you, *min presang.*"

Chapter Nine

A few minutes after the maid summoned Sydney from Nicolas's side, Sigrid moved across the tables to her vacated chair.

"Where has Siobhan gone? To nurse her baby?" Sigrid signaled to a server.

"She was summoned to Eirik's wife's birthing." Nicolas poured her a glass of wine.

"Good lord! Is she a midwife?" Sigrid's derision was clear.

"No. But his wife is English and apparently doesn't speak Norse. She wanted someone with whom she could converse," Nicolas explained.

"I'm glad to hear she's confined at last. And it's quite fortunate that the maid was aware that Siobhan speaks English!" Sigrid took a bite of the dish set before her. "This is delicious!"

"Sydney."

"Nicolas?"

"She goes by Sydney, not Siobhan."

"Oh. Well." Sigrid shrugged and helped herself to a bite off Nicolas's plate. "At the least, she hides her Irish heritage! Have you tried the venison?"

Sigrid dangled a forkful in front of Nicolas's lips. Her light blue eyes met his and her lips parted in invitation. Unwilling to make yet another scene on his first night in Christiania, Nicolas opened his mouth and allowed Sigrid to feed him.

"Very tasty," he mumbled, and sipped his wine. Deliberately changing the subject, he pointed his chin at Sigrid's empty seat. "How is Vegard these days?"

Sigrid's eyes darted to her husband. "His health is bad. But he refuses to die and leave me in peace."

"What are his complaints? I don't believe he used a cane, last I was here."

"The gout is most recent. Thus the cane. His only pleasures are food, wine. And my hand."

Nicolas choked. "I beg your pardon?"

Sigrid leaned close and whispered in his ear, her voice husky with drink. "He begs me to satisfy him, but it is akin to kneading biscuit dough. If he asks, I ply him with plenty of akevitt first. He falls asleep, and then I can stop."

"And that suffices?" Nicolas was appalled at her situation.

"I assure him the next day that he was hard as a cedar and came like a whale." Sigrid flipped a hand in front of her face. "I don't know if he believes me, and I don't particularly care."

Her hand dropped to Nicolas's thigh. "My memories of you inspired that particular description."

She leaned back into her chair and smiled across at Vegard. He sneered in return. Nicolas nodded a greeting to the old man. He didn't desire to make any enemies before understanding the political landscape at Akershus Castle. He was even willing to tolerate Sigrid's advances.

To a point.

He laid his hand over hers to keep it from drifting closer to his manhood. "Have you your father's ear?" Nicolas asked as his gaze shifted to Anders.

Sigrid straightened. "Do you mean in the quest for a king?"

Nicolas kept his tone casual. "In anything."

"I express my opinions. On occasion, he concurs. Other times he does not. Why do you ask?"

Nicolas gave Sigrid his best smile. "I only need to know whom I can trust, is all. And who might be my champion."

Sigrid's pale aquamarine eyes brightened with hope. "I might be able to help you. In anything you need. Anything at all."

"Thank you, Sigrid. That's very comforting to know." He squeezed her hand.

ഈൽൽ

Sydney hurried after the nimble maid. When they reached the second story hallway, she tried without success to appreciate the towering ceilings, carved wood paneling, intricate wrought-iron sconces and endless paintings that lined the window-casemented walls that she was practically running past. Behind heavy doors, she could hear screaming.

With a quick knock, the maid opened one.

"*Her er kvinnen!*" She put her hand in the middle of Sydney's back and shoved, slamming the door shut behind her. The woman on the bed stopped screaming and stared at Sydney.

"Are you English?" she demanded from amidst a massive mountain of pillows and lace.

Sydney approached the imposing brocade-canopied bed. "I'm American."

"Good Lord! I am surrounded by nothing but *barbarians* in my hour of need!" the woman wailed. She flopped back against the pillows and pressed one limp wrist against her brow.

Sydney shrugged. "Fine, then. If you've no need of me, I'll return to my husband and my dinner." She turned toward the door.

"No! No! I'm sorry! I just... I'm so... Ooohhhh!" The woman's face turned scarlet and she grabbed her enormous belly. "I'm gooooing tooo diiiiiieeee!"

The midwife heaved an exasperated sigh and crossed to Sydney. She placed her palm against her own chest. "Ingrid Olavsen."

"Sydney Hansen." Sydney extended her hand.

"*Du taler Norse?*"

"*Bare litt. Du taler Engelsk?*"

Ingrid nodded and held up her finger and thumb half an inch apart. "*Ikke forteller henne!*" Don't tell her!

Sydney laughed.

"What are you laughing at?" the natal beast on the bed snarled.

Sydney waved her hand in an offhand manner. "My Norse. I misspoke."

"Hmph." She glared suspiciously at the midwife.

"We've not been properly introduced, so that convention falls upon us. I'm Lady Siobhan Sydney Bell Hansen, wife of Nicolas

Reidar Hansen, Greve of Rollag."

"Lord Nicolas Hansen? Eirik's cousin?"

"I suppose so. And you are?"

"Lady Linnet Windsor-Worthingham, wife of Eirik Frederick Canutesen, Duke of Hamar."

Lady Linnet looked to be in her thirties. She was a comely woman with rich brown hair and gray eyes. But while her brow was ridged in permanent furrows, she lacked laugh lines.

"I'm pleased to meet you, Your Grace. What, precisely, do you wish from me?"

Linnet's eyes shifted back to the midwife. "I cannot understand a word that woman utters! I must have someone in attendance with whom I can communicate."

"I understand your concerns, but she is a midwife and I'm not. And my Norse is fundamental at best..."

"Have you birthed any children?"

Sydney swallowed, her mouth gone suddenly dry. "Three." *One that lived.*

"So then you know what hell I am going through!"

"Your Grace, birthing a child is not at all the same as delivering a child!"

Another pain gripped Linnet. She rolled on the bed and wailed, "I doooon't caaaare! Oooohhhh! God help meeeeeee!"

Sydney looked to Ingrid.

The midwife shook her head and rolled her eyes, lips puckered. "She will not *tillat* me *nær*," she complained.

Sydney considered her options. She really wanted to go back to her dinner and leave this obnoxious woman to her own end. She turned a little to the door, trying to convince herself the problem wasn't hers to solve. After all, Lady Linnet was a stranger to her. And a rude one, at that.

But.

This was her first night in Norway and at Akershus Castle with the royal family. And Nicolas had a great deal riding on the outcome of this journey. What she chose to do now would have an impact on his future. And hers. And their children's. She sighed and turned back to Her Grace.

When Lady Linnet's pain seemed to have passed, Sydney rested determined fists on her hips. "I'll help you as much as I'm able. But you must attend to what I say!" she declaimed.

Linnet's eyes focused slowly. Then she nodded, her muddled gaze riveted on Sydney.

Sydney waved a pointed finger in her direction. "This baby is going to come. You may help it, or you may hinder it. The choice you make may determine whether you live or die in the process!"

Linnet's eyes rounded. "I don't wish to die!"

"You needn't," Sydney quickly assured her. "But you must do as I—and Ingrid—tell you."

"Ingrid?"

Sydney huffed. "The midwife."

"Oh." Linnet had the decency to blush.

Sydney pulled a deep breath. "All right, then. First of all, lay on your side. And put that pillow between your knees." Linnet shifted awkwardly in the bed until she was in position. "Are you comfortable?"

"Yes." Linnet began to gasp.

"With this pain, Your Grace, I want you to relax."

Linnet glared at her. "Relax? How can I possibly relax when my very body is being torn brutally asunder?" When the birth pain strengthened, Linnet's body twisted and she cried out, "I cannot! I cannot! Ooooohhhh!"

Good Lord, Sydney thought. This had better be worth it.

Sydney walked around the bed so she was behind Linnet. She leaned close and rested her left hand on Linnet's belly. With her right hand she massaged Linnet's lower back. Linnet sagged as the contraction ended and her tension decreased.

"Close your eyes," Sydney whispered. "With the next pain, push your stomach against my hand when you breathe in. Can you do that?"

It took a few tries, but Linnet gradually gained a modicum of control over her body. And—thank God—she stopped screaming.

"You're doing very well, Your Grace," Sydney murmured.

"Thank you, Madam Hansen," she whispered.

Ingrid tapped Sydney on the shoulder. "*Er De en doktor?*"

Sydney shook her head, no.

"*Du har en presang.*"

Sydney understood *presang*, gift. "*Takk du.*"

A knock on the door preceded a maid with Sydney's dinner

tray.

"I'm hungry." Linnet whined, looking over her shoulder at the tray.

Sydney remembered Rosie's words when she birthed Kirstie and repeated them to Linnet. "Your body doesn't have time for food. You would just vomit it up."

Ingrid encouraged the fading fire back to life and set a pot of water to warm. She pulled an apron for Sydney and a stack of clean rags from her bag. Sydney heard her daughter in the hall before Maribeth knocked on the door. The clock on the mantel showed half past eleven. Sydney had come to Linnet's room at eight.

"Come in, Maribeth. Might you loosen my laces?" Sydney reached for Kirstie, crooning, "How is my darling girl? Are you hungry, sweetheart?"

Kirstie fussed and smiled and frowned as she fidgeted. Sydney sat near the bed and opened her gown. Kirstie latched on hungrily. She reached up to Sydney's face and Sydney kissed her small palm.

"How old is she?" Lady Linnet watched from the bed.

"Seven months."

"And you've not made use of a wet nurse? How very odd... I suppose it's because you're an American. How old are the other two?"

Caught off her guard, Sydney didn't look up. "They were born too early and didn't breathe."

When Kirstie was satisfied, Sydney kissed her and handed her back to Maribeth. "Might you bring me some cooking oil?"

Ingrid tapped Sydney's shoulder and pointed at Linnet. She made a circle with her forefinger and thumb, and pushed three of her fingers through the circle. Sydney nodded.

"Your Grace, Ingrid needs to examine you inside..."

"No. You do it."

"But I don't know how!"

"She can show you. I don't want that woman touching me. She stares at me oddly. And she mutters under her breath. I don't trust her."

Sydney slid her worried gaze to Ingrid. "*Hjelper meg gjør det?*" Help me do it?

Ingrid sighed and nodded, talking to herself. Sydney squelched her snicker when she recognized the words "stubborn" and "ignorant."

Ingrid showed her what to do. Sydney felt the baby's head pushing against a ring of tough flesh just wider than her three fingers. When she showed Ingrid, the midwife nodded and began to place the hot rags against Linnet.

"*Babyen kommer.*"

Maribeth returned with the oil and, between hot compresses, Sydney massaged it into the opening to Linnet's womb—the way the St. Louis midwife had done for her—then checked her again. As she did so, Linnet abruptly cried out. The baby's head pushed Sydney's hand back as it surged into the birth canal.

Panic overtook Linnet. Another pain caused her to curl on the bed, groaning and twisting.

"That's your baby!" Sydney cried. "Push it out, Your Grace, just as though you were using the chamber pot."

"But I'll soil myself!" she wailed. When another pain rolled over her, Sydney pushed her knee aside.

"I can see the head, Your Grace! Push!"

Lady Linnet's red face screwed tight as she finally bore down. Six straining pushes later, the baby's head emerged wet, bloody and cone-shaped. Ingrid jumped forward and wiped mucus from the infant's mouth and nose. Then she placed her hands over Sydney's.

Ingrid guided Sydney as she worked first one shoulder, then the other, through the tight opening. Suddenly the baby slithered into Sydney's arms. She cried out her own surprise.

"It's a boy! You have a son!"

Ingrid lifted the babe from Sydney and laid him on Linnet's chest. Linnet stared at his pinkening, slimy body in open-mouthed shock. He squirmed and threw his limbs wide before giving a wail of indignation.

Sydney trembled all over and her heart pounded so hard she was certain it could be heard in the hallway. God in Heaven—what an occurrence! Nothing she had ever experienced in her entire life felt like the moment Linnet's newborn child dropped into her waiting hands. She felt like she was floating, euphoric.

She fidgeted, shaking her hands in front of her. The elegant room suddenly felt too small to contain her. She didn't know what to do with herself. She wanted to laugh. She wanted to cry. She wanted to shout from the rooftops.

She wanted to do it again.

Sydney grinned like a lunatic at Ingrid. Ingrid smiled and nodded her understanding.

When Sydney finally went to search out her husband's chamber, the clock in the birth room said four-thirty. She was exhausted. She dropped her gown on his floor and climbed into his bed in her shift. She snuggled against Nicolas, seeking his solid warmth. He adjusted his position and made room for her.

"Was the birth successful?" he whispered.

"Mm-hmm." Sydney sighed and closed her eyes. "And now I shall become a midwife."

Before Nicolas responded, she was asleep.

Chapter Ten

July 20, 1806
Christiania

*T*he valet opened the door to the Great Hall and announced, "His Royal Highness, King Christian the Seventh, King of Denmark and Norway."

He stepped aside and swept his arm to the open portal. Nicolas bowed, as did his cousins Eirik and Espen, and his uncles Canute, Anders and Erling. Nicolas stared from under his brows at the unusual figure that entered the room.

Christian was a tall man with flowing brown hair, but he walked with furtive stoop, as though afraid of sudden attack. Once past the doorway, he stopped and straightened, looking down his long nose at the men.

"You may rise."

They did. Nicolas assumed that the younger man following Christian was his son—and the de facto king—Frederick VI. As Christian approached, Nicolas noticed that his ornate clothing was torn and repaired in places. And he had an odor about him, stale and unwashed.

"Who are you?" the king demanded.

The sweep of his glance made Nicolas feel unclothed. He stood tall, taller than the king, and introduced himself.

"I am Nicolas Reidar Hansen, Greve of Rollag. Great-grandson of your grandfather, Christian the sixth. My mother, Kirsten Marin Sven, is your first cousin."

"Are you an American?" Christian scoffed.

"I am, Your Highness."

One eyebrow lifted. "Are you barbaric in your ways?"

Nicolas glanced at his uncles. How should he answer that? One uncle nodded, another shook his head. No help from those two!

"I come from a young and wild land, Your Majesty. I have experience and skills which might be considered barbaric in such long-established realms such as Norway and Denmark."

"Oh? Really?" Christian's glance undressed him again. "I should very much like to hear more about these barbaric experiences."

Nicolas bowed, but did not respond. Frederick took his father's elbow.

"Would you like to sit, Father?"

"Well, of course I should like to sit!" he barked. "But you must make all those hideous creatures get out of my seat first!"

All eyes in the room turned to the empty chair.

"Of course, Father." Frederick waved his arms at the empty chair. "Off with you now! The King commands it!"

Christian strode to the chair and paused until his valet arranged the tails of his coat. Then he sank into the seat.

August 14, 1820
Christiania

"Do you remember your lessons?"

Espen Christian Canutesen, Duke of Lillehammer, addressed Nicolas while waving a sword in his direction. Blue sky slid along its steel blade in the late morning sunlight of the warm castle courtyard. Without warning, he flipped the sword, grip over blade, toward Nicolas.

Nicolas flinched, but his body remembered. He caught the sword by the pommel and his eyes flicked up to his cousin.

Espen smiled his approval. "Not a bad job."

Nicolas rotated the sword in his hand until he felt it settle. "There's not much call for swords in Missouri. Rifles and knives are the weapons of choice."

"Pity."

Nicolas sliced the air with a few broad arcs. It felt good.

"Care to test your skill?" Espen didn't wait for an answer; he lunged.

For the next quarter hour the two men parried, clashed, lunged and feinted. Nicolas fought from pure instinct at first. Sweat ran down his back and brow with the effort, and his lungs burned with the dust the pair stirred. But the longer they fought, the more sure his movements became. His balance shifted; his arm responded.

Finally, Espen stepped back and lowered his blade.

"Well played, Hansen."

"Thank you." Nicolas handed him the sword. "I needed the practice."

"Einar taught us well. Too well, as I recall, may he rest in peace."

Nicolas felt his face warm further at the reminder of his shame, but the cousins embraced and pounded each other's backs nonetheless.

"You look well for an old man of three and thirty!" Espen grinned.

"As do you!" Nicolas rejoined. "When, then, did your beard come in? When we were all of twenty, I recall your face was as smooth as a maiden's!"

"Right after I experienced precisely for what purpose those maidens were created!" Espen winked. "A purpose I enjoy whenever I'm able!"

"So you never married?"

"Not yet. There's time. I'm still searching, one by one." Espen sheathed the weapons; he didn't meet Nicolas's eye. "And you? I heard you lost your wife, but turned up here with another."

"My wife Lara died in childbirth seven years ago. Our son is with me. I married again and have a seven-month-old daughter."

"Are you happy, Nicolas?" Espen asked, looking askance at his cousin.

"That I am."

"But not happy enough, I venture, to stay in Missouri? The

prospect of kingship is seductive, is it not?"

"Are you a candidate as well?" Nicolas wondered if everyone knew why he was in Christiania.

Espen shook his head. "I wasn't asked and I would have declined. Apparently, a suitable wife is a requirement, and I have no interest in an arranged marriage for my career's sake."

"What about Eirik?"

"His wife, the Lady Linnet, is English. Need I say more?"

Nicolas chuckled. "No."

"But I understand that the birth of my nephew was eased by your wife's assistance. Be sure to thank her on behalf of the Canutesen branch of the Fredericksens!"

"I'll make certain you meet her soon, and so you may thank her yourself," Nicolas promised.

ɛɔႱଓ

"Å *min Gud!*" Nicolas fell back on the bed, panting, limbs thrown wide. "Å *min Gud i himmel!*"

Sydney curled toward him and sighed, her nether parts swollen and her limbs still tingling. "How decadent are we, husband? It's the middle of the afternoon!"

"The decadence lies not in the hour, but in the location. Finally! A full bed!" Nicolas stretched his legs. "I hoped we might 'christen' it last night, but the birth kept you away too long."

"Will we outrage your cousins if we share this room?" Sydney propped on one elbow.

"I'll not have you sleeping elsewhere!" Nicolas ran his knuckle down her throat and around her breast; she shivered as always at his touch. "Unless, that's what you prefer? After all these weeks, have you grown accustomed to solitude in bed?"

"No, indeed!" Sydney caught his hand and bit his finger playfully before sticking it in her mouth and drawing it out slowly. He watched her with widening eyes. "After all these weeks, I have grown deprived! Sleep is highly overrated."

Nicolas pulled her close and kissed her, his desire for her still obvious. "That's the perfect answer, wife. Tonight we'll work to eradicate your deprivation. As your loving husband, I am fully committed to your well being!"

Sydney giggled and kissed him deeply, teasing his tongue with hers. "Let's get everyone resettled, then, shall we?" she whispered against his lips.

He grunted and rolled on top of her. "I'll resettle now, wife, if you'll open up a bit."

Half an hour later, a considerably less deprived Sydney—with the help of her Akershus maid, Haldis—moved her things into the room previously assigned to Nicolas alone. Stefan's things were moved into the adjoining room, which had been intended for Sydney and Kirstie to share. That left Maribeth alone in the room across the hall. The shy maid looked as if she might swoon at such luxury.

When Sydney returned to her new bedchamber, she found Nicolas hunched over a large sheet of paper. He was writing names and drawing lines.

Sydney leaned over him. "What are you doing?"

"Charting." He didn't look up.

"Charting what? Is that a diagram of your family?"

He nodded. "Some members of this family were quite insane. Both Frederick's father and his uncle, King George of England, to name two." He paused and scowled at the document. "I wonder if that circumstance has been passed on to any of my cousins?"

Nicolas looked at her finally, his face still twisted in thought. "I'm trying to make sure that I know where each one is, relative to Frederick the Sixth. And to whom they are married."

"And then?" she prompted.

"And then I shall know who might be king."

Living Descendents of King Christian VI & Sophia Magdalen

Frederick V & Louise:
5 Deceased Progeny
Frederick V & Juliana Maria:
2 Deceased incl. Sebastian - <u>Leif's father!</u>
Anders & Johanna:
Sigrid & Vegard
Canute & Agnes:
Eirik & Linnet
(Espen)   **no heir**
Ellen
Elisa
Frederick V & Else Hansen (Mistress)
3 Deceased incl. Petra:
Dagmar
Didrick - Deceased
<u>Erling</u>
(Karl) & Ingeborg: **54**
Karla
Borg
Else

Marit Christiansen & Henrik Sven:
Kirsten & Reidar Hansen:
(NRH)

July 10, 1806
Rollag, Norway

Nicolas tried to doze in the carriage as he was driven to his mother's land. His head pounded, and his stomach clenched in rebellion at the unrelenting rock of the conveyance. Last night's ample akevitt still coursed through his veins.

He drank to avoid Christian.

The man who held the title of King of Norway was a man with strange predilections. He asked Nicolas endless questions about life in Missouri, wanting details about anything involving blood. Hunting, Indians, fatal accidents while taming the land, he asked about it all. And Nicolas could not help but see that the man fondled himself throughout. His arousal was unmistakable. As was his satisfaction.

In the middle of the conversation!

Nicolas shuddered. When Christian let his free hand fall on Nicolas's knee, it took all of his will-power not to knock it violently away. His voice was intense, sinister, seductive.

"You may be young, but you're already a real man, Nicolas. I admire that about you."

Nicolas swallowed, his throat gone dry. "Thank you, Your Highness."

"I'm a real man, as well." Christian's eyes lit disturbingly. "Everyone is afraid of me. And they should be. I might strike at any moment."

Nicolas refused to allow himself to show his fear. "Strike?"

"A mace, a sword, my hand, the choice of weapon is unimportant. The key is to hit often enough and hard enough to keep the populace in check. I attack whomever I wish, unprovoked, so that everyone will show me the respect I deserve!"

"I see." That was an odd way to rule a country.

Christian leaned forward, his voice dropped to a whisper. "I'm so much of a man, in fact, that I require lovers of both sexes to keep me satisfied."

Sweat began to trickle down the groove of Nicolas's back.

"I, of course satisfied them so completely, that many have died in the act." He began to giggle. "Can you imagine that? In the actual moment of sublime bliss they just... died!"

Nicolas glanced around the room until his eyes met Frederick's. His cousin stood and moved to them.

"Father? Are you finished with your meal?" Frederick stepped between Christian and Nicolas. Nicolas stood and gratefully gave his chair to Frederick. "You haven't eaten much."

"It's poisoned, you fool. Anyone can see that!" Christian pushed the plate away. "Give me your plate!"

Nicolas hurried to the other end of the table. He pulled up a chair and downed akevitt toasts with Eirik, Espen, and several lovely young ladies-in-waiting. He stayed there for the rest of the evening, not truly relaxed until Christian left the Great Hall without him.

Now he slumped in the carriage and regretted his decision to travel today. He pounded on the roof of the conveyance and the driver stopped. Nicolas clambered out just before he puked. Wiping his mouth on a handkerchief, he realized that there was nothing he had sampled in America that kicked a body as hard as akevitt. He would need to learn his limit or he might not survive the year. Nicolas sighed and considered turning back to Christiania. But he was already more than halfway to Rollag.

There must be a tavern there. He could get some small beer and maybe some soup. At any rate, he should at the least look at the land. His mother *would* ask about it when he returned. And the property would be his someday.

Nicolas pulled himself back into the carriage and banged on the roof. The carriage lurched forward.

But I don't know what the hell I shall do with it.

Chapter Eleven

August 22, 1820
Rollag, Norway

*N*icolas stood on the outcropping of granite and wiped rivulets from his brow with one sleeve. His linen shirt clung to him, nudged by breezes and gripped by sweat. For over two hours he zigzagged up the mountain on foot, the pathway existing only in his memory, until he reached this spot. He was three thousand feet above the valley.

His valley.

Nicolas shaded his eyes and followed the twisted, glittering rope of water that slithered through Rollag. Whitewashed structures, their moss-edged slate roofs reflecting glare from the midday sun, gathered like old women beside the Lagen River. A quilt of neat rectangles surrounded the tiny town; some dotted with livestock, others lush with crops nearing harvest. Rollag's three-story stave church, standing slightly above the fray, began sheltering worshippers barely a hundred years after William conquered.

He stretched taller, reaching toward the heavens, and felt his vertebrae pop in a satisfying manner. He inhaled the sharp bouquet of pinesap warmed by the intense summer sun. As he surveyed all that lay below him, his chest expanded with power.

He owned this.

Then Nicolas looked back over his shoulder at the towering peaks that wrapped around him, looming so high that trees gave up any attempt at climbing them. Even the gyr-hawks and white tailed sea eagles, whose sharp, mournful cries split the air around him, did not venture that high.

With an imperceptible shrug, these mountains could throw down a chunk of ice that would eliminate any trace of his existence. The understanding that no human could ever truly own them washed over him, numbing his fingers and toes. Nicolas suddenly felt very insignificant.

"But a partnership!" he said out loud, his deep vocals bouncing off the surrounding slopes. "A partnership! Allow me a bit of control, and I shall make you the most desirable mountains in all of Norway!"

He bent down and slapped both his palms, hard, on the rough rock beneath his feet.

∞⁣ℂ⁣ℰ

Anders looked up from his stein and squinted. The sun spilled around Nicolas as he entered the doorway of the ancient Rollag tavern, baptizing Anders with his elongated shadow. Anders signaled the serving girl for another stein of ale. Nicolas dropped into the seat across from him and grinned.

"God, what glory!"

"You've been gone for more than half a day! Where were you?"

Nicolas winked at the serving girl as she set down the ale, causing her to blush prettily. "I climbed the mountain and looked down on my dynasty."

"Your 'dynasty,' is it?" Anders smirked. "And what good is your dynasty to you?"

"How do you mean?" Nicolas drained his stein and waved for another. "Exertion like that makes a man thirsty. Thank you, my sweet." The serving girl giggled.

"I mean, you have these lands here, in Rollag, but you live in America."

"Yes?" Nicolas hoped his light tone did not betray his suspicions.

Anders smiled solicitously. "Perhaps there's a better plan."

Nicolas waited until the serving girl left the table, her hand trailing over the tabletop and her lashes fanning furiously with promise. Her cleavage seemed to have deepened.

"I was wondering how long you would wait before telling me why you insisted I come to Christiania," he said.

Anders laughed. "I forget how abrupt you Americans are!"

Nicolas drank deeply of the summer beer and found it light and refreshing. He helped himself to a bit of barbecued meat abandoned on Anders' plate. Then he met the older man's eyes.

"Come. Let's walk where there are no ears," Anders suggested. He dropped a few coins on the tabletop. The serving girl's disappointment was palpable.

The men left the tavern and strolled under a stand of trees along the Lagen River. Anders looked like a leopard, dotted with sunspots and every inch as dangerous. The gently rhythmic slop of water against land eased Nicolas's taught nerves.

"How much do you know of the situation here?" Anders asked.

"I know that through a series of unfortunate circumstances, Sweden has gained Norway," Nicolas began.

"True."

"And I know from your letter that the descendants of Frederick are searching for a candidate to take the throne and make Norway her own sovereign entity."

"True as well."

"What I don't know, is where I fit in." Nicolas stopped walking. "I'm not a descendent of Frederick."

Anders rested his hand on Nicolas's shoulder. "There are several possibilities, cousin. Are you ready to hear them?"

"I am." Nicolas folded his arms across his chest.

"No, Nicolas, you're not a descendent of Frederick. And you're an American. For that reason, there are many who feel you have no rights here. They want you to give up your land and go home."

"I didn't need to come all this way to do that!" Nicolas blurted.

"No, indeed. So it's obvious that I had other ideas, eh?" Anders withdrew his hand and rubbed his palms with anticipation.

Nicolas leaned against a tree. "You have my attention."

"There are also those who wish you to support them in their quest for the crown."

"And by 'support' I take you to mean my holdings as well?" Nicolas picked a loose piece of bark from the tree. It crackled loudly in the quiet afternoon.

"Yes, I'm afraid so."

"Who, specifically, has that hope?" Nicolas narrowed his eyes at Anders.

"Karl Fredericksen."

"The mistress's son? Erling's youngest brother?" Nicolas ran his hand through his hair. "How old is he now?"

"Fifty-four. But his wife, Ingeborg, is only thirty-three. And she has birthed an heir-apparent. Borg is already eight, so Karl only needs to hold the throne for ten years, maybe less."

Nicolas tossed the bits of bark aimlessly. "So he's the favorite, then?"

"Until now." Anders considered Nicolas. "Until you."

Nicolas attempted to sound uninterested. "Did you forget? I'm not Frederick's descendent."

"No. But you *are* a direct descendent of King Christian. And you *are* pure Norwegian otherwise."

"And?"

"And there are many who would back you as a *legitimate* heir, not one gotten off a mistress." Anders pulled a leaf from the tree above them. "Think about it."

Nicolas stared across the river. "I expect I'll have questions later. I wasn't prepared, so they don't come to mind presently."

"Of course!" Anders clapped his shoulder. "Are you hungry? How about supper?"

The cousins dined on *fiskeboller*—fish balls with boiled cabbage and vegetables. Dessert of Jarlsberg cheese and sliced apples finished the meal. They washed it down with more small beer and akevitt.

Nicolas retired upstairs to a small, clean room. He stripped off the dusty clothes of the day, shook them out, and draped them over the footboard of the bed. Then he washed, making use of the ewer of warm water that waited for him. He lay, naked and on a diagonal, across the narrow bed.

Silent mountains were visible through his window. They reigned saw-toothed and gray, hovering, crowned with moon-gilt and star-diamonds, robed with an arctic summer's lavender sky.

Their presence reassured him; he didn't feel alone.

And he prayed that God would show him what to do.

August 23, 1820

In the land agent's office, Nicolas listened politely while the wiry man who managed his lands extolled his own virtues.

"That is well and good, Herr Jenssen. But I believe it's time to do more, do you not?" Nicolas smiled. "While I'm here, I desire to raise the value of my land, and the conditions of my tenants' lives as well."

Anders turned and stared at him.

"Of course, Lord Hansen. Have you suggestions?" Herr Jenssen's lips widened but his eyes didn't return Nicolas's smile.

"I want to allot plots of land to be leased for logging. Once cleared, they can be used to pasture livestock. The current flatland pastures may then be cultivated for profit."

"Have you examined the land?" Herr Jenssen's tone made it clear he expected a negative response.

"I spent most of yesterday riding and walking through it. And climbing over it." Nicolas leaned forward in his chair, tapping his forefinger imperiously on the man's desk. "If we implement these changes, I believe it will benefit us both."

"Very well, sir. I shall see what can be done."

Nicolas leaned back and waved his hand. "Might I see the chart of current land usage? And the topography?"

"Now?"

"If it's not too much trouble."

Herr Jenssen sighed quite loudly to indicate it was, indeed, entirely too much trouble. "I shall need time to retrieve them, you understand. I wasn't expecting you. Sir."

"Very well." Nicolas stood. "My cousin and I shall enjoy an early lunch. Expect us to return in two hours." He extended his hand.

Herr Jenssen had no choice but to shake it. "Yes, sir."

They tried a different tavern this time. Anders considered him over a glass of stout while Nicolas grinned as though he had swallowed a whole flock of canaries.

Anders eventually lowered his glass. "What are your thoughts,

Hansen?"

"It's very simple, really. Whoever benefits from this land, whether it be me or the pretender, will benefit more richly if these changes are made. True?"

Anders answered slowly. "True."

"And I haven't made any decisions as yet, regarding my own path. In the event that I don't remain in Norway, then these changes must happen quickly. It's late August. Adaptations must be implemented before spring." Nicolas lifted his glass in silent toast, then sipped his beer.

Anders nodded. "That's good thinking. Very good thinking."

Their food was served; plates of smoked fish, sausages, cheeses and fresh bread. The men ate in hungry silence. When they were nearly finished, Nicolas asked, "Are there other candidates besides Karl?"

Anders set his fork down. "All of Louise's children have passed on except the youngest, Luise. She's seventy and unmarried. My mother, Juliana-Maria, has four living children: myself, Canute, and our spinster twin sisters, Ellen and Elisa."

"Why don't you or Canute take this role for yourself?" Nicolas did not want to make the mistake of assuming anything in this game. Anders' wry smile acknowledged what Nicolas guessed.

Anders dropped his napkin on the table. "I'm sixty-four, Canute is sixty-one. We seek a king who can hold the throne for some time. One who is not yet in his dotage!"

Nicolas chuckled. "You're far from dotage, cousin."

Anders waved his hand and pressed on. "As for heirs, I have only the one daughter. You're well acquainted with Sigrid. Of course, she has no children."

Nicolas startled, wondering for the first time if Anders knew of their intimate past. "And Canute?"

"Eirik and Espen. Eirik's wife is English, so Canute has been pressing for Espen."

"Does Espen aspire to the throne?" Nicolas asked, curious as to Anders' beliefs concerning his cousin's denied aspirations.

"It's best to assume that he does."

Nicolas drained his beer as he considered that twist. "That leaves Else's children," he prompted. "Are Karl's siblings still alive?"

"His brother Erling is sixty-two. His sister Petra is gone. She had a son and a daughter. The daughter lives in Paris, and the son is deceased."

Nicolas summed it up. "So Karl is overt, Espen is covert."

Anders lifted his glass in challenge. "And you, our American cousin, are the spoiler."

Back in the land agent's office, Herr Jenssen had the charts spread out on his desk in a hectic spill of paper. Nicolas used a charcoal pencil to sketch out the plot borders he wanted, based on the topography lines. He stepped back and considered his plan, nodding his satisfaction.

"I want the plots leased immediately," he instructed Jenssen. "That is of utmost importance. In order to facilitate that, I'll wave the first year's rents and taxes."

"Wave rent! And taxes?" As such, Jenssen's profits would be waved as well. "Lord Hansen, I must object!"

Nicolas stared him into silence. "I'll pay your percentage, Herr Jenssen, on every plot with a signed contract. Rest assured, I have no interest in seeing you starve."

"Uh, thank you, Sir." Jenssen swallowed audibly.

"In fact, if all the parcels are leased by November first, I'll pay you a bonus!" Nicolas tempted. "Your Christmas would be quite pleasant, I assure you."

"That was very impressive," Anders commended later, as his carriage rocked them back toward Christiania. Then he added with a wink, "Your Highness."

Chapter Twelve

August 21, 1820

*H*aldis shook her head. "*Jeg ikke forstår.*"

"*Du taler Engelsk?*" Sydney asked, though she already discerned the answer.

"*Ingen, Madam.*"

Sydney tried her best to voice her request in Norse, "You get midwife for me?"

Haldis frowned as her eyes flicked to Sydney's trim waistline. "Midwife? The woman who delivers babies?"

Sydney nodded, relieved to have made her request clear. "Yes. Ingrid Olavsen."

"When would you like her to come?"

"Today." Sydney smiled, hoping she looked encouraging. "You get Ingrid Olavsen?"

Haldis curtsied, obviously puzzled. "Yes, madam. I will summon Ingrid Olavsen today."

"*Takk du*, Haldis."

"*Velkommen*, Lady."

Ingrid came to the castle that afternoon. Sydney met her in the entry hall and led her to a private room on the first floor. She spoke in Norse as best she could.

"Thank you for coming, Ingrid."

"You're welcome, Lady. How may I help you?" Ingrid's eyes swept over Sydney's narrow-waisted body in an echo of Haldis's speculative gaze.

Sydney spoke with confidence, "Learn me to midwife."

Ingrid rubbed the amused smile from her lips. "Learn you? Do you mean 'teach'? Teach you to be a midwife?"

Sydney laughed at her own gaff. "Yes! Teach me. Please?"

Ingrid waved her hand around the well-appointed room of the castle. "You are the Lady Hansen, Grevinne of Rollag. Why do you wish to learn this?"

"In America, is no nobility. I want to help mothers, babies..." her Norse failed her at that point. She gave Ingrid an imploring look.

"Oh! You wish to be a midwife back in America?"

"Yes!" Sydney sighed her relief. "You teach me? I pay you."

Ingrid sat back in her chair and considered Sydney. For a long moment, she didn't speak. Then, "I saw your face when that Englishwoman's baby slid into your arms. It was *magisk*, was it not?"

Sydney nodded, having figured out the unfamiliar word. Frustrated by her lack of Norse, her mouth worked silently and her hands waved in mute circles. She already surmised that noble women didn't lower themselves to such menial tasks. But she wasn't noble—not really. And deep inside of her a need to do this had been awakened. How could she explain it?

"Nothing is the same!" she finally blurted.

Ingrid laughed. "You have the gift, Lady, that's sure. I never saw anyone with such ability and yet no training."

Sydney got the gist of the compliment. "Thank you."

Ingrid leaned forward. Her gaze pierced through the warm haze of emotion, straight to Sydney's reality. "If you are serious, it means you must come with me when I send for you. In the middle of the night, in the rain and in the snow, even during a dinner or ball here at the castle."

"Yes!" Sydney grinned. She would agree to anything—even if she only understood half the woman's words—because she wanted this so dearly. "I come!"

Ingrid nodded, narrow-eyed. "I shall send my girl, Agnes. She'll bring you to the birth."

"Yes. Good."

"When do you want to begin?"

"Today!" Sydney shrugged happily. "Why wait?"

"All right, then. I will expect you the next time I am called out." The corner of Ingrid's mouth curved. Clearly she wondered if Lady Hansen would follow through on her request.

"What, um, my dress?"

"Wear a simple, dark gown. Nothing expensive or fancy. And bring a *forkle* or two."

"*Forkle?*"

Ingrid traced the outline of an apron over her dress.

"Oh! I understand." Sydney stood and offered her hand. "Thank you, Ingrid. Thank you very much!"

"We shall see if you still thank me 'very much' in a month!" Ingrid laughed.

~~~

"She bade me fetch the midwife," Haldis whispered to the pierced wooden screen in the dark room. A single candle on each wall provided only enough light to ensure a body did not fall over the furniture.

"Why? Is she with child again?"

"No, sir, I don't believe so. She still suckles the babe."

There was an unmuffled grunt of disgust. "She doesn't use a wet nurse, then."

"No, sir."

"Has she had her courses since she arrived?"

"No, sir." Haldis blushed at the intimate question.

"And she sleeps in his bed every night?"

"Yes, sir." Her whisper was barely audible.

Several moments of assessing silence passed before she was dismissed. "Very well then. Be sure to let us know if anything changes. That's all."

August 22, 1820

Sydney pulled a dress over her shift as the clock on the mantle chimed softly, four o'clock. Nicolas was gone to his land with

Anders; Maribeth would care for Kirstie and Stefan until she returned. It was helpful that Kirstie ate solid foods now.

Sydney followed Agnes out of the fortress into the city. They walked for twenty minutes until they reached the house. Light glowed through the second floor window. Agnes led her up the stairs and handed her over to Ingrid. The room smelled of sweat, beeswax and wool.

"Welcome, Lady Hansen!" Ingrid smiled. "So you have come."

"Please, my name is Sydney. I say, I come," Sydney said in rudimentary Norse. She turned to the young woman in the bed. "Good morn, madam."

The woman nodded and closed her eyes.

"This is Mistress Arnesen. This is her second child, and her first birth was quick. She is already nearly open." Ingrid motioned for Sydney to come to the other side of the room. She held up her bag. "You will need a bag of your own. I recommend leather, it needs to be sturdy."

Sydney nodded. "I buy one today."

"Inside," Ingrid opened her bag, "You will need to keep a supply of rags. They are for soaking the mother's skin to soften it, remember? And for wiping the baby's nose and mouth before it breathes. The mother should have towels to clean and swaddle the infants, but if not, you will need rags for that as well." Ingrid spoke clearly and demonstrated with her hands to help Sydney understand.

"Yes."

Ingrid turned to face her, "You wash them out and use them again. It is a large *bekostning* only to begin."

"*Bekostning?*"

"Um…" Ingrid rubbed her fingers together. "Money?"

"Oh! Cost!" Sydney nodded.

Mistress Arnesen moaned and Ingrid moved to her side. She spoke to her softly and madam nodded. Ingrid looked over her shoulder at Sydney.

"I have *olje* in my bag. Would you bring it?"

Sydney dug in the bag and found the corked bottle. She handed it to Ingrid, but the midwife shook her head, pushing the bottle back toward Sydney.

"Please show me how you used it on Lady Linnet."

Sydney sat on the edge of the bed and gently spread madam's

legs. She poured a little of the deep golden oil over her finger tips; it smelled of olives. Gently, she massaged the opening to the birth canal, stretching it a little. "The midwife did for me when my baby born," she explained.

"And she used hot *komprimerer* as well? The hot rags, pressed against the skin?"

"Oh! Yes, she did one, two, one, two. Understand?"

"Yes, I understand." Ingrid checked the water heating in the fireplace. She placed several rags in the pot, then rung one out and handed it to Sydney. Sydney pressed it against madam's cunnus. Madam smiled her thanks, then winced with the onset of a birth pain.

Ingrid and Sydney worked together for the next hour, while Ingrid explained everything she did. Mistress Arnesen's birthing progressed rapidly. Her water broke over Sydney's hand as she massaged in the oil, soaking the sheets. With the next pain, the baby's furry head crowned.

"Do you remember Lady's birth?" Ingrid sat close to Sydney. She nodded, eyes wide with concern. Ingrid pressed a clean rag into Sydney's hand. "Do it again."

Completely focused, Sydney's lower lip slipped into her mouth and her teeth held it there. When the head emerged, Sydney determinedly wiped the baby's nose and mouth. She eased one shoulder, then the other, with the next contraction. The baby girl somersaulted into her guiding hands.

Ingrid told Mistress Arnesen she had a daughter and Sydney laid the newborn on her mother's chest. Ingrid showed Sydney when the cord stopped pulsing, and then she tied it close to the baby's stomach and again a few inches away. She let Sydney cut the tough cord between the strings.

Rags, oil, string, a knife. Sydney repeated the mental list until she could write it down. *And a whetstone to keep the knife sharp.*

Ingrid helped madam put the baby to her breast. "The sucking *årsaker* the womb to *sammentrek*." Ingrid tugged gently on the cord. "That pushes the afterbirth out."

Sydney figured out what Ingrid was telling her. Ingrid helped her deliver the afterbirth so she would become familiar with the feel of it.

"You must take care not to pull it too soon, or the mother can bleed to death," Ingrid warned. "That is the worst *feil* to make!"

On the way back to Akershus Castle, Sydney wondered if her feet truly floated over the pavement. Everything she saw seemed to be brighter, more colorful, portending good fortune for all. She stopped in a cobbler's shop and purchased a large leather bag with a broad shoulder strap. She planned to take a nap, and then shop for the other items later in the afternoon. She smiled up at the gracious midday sun, and hurried back to the fortress and her children.

August 27, 1820

Sydney was called out once more in the week that Nicolas was gone. She was surprised when she returned to find him in their room, hunched over the desk, working on his chart. He looked up when she opened the door.

"*Min presang!*" He stood to kiss her, his wheat-colored whiskers rough against her mouth. He smelled of smoke, road dust and pine. "I have so much to tell you!"

Sydney leaned into him. "And I want to hear everything, husband."

Nicolas turned to his task. "I'll tell you in a bit. It's late in the day, and I need to finish this. What shall I wear to dinner?"

"Dinner?"

But he was already too absorbed to respond. Tomas was putting away Nicolas's clothes and he held out a waistcoat and frockcoat for Sydney to approve. She nodded. Haldis laid out a gown for her and helped her dress. Maribeth came from the adjoining room with Kirstie and Stefan.

Stefan ran to his father. "*Pappa!* You're back!"

Nicolas pulled his attention away from his project and faced his son. "That I am! And what have you been doing?"

"I made a friend. His name is Leif and he lives in the stable."

"Does he? And does he speak English?"

Stefan shook his head. "I have to talk to him in Norse."

"*Og hvordan er det draen?*" And how is that going?

Stefan giggled. "*Det drar godt, Pappa!*" It goes well, Pappa!

Sydney reached for Kirstie. "Is she eating?"

"Yes, and very well, madam. But I think she misses the breast." Maribeth glanced at Tomas.

He watched her intently and blushed when their eyes met. He turned away.

"I'll nurse her once again after dinner. I'm not ready to stop any more than she is!"

"Very good. I'll not let her fall asleep too early, in that case. Come, Stefan!" Maribeth took the children.

Nicolas stood to change out of his traveling clothes. Tomas took away his soiled breeches and shirt, then handed him a clean towel.

Nicolas washed his face, neck and upper torso before donning a ruffled linen shirt and doeskin breeches. Tomas helped him into the waistcoat and stood aside with the frockcoat at ready.

Though excited to tell him about pursuing her new avocation, curiosity about his trip was still foremost in Sydney's mind. As Haldis helped her wash and change into one of her new gowns, she wondered why Nicolas was so quiet. Twice she attempted to draw information from him, but he brushed her off. Warmly, to be sure, but brushed her off just the same.

She supposed he would tell her later; but first, she had to sit through dinner.

Sigrid, who had not spoken a word to Sydney the entire week, sidled up to Nicolas as soon as he appeared.

"Darling! Did you survive your journey with my father? It was not too tedious, was it?" she murmured and melted against him.

Nicolas tried to unobtrusively scrape her off his person. "On the contrary, Duchess, it was very productive."

"I missed you at dinner. Conversation was not nearly as compelling without you!" she purred, sticking to him like cat hair.

Nicolas smiled and rubbed his knuckle under his nose. "After but a few days, you have become that accustomed to my repartee?"

"No." Her voice dropped in pitch and volume. "After thirteen years, Nicolas, I learned well how to miss you."

Sydney's pleasant expression did not change, but her grip on her husband's arm tightened. "Shall we go in?"

"Will you excuse us, Duchess?" Nicolas bowed to Sigrid, then led Sydney to their seats.

಄ଓଔ

Sydney rocked and hummed as she nursed Kirstie. The baby girl's blue-gray eyes were dark in firelight, just like her father's. Her lids drooped as she fought sleep to nurse longer. Sydney stroked her dark golden curls and kissed her forehead. Finally she succumbed and let go of the breast with a soft pop.

Sydney smiled as she laid her in bed. Each time, delivering the babies took her back to the moment that Kirstie slid out of her own body, pink and perfect. She was such a miracle.

"Beautiful," Nicolas whispered from the doorway to their room. Sydney looked up, her dress gaping open. "Come to me, wife. I have need of you."

Sydney happily obliged.

Nicolas undressed her slowly and his mouth tasted each portion of skin as he revealed it. His beard's roughness was a sensual counterpoint to the softness of his lips. Sydney trembled at his touch and her breath exhaled in small hums. She twisted her fingers in his hair, dislodging it from the leather tie and making him appear enticingly disreputable.

"Don't delay too long, husband. I have need of you, as well."

Nicolas lifted her and laid her, naked, on the bed. He stripped quickly. Climbing over her, urgent and ready, he took her with vigor. Sydney responded in kind, caught in a tumble of desire and need. She pushed against him, wreathed in his musky male scent. When she peaked, her eyes rolled back and, for a brief moment, she felt weightless. Nicolas's post-pinnacle sag on top of her pushed her back down to earth.

They lay entwined and unmoving. He dozed, snoring breathily against her temple. Sydney knew he was exhausted by his travels, and satiated with ample food, drink and sex. But he awoke after an hour, and, to her pleasant surprise, took her again.

Chapter Thirteen

August 28, 1820

*M*adam?" Haldis whispered.

Sydney opened her eyes; it was neither night nor day. "Yes?"

"Agnes is here for you."

"What time is it?"

Haldis looked at the clock on the mantel. "Almost five."

"Tell her, my husband, home, um, not talk..."

"What are you attempting to say?" Nicolas mumbled from the other side of the bed.

Sydney turned to him. "Tell Agnes that my husband just returned from a journey. Come back in four hours and get me. I shall come then." Nicolas gave Haldis the message.

"Very good, madam."

Nicolas opened one eye. "What do you mean 'get' you? For what?"

Sydney snuggled close to him. "I'll explain later. When we rise at a decent hour."

The sun was fully up when Haldis carried in a breakfast tray. Nicolas bounced from their tangled nest of blankets to relieve himself in the piss pot behind the screen. The clock chimed the half hour, and Sydney rolled over to make sure which hour it was half past.

Oh, good. Seven-thirty.

Tomas entered and prepared Nicolas's toilette. Emerging from the screen, Nicolas sat in front of the mirror. Tomas sharpened the razor while Nicolas lathered the brush. Haldis laced Sydney into a simple gown.

"What was that about this morning?" Nicolas asked Sydney in English, looking at her in the mirror.

"Agnes, the girl who came to fetch me, works for Ingrid Olavsen. She's the midwife whom I assisted on our first night here."

"Oh, yes. With Eirik's English wife. I remember. Why are you her concern?"

"She has agreed to take me on as an apprentice. I'm learning mid-wifery."

Nicolas spun to look at her, seriously risking his neck in the process. "You are *what?*"

Sydney leveled her gaze at Nicolas while Tomas, wide-eyed, held the straight razor in midair. "I am learning to be a midwife."

"Why?"

"So when we return to Cheltenham, women have a second option. You, of all people, must understand that! And, besides—" Sydney faltered.

"And?"

Sydney chewed her lower lip, begging Nicolas with her eyes not to laugh or poke fun. Or be angry.

"Sydney? Tell me!" he rumbled.

She pulled a deep breath. "And because it is the most amazing experience in the world to, to, guide a brand new baby—a brand new *life*—from its mother's body into a sudden and independent existence of its own!" Sydney's voice lifted and she pantomimed the actions as she spoke. "Truly, Nicolas, there is absolutely nothing else on earth like it!"

Nicolas turned back to the mirror. "I see."

"I have helped deliver two more babies since Lady Linnet."

Nicolas did not respond.

"I wanted to tell you last night, but I did not have the opportunity."

Nicolas's eyes met Sydney's in the mirror. "I'm not sure that I approve."

"Approve?" Sydney was confused.

"In our position it might not be appropriate."

"Our position? What do you mean, 'our position'?" Sydney stepped behind her husband and frowned at his reflection. His eyes flickered to the desk.

Sydney crossed to it and stood over his chart of the royal family. There were three circles: one around Karl Fredericksen and the notation '54', one around Espen Canutesen and 'no heir', and one around three initials, N.R.H.

Sydney spun to face him.

Nicolas regarded her with his unflinching blue gaze. Tomas glanced at Haldis and uncomfortably shifted his feet. Challenging what she saw, Sydney jutted her jaw.

"What is inappropriate about learning a skill that is needed in the Territory?"

"Sydney, you must discuss these things with me first. It's of the utmost importance!" Nicolas scowled.

"That's what I'm doing now, Nicolas." She tipped her head toward the chart. "It's a good policy for *both* of us, is it not?"

He turned in the chair to face her again. "But you have already set yourself on this course!"

"Are you set on a course?" Sydney glared at her husband.

"This discussion is not about me." The scar on Nicolas's cheek whitened in a face that was reddening but not from his shave.

"Are you forbidding me to continue?"

Nicolas ran his hand through his hair. "Yes! No. I don't know!"

Tomas backed away from Nick's chair. Haldis busied herself with straightening the bed and the room. Neither one of them looked at the couple.

Sydney narrowed her eyes and rested her hands on her hips. "Agnes will be back to fetch me at nine if the babe is not yet born. May I go with her?"

Nicolas regarded his wife darkly. "Are you expected?"

"I was expected at five this morning."

Nicolas stared at Sydney for a silent minute, then waved to Tomas to continue his shave.

"You may go this day. But we will need to discuss this matter at more length before you continue."

"Yes... *Sir*."

Nicolas's eyes jumped to hers. She smiled sweetly and went to check the supplies in her leather bag. "I'm going to feed Kirstie now. I'll be in the next room if you need me."

Nicolas's eyes followed her out of the room.

ဪ

"They argued this morning."

"Oh? What about?"

"It was in English. But Tomas said it was about her becoming a midwife."

A sharp hiss of inhaled breath. "She wants to be a midwife? Good Lord! She's more colonial than we first thought!"

Another voice, "This will most certainly not do. Not at all."

"Was it resolved?" the first man asked.

"I do not believe so."

"Did he try at all to dissuade her?"

She shrugged. "Tomas didn't tell me. But he had her look at a chart he made."

"What's on the chart?" the first voice asked.

"Names."

"Whose?"

"The royal family—with lines and circles."

"Was there anything else?"

Haldis nodded, unsure if they could see her. "She does not seem pleased that he may be king."

"And him?"

She thought a moment. "I think he might like to be."

"Interesting. Thank you, Haldis. You've done well today."

ဪ

Sydney sat on a bench in the garden and squinted at the overcast sky. Heavy, uneven clouds in mottles of gray and lavender obscured the sun, and a wet breeze redolent of both sea salt and rain water swirled around the manicured grounds. A few brave drops darkened the footpath.

"It's an unusual day for a walk, husband."

"It was important that we talk out here. The walls have ears, Sydney," Nicolas said, his voice low.

"Ears?"

"And eyes. Nothing, not one single thing, that passes between us is private inside the castle."

Sydney frowned. "Who is listening?"

"Everyone."

"Are you sure?" Sydney glanced over her shoulder at the ancient castle walls behind them.

Nicolas shrugged and took her hand. "It's always safest to assume so. If we need to talk privately, we must do so out in the open. Then no one can get close enough to eavesdrop."

"All right."

"Make no mistake, Sydney. I am absolutely serious about this." Nicolas leaned closer. "This may concern life and death matters."

She nodded.

Nicolas pressed his lips to her ear, eyes lowered. "Do you *truly* understand me?"

Sydney rolled her eyes. "Yes, Nicolas. I do. Anything that we say or do in the castle will be public knowledge. I may be American, but I'm not unaware of royal intrigues."

She smiled warmly up at him, then, looking for all the world like a contented, loving wife. "And might we use that to our advantage?" she whispered.

Nicolas ran his hand through his hair. "Oh, yes, indeed we shall. It will be our most powerful tool."

"And we speak in English when we need to be private, then."

"And Norse when we wish them to hear us? Perfect, *min presang*." Nicolas laughed.

Sydney considered her husband. "Did you discover what they want from you?"

"I did." Nicolas stood in front of her and rested his hands on his hips. "There are those that wish me to relinquish my holdings here and go back to America. They don't consider me to have any rights at all in this land."

"And?"

"And then there are those that wish me to support the favorite candidate in *his* quest for the crown."

"Is the favorite Karl or Espen?"

Nicolas shrugged. "That's not determined as yet. Karl is Frederick's son, true. But by the mistress, not the wife. The fact that he has an heir helps him some."

"And Espen?"

"Not married, no heir. And, he told me he has no intent to marry for the purpose of advancing his career. But he is a legitimate descendent of Frederick. And his father backs him strongly."

Sydney nodded and waited, nervously spinning her garnet wedding ring around her cold finger, its deep color that of dried blood. In the dim day, the stone refused to flicker, as though it sensed her mood.

"And then there are some..." Nicolas ran his hand through his hair again, and squinted up at the lowering sky. "Some who want me to claim the throne."

Her heart lurched, though the statement wasn't a surprise. Why else would they be here? She kept her voice level. "On what basis?"

Nicolas held up fingers and marked them as he spoke. "I am a direct descendent of Christian the sixth. I am Norse. I have an heir."

Sydney stared hard at her husband. "Do you wish to be the king of Norway, Nicolas?"

He didn't answer. He stared at the gravel path.

"Nick?" she prodded.

He jerked and fixed her with an intense stare. "I think not."

She pulled a steadying breath. His eyes, dark as a midnight sky, didn't move from hers. "Do you know why I insisted that we accompany you on this journey?" she murmured.

His expression softened. "You said that you could not live without me."

"Well, there is that." Sydney smiled and stood to face her husband.

"Is there aught else?"

Sydney pinched her lips between her teeth and nodded.

"What is it, Sydney?"

She lifted her chin. "I didn't want to be left behind, should you choose to stay."

"What!" Nicolas stepped back, hands flying out to the side. "How could you believe that I would do such a thing?"

"I never believed you intended that. But politics, royalty and ambition are a dangerous—and seductive—mixture."

"And?" he barked.

Sydney grasped his arm. "And there was no way to anticipate

what sort of pressures they might have put on you."

"I'm not a weak man, Sydney!"

"No, Nicolas, you most certainly are not! But you are only *one* man; perhaps against many." Sydney slid her arms around his waist, under his frock coat. "I believed it was safer for us to be here with you. Was I wrong?"

His jaw clenched, making the scar visible, and he stared down at her.

"No," he finally whispered. He pulled her close against his large, warm, and very solid chest.

Chapter *Sixteen*

*N*icolas waved his hand in concession and leaned on his thighs, panting and sweating.

Espen straightened, lowering his blade. He wiped his brow on his sleeve and retrieved a jug of water. After several gulps, he handed it to Nicolas.

"Is it the weather? Or the exertion?" Espen asked.

"Both!" Nicolas shook his head. "I fear the journey has sapped my stamina." He finished the water in the jug.

"Your skills are still evident." Espen's tone held a touch of envy. "You always bested me as a youth."

"Ha! I fear my 'youth' is a stranger to me now!" Nicolas grinned and handed the borrowed sword back to Espen. "I need to order a blade of my own. Perchance I shall do so this afternoon."

"I can take you to an excellent craftsman. His steel sings."

"I accept. Thank you." Nicolas slapped his cousin's shoulder. "And now I shall go discern what mischief my son might be up to!"

Nicolas found Stefan in the stable mucking out stalls. He was conversing in easy Norse with another boy. Nicolas stood in the shadows and listened; it was remarkable how quickly his son was acquiring the new language.

"Stefan! Do you miss your chores at home so completely, that you do them here?" Nicolas asked in English, chuckling.

Stefan's bright blue eyes lifted. His wavy auburn hair was tied back with a thong like Nicolas's. It made him look much older than his nearly seven years.

"*Pappa! Jeg hjelper Leif slik han kan leke med meg.*" I am helping Leif so he can play with me.

"*Slik du foretrekker jeg taler til du i Norse?*" So you prefer I speak to you in Norse?

Stefan shrugged and continued in that language, pointing to the next stall, "That's Leif. He's twelve."

"I'm almost thirteen!" a voice dithering on the cusp of puberty declared. The boy, with cropped ash-blond hair and brown eyes, appeared at the stall door. "Just seven and a half more months!" His eyes rounded when he saw Nicolas. "Your Highness."

Nicolas shook his head and sat on a bale of straw to get closer to the boy. He was not much taller than Stefan, painfully thin, and clothed in apparel obviously discarded by a much larger person. Wiry muscles, fruit of his stable labors, were all that kept the boy from looking like a mere assortment of knobby joints.

"I'm not the king, Leif. You may call me 'Nicolas' until I am."

"Yes, Sir. Thank you, Sir."

Nicolas looked around the stable. There were two wide corridors with eight stalls on either side of each corridor. "Do you have to clean out all thirty-two stalls by yourself?"

"Not anymore!" Stefan's voice bounced out from where he had gone back to work.

Nicolas smiled. "And when my son is not around?"

"Yes, Sir. But I only do half each day. And sometimes there are empty stalls." Leif frowned and his voice increased in urgency. "But I do other work, too! I don't waste my time in idle foolishness."

Nicolas bit his lip and wondered who had chastised him with those particular words.

"Of course not! Not a strapping lad such as yourself!" Leif pushed his chest out a little at Nicolas's assessment. "Do your parents work at the castle as well?"

The chest deflated. "I don't have parents. I'm a bastard orphan." That parroted phrase was not so amusing.

"How is that?" Nicolas asked softly.

"My father's name was Sebastian Fredericksen. He was the king's brother. He promised to marry my mother, but I guess he forgot to. He died when I was three, my mother said."

Nicolas looked kindly at the boy. "And your mother?"

"She worked in the castle until she got sick."

"How long have you been alone?"

"I'm not alone! The grooms watch out for me. They let me sleep in the tack room and bring me food. I've been earning my keep for three years, now!" Leif's serious expression was far too old for a boy his age.

Stefan emerged from the stall. "Done! Can we play now?"

"I have to finish this one first." Leif turned back to his work.

Nicolas stood and offered the boy his hand. "It was a pleasure to meet you, Leif."

Leif looked from Nicolas's hand up to his eyes and back again. He wiped his hands on his filthy breeches before shaking Nicolas's hand.

"Yes, Sir."

September 5, 1820

As they dressed for dinner, Sydney debated whether or not to mention the date. She paced in the bedroom, checked her hair in the mirror, then rechecked her hair in a different mirror. She changed her slippers. Then she changed them back.

While Tomas shaved him, Nicolas's eyes followed her in his mirror. "Sydney?"

She spun around to look at him.

"What's bothering you?" Nicolas stopped Tomas and turned to face her, lather still adorning one side of his face in a white half-beard. Sydney's lower lip tensed and her eyes widened.

"Sydney?" Nicolas stood and approached her. "What is amiss?"

Sydney shook her head. "I'm afraid to say anything."

Nicolas gripped her arm. "What is it?" He glanced around the room. "Are we in danger?"

"No, Nicolas. We're not. It's nothing of that sort."

Nicolas relaxed his grasp. "Then what is it?"

Sydney drew a deep breath. "Do you know the date?"

Every muscle in Nicolas's body visibly eased, and a faint smile lifted his soap-frosted cheek. "Is that all?"

Sydney nodded as she watched her husband closely. What if Nicolas intended to behave the way he always had before: waking early on Stefan's seventh birthday—the anniversary of his wife's death—with the intent to drink himself senseless? Without Rickard here to watch over him, Nicolas could literally kill himself with such foolishness.

"Yes, I'm aware. Today is September fifth. Tomorrow is Stefan's seventh birthday." Nicolas returned to the dressing table. He sat and faced the mirror and gave Tomas permission to resume his shave.

"In fact," Nicolas caught Sydney's eyes in the mirror, "I have a gift for him."

"You do?" Sydney sank into a chair as a surge of relief pulled the strength from her legs.

Tomas wiped flecks of lather from Nicolas's face, and applied a scented lotion to his newly smoothed skin. He gathered his tools and left the room, wet towels tossed over his shoulder and careful not to slop soapy water on the carpet. When they were alone, Nicolas crossed to Sydney's chair and kneeled beside her.

"I know that my behavior in the past has not been—gentlemanly—to state it in the least of terms. But my grief has been put to rest. I have you, now. I have Kirstie. And I have Stefan." Nicolas smoothed Sydney's hair. She grasped his hand and held it against her cheek; his fingers were cool and trembled slightly.

"Forgive me, Sydney. I should have said something."

"There's nothing to forgive, Nicolas," she murmured.

"Yes. There is."

"Then I forgive you, husband." Sydney kissed him tenderly. She rested her forehead against his. "I love you."

"And I you."

Sydney sat back and considered her husband curiously. "So what did you get for him?"

Nicolas retrieved a small leather pouch from his dressing table. He pulled the drawstrings open and handed it to Sydney. She upended it, and a heavy gold ring rolled into her palm.

"It was my great-grandfather's. King Christian the Sixth."

The ring was a signet ring, the kind used to stamp sealing wax. It was made of deep yellow gold, and large enough to fit over two of Stefan's fingers. King Christian's crest was carved into the oval face.

"I know he cannot yet wear it, so I planned to put it on a chain for him. What do you think?" Nicolas's navy eyes probed Sydney's.

"I think it's perfect."

"Do you, then?"

"I do! And I got him a gift as well."

Sydney pulled a small shield from the wardrobe, with the Hansen crest painted in bright blue and yellow, and handed it to her husband. She also retrieved a scabbard and short sword made, and dulled, for Stefan.

"Sydney!" Nicolas exclaimed, a smile lighting his face. He pulled the blade from its sheath and held it in front of him. "This is a wonderful gift. What made you think of it?"

"I saw you in the courtyard, practicing with Espen. I thought it might be something that you could teach Stefan to do."

Nicolas's jaw clenched as he nodded. His lips pressed together as he stared down at the gift in his hands, turning it over and over again.

"It's past the time for me to start his training, in the way a father should." Nicolas' voice was thick. He raised wet cheeks to his wife. "But not too far past, I think."

September 6, 1820

Stefan was beside himself with the gifts. He leapt around the bedroom, imitating his father's moves and fighting imaginary dragons with great exclamations of threat and victory.

"Can we start today, Pappa?" he shouted.

"We can. You may watch my practice with Espen, and then I shall teach you."

"And Leif, too!" Stefan huffed.

Nicolas frowned and glanced at Sydney. "Won't that interfere with his work?"

Stefan shook his head, further frustrating Maribeth's attempts to corral his unruly auburn locks with a leather thong. "If I help him we can get done before lunch!"

Sydney nursed Kirstie by the hearth. "Would Leif be allowed to learn swordplay?"

Nicolas considered his son's exuberance. "I would rather not ask, in the event the answer is no. Besides, I believe it would be good for Stefan to have an adversary of his own size and ability to practice with."

Stefan stilled and pushed wavy hair from his eyes. "Is that a yes, *Pappa*?"

"That's a yes, son."

Stefan jumped down from the chair that had stood in for a mountaintop. "Can I go tell Leif?"

"Yes, go on then!" Nicolas laughed.

When he was out of earshot, Nicolas turned to Sydney. "I'll pack them both a lunch. The 'bastard orphan' does not give off the impression that he eats regularly."

"Is it only what the grooms bring him?"

"That's how he described it."

"Hm." Sydney's chubby, healthy daughter grinned and waved hands creased at the wrist. "Make sure you take enough for him to have a snack after the lesson, as well."

"I thought the same."

ℬ☪

Sydney intended to watch Stefan's first sword lesson, but before lunch she began to feel a familiar pain deep in her core. She ate heartily anyway, hoping food might discourage the expected headache. It did not.

Sydney summoned Haldis, and then climbed into bed. When Haldis came to the room, Sydney tried to explain what was wrong, but ended up simply showing her the blood. Haldis' look of confused worry turned to one of understanding competency. She gave Sydney a hot stone to place against her abdomen and cold cloths for her brow. She held the basin while Sydney vomited her noon meal. She closed the curtains to darken the room. And she brought Sydney endless cups of willowbark and chamomile teas.

Sydney lay on her bed, curled around the comforting warmth of the hot stone, eyes closed. All she could think about was breathing in. Exhaling took care of itself.

"*Min presang?*"

"Hm?" Sydney did not hear him come into the room.

Nicolas stroked her cheek. He smelled of outdoors, straw and sweat. "Is it very bad?"

Sydney nodded. Her skin was hypersensitive to the brush of her sheets, causing gooseflesh when she stirred. Light hurt her eyes. Sound made her head throb. And the pain in her womb was unrelenting. One hot tear slid from under her lid.

"Where is the worst pain?" he whispered.

"Low on my back." Sydney sniffed, but could not muster the will to wipe her tears.

"Turn over."

Sydney rolled slowly onto her stomach. Nicolas pushed back the covers and lifted her shift. His strong hands were so warm. He massaged her back and she moaned her gratitude. Slowly, her muscles relaxed and her body melted into the mattress. In less than thirty minutes, she was asleep.

§つCЗ

"Yes, Haldis? Why have you come in the middle of the afternoon?"

Haldis curtsied. "Beg your pardons, sirs. I wanted to let you know that Lady Hansen is not with child."

"No? Her courses have returned?"

"Yes."

"Thank you, Haldis. We do appreciate your diligence."

"Your servant, sirs." Haldis curtsied again and left.

He sighed deeply and downed his akevitt. "His wife is a problem. I thought you said he was a widower?"

"That was his circumstance when I wrote to him, two years ago. I was not aware he remarried until I received his second letter."

"She is not connected at all."

"And she is not Norwegian. Or Danish. She is not even Swedish!" The observation was punctuated by a derisive snort.

"No, she is American," he sneered. "And a Scots-Irish mutt."

"And yet, he seems quite taken with her. Perhaps she beds well?" He shrugged. "She does have a decent arse."

"Everyone knows the Scots and the Irish make good whores."

He tossed back his head and laughed. "Our Viking forefathers knew that. They bedded them repeatedly for centuries!"

They fell silent, deep in thought.

"And so, how shall we handle this, should he come around?"

Fingernails cadenced on the tabletop. "He needs to send her home for some urgent reason…"

"Of course! To settle his holdings there!"

"Yes! Under his expressed written instructions, to be sure. He can send for her later, when the situation here is resolved."

"That could—*should* take years. Very good thinking! In the meantime, we can place our own candidate in front of him."

"She must be young and very comely. And ambitious enough to do as we bid."

"Once a child is conceived, we will arrange a quiet divorce."

"And a very royal wedding!" With a dismissive wave of his hand he added, "The order of which is unimportant."

"We are agreed then?"

"We are."

"Oh, dear."

"What now?"

"She's Scots-Irish! Do you suppose she's a papist to boot?"

"Oh, Lord have mercy!"

September 10, 1820

Tomas handed Nicolas an envelope. "From Sir Anders."

"Thank you, Tomas." Nicolas withdrew the parchment. He nodded as he read it. "The game is on," he said in English.

Sydney lifted her leather bag to her shoulder and held up one hand to Agnes waiting for her at the door. "What do you mean?"

"Anders has called a meeting of all available male members of the family for the purpose of officially naming candidates for the throne." Nicolas raised clear blue eyes to his wife. "You know what this means, don't you?"

"I do."

"Are you ready?"

Sydney smiled softly. "I am."

Chapter *Seventeen*

September 11, 1820

*S*igrid stood at her window and watched the couple strolling in the garden below. Dark-haired and slim, she held his arm and lifted her mouth to speak to him. Tall, broad and blond, he bent his head to hers.

They stopped walking and spoke urgently to each other. Arms moved to punctuate statements, while hands fisted. He seemed to be trying to convince her of some point; she was unsure. Finally, she nodded.

Then they kissed. Sigrid turned away.

If she hoped to entice Nicolas back to her bed, she must work harder at the task. The night Sydney was not at dinner, Sigrid sat with Nick and they reminisced, laughing together over multiple glasses of wine and akevitt. She let her hand fall casually to his thigh, then squeezed it purposefully to make a point. There was no doubt about his arousal; she could see the bulge through his breeches. But he didn't follow her when she left the Great Hall. And when she went back to look for him, he was gone.

She couldn't help but look out her window again. Nicolas and Sydney sat on a bench now, their heads close together. Sigrid felt a stab of loss. She never admitted she loved him when he was nineteen.

Now that he was thirty-three, she was consumed by him.

A rapid knock startled her. "Come in," she called and turned to the door.

"Are you occupied?"

"No, Father. Please come in."

Anders crossed the room and stood beside her. He looked out the window. "Have you had opportunity to talk with him?"

Sigrid shook her head. "Not so one would notice. Only twice since he arrived."

"Pity."

Sigrid could not stop herself; she watched the couple as they huddled together.

Anders sighed heavily. "He seems the perfect candidate. He is a direct descendent of Christian the sixth, he is Norse, and he has an heir. There is just the one thing, really."

"What one thing is that?"

Anders faced his daughter. "His wife. She's an American commoner."

Sigrid understood his point.

"Perhaps he can be convinced to send her back to America?" Anders speculated.

Sigrid waved one hand. "Certainly there would be cause?"

"Undoubtedly. And once she's gone"—Anders lifted one brow suggestively—"his eye might wander. He only needs to choose someone from the royal line. He has an heir, so her age does not matter."

Sigrid was silent. Could he really mean... *her?* Hope warmed her blood.

"How is Vegard these days?" Anders asked, startling her anew.

She sighed. "The same as he has been this past decade: fat, gouty and sleepy. Some days I can barely wake him. And his sight is failing him."

"You paint a bleak portrait, daughter!"

"He is bleak."

Anders appeared to have a new thought. "Nicolas has remarried. If you were widowed, you would remarry as well, would you not?"

Sigrid faced her father.

"Yes," she answered carefully. "I would be amenable to that."

Anders smiled. "Good."

As he left her room, he spoke over his shoulder, "I hope you have more opportunities to renew your friendship with Nicolas. Let me know if I might assist that endeavor in any way."

"Thank you, Father." Sigrid's face heated. Then her thighs heated.

"It is my pleasure, Daughter." With a wink, he was gone.

September 20, 1820

The men of the royal family met in a room off the Great Hall. They greeted each other pleasantly, then grouped beside their preferred, though as yet merely assumed, candidates. Some men were openly solicitous in their attentions, others held back, waiting to see which way the wind might blow.

Servants set bottles of akevitt and pitchers of beer in the center of the table and glasses at each seat. Anders stood, cleared his throat and clinked two glasses together to begin the meeting. After jockeying for position, everyone settled around the table.

"Thank you all for being here. I believe that our purpose today is clear." Anders made eye contact with each man. "It's time for Norway to regain her identity. And that means placing a Norseman on the throne in Christiania. Everyone here is a member of the royal family, and for that reason, under consideration. Are we agreed, thus far?"

The men nodded and exchanged veiled glances.

Erling spoke up next to Anders. "Perhaps it would be helpful if each of us stated our qualifications? We may not all be familiar enough."

"Or even our desire to take the throne!" Canute Fredericksen added.

"Canute, you make a good point. Shall I begin?" Anders looked around the table; a couple men waved permission. "You all know me; Anders Fredericksen, Duke of Stavanger, and son of Juliana, King Frederick's second wife. At sixty-four I, personally, have no aspirations to the throne. But I love Norway with all my being and I want to see her come into her own in my lifetime."

He lifted his glass as a rumble of approval swelled and subsided. "Until the 1348 plague, Norway was the strongest of the

Scandinavian countries. Our Vikings ruled the North Sea! We settled in Iceland and Greenland, Scotland, England, North America. France was our stronghold. King William was of our lineage; Viking courage made him a conqueror!"

Another murmur of agreement circled the room.

"Gentlemen, it is the year 1820! For centuries we have lived under a Danish king. Now we have been given to Sweden as a spoil of war." Anders shook his head in warning. His blue eyes darkened as he gazed at the men. "We are more than that, are we not?"

The murmur grew louder and morphed into table-pounding support.

"Do you share my dream? Are there those among you who would step forward and lead Norway as her King?"

"I shall!" Karl Fredericksen stood. "I am King Frederick the Fifth's son, and brother to King Christian the Seventh."

"His illegitimate half-brother," someone muttered.

Karl's piercing gaze rounded the table. "The 'legitimate' line has had its turn, has it not? And we are where we are today, as a result!" he bellowed.

"How old are you?" someone else asked.

"I am a strong and sound fifty-four years of age. And, I have an heir of eight years, who will reach the age of majority before I reach years equal to my brother's today!" Karl pointed at Anders. "There is no doubt as to the vitality of our line."

"And your wife?" Anders prompted.

"Ingeborg is second cousin to Caroline Mathilda, King Christian the Seventh's wife."

"Thank you, Karl." Anders faced the room. "I propose to this assemblage that Karl Fredericksen be nominated as a candidate for King of Norway."

The glasses on the table bounced with thumps of approval.

"Thank you." Karl bowed, and then sat. Canute Fredericksen was next; he stood and spoke loudly.

"I am Canute, *legitimate* son of Juliana, King Frederick's second wife, and full brother of Anders. I am sixty-one and do not seek the throne for myself, but for my son, Espen."

"Father!" Espen blurted. "Am I not to decide for myself?"

Canute didn't pause. "My son is well-educated and a direct descendent of the King. He is thirty-three, and in fine health. He would hold the throne for enough years to firmly establish Norway in her own right!"

"Father!" Espen stood, red-faced with anger.

"All you lack is a suitable bride!" Canute now acknowledged his son's presence. "That's easily provided."

Espen shook his head. "I have told you repeatedly! I do not desire to marry simply for political reasons!"

"Then fall in love with an aristocrat!" Canute bellowed, his face mottled.

"What about Eirik?" Espen pointed at his silent brother. "He has a wife *and* a son!"

"An English wife!"

Shouts of dissent swirled around the room.

"Gentlemen!" Anders waved his hands in the air. "Let's not argue amongst ourselves!"

"I propose to this assemblage that Espen Canutesen be nominated as a candidate for King of Norway!" Canute shouted.

All eyes shifted to Espen. He glared first at his father, then at the assembled faces eyeing him with varying support. He nodded and dropped into his chair, pressed into acquiescence. Tentative palms hit the table in approval.

Introductions continued, but no one else volunteered to be a candidate. Nicolas remained quiet, watching and listening to the other men.

At last, Anders turned to him. "And that leaves our American cousin." Nicolas made eye contact around the table. He stood slowly and bowed deeply.

"Gentlemen, I am Lord Nicolas Reidar Hansen, Greve of Rollag, great-grandson of King Christian the Sixth, great-nephew of King Frederick, cousin to King Christian the Seventh. My father was pure Norse, so my bloodlines are acceptable. I am also thirty-three years of age. I spent a year here in Christiania when I was nineteen.

"I have been educated at universities in Philadelphia and Boston. Life in the American wilderness has made me strong, both in body and in resolve. I, too, have a son, an heir. He is intelligent and personable."

Anders smiled, obviously pleased with Nicolas's words. "And you are willing to be considered as a candidate?"

"I am."

"What about your wife?" Karl asked.

Nicolas met his gaze. "My wife is beautiful, intelligent, and capable."

"And her background?" Karl pressed.

"She is American."

"Of what lineage?"

Nicolas straightened. "Her father is Scots, her mother is Irish." Someone snorted.

Anders stepped beside Nicolas. "I propose to this assemblage that Nicolas Hansen be nominated as a candidate for King of Norway."

Pounding palms filled the room with thunder. Nicolas nodded his acknowledgment and sat.

"So we have three candidates. What's next?" Espen asked.

"Who makes the decision? And how is it to be made?" Canute looked to Anders.

"That's ours to determine."

"Are there any ideas?" Erling opened the discussion.

Eirik faced Nicolas. "How are leaders selected in America?"

Nicolas lounged in his chair. "Well, once the candidates are chosen, they spend the next months telling the people why they are the best choice. Then the people vote."

"The commoners elect your king?" Canute was aghast.

"President. Yes and no." Nicolas straightened and leaned on the table. "The Congress selects the President, and generally they go along with the wish of the populace. But they may vote with their conscience, if they seriously disagree."

"Then that is what we shall do!" Anders smacked the table. "We shall place our candidates before the people throughout the winter, and ask them to choose. Then, this group shall act as a congress, and decide in spring."

"So, we are free to follow the people, or not?" Canute clarified.

"Yes. Though, the wisdom of selecting the people's choice needs not be explained!" Anders chuckled.

"And will the candidates, themselves, be allowed to vote?" Karl looked at Nicolas and Espen.

"In America, the candidates may vote. Generally it's not enough to change the outcome." Nicolas glanced around the table.

"But this is a considerably smaller group."

"I believe the candidates should be allowed to vote," Anders decided. "There is always the chance they could choose other than themselves!"

"I second that!" Eirik called out. Agreement wafted toward him.

Anders rubbed his hands together. "I will commence the planning of a series of candidating opportunities. Balls, dinners, hunts—whatever I can conceive—and invite the aristocratic society of Christiania to participate. By April, we should be ready to vote. Are we agreed?"

The pounded approval lasted nearly three minutes.

September 25, 1820

The castle door opened and a woman swept inside. She pushed the ermine-trimmed cloak off her shoulders to reveal a dark red gown with silver embroidery. Her deep walnut hair was parted and brushed back, held in place by a pearl and silver snood. She was stunning.

"Oh, my! I had no idea I would be greeted in such a manner!" She smiled coquettishly as her face followed her black-lashed eyes around the waiting dinner crowd. Her Norse lilted with a French accent. "Is Karl Fredericksen here?"

Karl stepped forward, squinting. "Dagmar?"

"Uncle! It is indeed your own niece! I have come from Paris!" Her voice was deep and smooth, like a dark pool in an old forest. It rippled with her laughter. "I hope you are pleased to see me?"

"Of course!" Karl took her hands and kissed her cheeks. "I wish I knew you were coming! How long will you bide?"

"I shall winter here. I understand much is under consideration!" Dagmar glanced at Nicolas. He dipped his chin in greeting.

Anders joined Karl. "Indeed it is! May I welcome you to Akershus Castle, *Mademoiselle?*"

"Uncle Anders?"

"One and the same."

"You are looking well, Uncle!" Dagmar tipped up on her toes and kissed Anders' cheek.

"As are you, my dear. Come, join us for dinner. I shall have my butler assign staff to settle you in."

Dagmar turned and waved her hand toward the door. Two servants waited there with luggage. "There's no need, Uncle. I have my maid and footman with me. They are accustomed to my peculiarities and care for me quite well. I do appreciate your offer, but shall not require any additional servants. If they could be shown to my rooms, that would suffice."

"Of course!" Anders clapped his hands and a butler appeared at his elbow. He spoke in the man's ear, then turned and took Dagmar's arm. "Shall we dine, *Mademoiselle?*"

Dagmar curtsied, slid her hand into the crook of Anders' arm, and followed him into the Great Hall.

Willowy; Sydney thought Dagmar embodied the word. Everything on her was long, lean and graceful. She swayed as if blown by a breeze. Her throaty laugh sounded like birds. Sydney looked up at Nicolas. He stared oddly at his cousin as they followed her into the Hall.

"Captivated?" she murmured in English.

"Who would not be?" Nicolas turned to her. "Unless they were married to the most exceptional woman in the room, of course."

"Of course. Very politic remark, Lord Candidate." Sydney squeezed his elbow.

ഇ⊙ⴷ

Dagmar carried a fan as an expressive extension of her arm. She sashayed toward Nicolas after dinner, and tapped his chest with its folded tip. Her gaze slid slowly over every inch of him.

"We have not been introduced. I am Dagmar Lunde, Duchess of Steinkjer. My mother, Petra, was Karl and Erling's sister."

Nicolas bowed. "My pleasure, Your Grace. I am Lord Nicolas Reidar Hansen, Greve of Rollag, great-grandson of King Christian the Sixth."

"And an American, by your accent, eh?" Dagmar moved the fan tip back and forth on his chest.

"*Oui, Mademoiselle.*" Nicolas reached for Sydney. "May I present my wife, Grevinne of Rollag, Lady Siobhan Sydney Bell Hansen?"

"You are married? Hm. What a shame."

"And happily, so it seems," Sydney said in Norse as she slipped her arm around Nicolas's waist.

"So you say. He has not said a word!" Dagmar's fan ran down Nicolas's body.

"I would expect my contentment to be so obvious, that words are not necessary," Nicolas parried.

"*Touché*, Cousin." The fan withdrew. "Perhaps you would introduce me to those I need to know?" Dagmar's lashes fluttered over her cheeks, then lifted. "I have been away so long, I feel like a stranger. You, of course, understand that?"

Nicolas glanced at Sydney; she squeezed his waist. "I'll check on the children. Take your time."

"I shan't be long," he promised. Sydney smiled at him in a way that assured he would not.

Nicolas offered Dagmar his arm. The couple walked through the room at a casual pace. "Are you aware of the search for a Norse king?" he asked.

"I am. That's why I came. It seemed far too delicious to stay away!"

"Then you know that your uncle Karl is a candidate?"

"Yes. But I don't know who else."

Nicolas pointed with his chin. "Espen Canutesen."

"Is he?" Dagmar stared at her cousin. "Is he married?"

Nicolas chuckled. "No. And he seems oddly opposed."

"Really?" Dagmar turned back to Nicolas, her delicate brow wrinkled. "Has he had any prospects?"

Nicolas shrugged. "I have only been in Christiania since August. But none that I have seen or heard of in that time."

"Interesting. He is not unattractive. Not at all. Introduce us, would you?"

Nicolas happily led her to Espen's side. Espen turned toward them when he sensed their approach. His eyes swept over Dagmar, but showed no light of interest.

Nicolas bowed. "May I present your cousin, Her Grace, Dagmar Lunde, Duchess of Steinkjer?"

Dagmar dropped to a deep curtsy and faced the floor. She lifted her face and looked at Espen from under her dark lashes. Pink lips parted and curved in a slow smile as she rose and spread her fan. "It's my pleasure, Espen. It has been far too long."

Espen looked at his cousin as if he was puzzled. "Dagmar?"

She swirled the fan and snapped it shut. "You look wonderful, Espen." Her sultry voice was mesmerizing.

"Thank you, Duchess. You look rather amazing yourself."

"Please call me Dagmar, Cousin. I hope you will find time for me. I should very much wish to re-establish our childhood friendship." The fan re-opened and fluttered. "And perhaps find new ground?"

"Yes. Yes, I—I believe, I would enjoy that." Espen blushed, obviously caught off guard. "I shall send for you."

"I look forward to it." Dagmar held out her hand.

Espen took it and pressed it to his lips as his eyes met and held hers. Nicolas cleared his throat. Dagmar pulled her hand away and grasped Nicolas's elbow.

"I'm tired," she sighed.

"Do you wish me to escort you to your rooms?" he asked.

"Yes. Thank you."

He tipped his head toward Espen. "You may have caught his eye, after all. I cannot remember the last time I saw him blush!"

Dagmar glanced back over her shoulder, though they were gone from the Great Hall. "Truly?"

Nicolas led Dagmar to the same hallway where his rooms were. As he said good evening in front of her door, she stopped him from leaving.

"Are there only two candidates, then, for the throne?" she asked.

"No, *Mademoiselle* Duchess. There are three."

"And who is the third?"

Nicolas grinned. "The American. Have a pleasant sleep, Your Grace."

Chapter Eighteen

October 1, 1820

*S*ydney dressed for the Ball in a forest green dress trimmed with white lace; the fit of it caressed the arcs of her slender form and made Nicolas ache to do the same. The color echoed her gray-green eyes in a way that caught the casual observer and required a second, more studied consideration. Haldis coiled Sydney's nearly-black hair around her head, exposing the white skin of her graceful neck. A single pearl dripped from a green velvet ribbon around her throat.

Though her scar prevented her from wearing revealing gowns, the effect of her refined beauty was even more pronounced.

Nicolas shrugged into a skirted coat of navy blue over a brocade waistcoat shot through with golden threads. Since arriving in Christiania, he had gold buttons made with the Christiansen's royal crest, and Tomas sewed them meticulously in place. His lace linen shirt, tan breeches and cream-colored hose completed the look.

"You are definitely the most handsome of the choices," Sydney stepped behind him as he examined himself in the mirror. "In case that helps your cause!"

"Hm. If it were only that simple," he said, smirking at her reflection. Then his countenance softened. "I have made a decision about something."

"What might that be, husband?" Sydney's eyebrows lifted and her tone was too light. He turned to face her.

"I believe it's important for me to pay a visit to my father's family."

"Oh!" Her shoulders sagged in apparent relief. "Is that all?"

Nicolas kissed her forehead. "It's a bit of a journey, I'm afraid."

"Where are they?"

"Arendal. It's to the south and west. I believe it will take three or four days to get there."

"You believe?" Sydney's brows dipped. "Have you not been there?"

Nicolas rubbed the back of his neck. "No. I didn't see a need when I was here last."

Sydney's demeanor shifted. "And now that you might be king, you do?"

"Well, yes. To make a fine point of it." He ran his knuckles up her arm. "How would they respond to know that one of their own was a candidate, but did not care enough to present himself in person?"

Sydney's mouth shaped into a half-serious pout. "You have a point," she conceded.

"And then"—how might he explain it?—"I feel strangely drawn. When I was a careless lad of nineteen, not here of my own choosing, it didn't occur to me. But now..." he faltered.

"Now that you have family of your own, you understand the importance of those connections?" Sydney suggested.

"Yes!" He smiled at her. "That must be what it is."

"And campaigning along the way, enlisting their aid in your quest; these are merely side endeavors?" Sydney's amused expression belied her true thoughts. Nicolas laughed.

"*Min presang!* What wonderful ideas you have!" He pulled her close and kissed her well, inhaling the warm rosy scent of her. His hands traveled, mapping her body with no conscious thought.

Sydney's eyes drifted open, though not completely. "Who will go with you?" she whispered.

"I shall go alone, and take Tomas to valet for me. Though I wish for Stefan to see, he is too young for this particular journey. Besides," he smoothed Sydney's brow with his lips, "I can travel faster if I travel lighter."

"When will you leave?"

"Soon. It's already October and the winds are colder by the day!"

Sydney's arms tightened around his waist. The clock chimed the hour, softly intruding on their momentary silence. Nicolas lifted Sydney's chin with his knuckle and waited for her dark lashes to lift and reveal the deep green of her eyes.

"Are you ready?" he asked.

"Yes." Her voice surprised him with its warmth. "But I suppose we must attend the Ball first."

It took him a moment to grip her meaning; then it took the weight of every one of his responsibilities to lead her away from their bedroom.

₭₳₮

Sigrid waited at the foot of the stairs. Her golden dress complemented her fading blond hair and pale skin. Multiple strands of pearls circled her throat. Vegard stood next to her, with a cane and a scowl. Silver buttons strained to close his waistcoat across his ample stomach, and folds of his throat rolled over a lace collar.

"I'm going to sit down," he grumbled as Nicolas and Sydney descended. "I shall meet you inside." He limped away, wincing and relying on the cane.

"Good evening, Sigrid," Sydney spoke in Norse. "That is a beautiful dress."

"This?" Sigrid looked down and waved her hand. "I found it in the back of my wardrobe. I had not worn it in years. I believe the last time might have been when you were here, Nicolas."

"Oh, really?" Nicolas glanced around the crowd, not at her. "On what occasion?"

"If memory serves, it was the state dinner with King Christian and King William of Prussia." Sigrid grinned and rested her hand on Nicolas's chest, pulling his attention to her. "Do you remember that aristocrat from Moscow?"

Nicolas slapped his forehead. "I had forgotten about him!"

"He kept pouring beer in his cup and never figured out—"

"—that it had a leak! By the time he got up to leave, his lap was soaked!" Nicolas laughed. "He appeared to have pissed himself!"

Sydney was barely able to follow the conversation. "He was not aware?"

"No!" Nicolas wagged his finger at Sigrid. "And you played him along!"

Sigrid giggled behind a guilty hand. "He was so drunk, he had no idea he was the joke of dinner!"

"You made him believe you wanted him."

"He flirted with me all through dinner!"

"And he responded, did he not?" Nicolas sniggered.

"He did! He was hard. And proud. And tiny!" Sigrid waved her hand, smiling seductively. "So different from—oh."

Nicolas frowned and grabbed Sydney's arm, his face heated. "I believe my presence is required. Will you excuse us, Duchess?" He pulled her into the Great Hall.

"At least you had the decency to blush," Sydney muttered, her deep irritation obvious.

Fifty prominent citizens of Christiania were invited to Akershus Castle, for the purpose of becoming familiar with the three men on whom their future might rely. Nicolas, Karl and Espen stood in a line and greeted each one of them. Following an elaborate dinner, the tables were pushed against the walls and musicians, who played quietly through dinner, now provided dance music.

Sydney knew Nicolas would not be able to stay by her side. He was on display and must be available to all the guests. Even so, it seemed Sigrid was taking more than her share of turns as his partner. When Nicolas came to Sydney, and gratefully accepted a glass of beer from her, she expected to dance with him. But Sigrid sidled up to him, whispered in his ear and tugged at his sleeve.

"I am sorry, *min presang*, duty calls," Nicolas handed Sydney the drained glass. He disappeared into the press of revelers with Sigrid on his arm. Sydney sighed and turned away. With a start, she noticed Vegard watching her. He sat against the wall, hands on his cane, his rheumy eyes fixed on her.

Almost imperceptibly, his expression changed. Under his sad gaze, an understanding smile lifted one corner of his mouth. His chin dipped in a small nod, then he shrugged. Shaken, Sydney looked away.

She searched the room for Nicolas, and found him in Sigrid's arms, whirling and laughing. Navy eyes matching navy frock coat, blond hair combed back and tied at the nape, taller than anyone else in the room, he was so beautiful that it made Sydney's heart hurt. She looked back at Vegard, but his head was propped against the wall and his eyes were closed.

"Lady Hansen?"

Haldis' voice invaded Sydney's thoughts. She turned toward it. "Yes?"

"Agnes has come."

Sydney nodded, relieved at the interruption. "I will tell Lord Hansen. I will come."

Haldis nodded. "Yes, Madam."

Sydney pushed through the room until she caught Nicolas's eye. She waved him to her.

"Yes?" he asked, breathless.

Sydney raised her voice to be heard. "A baby. I am going out."

"Good! Fine! I shall see you later, then!" He kissed her hard on the mouth, then was swept away, only the pale gold of his hair visible above the crowd.

Sydney walked quickly to their rooms, chanting under her breath, "He loves me. He loves me. I know that he loves me."

Haldis scurried to keep up with her. "*Jeg tigger din benådning, Dame?*" I beg your pardon, Lady?

"*Det ikke er noe.*" Sydney muttered. It is nothing.

Sydney opened the door to the children's room. Maribeth sat close to the fire, and Tomas was with her. Their heads turned in tandem toward the door. Tomas jumped up, knocking over his chair. He fumbled to set it aright.

"Good evening, Lady Hansen."

"Good evening, Tomas." Sydney looked for her children. Stefan and Kirstie were asleep in their beds. "I have been called out to a birth and I wanted to check on the children first."

"They ate dinner and went to bed without a problem," Maribeth spoke in Norse. "I believe Leif keeps Stefan busy enough that it wears him out."

"Your Norse is getting better. Practice helps!" Sydney commented.

Maribeth blushed at Sydney's words and glanced at Tomas. "Yes, ma'am."

"And Lord Hansen?" Tomas asked.

"He will be late."

"I shall be available for him when he returns." Tomas bowed.

"Thank you, Tomas."

Haldis helped Sydney change from her ball gown into a plain woolen dress, then retrieved the fur-lined cloak from the wardrobe. Sydney shouldered her leather bag and followed Agnes into the cold October night.

October 2, 1820

"Take a walk with me, husband?"

Nicolas moved carefully. He set his coffee cup on the breakfast tray before Haldis carried it out, and squinted through the leaded window at the colorless day. "Is it necessary?"

"I simply desire your presence. And your undivided attention." Sydney faced him with a determined smile. "Will you escort me, my love?"

Nicolas swung his gaze back to hers. Her choice of words was unusual; she must have something to discuss with him. *I hope it's not last night.*

"It would be my pleasure." He smiled and waved at Tomas. "As soon as I have my shave."

Wrapped in cloaks against the sporadic wind, Nicolas and Sydney pressed against each other on the garden bench. The sky was a soft gray, the sea's horizon indistinct. Fifty feet of dead flowers in all directions protected their conversation. He waited for her to start, absently watching her spin her wedding ring around her pinkening finger.

"I love you."

Surprised, Nicolas responded, "I love you, too. What is amiss?"

Sydney took his hands in hers and pinned him with eyes as gray as the day. "We need to decide on what flirtations are acceptable."

"Ah." Nicolas shifted his weight and cleared his throat.

"You are in a very public position, husband. And I understand that well. And I am willing to let go of some conventions, so that you may achieve your goal here. But we must decide, together, which conventions those are." Sydney did not blink.

Nicolas nodded and scrubbed one hand over his chin. "That is sensible."

"Thank you."

"Have you already considered what—conventions—you can bide?"

"Yes, some." Sydney adjusted her position so she faced him squarely. "You will have to dance. You will dance with ingénues and dowagers. You will smile at them, and make them believe that you are nothing without their support. You will kiss their hands, their cheeks, and you will lead them on your arm. They will not be able to keep themselves from adoring you."

Nicolas lifted one brow. "Adoring me?"

"Last night, you were the most handsome and intelligent man in the Hall—"

"Sydney! You exaggerate!" he interrupted.

Sydney faced her lap, biting back her smile. "I do not."

"Well, then, you must admit to some bias?" Nicolas lifted her chin with a wind-reddened knuckle. "You do love me, or so you said."

"I do," she assured him. "But that does not negate what I'm saying. You are uncommonly handsome and exceptionally intelligent. You always will be. It's your blessing. And your curse."

"How is it a curse?" Nicolas was fascinated by her logic.

"Because, husband, some of those women will want to speak to you in private. They will pull you to a corner of the dance floor, into a room, or even a curtained window casement." Sydney's raised eyebrow mimicked his. "And they will touch you. Boldly."

Nicolas cleared his throat and felt his face flush. "I believe I can handle that. Should it occur, that is."

"Nicolas, it's not you that I worry about."

"No?" Relief warmed him; she wasn't angry. "Then what?"

"You need the support of their brothers, their husbands, and their fathers, even more than you need them. If you are too successful at gaining their adoration, you risk the wrath of their men."

Nicolas nodded. "You make a very clear point, *min presang*."

"*Takk du.*"

Nicolas smiled. "And what, then, is your advice?"

Sydney's steel-gray gaze held no glint of amusement. "Always be in sight. Never disappear from the gathering. Whatever you may decently do in public, I can bide. It is the thought of you cloistered with another woman that, that—" her voice broke.

Nicolas slid his arms under her cloak and wrapped them around her. He felt her ribs jerk spastically, though she didn't make a sound.

"Sydney, I want you to remember this: you are 'my gift' and always will be. You brought me back to life. You taught me to father Stefan, and gave me a daughter to worry over for the rest of my days."

Sydney grunted at the joke.

"There is not a woman on this earth who can change any of that. Ever. I swear this to you."

Sydney nodded, her face pressed against his chest.

He rested his chin on her head. "Whatever happens, *min presang*, always remember that."

"I can weather this storm," she whispered, "so long as your heart remains unchanged."

October 5, 1820

Sydney turned around in front of the mirror, inspecting her riding habit. She smiled at the image. Made of burgundy wool and trimmed in black fur, it highlighted her flawless skin and dark hair. The skirt was split and sewn into two wide legs so she could hook one over the pommel of the side-saddle. The knee-length jacket had two slits in back to allow it to drape over her steed's rump.

"I'm so excited, Nicolas! I've missed riding so much!" She reached for the matching black fur hat perched on the bed.

"Have you hunted before?" Nicolas shrugged into a doeskin coat. He wore tall black leather riding boots, polished to perfection by the vigilant Tomas.

"A few times, back in Kentucky." Sydney returned to the mirror and fiddled with the hat. "I only wish I could ride astride today. I have never been particularly good at side-saddle."

Nicolas lifted her heavy braid aside and planted a soft kiss on the nape of her neck. "Your 'not particularly good' is someone else's 'quite skilled' I would venture. You'll do fine."

Sydney smiled at Nicolas in the mirror. "Are you ready?"

The horses were saddled and waiting outside the stable. Leif waved Nicolas over.

"I picked this one special, Sir. He's a beauty, isn't he?" The tall dark stallion eyed Nicolas warily. Nicolas offered his fist and the horse sniffed it, pushing his hairy muzzle against it. He snorted and stamped one hoof. Leif beamed.

"That means he likes you, Sir!"

"And I like him. Thank you, Leif." Nicolas turned to Sydney. "Have you a steed yet?"

Sydney was about to say no, when a groom tapped her on the shoulder. "Lady? Will you follow me?" Her heart sank when she saw the gelding selected for her. Head down and one rear hoof cocked, he appeared to be asleep.

"Is there another horse?" Sydney did not know the Norse words to be more specific.

"He is gentle, ma'am. Have no fear." The groom held his hands for her foot.

With a sigh of resignation, Sydney stepped into it, and he lifted her onto the saddle. She hooked her leg around the pommel and arranged her coat. She glanced at Nicolas and saw his sympathetic expression.

"Next time, I'll let them know that you're an expert rider," he said in English.

Sydney shrugged. *"I dag jeg vil nyte jakten."* Today, I will enjoy the hunt.

Anders rode out first with his brother Erling. Karl and his wife Ingeborg followed. Eirik and Lady Linnet came up behind Nicolas and Sydney. Sydney wanted to tell Eirik to hold his reins more loosely, but was not sure how he might respond. She decided, instead, to ask, "How is your son?"

"He is well and healthy, thank you."

"Such a bonny boy!" Linnet puffed up. "The wet nurse says she has never seen such a good baby!"

Several more people joined them; some were guests at Akershus Castle, some lived in Christiania. As they left the castle, another couple cantered to the front of the group. Espen rode a bay gelding, and Dagmar, on a matching mare, rode at his side. She was resplendent in a deep purple riding habit and matching cloak.

Nicolas shot Sydney a look and nodded. She nodded back.

Conversation was loud and spirited as the hunting party rode through town. The kingly candidates were introduced to those who did not yet know them. Questions of lineage, education, and heirs were asked so often, that Nicolas joked that they should publish handbills with the answers! When they left the city behind, the dogs were released and the hunt began. They quickly picked up a scent and the chase was on.

Even though her mount was sluggish, Sydney loved riding. Head high, she breathed in the sap-filled scents of the dying autumn forest. The dry swish of dead grass and the snapping of twigs made for a loud pursuit. The wind chilled her cheeks and nose; she was glad she brought her leather riding gloves on the outing.

Nicolas was far ahead of her. She could see him standing in his stirrups and sighting his rifle. She saw the puff of smoke a full second before the sound reached her. He shook his head, and sat to reload. Several other shots went off, and were followed by a cheer. Sydney caught up and saw the downed buck.

"Better luck next time." She smiled at her red-cheeked husband.

"I've spent so much time with the sword, my shooting is off. But I'll improve!" He grinned at her, his blue eyes alive with energy. "I must prove myself a warrior!"

Sydney laughed.

The dogs bayed again, and took off in a jostling pack. The hunters followed, crashing through forest, splashing through streams. This time it was a boar, tusked and angry. Sydney could smell his musk. Nicolas brought him down with one shot.

"Vindicated!" He winked at Sydney, and wiped his brow in exaggerated worry.

Her attention was diverted by the stomping of iron-shod hooves on dead leaves. Eirik's mount was prancing off to one side of the group. Eirik had his reins pulled back so far, the animal's chin was pressed against its neck and he could not close his mouth. He kept bumping into Lady Linnet's delicate black mare as he fought Eirik for control.

"Eirik?" Linnet squealed and held her saddle with both hands.

"Hold! Hold!" Eirik demanded.

"Loose him!" Sydney shouted, reflexively in English.

"*La ham løsner!*" Nicolas repeated. Eirik seemed not to hear either of them.

"Hold!"

He kicked the stallion and pulled the reins to one side. The animal bucked then reared, jaw foaming and hooves beating the air. Eirik tumbled backward from the saddle, thumping Linnet's mare's rump on his way to the ground. The mare bolted. Linnet, in a tangle of limbs and leather, held on. Eirik lay in the leaves, the wind knocked out of him.

Sydney did not stop to think. She jumped from her gelding and walked steadily toward the stallion, talking softly and holding out her hand. Freed from Eirik's torment, the animal had calmed some, though his eyes rolled. Sydney grabbed the dangling reins, patted the horse, and quickly mounted him astride. She turned him in a circle to establish her control, then aimed him to follow the mare. She tapped his ribs with her toes. He trotted at first, then shifted into a smooth ground-eating canter.

Sydney had no trouble pursuing the mare with the screaming beacon on her back. Once clear of trees, she gave the stallion his head. His gate stretched and his ears flipped back as he ran for the thrill of it. No obstacle slowed him; he took them in stride, gliding high over logs or ditches. Sydney felt at one with the horse and relished the incumbent sense of freedom.

She was disappointed when he caught up to the heaving mare. Sydney reached over and grabbed the exhausted steed's bridle, then slowed both mounts to a stop. Only then, did Linnet open her eyes.

"Good Lord! It's you!" Her gaze swept Sydney. "What are you doing riding like a man?"

"Saving your hide, Your Grace!" Sydney snapped.

"But—it's not proper for you to ride that way!"

"You are most welcome, Linnet." Sydney raised an eyebrow. "It was my pleasure to come to your aid."

Linnet snorted and straightened her hat.

Sydney turned the horses and walked them back toward the hunting party. They were met halfway by the assemblage. Eirik sat awkwardly on the abandoned gelding's side-saddle.

"Linnet? Are you all right?" He jumped to the ground and loped to her side. "I was so worried!"

The stallion snorted and tossed his head. Sydney dropped the mare's reins and turned her mount away from Eirik. She rode around to the other side of the group. Dagmar came up beside her, eyes sparkling.

"That was very impressive, darling. Who knew you could ride like that?"

Espen frowned. "I have never seen a woman of good breeding ride astride."

"Neither have I, but I think she's fabulous!" Dagmar fluttered her eyes at Espen. "And she certainly saved the day, did she not?"

Nicolas nudged his mount toward them, smiling broadly. "You're a hero, wife!"

Anders followed close behind. "Did you know of her horsemanship?"

"I did. She was raised to handle horses. And she is gifted in it."

Sydney returned Nicolas's proud grin. "Thank you."

Erling considered the angle of the sun. "I believe there is daylight enough to continue, if anyone is amenable?" he addressed the group.

"We shall head back." Eirik patted Linnet's leg. "I believe we have had enough excitement." He approached Sydney on the stallion. The horse bobbed his head and snorted.

"Eirik, you ride the gelding back. Sydney will stay where she is," Anders decreed.

"But, the saddle! It is a woman's!"

"So you should be able to manage easily. Do you know the way back?"

Eirik straightened his shoulders in an attempt to save face. "Yes, sir. I shall see my wife safely home."

"Fine!" Anders signaled the master of the hounds and he whistled for the dogs. He sent them off and the party followed.

Sydney knew she was being watched. She leaned to Nicolas and whispered in English, "Am I an abomination?"

"You very well might be," he answered in kind. "So sit up straight and make them respect you."

Smiling broadly, she did just that.

Chapter Nineteen

October 10, 1820

*N*icolas pulled his cloak closer and turned away from the pelting rain. He and Tomas had been riding from dawn to dusk for four days, two of those days in freezing rain. They hoped to reach Arendal before nightfall.

"If we shall even be able to tell when night falls!" Nicolas muttered.

"I beg your pardon, Sir?" Tomas asked and twisted to see him. Nicolas realized he had spoken in English. He shook his head.

"Nothing, Tomas," he said in Norse. "Only the frozen mumblings of a starving peasant!"

"Peasant?" Tomas scoffed. "As you wish, Your Highness."

Nicolas laughed at that. "Elevating your own state, are you?"

Tomas grinned from under his hood. "It's the delirium of deprivation, Sir. Pay me no mind."

The brief exchange lifted Nicolas's spirits some. He shifted in his saddle and wondered yet again if he should have chosen to travel by carriage. *No*, he thought. *The journey is long enough as it is.* Horseback was faster, especially in the rain; there were no wheels to sink into the mire that passed for a road. That was a good thing, because the distance from Christiania was farther than he realized.

Nicolas rode a magnificent chestnut gelding who seemed impervious to the weather. He sported a white blaze down his muzzle and three white hocks. The horse considered the foggy landscape around the road with cheerful interest. His ears constantly flicked drops of water and his sodden tail stung Nicolas's legs when he swung it around. Tomas's gray mount was soaked black with the rain and stomped along beside, snorting his displeasure with every mud-caked step.

"What time do you suppose it might be?" Nicolas asked.

Tomas squinted at the low, featureless sky. Gray and indistinct, it offered no hint as to the position of the sun, nor the direction they were headed.

"Four o'clock, Sir."

Nicolas shifted a disbelieving gaze to his valet. "And how did you reach that conclusion?"

Tomas pointed in front of them. A faint light glowed in the gloom, joined suddenly by another. "They are lighting the lamps."

"Could it finally be Arendal?" Nicolas sat straighter. "And how quickly do you suppose we might find out?"

The men kicked their reluctant mounts to sloppy trots and soon reached the village. Nicolas led the way to a large inn with a sign advertising, "Lodging ~ Clean." A surprised stable boy jumped up from his sheltered seat near the front door and took both horses to a barn behind the inn. Tomas held the door for Nicolas and they stepped into the blessedly dry warmth.

Nicolas inhaled the beery smell of the room, spiced with akevitt and acrid wood smoke. The décor was sturdy, rugged. They peeled off their wet cloaks and hung them on hooks near the fire where they immediately began to steam, returning tendrils of borrowed fog. A robust middle-aged man rocked toward them, a smile splitting his round, red face and displaying an astonishing lack of teeth.

"Welcome!" He slapped Tomas on the shoulder. "You are hungry?"

"Hungry, thirsty and in need of lodging," Nicolas replied. "Have we reached Arendal?"

"That you have! And on a wicked night, I'm a-feared."

"Have you rooms available?"

"Only one tonight. But it's the best room we have!" His gaze checked Nicolas for objections to the higher cost.

Nicolas kept his face intentionally passive. *Of course it is.*

At Nicolas's silence, he added, "But maybe tomorrow we'll have another?"

"Thank you, sir, but I anticipate that we should only need the one night. Rest assured, however, we will let you know if we discover our needs have changed." Nicolas smiled politely.

Thus placated—at least as much as was possible for now—the proprietor showed them to a table. A parade of food and drink followed. Sausages, cheeses, fish stew, bread, and fruit tarts were presented with apparently bottomless steins of beer and flagons of akevitt. Nicolas and Tomas ate and drank their fill and then some, so relieved were they to be warm and dry. When their saddlebags were carried in by the stable boy and taken to their room, the men stumbled behind him, up the narrow wooden staircase, and to the 'best room.'

Nicolas swayed in the center of the floor and stared at the small bed. He lifted one brow at Tomas.

"I am not sleeping in that," he pointed with his whole arm, "with you."

Tomas waved his hands, almost knocking himself off balance. "I shall sleep on the floor. In fact, I believe I shall begin now." He sunk to his knees on the hearthrug.

"Some valet you are!" Nicolas snorted. He dropped his frock coat, waistcoat and breeches on the floor and, clad only in his shirt, climbed diagonally between the sheets. Even so, his feet stuck out from the covers until he curled on his side.

Both men began to snore at the same time.

October 11, 1820

A blade of sunshine cleaved Nicolas's skull leaving him, unexpectedly, still alive. He turned away from the murderous shaft and tried to pry his tongue from the roof of his mouth. His eyes opened with less effort and he saw that, while he was presently alone in the room, Tomas had been busy. His formal clothes were laid out across the small table, and steam rose from the pitcher on the washstand.

The door latch clicked and Tomas entered with a tray bearing two mugs of coffee and fresh rolls. When the rich scent of the brewed beverages reached Nicolas, he inhaled deeply, appreciative of Tomas's efforts. This proved to be a mistake.

Nicolas rolled off the bed onto all fours and puked into the piss pot which Tomas—thank the Lord—had already emptied. When his stomach felt he had been sufficiently punished for last evening's abuse, the retching stopped. He sat back against the bed frame. Tomas handed him a warm, wet towel to wash his face.

Thus renewed, Nicolas held out his hand. Tomas placed a warm roll in his palm. "I'll have that coffee now, as well," he croaked. Tomas pushed a hot cup into his grip.

Nicolas, from his seat on the cold wood floor, considered the valet as he chewed. Despite his industry, Tomas' face was colorless down to his lips. A clammy sheen reflected the morning light.

"How are you this morning?" Nicolas asked him.

He nodded toward the piss pot. "It is a shame no one was around to empty it for me. Before."

Nicolas snorted his amusement and one side of Tomas' mouth curved in rueful acknowledgement.

"I'm preparing you a bath downstairs," he continued, retrieving both the piss pot and the wet towel. "I shall shave you afterwards."

"Have you found out anything concerning our destination?" Nicolas asked before popping the last bite of bread in his mouth and draining his coffee cup.

Tomas nodded. "Yes, sir. The Hansen estate is further west along the main road, about a mile or so. They say it's obvious, built on the edge of a cliff."

"Thank you, Tomas."

Two hours later, bathed, brushed, and polished within an inch of his sanity, Nicolas caught his first sight of the ancient Hansen homestead. Reining the chestnut to a stop, his narrowed gaze took in every detail.

Hansen Hall was built on the top of a bluff. Cobbled together in fits over the last several centuries, it was dominated by a round tower built of rough stones. Its turreted top stood three stories over the road, and five over the empty moat that dipped around it. There were no windows in the tower, only the vertical slits which allowed archers to defend the inhabitants.

Viking archers.

Nicolas felt their unseen presence in the breeze that stroked his cheek and he rested his fingertips there; a thrill tingled up his spine and his belly clenched with recognition. He nodded his silent respect to those whose restless blood he shared.

Extending off one side of the tower was a two-story structure, built centuries later of quarried stone. This addition had glass windows, leaded in a multitude of small diamond-shaped panes. Peeking over the flat roof of the medieval façade were several tall chimneys, all spouting gray smoke like a row of flags. Slanted slate roofs declared the presence of a modern wing behind the tower, creating a courtyard in between, perhaps.

Nicolas breathed in the North Sea. Over the cries of single-minded gulls, he could hear waves impaling themselves below the cliff. He wondered how far down the water was.

"Shall we go on, my lord?" Tomas prompted.

Nicolas started, forgetting the valet was there. "Yes. Yes, let's do," he answered.

Their horses' hooves crunched up the drive made of crushed white stone and shells. The main entrance was centered in the medieval section, in an arched alcove at the end of the moat bridge. A heavy wooden door stood under a carved "H" which had, on either side, sculpted friezes. With Thor on one side, and Christ on the other, they proved that Christianity had reached Norway centuries earlier.

Nicolas swung his leg over the gelding and dismounted. Tomas took the reins and Nicolas climbed to the massive portal, the scooped stone steps worn down in the middle by thousands of feet. He grabbed the round iron knocker and thrust it against the planks. He heard the sound echoing beyond.

The door was pulled open by a surprised butler. His eyes swept over Nicolas's finely tailored attire. "May I help you, sir?"

"Is your master at home?"

"He is."

"Would you be so kind as to inform him of my presence?"

An infinitesimal change flickered over the butler's countenance when he heard Nicolas's accent. "And how shall I announce you?"

"Lord Nicolas Reidar Hansen, Greve of Rollag."

The man's eyes did not flinch at Hansen; it was a common name after all. But the title pulled him up sharp. "Of course, my lord. Won't you please come in? I shall send a man to see to the horses."

෨෦෬

Nicolas waited in a drawing room full of ancient works of art and craft. He was admiring a lethal looking iron sword when he heard approaching footfalls.

"Lord Hansen?"

Nicolas turned to face a tall white-haired gentleman. His slender frame stooped a little around the broad shoulders, but the way he moved proved a physical past. Blue eyes, clear and intense, met his without blinking.

"I am Edvard Aleksander Hansen, Ninth Greve of Arendal. How may I assist you?"

Nicolas bowed. "I am the firstborn son of Reidar Magnus Hansen, grandson of Martin Gunnar Hansen, and great-grandson of Eskil Brander Hansen."

"Uncle Martin?" A slow smile drew back the wrinkles in his cheeks like drapery. "My father, Roald Petter Hansen, was his older brother."

"Did you have opportunity to meet him?" Nicolas asked.

"Yes. He came here when I was in my twenties. I recall him well." Lord Edvard waved Nicolas to a chair and moved deliberately to a sideboard. He lifted a bottle of akevitt in silent question.

"Yes, thank you. Cousin."

"Cousin," Lord Edvard whispered, pausing. Then he chuckled. "Now your accent makes sense."

"Is it so noticeable?"

Lord Edvard's sideways glance squelched that hope. He handed Nicolas the glass and sank into an upholstered armchair.

"To unexpected family?" He lifted his drink. Blue veins showed through large, onion-skinned hands knobbed with arthritis.

"To your health, Lord Edvard!" Both drained their glasses.

"So, young Nicolas, why are you here?" Lord Edvard set his glass on a small side table, a slight rattle betraying a tremor.

"To meet my family and see my ancestral home." Nicolas ran his knuckle over his upper lip. "I had hoped my son might come with me, but the journey was too difficult for a seven-year-old."

"From America? Yes, I see that."

"No, sir. From Christiania. My wife is there as well, with our infant daughter."

Lord Edvard sat back in his chair, his expression changed. He stared at Nicolas for a long, silent time, lips drawing tight, then puckering.

"So, young Nicolas, why have you brought your family to Norway, then?"

Nicolas leaned forward in his chair. "That question requires a very complicated answer. Might I impose on your hospitality, cousin, and bide here a day or two? I shall tell you everything you wish to know."

Lord Edvard tipped his head.

Nicolas leaned back again. "Perhaps you can give me some advice for the situation I am currently facing. And," he waved his hand around the room, "tell me the Hansen story, eh?"

୫୬୦୪

At dinner that evening, Nicolas met the Lady Olina Berg Hansen, Edvard's wife of forty-one years. Tall and white-haired like her husband, she was a bit hard of hearing and had the tendency to speak so softly that Nicolas could barely hear her. He found himself smiling and nodding a lot, then turning his attention back to Lord Edvard's narrative.

The Hansen family's story was arresting, and Nicolas wondered if his father knew of Norway's failed attempt to settle Greenland, the devastating effect of the Black Death, or how Denmark's king became ruler of the much larger country.

Sitting in the dining hall of the medieval wing lent an aura of supernatural realism to Edvard's tales. Nicolas considered the possibility the shadows from the flickering lamps were actually the shades of long-dead Hansens, listening and passing judgment on Nicolas's worthiness to carry the name.

After a long pause, while the dinner dishes were cleared away and dessert was served, Edvard turned a sharp gaze to Nicolas. "And now, Nicolas, it is your turn."

"Sir?"

"Why have you brought your family to Norway?"

Nicolas took a bite of the rum pudding, chewing slowly. He sipped the black coffee laced with akevitt.

"I might be elected King of Norway," he stated simply. No point in evading the truth.

"You—what?" Edvard nearly spit his coffee. "How?"

"On my mother's side, I am the great-grandson of King Christian the Sixth. The royal family is attempting to reclaim the throne from Sweden and I was summoned to Christiania to be considered as a candidate."

Edvard stared slack-jawed at his wife.

"What is it, dear?" she asked.

"Our cousin Nicolas, here, might become King of Norway!" he said loudly.

"Oh my!" Her cloudy brown eyes shifted to Nicolas. "Isn't that wonderful?"

"Thank you, Lady Olina." Nicolas dipped his head in acknowledgement.

"Tell me everything, Cousin!" Edvard demanded. "And do not leave one single thing out, do you hear me?"

October 12, 1820

Late the next morning, Nicolas, with Edvard's blessing, explored the hodge-podge manor. Once inside the building, the transition from the ninth-century tower, to the fourteenth-century hall, to the modern eighteenth-century sleeping rooms and kitchen, was not as disjointed as it was on the exterior. Generations of mistresses had worked to make the interior décor seamless and inviting. They had done well.

At the end of one windowless passage on the ground floor lurked an unusual door. Set deep into the wall, there were carvings all around it. Nicolas leaned closer to make them out. They appeared to be Christ with His cross; perhaps the 'stations' Sydney had told him about once. He was taken aback for a moment, considering that his predecessors were papists. Then he smacked his hand to his forehead: Martin Luther sparked the reformation in 1517, two centuries after this wing was built.

Nicolas tried the handle. It was stiff and the latch clanked, iron echoing down the hall. He dragged it open and discovered a small chapel. The faintest smell of ancient rot underlay the cold, damp odor of stone. Wooden benches, black with age and use, sat in perpetual formation; faithful, waiting.

Gravestones paved the floor. Centuries of shoes had worn away the finer details of the carved stones, but some information was still legible. Nicolas walked slowly to the front, engrossed in the names and dates he could decipher. The closer he was to the front, the older and more worn the stones.

When he reached the railing that separated mere humanity from the priests, the stones were once again readable. He stepped over the railing—after all the chapel was obviously not in use anymore—and went to the very front.

"Rydar Martin Petter-Edvard Hansen, born 1324, died 1401," Nicolas read out loud. "I expect I am named for him."

He turned to the stone set alongside. "Belovd Wyfe, Grier MacInnes Hansen, born 1328, Scotland, died 1401."

These were the first, the oldest, graves in the chapel.

"He built it, you see." Lord Edvard's deep voice, breathy with age, floated over the musty past to Nicolas. "He came home from Greenland after the Black Death. No one was left, so he reclaimed the land; brought it back from death."

Nicolas turned to face his elder relation. "Of course they had children."

"Seven. Five that survived infancy. Four sons and a daughter." Lord Edvard pointed to stones along the outer wall. "They are all there, with their wives."

"So we have Scots blood?" Nicolas grinned, one eyebrow cocked.

Edvard coughed a laugh, wheezing a bit. "It's very likely that one of our own Viking warriors spawned her great-grandmother, don't you know!"

Nicolas laughed with him; jarring sounds in this somber and silent tomb. He turned back to the graves. Even though he was a staunch Lutheran, he crossed himself in imitation of his Catholic wife.

"God has blessed you both abundantly," he murmured. His throat tightened and he brushed unexpected tears from his cheeks. Being here, at these graves, moved him more than he would have thought possible. His connection with Norway thrummed through his soul, deep and insistent.

"Rest in peace, father," he whispered, touching the stone lightly. "You've done very well."

After a moment, he stepped back over the railings and took Edvard's arm. His throat clearing echoed in hollow reverberation.

"So who built the new wing?" he asked, closing the chapel door behind them.

Nicolas and Tomas remained in Arendal for four days. When they left, Nicolas had Lord Edvard's pledged fealty, plus his advocacy with the surrounding aristocracy. They took time with the journey back to Christiania, stopping at the largest establishment of each village they passed through to press Nicolas's case. Countless akevitt toasts, impromptu speeches and back-thumping promises later, they plodded into Christiania, exhausted, surfeited and filthy.

"But worth every moment," Nicolas groaned, slipping into a hot bath. "As Tomas will undoubtedly be asked to confirm."

Sydney handed him the soap. "And Lord Edvard?"

"With his very valuable help it is apparent that I have won the southern lands." He scrubbed his face and dipped under the water. When he surfaced, Sydney kissed him.

"Well played, husband."

Chapter Twenty

October 23, 1820

*S*tefan? Hold on there, young man!" Sydney grasped Stefan's coat as he tried to leave the bedroom. "You have not had your lessons since we arrived in Christiania!"

"But I need to go, *Mamma*. I need to help Leif!" Stefan's bright blue eyes were sincerely concerned. "And then we have our sword lessons with *Pappa*. And he promised to teach us to ride like hunters!"

Sydney looked to Nicolas. His eyes were narrow and his lips pursed. "What are you thinking?" she challenged.

Nicolas rubbed his dark gold whiskers; soft rasping filled the silence. He ran both hands through his hair. "A heretical thought, to be sure."

"Oh? And what might that be?" Sydney rested one hand on her hip; the other still leashed Stefan.

"The boy is learning Norse. He is working hard. And he is gaining skills," Nicolas posited. "If we ensure that he reads, in both languages, every day, I believe we can catch up on his arithmetic later."

"On the voyage home?" Sydney's sarcastic tone was unmistakable.

"Or we can hire a tutor here, if need be."

"Say 'yes,' *Mamma!* Please?" Stefan hopped up and down.

"You need to read every night before bed," Sydney declared, pointing at her growing stepson. "I will buy Norse books today. And your father and Maribeth have books in English."

"I promise!"

"And you need to write reports about the books, so we know you have truly read them," she added.

"I will!" Stefan nodded earnestly; his perpetually wavy auburn hair escaped the thong.

"All right then." Sydney let go of his coat. "Go on!"

"Thank you, *Mamma!*" Stefan ran out the door, spun, and ran back to hug her. "I love you!"

Then he was gone.

Sydney grinned at Nicolas with unrestrained joy. "That, husband, was well worth the compromise!"

Tomas entered the room. "Excuse me, sir. But an important letter has arrived for you." He handed Nicolas an envelope. "The messenger is waiting for a response."

Nicolas broke the seal and opened it, nodding as he read. "Thank you, Tomas. Please tell the messenger that I will arrange for payment by the end of the week."

"Very good, sir." Tomas left the room.

"Do we need to walk in the garden?" Sydney asked.

"No. It was from my land agent. All my land is leased."

"The new plots?"

"Yes. I now have twice as many tenants. Hence, the land has doubled in value, as has my standing." He slapped the papers against his hand in sharp confirmation.

November 5, 1821

Nicolas downed his akevitt and followed it with a gulp of small beer. The tavern was quiet in the midday. Low clouds, threatened snow and seemed to warn patrons away. That suited Nicolas fine; he had taken a round-about route to ensure he wasn't followed here.

A carriage stopped outside and a gentleman disembarked. The family resemblance made Nicolas smile. He waited until the carriage was gone and the man disappeared into the office door across the street.

Nicolas paid his bill, and left the tavern, entering the establishment designated, "Matias Ivarsen, Lawyer."

೮೦౧೮

Stefan and Leif practiced their swordplay while they waited for Nicolas. When he returned to Akershus, he watched them for several minutes. The difference between the boys was striking.

Stefan, at seven, was over four feet in height. Leif was five feet at twelve years. Stefan's body was rounded, sturdy. Leif was thin; his bony shoulders showed through his shirt, and his hand-me-down clothes hung on his frame. When Stefan looked at the world, his eyes rested. Leif's eyes darted. One boy was safe; the other never had been.

"*Pappa!* Did you see us?" Stefan pushed his hair back.

"I did. Leif, you are showing great promise."

"What about me?" Stefan frowned.

"You are doing very well for a seven-year-old. But Leif is doing very well for a twelve-year-old."

Leif stood as tall as he could stretch. "Thank you, Sir."

"In fact, I believe you are ready for this." Nicolas pulled a short steel sword, like Stefan's, from behind his back.

Leif dropped his wooden blade, eyes round as the autumn moon. "For me?"

"For you."

Leif handled the sword like it would break. "I can use it every time?"

"Of course. It belongs to you."

Leif sat down, hard, on the ground. He sniffed and wiped his nose on his sleeve. He cleared his throat. He sniffed and wiped again, leaving dirty streaks down his cheeks. Nicolas pulled his attention away to give the boy privacy.

"Stefan, would you like to parry with me first?" He pulled his sword from its scabbard.

Stefan lifted his blade and turned sideways to Nicolas. They jabbed, countered and feinted. Careful not to be too aggressive, Nicolas challenged Stefan to see how far he could go. When Stefan began to pant, he stepped back and lowered his blade.

"Very well done, son." Stefan looked extremely pleased with

himself. "Leif? Are you ready to give a try?"

Leif nodded, pushing himself from the ground. He jumped to the *en garde* position. "Yes, Sir. I'm ready."

Nicolas began as he had with Stefan, then intensified his movements. When Leif disengaged, Nicolas grinned. "Good move."

When Leif lunged, he nearly cut Nicolas's thigh. Nicolas jumped back. "Excellent!"

When the blade lowered and seemed to grow heavy in the boy's hands, Nicolas let Leif touch his chest. "*Touché!*"

Leif stepped back, breathing hard. Then he bowed. "Thank you, Sir," he huffed.

Nicolas sheathed his sword and looked at the sky. "I am afraid it has grown too late to ride today. Perhaps tomorrow?"

Leif nodded and held his sword toward Nicolas.

"What are you about? The sword is yours to keep."

"Will you hold it for me, Sir? If I hold it, it will be taken from me." Leif's embarrassed concern showed in the crease of his young brow and the heightened flush of his cheeks.

Nicolas felt his own face grow hot at his unthinking blunder. "Yes, Leif, I will hold it." He accepted the blade, placed so carefully in his hand. "I shall see you tomorrow."

November 13, 1820

Invisible in the darkened room, the clock on the mantle chimed three times. Sydney turned over in bed yet again, and sighed, kicking the tangle of covers. She punched her pillow, unable to relax, her mind dragging her in directions she did not wish to go.

The bedroom door opened and closed; Nicolas crossed the room and slumped into a chair. Pungent cigar smoke stung her nostrils. She sat up, and his head jerked in her direction.

"When did you return?" he grunted.

"Eleven. The pains were false."

"What time is it?" Nicolas twisted to see the clock.

"After three."

He slumped back in the chair, eyes closing, and held out his hand. "Come to me."

Sydney hesitated, then slid from the bed, her jaw set. A winter draft seeped through the windows and hovered over the carpet, chilling her bare ankles as she tiptoed to him. Nicolas grasped her hand and pulled her across his lap; she felt his hardness beneath her. When he kissed her, she tasted the akevitt and cigars that occupied his evening. And his skin reeked of Sigrid's perfume.

Nicolas rested his forehead against Sydney's cheek. "That woman torments me, *min presang*. You have no idea."

"I don't know how to respond to that, Nicolas," Sydney whispered.

Nicolas pushed her off his lap, but still held her hand. He unfastened his breeches and pushed them out of the way. "Love me. I've had too much to drink to stand, but I need you mightily," he rasped.

He lifted Sydney's nightgown and took hold of her hips. He turned her around and worked his knees between hers. Sydney tipped forward and grabbed Nicolas's knees for support as she straddled his thighs. She gasped as he pushed into her from behind. He lifted her, then pulled her close, seemingly without effort. His fingers cut into her as he pressed deeper. He moved in and out of her, exhaling violently with each thrust, until he peaked. With a moan, his hands fell away and he melted into the chair.

"Thank you," he breathed.

Sydney climbed from his lap, both furious and aroused. She rearranged her nightgown and walked stiffly to the bed, slipping between the cold, smooth sheets. When she heard him begin to snore, she cried herself to sleep without a sound.

November 27, 1820

Sydney sighed as Haldis laced her into yet another ball gown. There was a time in her life when she considered dressing up and attending social functions as pleasant diversions from everyday life. Now that it had become her everyday life, she was not so pleased. She looked forward to Agnes's plain face appearing at her door and summoning her to another birth.

She watched Nicolas dress. He had ordered new clothes since they arrived, and he looked magnificent. Sydney never took for granted that this tall, handsome and intelligent man was hers until death did them part. She thanked God for him every day, and prayed for him every night. She looked to his best interest at all times. She strived to hold on through this storm, until their life was settled.

"*Ha du noensinne ville til å være en droning?*" Sydney asked Haldis. Have you ever wanted to be a queen?

Haldis stared at Sydney's reflection in the mirror. "*Hver liten pike gjør.*" Every little girl does.

"*Ingen. Hver små pikebehov til å være en prinsesse.*" No. Every little girl wants to be a princess.

Haldis shrugged, finding the distinction unimportant.

Sydney examined her own image in the large glass. She looked perfectly assembled, confident, and very somber. Did she want to be a queen? Would having Nicolas for a husband be worth the burden of royalty?

"Are you ready, wife?" Nicolas's deep voice shattered her ruminations.

"I only need my shawl." The castle was drafty and winter came strong in Norway. Sydney took Nicolas's arm. "You look very handsome tonight, husband."

"And you are so beautiful, I am tempted to not go to dinner at all!" Nicolas nuzzled Sydney's ear.

"I am afraid I need my sustenance, if I am to keep up with your other activities!" Sydney smiled.

The regular royal crowd attended dinner: Anders and Erling, Karl and Ingeborg, Eirik and Linnet, Espen and Dagmar—who had become his steady companion, Sigrid and Vegard—who did not always come down to dinner. Plus, of course, the press of Norwegian aristocrats and countrymen who came to observe and dissect the three kingly candidates.

The first course was tomato soup with basil. It was one of Sydney's favorites. She savored the warm, rich flavor and thought about Addie's garden in Cheltenham. A wave of homesickness engulfed her. She swallowed the lump in her throat with another spoonful. She wondered if Nicolas was ever homesick. Before she could ask him, the next course was served and Sydney was pulled into conversation concerning a Norwegian flag.

"How did America choose her flag? It is very unique," a middle-aged man asked politely.

"The, bands, red and white," Sydney pantomimed stripes, "are for the thirteen first... I do not know the word. Pieces of America."

"*Stater*," the gentleman offered. "*Forente Stater.*"

"That is easy! *Takk du.*" She gave him her warmest, most politic, smile.

"And the stars?" inquired his dinner companion, a woman with the reddest hair Sydney had ever seen.

"One for each, state, that is a piece of America. There were twenty-two, but Maine was added in March of this year. We hope Missouri will be twenty-four."

"Missouri? Where is that?" the man asked.

"Almost in the middle of the—" Sydney spread her hands sideways in front of her, showing something large. "Land?"

"The middle of the continent?" the woman suggested. "How far is that from the ocean?"

Sydney screwed up her mouth. "I believe that it is almost a thousand miles."

The man chuckled. "Certainly not, Lady. You must be mistaken."

Sydney waved to gain Nicola's attention. He sat across the table, listening to a warbling matron and nodding intently. He apologized for the interruption in mid-sentence, and turned to Sydney, amusement lighting his cerulean gaze.

"Yes?"

"How many miles is it from St. Louis to Baltimore?" she asked in English.

"Nine hundred and fifty miles. Why do you ask?"

"How wide is the continent?"

Nicolas ran his hand through his hair. "The best guess is close to three thousand miles. Perhaps a bit less."

Sydney turned back to her inquisitors. "I was mistaken."

The man nodded, condescending. "I thought so."

"Missouri is nine hundred and fifty miles from the ocean. And it is one third, not in the middle."

"What?" The woman's jaw dropped.

"The continent is…" The man frowned as realization sunk in.

"Almost three thousand miles wide," Sydney finished the sentence. She felt a surge of pride. "It is very big. And very, very beautiful."

The couple fell silent.

"What is Norway's flag?" she asked, careful not to seem smug.

"I cannot think of it."

"We currently haven't a flag. But there has been discussion of late that we should have one," the woman explained.

"Yes, yes. The *Storting* is looking into the idea," the man added.

"*Storting?*"

"The Great Assembly? Our parliament."

Sydney nodded her understanding. Her eye, however, was drawn to the other table. Vegard was in some sort of distress, pulling at the neck of his shirt. He clutched his throat and his face grew red as the soup. He tried to stand and promptly toppled sideways to the floor. Sigrid screamed.

Sydney hurried around the table and knelt beside Vegard. His pupils were so dilated that his eyes held no color. He blinked and squinted, and batted his hands at the air.

"Vegard?" Nicolas shouted over Sydney's shoulder. "Can you talk, man?"

"They are trying to kill me!" his voice was husky and dry, painful to listen to.

"Who?"

"THEM!" His hands fell to the floor. "Where am... It's you?" He frowned at Sydney. She cradled his head in her lap. "I'm so sorry..." he rasped.

Sydney rested her fingers against his neck. "His heart is beating way too fast!" She looked up at Sigrid, standing with fingers pressed against her lips, pale blue eyes wide in an even paler face. "Has this happened before?"

Sigrid shook her head.

"C-can't b-breathe," Vegard's voice was no more than a strained whisper. Sydney loosened the neck of his shirt as he writhed in panic.

"Try to relax, Vegard," Sydney spoke in a calm voice and stroked his hair. "Relax and you will breathe."

Vegard gasped and his eyes rolled back. He fell limp for a moment, then gasped again. He opened his eyes and searched for Sigrid, then his gaze went to Nicolas, and then to Sydney.

"I am sorry..." he wheezed. "I was never man enough..." Another wheeze. "To keep her..." He coughed blood. "From him..."

Another cough, more blood, and Vegard's body voided. His sightless eyes gazed at beings no living person could see.

Sigrid screamed again, swayed and fell. Nicolas caught her, and with Anders' help, carried her to a bench at the other end of the Hall. Sydney closed Vegard's eyes. His final words tore at her heart and her shoulders began to shake. A loud sob escaped, though she struggled to contain it. Her breathing was as coarse as the dead man's had been.

She felt hands under her arms lift her to her feet and guide her to a chair. A glass was pushed into her hand and lifted to her lips. The akevitt burned her chest and set fire to her stomach; but it made her aware. Tears dripped from her cheeks and left dark spots on her satin gown.

Loud whispers of 'poison' wafted around her, along with speculation as to the kind.

Henbane?

More likely deadly nightshade. The berries could have been hidden in the soup.

Why him?

Sydney craned her neck and searched for Nicolas. He stood across the room near Sigrid, jaw jutting, hands on his hips. She wiped her cheeks, ineffectually. *Look at me.*

Nicolas turned as though he heard her thoughts. He crossed the room quickly and knelt at her side.

"*Min presang*? Are you ill?" His critical gaze skimmed her face.

Sydney shook her head, unable to stop crying. "Please take me to our room, Nicolas."

"Yes, of course. Can you walk?"

She nodded and Nicolas helped her, unsteady but determined, to her feet. "Your gown is ruined, I am afraid."

Sydney saw for the first time that Vegard's blood, piss and shit splotched her skirt. "This is what a life ends up to be?" she whispered.

Nicolas's arms surrounded her shoulders and parted a path through the scandal-frenzied crowd. He did not loosen his grip until they were closeted in their room.

Later that night they made love, with more intensity than they ever had before.

Chapter Twenty One

November 28, 1820

*S*ydney sat by the fire in her nightdress and dressing gown. She nursed Kirstie only twice a day now, mornings and evenings. After the hysteria of the previous evening, they slept a little later, and her daughter was hungry. Nicolas picked at the breakfast tray, looking for any tidbits he might have missed, then sat at the desk. When she finished, Sydney set Kirstie on the floor and she promptly crawled away.

"I heard the word 'poison' last night," Sydney finally broached the subject. "Who would want Vegard dead?"

Nicolas shook his head. "Only Sigrid. But she would never kill him."

"Maybe it was not meant for him?"

"I thought of that." Nicolas turned to his chart. "Who sat near him?"

"Let's see, on the one side was Lady Linnet, and that man who owns the bookstore."

"And on the other side were the spinster twins, Ellen and Elisa Fredericksen." Nicolas watched his daughter crawl toward him.

"Sigrid was opposite him, between Eirik and Canute."

"There are no clues there. I mean, Karl, Espen and I were seated elsewhere."

Sydney gasped. A prickle of fear stung her skin. "Do you think someone might want you dead?"

"The throne is a tempting prize," he conceded. Kirstie grabbed his leg.

"Do you believe your life is in danger?" Sydney clutched her dressing gown, eyes wide.

He paused, frowning. "I didn't."

"And now?"

Nicolas stared at the floor, his expression unreadable.

"Nick?" It was almost a sob.

His eyes rose to meet hers. "Now, I think our game might be more dangerous than we anticipated."

Kirstie pulled herself to stand, her chubby fingers grasping the hem of Nicolas's breeches. Nicolas patted her soft, gold-brown curls. "But that's a *very* extreme consideration, Sydney. Perhaps it was simply Vegard's ill health that took him."

Sydney leaned back in her chair, not believing it for a minute. "Perhaps you are right."

"He was not well in 1806, remember. And he was most certainly not at all well before last night. Do not stress yourself, *min presang*. I shall talk to Anders about precautions, though I don't feel I am in any danger."

"Please do, Nicolas." She leaned forward and speared him with her gaze. "We cannot lose you."

Kirstie let go of Nicolas's leg and stood. Her parents stared at her.

"Are you going to walk today, *liten datter?*" Nicolas grinned. Kirstie bounced a little on bent knees, then moved one foot forward.

Sydney pushed from the chair and hurried over to crouch in front of her daughter. "Come to *mamma*, little one!" She held out her hands. Kirstie smiled and moved her other foot.

"Come on, come to *mamma.*" Sydney wiggled her fingers.

Kirstie seemed to decide, right then, to walk. She took three more steps and fell, giggling, into Sydney's arms.

"Will you look at that!" Nicolas beamed. "See if she will come to me!" He leaned elbows on his knees and held out his hands. Sydney turned Kirstie around and set her on her feet facing him.

"Come, *liten datter*, come to your *pappa!*"

Kirstie took four steps and grabbed Nicolas's huge hands. He swept her into the air over his head. "That's my girl!"

She chuckled and kicked, fist in her mouth. He set her in his lap and tickled her tummy, causing her to laugh and wiggle.

Stefan opened the door from his adjacent room. "I'm going to the stable now."

"Stefan! Look what Kirstie has learned!" Nicolas set her down and she toddled to Sydney.

"Good. 'Bye."

Sydney laughed, lifting her delighted daughter. "Well, *he* was not impressed!"

December 12, 1820

Vegard's funeral had been held just two days after he died. Sigrid wore black, including an obscuring veil, and appeared to dab her nose. Only those very close to her could detect the tiny flask in her handkerchief. By nightfall, her words were badly slurred and she could barely stand. Once her maid helped Sigrid upstairs to her apartment she did not reappear for a week. When she did, her skin was an unhealthy splotch of crimson.

The sun finally showed itself this early afternoon, swinging low and yellow around the horizon in its short winter's path. The sky was lavender and orange. Christiania's snow cover was crusted hard and slick on top, all loose powder blown away.

Sydney found Nicolas with Stefan and Leif. The boys were riding hunters and learning to take jumps in the corral. She stood next to him and shaded her eyes against the glare of the weak sun off the icy snow.

"Why is there a statue of a naked woman in our chamber?" she asked.

"They came?" Nicolas's deep blue eyes betrayed his excitement.

"They?" Sydney's heart sank. "There is more than one?"

"A mermaid and a dragon. They are antique bow carvings from Viking ships."

"Husband?" One brow lifted. "The question remains."

"I bought them." Nicolas grinned.

"Why?"

"Would you accept that they are a first anniversary gift for my

168   *Kris Tualla*

beautiful wife?"

"Not if you expect there to be a second anniversary," Sydney half-teased.

"Fair enough!" Nicolas slipped his arm around her waist, his blue eyes dancing. "I wanted them. Trust me, *min presang*, there is a precise method to my madness."

"What are we to do with them?"

"Nothing for now. Simply enjoy them."

Sydney scoffed. "And later?"

"They go back to Missouri with us. That is, if we do."

Sydney rested her hand on Nicolas's back as she watched their son take jumps on the hunter. "I do trust you not to have lost your mind. Barely."

In their room after dinner, Nicolas ran his hands over the rough statues. They stood taller than Sydney and were crafted from the trunks of ancient oaks. Each was too heavy for one man to move by himself. "Beautiful," he whispered. "These are perfect."

"Perfect, are they?" Sydney looked askance at him. "I suppose I should be glad that the only women you pay for these days are old and made of wood!"

December 6, 1806
Christiania

"I love it when a man plays music!" Sigrid breathed, snuggling under Nicolas's arm.

In deference to visiting dignitaries from Russia, a feast honoring St. Nicholas had been planned. A tippling Muscovite aristocrat wooed Sigrid aggressively all through dinner, until Nicolas rescued her. They stood outside the Great Hall, in the shadows, and listened to the strains of the fiddles.

"Do you?" Nicolas looked down at her.

"Mm-hmm." Sigrid's eyes closed and she slid her hand down her throat, over her décolletage and to her waist. Nicolas strongly desired to trace that path with his tongue. "There is something so completely sensual about it," she murmured.

"I was thinking about taking up the Hardanger." *For at least half a minute, now.*

Sigrid's eyes opened and met his. "Why, that would be

wonderful! I would adore it if you could play for me!"

Nicolas warmed deep in his belly. "Then consider it done."

"I know a shop where they make the most beautiful fiddles! They are painted and inlaid with mother-of-pearl!" Sigrid grabbed his hands. "I shall take you there tomorrow! It will be my Christmas gift to you!"

Nicolas shook his head. "You don't need to buy me a gift!"

"But I want to! And I will pay for your lessons as well!"

"Does it mean that much to you?"

Sigrid smiled a smile that Nicolas recognized well from their experiences in bed. "I would be completely undone watching you, naked as the day you were born, stroking a Hardanger by firelight."

"Then I shall learn as quickly as I can!" Nicolas promised. After all, it was not often that a nineteen-year-old lad could impress a married woman of twenty-seven with his skill at seduction.

Christiania
December 25, 1820

Nicolas hefted his bow and pulled it over the strings of his Hardanger fiddle. He was not exactly certain how he came to be in this position; he had never played for anyone outside his family! Even then, it took a substantial amount of coaxing from Sydney before he truly felt comfortable doing so.

Now he stood in the Great Hall, amidst several musicians, preparing to play for a group of visiting dignitaries from Moscow. His lips twitched at the irony.

"Do you know *O Hellig Natt, O Hellig Barn?*" the music master asked.

"Yes," Nicolas nodded.

The master waved his hand and set the beat. On cue, the musicians launched into the song. Nicolas kept up and hoped no one in attendance could actually hear him play.

When the song ended, Nicolas heaved a relieved sigh and looked for Sydney. She sat on the edge of her chair, beaming at him. He could not help but smile in response.

I love you, she mouthed.

He winked at her, suddenly quite pleased to have played.

The next morning Sydney snuggled against Nicolas, seeking his warmth. He shifted to accommodate her. The sun was not going to come out today, choosing to hide behind a flurry of white confetti thrown sideways by the wind. That was fine with her. The revelry of the past week had worn her down.

Christmas in Akershus Castle consisted of endless dinners, balls and hunts. They attended church on Christmas Eve in a stave structure which existed centuries before Martin Luther reformed, and took the children in spite of Anders' disapproving glare.

Yesterday, Sydney insisted that Nicolas sit alone with her and the children for an early dinner, even though there was a banquet planned in the Great Hall. They exchanged gifts before tucking Stefan and Kirstie into their beds.

"You may be a candidate for the throne of Norway," Sydney told him. "But you are a husband and father first."

Now Sydney fingered her new gold cross on its braided chain. She smiled. The gift was perfect. She gave Nicolas a leather-bound book of blank pages. His name was impressed in gold leaf on the front.

"For your thoughts and memories," Sydney explained. "Stefan is too young to understand what choices you face, and why you choose as you do. This is a way for you to let him know."

"That is very thoughtful, Sydney. I would not have considered it myself. Thank you."

Last night after he played his fiddle for her in the Hall, they made love in front of the fire, lying on the rug and wrapped in her fur-lined cloak. Half his body was illuminated in the orange light, the other half disappeared into shadow. His eyes were black with desire. His hair tumbled freely over his shoulders; he looked like a wild Viking and took her with as much urgency.

Afterward, they lay wrapped in the cloak and whispered to each other, reaffirming their relationship and their path.

Then he took her again, slowly that time. Coaxing her response, building her pleasure, a lover constructing a pyre intended to flame out, consuming them both with its heat.

"If you keep touching me, I shall be forced to reciprocate," Nicolas mumbled as she pressed her chilled thighs behind his.

"Even after last night?" Sydney kissed his shoulder.

Nicolas's answer was to pull her hand around to his groin. "What do you think, wife?"

A quick knock on the door and the entrance of Tomas and Haldis halted their play. The breakfast tray smelled wonderful and Sydney's stomach growled, rumbling against his back.

Nicolas chuckled. "If it's not one appetite, it's another, eh?"

She stayed under the warm covers to put on her cold dressing gown, then pulled back the bed curtains. The clock chimed nine.

"We slept late today." She slid her feet into the slippers by the bed.

"The whole castle has. It must be the weather." Haldis picked the cloak off the floor and hung it in the wardrobe without comment.

Nicolas and Sydney sat down to breakfast while Haldis straightened the bed and the room, and Tomas prepared to shave Nicolas.

"What is on the agenda for today?" Nicolas asked.

"Only dinner tonight at eight, sir." Tomas stropped the razor. A hesitant knock drew their attention. Haldis answered the door.

Agnes bobbed her head in apology. "I beg your pardon, Miss. No one answered the front door."

"Lady?" Haldis turned to Sydney.

"Yes, I shall dress and be right there."

"Very good." Agnes backed away.

Haldis closed the bedroom door. "The gray wool, as usual?" She moved to the wardrobe.

"Yes, thank you."

Nicolas watched her, his expression carefully blank. His pressed lips made a colorless crease in his face; his eyes were dark under a lowered brow.

Sydney followed Agnes through the snow-muffled streets of Christiania, their sabots silent in the flurry. Flakes stung her cheeks. She held the fur-lined cloak closed with one hand, her leather bag against her body with the other.

"How far?" she called to Agnes.

"About half a mile." The words floated back between gray stone buildings.

Sydney pulled her toque over her ears. The cold here was

different than Missouri; it seeped into everything, relentless and grasping. The sun stayed so low on the horizon, that her appearance was wispy and hazy. Sydney could not remember the last truly blue sky she had seen.

Agnes turned down an alley and knocked on a door. A young boy cracked the door open.

"Yes?"

"We are here for your mother." Agnes pushed on the door.

The boy stepped back. He looked Sydney up and down, slammed the door behind them and dropped the crossbar. "She's upstairs."

Sydney left her sabots by the door and climbed the wooden staircase to a small landing. One of the two doors was closed, through the other she saw an assortment of children huddled on a bed. She knocked on the closed door.

Ingrid answered. "Oh, good! I was afraid the weather might hinder you."

Sydney stepped in and shrugged off her cloak. "Is she close?"

"I believe so. Go on and check her, and tell me what you think."

Sydney rinsed her hands and approached the woman groaning on the narrow bed. "Good day, Madam. My name is Sydney. I will check your baby." She ran her fingers over the woman's legs. "Is that acceptable, Ma'am?"

The woman grunted.

Sydney held her breath against the scent of unwashed cunnus as she pushed the woman's knees apart. In the castle, few bathed in the winter; in a household like this one it was even less likely. She slid her fingers inside and felt the baby's head, it should enter the birth canal with her next pain.

She told Ingrid.

They laid hot cloths on the woman and prepared to deliver the child. It was her fifth birth and they expected it to go quickly. The woman began to strain and Sydney crouched at the foot of the bed while Ingrid held the clean rags. A dome of swirled red hair pressed and receded, pressed and receded.

Finally, it emerged.

Ingrid handed Sydney a rag and she wiped mucus from the squished nose and swept through the mouth.

"Do not push," Ingrid instructed. "Let her help the baby out."

Sydney worked one shoulder, then the other, and the tiny baby girl squeezed out. Sydney rubbed her with the rag until she gasped and cried.

The mother leaned up to see the child, then slumped back on the bed. *"Enda et forbanner pike."* Another damn girl.

Ingrid swaddled the baby and handed her to the mother while Sydney waited for the afterbirth to expel. She tugged gently on the cut cord. "What is her name?"

The mother stared at her daughter. "Nora?"

"I like it." Sydney smiled and looked at Ingrid. "Do you?"

"It is a beautiful name for a beautiful girl." Ingrid stroked the drying red hair. The woman grimaced and grunted. "It is the afterbirth."

"It hurts more than I remember."

Sydney gave another tug and felt the organ release. She pulled it out and wrapped it in a rag. Water gushed from the woman.

Ingrid took the refuse from Sydney. "Check her again!" she demanded.

Sydney spread the woman's legs and inserted her fingers. She felt a foot. "There is another baby!"

The woman's eyes rounded. "There are two of them?" she squealed. "Twins?"

"Yes. But this one comes out wrong." Knowledge of Nicolas's experience sank like a hot stone in Sydney's stomach. "What do we do, Ingrid?"

"We turn the baby. Can you push the foot back in?"

"I believe so..." Sydney pushed and the babe responded, withdrawing its appendage. "What now?"

Ingrid got the woman up on all fours on the bed, her belly hanging down.

"Reach inside and see if you can push the baby's bottom away from the opening," she instructed.

"Will you do it?"

Ingrid shook her head. "A midwife must know how to do this."

Sydney forced her hand into the womb. The woman screamed her pain into a pillow while Ingrid rubbed her back and spoke encouraging words in her ear. Sydney felt the buttocks and pushed them toward the front of the woman's body. The baby squirmed and resettled.

A powerful contraction squeezed Sydney's hand with a strength that surprised her, cutting off her circulation. The woman began to cry in loud gasping sobs.

When her womb relaxed, Sydney pushed on the baby's knees. It squirmed again. If Sydney had not had her hand there, it might have slid back into the upside down position. Sydney pushed yet again and the shoulder slipped into the opening.

Sydney sat back, wiped perspiration with her forearm, and shook out her hand. "Do not move. Almost."

The woman wailed and Ingrid comforted.

Sydney leaned forward and put her hand inside the woman again. She closed her eyes and pushed the baby with as much force as she dared, in spite of the mother's screams.

Her fingers walked along the shoulder, the neck and under the chin. She hooked her fingers under the chin and pulled the head toward her. The skull finally rested against the gateway to the canal.

"Push," Sydney rasped.

The woman dropped to her side and strained. Ingrid held one leg in the air.

"Push, again." She did. Again. Again. Again. Another swirled head of red appeared.

"The head is here. One more push." Sydney wiped sweat again from her forehead.

"Can't," the woman gasped.

"One more push, the baby will come," Sydney soothed.

The woman shook her head, "Can't." She began to sob.

Sydney looked to Ingrid, who only raised one eyebrow and waited. So she moved to the woman's head and wiped her brow with a damp cloth.

"You have a beautiful daughter." The woman's irregular gasps punctuated Sydney's words. "You have another child with red hair waiting to be born. Does your husband have red hair?"

"Yes," she whispered.

"Is he handsome?"

"I think so." She smiled a little.

"Do you think this one is a boy?"

Eyes underlined with blue quarter-moons snapped to hers. "Could it be?"

"They were in different sacks," Sydney explained. "It is

possible."

The woman wiped her eyes. "I am so tired," she sniffed. "It hurts so much."

"I know. I've birthed children myself." Sydney wiped her forehead again. The woman winced.

"Is it another pain?" Sydney asked.

The laboring mother nodded.

"If you work with it, your baby will come," Sydney assured.

"All right," the woman grabbed her knees. She drew three deep breaths and pushed, her face as scarlet and squished as the babe's.

"Stop, now and rest." Sydney wiped the nose and mouth. "Let me do it." One shoulder, another shoulder, a red-headed boy. "You have a son!"

"Show me!" The woman looked over her belly.

Ingrid swaddled the infant and handed him to his mother. "What is his name?"

"Nils, I think. I shall have to ask my husband."

"Nils and Nora. They go well together." Sydney tugged at the afterbirth.

Thump-thump-thump.

"Gjertrud?"

Sydney pulled a sheet over the woman's legs and nodded.

"Come in, Alfred."

A red-bearded visage seeped around the door. His jaw dropped. "Is it the babe?"

"It's twins, Alfred. A boy and a girl." Gjertrud's voice wavered, her expression unsure. "They've red hair."

"Red-headed twins?" He crossed the room and stared at the babies. He slapped the top of his head. "Twins?"

"Are you angry?"

"No. Only surprised is all."

Alfred stared at his children. "I suppose we shall need to name them."

Gjertrud glanced at the women. "I had thought that the girl could be Nora."

"I can bide by that. And the boy?"

"Nils. After my grandfather?"

Alfred nodded and sank to the edge of the bed beside his wife. "Nils and Nora," he whispered. "Six children. How will we do?"

"We will do fine, Alfred. Somehow," she said.

Sydney packed her leather bag and looked out the window. The world was white. "I need to go," she said.

The woman turned to Sydney. "Thank you so much."

Agnes waited at the table by the door. Sydney slid her sabots over her slippers and pulled her cloak around her.

"Lead me to the castle?" she asked and pulled her toque down over her ears.

Agnes nodded and they stepped into a world with no features.

Chapter Twenty Two

December 26, 1820

*I*n good weather, the half-mile walk would take about ten minutes; Sydney thought they had been walking for almost half an hour. Her sabots were caked with packed snow becoming ice, and her slippers were soaked. Her toes had gone from aching cold to stinging burn to unfeeling. She had the back of Agnes' cloak clenched in her gloved hand, though her stiff fingers grew numb as well. Snow caked her lashes as wind pelted them with icy confetti.

The women made their dogged way in the swirling snow that hid the world from them. They felt their way along buildings, then crossed empty space when they reached an intersection. They made two wrong turns and had to back-track when they discovered their errors.

Lacy, lethal, flakes blew past them, into them, around them, and under their skirts, carrying the storm's frigid touch. Sydney pulled her toque as low as she could over her ears. She tried to bury her stinging face in the collar of her cloak, but her breath froze on the fur. Agnes stopped and turned to her. They huddled close and rested, the steam of their breath warming their faces.

"Are we hopelessly l-lost?" Sydney's voice spit past her chattering teeth.

Agnes shook her head. "This is the bakery that is in front of the fortress. We should be but ten yards from the gate."

"Thank the Lord."

Agnes stepped into the street. At least, Sydney assumed it was the street. She sunk into snow up to her knees, wetting her hose to her garters. The pretty white stuff was heavy and resisted her intrusion. She could not lift her knees high enough to take a clean step, so ended up kicking through the freezing banks.

The women pushed each other forward, arm in arm. Finally, the towering stone wall of Akershus Fortress appeared in front of them. But no gate.

"Which way is the gate?" Sydney shrieked over the wind.

Agnes looked one way, then the other. She pulled Sydney to the left. They stumbled next to the wall, and in its protection, until they reached the end.

They stood on the cliff that overlooked the harbor.

"No!" Sydney sobbed. She turned and stumbled back in the other direction, crying openly. She was exhausted. Her feet were numb, her face frozen. Her lungs burned with the frigid air. Her fingers bled as she grabbed the stone wall and put one foot in front of the other. Agnes followed, her fingers now gripping Sydney's cloak.

Step, grab the wall. Take a breath. Step, grab the wall. Take a breath. Step, grab the wall. Do it again. Sydney's eyes were on the invisible ground, her legs moved only by strength of her will; they had no will of their own. She squinted against snow pellets that pushed past her lashes and picked at her eyes.

Pushed beyond her ability, she stumbled. With a desperate cry, and no strength to catch herself, she fell, face first into the burning cold.

Steel arms wrapped around her waist and lifted her. They cradled her and carried her through the indiscernible landscape into the castle. The warmth inside burned her cheeks.

"Sydney? Sydney!"

She felt Nicolas's voice vibrate in his chest.

"C-cold," she pressed her face against his bulk. "Ag-agnes?"

"She is being cared for."

Haldis helped Nicolas undress her and wrap her in blankets. They sat her with her back to the fire and bathed her feet in cool water.

"That is too hot!" Sydney yelped and pulled her feet back.

"No, Sydney. It's cold water. It only feels hot to you." Nicolas pushed her feet back in. "It is good that you feel it. Might you wiggle your toes?"

Sydney obliged, though she could not tell if she succeeded. "Are they moving?" she whispered.

"They are." Nicolas immersed his hands in the basin and massaged her. Needles jabbed her thawing feet. She shivered uncontrollably and whimpered, unaware.

Haldis left and returned with a bowl of beef stew and a mug of wine, heated with the fire poker. Sydney's hands shook, but she spooned the warm stew nonetheless, grateful to have it. As she ate and drank, she warmed. Nicolas hovered around her, silent, touching.

"Is Agnes all right?" Sydney asked again.

"She is fine."

"She will stay the night at the castle," Haldis added.

"Good."

"Det vil være all, takker du," Nicolas instructed Haldis. That will be all, thank you. She curtsied and shut the door behind her.

"Sydney!" Nicolas switched to English. "What were you thinking?"

"We did not know how bad the storm was until we were out in it. Then we had no choice but to keep going and find our way back."

Nicolas shook his head in denial of her words. "This is not Missouri! The winter storms here are *much* colder! And they kill more easily!"

"It was not intentional." Sydney's lip trembled. "I did not try to die!"

Nicolas ran fists through his hair and rested them on his hips. "I know that, *min presang*. But..." His voice caught and he rubbed his face, hard. When his hands came away, his cheeks were wet.

One of Sydney's hands emerged from her blanket cocoon and reached for him. After a moment's hesitation, he took it and knelt beside her. He turned it over and kissed her palm. She felt the smooth, damp skin of his jaw. Her chest constricted with the realization of what nearly happened to her, and what it would have meant to him.

"I am so sorry, Nicolas," she whispered.

He nodded and pressed his forehead against her arm. She kissed his hair and rested against it. After a long silence, his voice startled her. "Did the birth go well?"

She had forgotten all about it. "It was twins. One was coming out wrong."

Nicolas sat back and stared at Sydney, his eyes black and his expression fearful. "And?"

"And I turned the baby."

"You *did?*"

Sydney nodded. "Ingrid made me. She said any midwife would need to know how."

"Will the mother survive?"

"She was fine when we left, and nursing both babes."

"Truly?"

Sydney smiled, and a shiver passed through her. "Truly."

Later, Nicolas summoned Haldis back and ordered tea and biscuits for Sydney. He forced her to finish both, then tucked her in bed with a hot stone at her feet. He sat with her until she drifted off to sleep in the early gloom of the swirling winter night.

₧₧

"Was she found?"

"Yes, they made their way back to the gate eventually."

"Thank you, Haldis."

She curtsied and left.

He shook his head, muttering, "This is unaccaeptable."

"I agree. Acting as midwife for a common tailor's assistant? For the love of God, acting as midwife at all!"

"And the way she rides. Astride! After she saved Eirik's wife, she has ridden astride on every hunt."

"It's unseemly, even for a commoner."

"If Nicolas intends to be king, he must be made to see these flaws!"

"So, then, what do we suggest? I mean, if she changes her ways, what then? Do we still try to make him send her away?"

"I think we must."

The men were silent.

"Vegard. That was nice work."

He sounded shocked. "You are of a mind that was *my* doing?"

A shrug. "It frees Sigrid. She is of the correct lineage."

"But she is past the age to produce an heir!"

"True. But he has an heir."

"We agreed on a younger woman."

He paused and leaned forward. "We did. But I know you well." He shook his head. "Perhaps, too well."

"I would never be so foolish as to admit to murder."

"Of course not."

"Not even to you."

"I would not expect you to."

A sideways glance. "But, we *do* understand each other?"

He smiled.

January 8, 1821

Nicolas, Karl and Espen entered the front door of the Cathedral School of Christiania. Lacking a building of its own, the *Storting* met in a tiered lecture hall there. About a hundred men, representing towns, rural districts, and the military, stood around the room in this, their first gathering in months. They talked, laughed and argued with each other until one man stepped to the podium. Nicolas urged his companions in that direction.

"May I help you gentlemen?"

"We have come from Anders Fredericksen," Karl began.

"Oh yes! Our three royal candidates!" The man stuck out his hand. "Welcome to the *Storting*! I am Lord Wilhelm Christie, Speaker."

"Sir Karl Fredericksen, Baron of Moss." Karl shook Wilhelm's hand.

"My pleasure, Sir Karl."

"Espen Christian Canutesen, Duke of Lillehammar."

Wilhelm tipped his head. "My pleasure, your Grace."

"Nicolas Reidar Hansen, Greve of Rollag."

"Ah! The American. I have heard about you!" Wilhelm shook his finger at Nicolas. "It is most pleasurable to finally meet you, Lord Hansen!"

"I trust that what you have heard is complimentary?" Nicolas smiled.

"Most of it," Wilhelm said, one side of his mouth lifting. "If you gentlemen would not mind taking a seat in the front row, I shall introduce you."

The three candidates sat, and Wilhelm pounded his gavel on the podium. The men in the room walked up the steps and sat in seats that seemed to be assigned.

"Welcome, gentlemen, to today's session. I trust your holiday celebrations were exemplary and you all have returned, prepared to do business!"

Mumbles and chuckles swirled around the walls and dissipated.

Lord Wilhelm Christie continued, "I am pleased to announce that our royal candidates have joined us. I shall ask each of them to introduce themselves, and give us all a brief exposition on their personal qualifications for ascending to the soon-to-be restored throne of Norway."

Applause peppered the air as necks craned to get a clear view of the three royal strangers. Karl stood first and approached the podium.

"Good day, sirs. I am Sir Karl Fredericksen, Baron of Moss," he began.

Karl told the assembly about his mother and his relationship with his father, King Frederick. He talked about his education, and his military experience. He smiled as he told them about his young wife and children.

And then he spoke of Norway.

He told of his love for the people, sturdy and strong. His love of the land: deep clear fjords clawed by God's own fingers into the most magnificent mountains to be found anywhere. And the North Sea, the cold, turbulent and unforgiving source of so many of their citizens' livelihoods. He spoke of his understanding of Norway's past and his hopes for her future. His words silenced the men; a few wiped their eyes. He talked for more than half an hour and when he finished, they stood and thundered their approval.

"Shall we crown him today?" Espen said under his breath.

Nicolas wished to go last, so he spoke in his cousin's ear, "It is your turn to impress them."

Espen shot him a wry smile, and then stood. He shook Karl's hand and slapped his shoulder as they passed each other. He took the podium and spoke for barely ten minutes. Many of his points were similar to Karl's. The applause was polite.

Nicolas could no longer avoid this moment. He stood, walked to the podium, and turned to face the assemblage. He made silent eye contact with as many as he could while they quieted and waited for him to speak.

"My name is Nicolas Reidar Hansen, Greve of Rollag," he began. "I am the great-grandson of King Christian the Sixth. I am royal by heritage and Norse by birth. My grandmother, King Frederick's sister Marit Christiansen, emigrated to America as a young bride, and birthed my mother, Kirsten, in Philadelphia. Kirsten married Reidar Magnus Hansen, a man of pure Nordic blood, and I am their firstborn."

Nicolas paused and shifted his stance. "It never occurred to me that I would be in the position that I find myself today. When Anders Fredericksen's letter reached me, a full year and a half after he sent it, I began a journey to learn who I am."

Nicolas smiled. "I know I am an American. You know it, too. You can hear it in my accent, can you not?" Heads bobbed and several men chuckled. "As an American, I have been raised to believe that all men are created equal, and they all deserve the same level of respect. So from that standpoint, it is difficult for me to think of becoming a king."

A murmur rippled through the assemblage.

"But, I have discovered that I am also Norwegian. Her mountains are my shoulders, her rivers my veins, the northern lights, my soul. I felt it when I came as a youth, but now I understand it. I love this country."

Applause approved his words.

"If I am elected as king, I will combine my American experience with Norse traditions, and do everything in my power to give all the citizens of this magnificent land equal opportunity for individual success. That will be my legacy."

More applause, but not enough to drown out some grumbling dissent.

"It is my deepest honor to stand before you today. I thank you for your consideration." Nicolas returned to his seat as several members of the *Storting* stood in response to his words.

Lord Wilhelm Christie returned to the podium. "Thank you,

gentlemen, for your heartfelt and impressive words." Nods of acknowledgement followed. "At this time, I would like to entertain a motion that these three candidates become members of the *Odelsting* until a king is elected, or the idea is abandoned."

Three hands went up. "I make that motion," one man said.

Another called out, "Second."

"Is there any discussion?" No one spoke.

"All in favor?" Wilhelm looked around the auditorium at the raised hands.

"Opposed?" A few hands wavered.

"Then the motion is carried." He banged his gavel on the podium. "Welcome, candidates, to the *Storting*."

Karl turned to his cousins. "This will be the true test, eh?"

"That it will," Nicolas concurred and slapped Espen's back. "Are you ready?"

"What is the *Odelsting*?" Sydney asked as they dressed for dinner.

"The lower house of the *Storting*. Three fourths of the members belong there."

"And the other fourth?"

"The upper house, the *Lagting*." Nicolas slid his arms into the frock coat that Tomas held at ready.

"What is the difference?" Sydney held the bedpost while Haldis laced her dress.

"Bills are submitted to the *Odelsting* first, and then to the *Lagting*. The upper house is the elite."

Sydney snickered. "So possible future kings are not elite?"

"I believe they want to keep an eye on us. They've no intention of letting us have too much power as yet!" Nicolas grinned. "And in the end? Perhaps none at all!"

January 11, 1821

Nicolas left the Great Hall behind Sigrid. He felt like a nineteen-year-old again. She reached back for his hand and pulled him into a window casing behind heavy brocade curtains. An icy draft seeped through the glass and chilled his spine.

"What have you learned?" he whispered.

"Espen and Dagmar."

Sigrid pulled his ear down to her mouth. His ear was cold and her breath was warm.

"He goes to her room late at night."

"How often?"

"Almost every night. But he doesn't sleep there. He goes back to his own room." Her tongue flicked into his ear.

"Sigrid." Nicolas turned to face her. Her lips touched his.

"What?" She did not move away.

Nicolas could barely see her by the snow-reflected starlight. Her eyes were black pools in a pale landscape. Her hand moved up his thigh; she knew his body. He grabbed her wrist.

"Stop."

Sigrid shook her head. "Vegard is gone. I am finally free of him." She rubbed him deliberately.

"But I am not free!" Nicolas clenched his jaw and cursed his responsive manhood.

Sigrid kissed him hard, biting his lip and pulling back with her teeth. He tasted blood. "Do you know how much I desire you?"

"Sigrid!" Nicolas pulled her hand away from his groin. "Thank you for the information. Now I need to go." He threw the curtain aside and strode into the hall, seeking the respite of his chamber without looking back.

Sydney was there. Her leather bag slumped by the fireplace and she was hanging her cloak on the wardrobe door.

"I'm so glad to see you! Might you unlace me?" She lifted her hair out of the way. Nicolas came to her and managed to loosen the laces enough for her to take the dress off. She stood in front of the fire, in her shift, and brushed her hair.

Nicolas sat on the bed and watched her. She looked so beautiful in the warm, orange light, her breasts and hips outlined in gold. She turned to look at him over her shoulder and smiled.

"How was dinner?"

Nicolas stared at her. "I found out something. Maybe something useful."

The brush lowered, as did her voice. "Oh?"

"Sigrid told me that Espen visits Dagmar's room nearly every night. He does not sleep there, though. He returns to his own room."

Sydney relaxed. "I'm not surprised. I have seen the looks that pass between them. So if he marries her, he improves his situation?"

Nicolas nodded. "I would think so. Before the people can back him, they need to know he will produce an heir."

"What will you do with this information?"

"I imagine I will ask him straight out about his intentions. That should push him into some sort of action." Nicolas ran his hands through his hair and rubbed his face. His pulse surged. "There is something else. When she told me, she pulled me into a window casement."

Her jaw fell open. "What?"

"She whispered it in my ear, then before I knew what she was about, her hand was on me."

Sydney grabbed her throat and her breaths came in gasps. "Did she—did you—how far?"

"I pulled her hand away and left her there. I swear to you, I didn't touch her."

Sydney grabbed her nightgown from its hook in the wardrobe and jerked it over her head.

"Sydney?"

Her steel-gray gaze sliced toward the chamber's door and then came back to him. "Do not speak to me," she said loudly in Norse.

She walked around the end of the bed and climbed in. She dragged the covers to her chin. Nicolas stoked the fire, blew out the candles, and got into the bed.

"*Min presang?*" He reached for her but she pushed his hand away. "Sydney?"

She sat up in the bed. "Are you having an affair with her?"

"No! Of course not!" he bellowed.

"How can I know for sure? How can I trust you after this?" she cried.

Nicolas climbed to his knees and grabbed her shoulders. He pulled her close to whisper English in her ear. "We are as we have always been. My heart is unchanged."

"You have wounded me, husband," she answered in kind.

Nicolas spoke in her ear, "Your wound is my wound ten times over, *min presang*. Please believe me. I beg your forgiveness."

Sydney pulled away and looked Nicolas in the eye.

"I shall leave you if you allow her to touch you again!" she exclaimed in Norse, though he knew she meant every word.

Then she took his hand. "Her attempt to seduce you will remain fixed firmly in my mind while we are here," she whispered. "I cannot change that."

"I understand."

"The end had best be worth the journey," she murmured. Then she turned away and curled up to sleep on the far side of the bed.

January 13, 1821

The sun climbed high enough in the southern sky to skim the fortress walls and bless one corner of the courtyard with her smile. Nicolas and Espen rested there, sweating in spite of the below-freezing air. Taking advantage of a break in the weather, the two men relished the opportunity to be outside and practice their swordplay.

"Might I ask you a personal question?" Nicolas's breath clouded around his face.

"It will come at a cost!" Espen chuckled.

"And that is?"

"Lose the next round."

Nicolas laughed. "I will probably do so in any case! It seems too easy to lose the skill and too difficult to regain it."

"Even so." Espen grinned. "What do you wish to know?"

"Dagmar."

The grin faded. "Ah."

"You appear to be a good match," Nicolas prodded.

Espen shrugged. "She is my cousin."

"But your father and her mother were only half-siblings. It is not too close." Espen stared at the lines his sword tip traced in the snow. "She is of acceptable bloodlines for the king of Norway. Might you consider her?"

"Consider her?" Espen stalled.

"For marriage."

Espen looked pained. He traced more lines in the snow. "No. I do not believe so."

Nicolas squinted at the pale sun, low in the yellow-gray sky. Soon they would be in shadow. "Is it too personal to ask why not?"

"All I can say is, there would never be an heir." His voice strained thin. He swallowed and sniffed. "Such a marriage is impossible."

"Without a wife, you will not be selected."

Espen's head snapped up. "And you think *you* are the one? Not with *your* wife!"

"What do you mean?" Nicolas blurted, taken aback.

"A Scots-Irish mutt? You should hear what they say. With that millstone around your neck you are sunk, cousin!" Espen stood, inexplicably angry. "Hand it to Karl, then. I am done in for today." He left the courtyard without looking back.

Chapter Twenty Three

January 15, 1821

*N*icolas sat in the outer room of Anders' apartment and accepted a golden glass of akevitt. A blurry-edged patch of pale morning sunshine glowed on the carpet between clouds.

Anders perched on a chair facing Nicolas. "How are you doing, son?"

"I am in good health. Thank you, sir."

"And your family? I noticed your son spends quite a bit of time in the stable."

Nicolas chuckled. "It's a struggle to get him to do chores at home, but here he volunteers! He has befriended a stable hand and once the boy finishes his work, he can play with Stefan."

"Ah! Of course." Anders smiled. "How is his Norse?"

"He has grown to be fluent."

"Excellent. Would you care for a cigar?" Anders stood and gestured toward the humidor.

"No, thank you."

Anders sank back into his chair, still smiling. "So. Have you been planning your reign as king?"

Nicolas laughed outright. "*My* reign, is it?"

"It could be."

Nicolas's smile faded. "Do you truly think so?"

"Don't you?" Anders sipped his akevitt.

Nicolas waved his hand. "I had considered Karl the most likely candidate."

Anders leaned forward and dropped his voice. "Do you want it? I mean really want it? For yourself?"

Nicolas hesitated. "And if I do?"

Anders leaned back as though what he was about to say was of little consequence. "There is one, small, issue."

Nicolas clenched his jaw, then forcibly relaxed it. "What might that be?"

"Your wife. She is a very charming and beautiful woman—do not misunderstand me." Anders' warm tone was obviously intended to pull Nicolas along. "But, to be honest, midwifery is not an avocation usually pursued by someone of royal standing."

Nicolas conceded the point. "I understand that. She expects to use the skill in Missouri."

Anders frowned, puzzled. "She expects to return? Does she not believe in your candidacy?"

"I, well… Of course she does." Nicolas chose his words with great care. "But, I had not considered that perspective…"

"If she understands that you might be king of Norway, then she should act like a queen now." Anders refilled Nicolas's glass, his voice as smooth as the liquor. "Riding astride, and delivering babies? These hardly put forth a royal image."

Nicolas stared into his glass. The pale liquid shimmered gold in a brief shaft of sunlight. He raised wary eyes to Anders. "What do you suggest?"

"Explain your situation clearly to her. Tell her, gently of course, how her actions are a detriment to you attaining your deserved position. She is an intelligent woman. I am sure she will understand."

"And if she does not?"

Anders raised one eyebrow. "You intend to be king. Rule your own house first."

Nicolas drained his glass and set it on a nearby table. "I shall do so." He stood and offered his hand to Anders. "Thank you, sir, for your sage advice."

Anders stood as well. "I have faith in you, Nicolas. Don't let me—or Norway—down."

৪০০৪

Sydney was with Stefan and Kirstie in their room. Nicolas came in and squatted.

"Come to *Pappa, liten datter*." He held out his arms. Kirstie grinned and wobbled across the rug. He swept her up and held her over his head while she squirmed, giggled and chewed her finger. He lowered her into his arms; she grabbed his nose.

"What did Anders want?" Sydney handed Stefan a book and pointed to the page. "Start here and read to the end of the chapter."

"Then can I go to the stable?"

"After you tell me about what you read." Sydney turned back to Nicolas and waited.

"Where is Maribeth?"

"She is at lunch. Why?"

Nicolas tilted his head toward the door to their room. "Let's talk in there."

Sydney followed him through the portal and he set Kirstie on their floor. Haldis nodded her greeting as she remade the bed with clean sheets.

Sydney sat near the fire to make sure Kirstie did not get too close. "All right, tell me," she said in English.

Nicolas ran his hands through his hair and stood in front of Sydney. "Anders believes I could be king."

"We knew that, did we not?"

"I suppose we did. But this time he made it very clear."

"And are you pleased with that revelation?" Sydney probed.

Nicolas nodded.

"So why do you not look happy, husband?"

"Anders has some concerns."

"If I were to guess, should I guess that those concerns are centered on me?"

Nicolas smiled. "Have I ever told you how much I admire your intellect?"

"No." Sydney chuckled. "But you may commence now."

Nicolas's smile faded. "Unfortunately, you are correct."

"Hmm. So what precisely are my transgressions?"

Nicolas turned to the window. The midday light made his blue eyes glow, he could see it in his reflection. "To begin with, he feels that midwifery is not pursued by those of royal standing. It is beneath them."

Sydney pressed her lips together and crossed her arms. "And?"

"And I must tell you to stop."

"Are you?"

"Am I what?"

One eyebrow lifted as Sydney's voice grew more insistent. "Telling me to stop?"

Nicolas glanced at Haldis, and back to Sydney. *"Medlemer av den kongelige familien ikke leverer babyer. Det er ikke passende."* Members of the royal family do not deliver babies. It is not appropriate.

Sydney stood. *"Hva hvis vi drar hjem?"* What if we go home?

"Vi er hjem." We are home.

"No." Sydney switched back to English. "I am not home."

"Sydney."

"Nicolas?"

His voice became louder. *"Du må gjøre skuller jeg sier."* You must do as I say.

Sydney raised her chin, eyes glittering. "Would you truly take this from me?"

"It has become necessary."

Sydney clenched her jaw and sniffed pointedly. "Please don't do this, Nicolas," she whispered.

"It is not my intent to upset you."

"You have."

"That is regrettable. But this course is necessary."

Sydney sank to her knees in front of her husband. "Nicolas? Please?"

"No, Sydney. I'm sorry."

"That is your final decision?"

"It is."

Sydney climbed slowly to her feet and glanced toward Haldis before she stared somberly at her husband. *"Jeg er din kone. Jeg blir ventet til å adlyde deg."* I am your wife. I am expected to obey you.

She leaned forward. *"Men jeg kan ikke være glad om det."* But I can't be happy about it.

"Min presang." Nicolas reached for her, but she stepped to the

side. Kirstie sat still, staring at her arguing parents with wide eyes. Sydney picked her up and settled the worried toddler on her hip.

Stefan opened the door. "I finished!"

Sydney crossed to him quickly. "Come tell me about the book." She guided Stefan back into his room and did not look back.

‽‽

"They fought?"

"Yes, sir. About her being a midwife."

"And how did it end?"

"She begged him on her knees."

He made a disgusted face. "Did she?"

Haldis nodded.

"Did he remain strong?"

"He must have, because she was very angry at him."

"Is she still angry?"

"They have not spoken since. At least, not in my presence."

"Thank you, Haldis."

January 20, 1821

Sydney sat cross-legged on the garden bench. Eyes closed, she curled inside her fur-lined cloak, sabots waiting on the packed snow of the path. Stars spattered the moonless sky. She fingered her rosary; the familiar feel of the rounded glass beads soothed her soul as she prayed the petitions of her youth.

"Father in Heaven, I am so afraid," she whispered in the dark. "I am afraid of losing my husband. Please make him strong in his vows; so many here wish to see him break them."

Sydney's fingers moved to another bead. "He has always been an honest man. Please, Father, hold him to his word."

Her breath condensed around her face, rising like a spectral crown. "Please protect me, Father, from those who wish me harm. And protect our children."

She crossed herself and moved back to the first bead. Once again, she prayed through her rosary, finding solace in both the repetition of the words, and her faith in her Listener. In time, the irrefutable Nordic winter night seeped through her cloak. Her teeth clattered in spite of her clenched jaw. She shivered and unfolded her stiff legs, pushing her slippered feet into the sabots. Then she looked up.

Curtains of undulating color hung in the sky. Glowing blue, green and red, they spanned the heavens. Sydney's mouth dropped open and she sank to her knees in the snow. She had never seen anything so beautiful.

She watched it, silent, spellbound, no longer aware of the cold. Her vision was filled with the unexpected celestial glory. She remained on her knees until the lights faded, as quickly as they had appeared. Sydney crossed herself again.

Thank you, Father.

She rose from the snow and made her way back into the castle, her spirit at peace.

January 22, 1821

"Would you object to my hiring a Norse tutor?" Sydney asked Nicolas while they dressed for dinner.

Nicolas turned from the mirror. "For what purpose?"

"If I am to be the wife of the king of Norway, then I should be fluent in the language, culture and history. Should I not?" Sydney's innocent gaze met his while Haldis laced her gown.

Nicolas stared at her, trying to discern her true motive. He slipped his arms into the waistcoat Tomas selected. "Yes. That would be quite helpful."

"I found an advertisement posted at the lending library today, when I was picking up books for Stefan," Sydney explained. "If it is amenable to you, husband, I can arrange lessons in the afternoons. At the library."

"Why not here? At the castle?" He donned the matching frock coat.

Sydney stepped closer and laid her hand on his chest. "At the library, there are history books and maps. Resources that may be helpful."

"Oh, yes. Of course." Nicolas stood still while Tomas brushed his coat skirts.

"So, may I have your permission?"

Nicolas clenched his jaw and squinted. She regarded him with a pleasant expression. "Is this truly your desire?"

"It is. Why would it not be?"

"I am not sure how I feel about it, but you may proceed for now," he acquiesced. "We shall see how it goes, eh?"

"Thank you, Nicolas." Sydney bobbed her head in a pseudo-curtsy.

"You are welcome, Sydney. Shall we?" He offered his arm.

Sydney indicated an empty corner as she took the proffered appendage. "Where did the statues get off to?"

"I sent them to be restored. Refinished. Why?"

"I had only hoped that they found a new home."

Nicolas chuckled. "No, Madam. They are still mine. And I have every intention of keeping them as close to my heart, as they have grown."

Agnes appeared right before dessert. She stood outside the Great Hall while Haldis came to fetch Sydney. Nicolas saw the maid in the doorway, and then looked at Sydney. He shook his head, no.

Sydney drew a deep breath. "*Jeg har ikke hatt tid til å forklare til henne. Jeg kan vær så snill og gjøre det nå?*" I have not had time to explain to her. May I please do so now?

Others at the table exchanged glances; some uncomfortable, some condescending.

Nicolas waved his hand. "*Selvfølgelig du kan.*" Of course you may.

"*Takk du.*" Sydney stood and followed Haldis into the hallway. She bent her head close to Agnes and spoke for several minutes. Nicolas wondered what was delaying her return to her seat. He was about to follow after her when she turned and hurried back to the table.

"Is everything settled?"

"Yes, Nicolas."

Her answer was oddly flat. Emotionless. Maybe it meant less to her than he thought.

February 2, 1821

A special feast was planned, ostensibly for Nicolas's thirty-fourth birthday; but Sydney knew it was simply an opportunity for

Anders to push his favorite candidate to the forefront once again. She took another bite of the fabulous confection created in Nicolas's honor and wondered if it would stay down. Already, the dull instruments of her agony were pushing against her lower back, and a vague pressure was building behind her eyes.

Nicolas was on the dance floor with Sigrid; she pulled him there after offering an embarrassingly complimentary champagne toast. Sydney graciously turned down another offer to dance, and pressed fists against her back. Soon she would need to go and swath herself with rags.

"I suppose I should do so before I stain my gown," she muttered and pushed her plate away. She had no desire to move.

Karl and Ingeborg were dancing now, as were Espen and Dagmar. Dagmar's French gowns hugged and accentuated her lithe form and she hovered in Espen's embrace. She lifted her lips, inviting a kiss. Espen declined, and glanced around nervously.

"Oh, go on, Espen," Sydney whispered to no one. "She is lovely."

Invited again, he hesitated.

The third time, he acquiesced, taking her full lips in his. Sydney held her breath. The kiss was tender, inquisitive, bidding. When it ended, Dagmar's slow smile of triumph made Sydney feel as though some large barrier had just been traversed.

Good for you, Duchess, she thought, forcing herself to stand. Just in time, she realized. She stepped carefully toward the doorway and tried to catch Nicolas's eye. He saw her and excused himself from the dance.

"*Min presang*? You are ill." His concern was evident.

"It's only my course. I shall survive. I always do."

"I'll escort you to our room, then, and make certain Haldis does her duty." Nicolas grasped her elbow

Sydney intended to say no, but a wave of nausea and dizziness caused her to rethink. She leaned her head against his arm, the wool of his skirted coat rough against her cheek. The warmth of his body, augmented by the effort of dancing, seeped through the fabric.

She closed her eyes and stumbled.

He lifted her, wordless, and held her against his chest. The silk brocade of his waistcoat was slick on her skin.

She watched the transient light of passing candles move over the smooth plane of his jaw. Secure for the moment, she closed her eyes and melted into him.

February 13, 1821

Sydney sat in the lending library, as she did every Tuesday, Wednesday and Thursday afternoon, reading a novel about a Viking warrior and a pagan witch. She found it far-fetched, but it did stretch her knowledge of the Nordic tongue. These afternoons were proving profitable after all.

Agnes's whisper drew her attention. Sydney grabbed her cloak. "How far this time?"

"Just around the corner, Madam."

"Good. I have less than three hours left."

೫)೦ಪ

Nicolas watched Tomas in the mirror, stirring soap in the mug. Foamy waves of lather worked their way up the brush and spilled over their porcelain banks.

"Tomas?"

The valet jumped. "Yes, my lord?"

"Do you mean to beat the soap into submission?"

Tomas looked down at the mug. "Oh, Lord. I've made a mess. Forgive me, sir." He held the mug over the basin and wiped it with a towel.

"It's of no matter, Tomas."

The younger man shook his head. "I was thinking of other things. I didn't notice." He picked up the razor and turned to Nicolas. "Are you ready, my lord?"

Nicolas eyed the blade, vibrating in Tomas's trembling hand. He pushed the hand down, out of harm's way. "What has you so unnerved, Tomas?"

"N-nothing, sir."

"I believe it is something. And I have no desire to put my life at risk before discovering what that 'something' might be."

The corners of Tomas's mouth tugged downward. He sniffed and lifted his chin. "I do not wish to burden Your Highness."

Nicolas turned to face Tomas directly. "I am not anyone's

'highness' as yet. Please, tell me what is bothering you."

The mug and razor dropped to Tomas's sides and his shoulders slumped. Despair weighted his young features. "It is my sister, sir," he whispered.

"What is her situation?"

Tomas blushed and looked away from Nicolas. "Her husband. He lost his job. And he has been spending his days at the tavern."

Nicolas laid his hand on Tomas's arm. "Is there more?"

"He is frightened, I believe. Frightened that he will not be able to provide for my sister and their children."

"How many children do they have?"

"Four."

"I do understand his concern," Nicolas said kindly. "But spending money in a tavern is not helpful."

Tomas shook his head. "No, my lord. Neither is his frame of mind afterward."

"Tomas?" The valet's eyes lifted, but his chin did not. "Is he hurting the children?"

Tomas shook his head again, his voice barely discernible. "Only my sister."

"Does he hit her?"

Tomas nodded.

Nicolas pulled a deep breath and leaned back in his chair. "What was his job?"

"He is skilled in iron work."

So he was strong. *Skitt.* "Why did he lose his job?"

"He worked with a man who promised to give him the business when he retired. Only he never put it in writing." Tomas sank into the desk chair. "He was killed last month. Kicked in the head by a horse. His son claimed the business and put it up for sale."

"And your brother-in-law does not have the resources to buy it, I would assume?"

"No, sir."

Nicolas considered the young man. "Tomas, we must do something to rectify this."

"We?" Tomas's eyes rounded.

"As I see it, there are two problems we need to solve." Nicolas held up two fingers and grabbed one. "The first is to let this man know—what is his name?"

"Olan."

"Let Olan know that he may not waste money or beat his wife because of his own fears."

"You said 'we', my lord."

Nicolas grabbed the second finger. "And the second is to find him new employment. Perhaps here, at the castle. That way you could keep watch over your sister."

"How will you, I mean, can you..." Tomas's mouth continued to work but no coherent sentences emerged.

Nicolas patted his shoulder. "We shall skip the shave this evening. Tomorrow you will show me where they live. Then leave everything to me, eh?"

"Y-yes, sir."

February 26, 1821

Nicolas snored softly as the clock chimed midnight. Sydney collected her cloak and sabots, and shut the bedchamber door behind her. In the kitchen, she stirred the fire and set a pot of water to heat.

She was sipping the last of her tea when the soft knock came. It was almost half past twelve Sunday night; or rather, Monday morning.

"I thought tonight I might get back to sleep." Sydney grinned as she wrapped her cloak around her and slid into her sabots.

Agnes nodded her agreement and smiled shyly. "Three nights in a row! None of us are sleeping much!"

"How is the night?"

"Windy, with an ice ring around the moon." Agnes stepped out the door.

"At least there is no new snow!" Sydney crossed herself and kissed the rosary she kept in her bag as the women made their way between four-foot mounds of gritty snow piled on either side of the path.

෨෦ඏ

"Sir?"

"Come in, Haldis."

"I have news."

He waved his hand for her to continue.

"She has not stopped."

"Stopped?"

"Being a midwife."

"Really. When is she doing this?"

Haldis held up one finger at a time. "Friday, Saturday and Sunday nights."

He frowned. "What time?"

"She goes to the kitchen when the clock strikes twelve and has a cup of tea."

"And?"

"And the girl, Agnes, fetches her."

"Every time?"

Haldis shook her head. "No. If Agnes doesn't come, she goes back to bed at half past midnight."

He steepled his hands in thought. "How did you discover this?"

"She has begun to take naps." Haldis held up fingers again. "Saturday, Sunday and Monday usually. I wondered why she was so tired, of a sudden. So I stayed up to watch her."

He nodded and smiled. "Very good work, Haldis."

"Thank you, sir." She bobbed a curtsy.

"You may go." He stood and went to his brother's room. He repeated the maid's story.

"Does he know?"

"He must. Unless, of course, he is sleeping elsewhere."

"Do you believe he might be?"

"There is only one way to be sure. Ask his valet, Tomas."

Chapter Twenty Four

March 2, 1821

Nicolas looked up from the desk when Tomas's shadow darkened its surface. "Yes, Tomas?"

The valet glanced at the open bedroom door, and then crossed to close it. He returned to Nicolas's side. "May I sit, my lord?"

"Of course."

Tomas pulled a chair next to the desk. "I have been asked about you," he whispered.

"Have you?" Nicolas leaned back. "In reference to what?"

Tomas kept his voice low. "They want to know where you sleep."

"I see." Nicolas wiped his mouth and ran his hand through his hair. "What did you tell them?"

Tomas blushed. "I said... I said that you slept with your wife, as far as I knew."

"Did that satisfy them?" Nicolas queried.

Tomas shook his head. "No. I am to watch you."

"Every night?"

"That is the odd part, sir. Only Friday, Saturday and Sunday nights."

Nicolas stood and paced in a circle. Then he turned back to Tomas. "Then I suppose I shall oblige their curiosity."

"Yes, my lord?" Tomas looked confused.

"Do not concern yourself, Tomas. Just tell them exactly what you see. Can you do that?" Nicolas sat down in his chair and stared at the valet. "Whatever it might be?"

"Yes, my lord."

"Good. Now, I have to wonder, why did you tell me?"

"My sister."

"Ah. So the situation has improved?"

"Oh, yes sir! Olan has not laid a hand on her. In fact, he treats her better than ever."

Nicolas ran his forefinger under his nose and grinned behind his palm. "Did she have an explanation?"

Tomas struggled to suppress a smile. "Seems he was visited."

"Visited?"

"Yes, sir by a ghost." He giggled, then clapped his hand over his mouth.

"A ghost, you say. Must have been a fierce one!" Nicolas snickered.

"A Viking warrior dressed in wolf furs and a huge horned helmet. He was eight feet tall with his hair in flames!" Tomas hooted, unable to contain his glee. "Threatened Olan with a six-foot sword, he did; said he'd separate his bollocks from his body if he laid one more hand on his wife or the children. Made Olan piss himself!"

Nicolas's mirth burst out and filled the room. The two men laughed together, wiping tears and holding their sides. Tomas's relief was clear. Relief at both his sister's improved situation, and at Nicolas's understanding of his unpleasant assignment.

He sobered finally and bowed to Nicolas. "I owe a debt, my lord, which I cannot repay."

"No, Tomas." Nicolas patted his shoulder. "Your concern was for your sister, not yourself. I am glad I could help."

"Thank you, sir."

"Does he have work yet?"

Tomas shook his head.

"Then have him come to the castle. I will give a word of recommendation for him at the forge."

"Thank you again, sir." Tomas's voice was pinched. "I swear this to you, my lord. You have my loyalty from this day forward. I am *your* man."

"Thank you, Tomas. That means more than you can know." Nicolas offered his hand.

Tomas shook it, blushed, and walked to the door. He paused before he opened it. "Sir?"

"Yes?"

"I do not need to tell them. If you should sleep elsewhere, I mean."

Nicolas sighed. "I appreciate the gesture, Tomas. But rest assured, you may be honest. That is the best course of action at this time."

"Are you certain?" Tomas frowned.

"I am. But thank you just the same."

ॐ⊂ॐ

The bedroom door clicked. Nicolas felt for the warm spot Sydney left behind in their bed. He got up and pulled on a pair of drawstring breeches, and wrapped his dressing gown around his bare chest. He opened the door, closed it solidly, and headed toward Sigrid's room.

March 14, 1821

Nicolas sat on a low stone fence. Though this spring day was pleasant enough, the rocks still harbored the cold of winter, and pushed it through his breeches. The sun shone between small, scudding clouds and the breeze was as much cool, as it was warm.

Nicolas shared his lunch with Stefan and Leif while they watched the castle's farrier shoe the Akershus horses. Leif sat next to Nicolas and subtly mimicked his gestures. Nicolas pretended not to notice.

"Should I get the next horse?" Stefan hopped up.

Leif nodded. "Go ahead. It's the bay in the fourth stall."

"I know!" Stefan frowned. He marched toward the stable.

"He's a hard worker," Leif commented to Nicolas. "For such a young boy."

Nicolas struggled not to smile. "Yes, well you would know. Being thirteen and all."

The farrier's assistant carried out an armload of horseshoes, hefting the various sizes of u-shaped irons onto a sturdy plank table. He glanced at Nicolas and paled.

The farrier barked at him, "Olan!"

He dragged his eyes to his superior. "Yes, sir?"

"Give me a hand, will you?" The farrier pointed at the shoe. "That one. It needs to curve more."

Olan grabbed the hammer and pounded the shoe on the anvil while the farrier held it with long tongs. In five powerful strokes he had the task accomplished.

"My thanks." The farrier nodded and carried the shoe to its new owner, the bay gelding whom Stefan held in place. Olan stared at Nicolas, eyes and mouth open wide.

"Have you business with me?" Nicolas inquired politely.

"I beg your pardon, sir, but have we met before?" Olan fidgeted with his leather apron.

Nicolas shrugged. "It's possible. I'm a candidate for the throne of Norway. I have been on public display for months."

Olan shook his head. "I think it's something else."

"What could it be?" Nicolas looked as pleasantly innocent as he could. "Have you traveled abroad?"

"No, sir."

"Then I have no answer for you."

Olan turned and walked toward the forge, glancing over his shoulder and scratching his head.

Leif shaded his eyes and squinted up at Nicolas. "What was that about?"

"He thought he knew me. But he has never met me." Nicolas handed Leif half of his sandwich, which the boy devoured in two bites. "Are you ever going to put on weight?" Nicolas teased.

"I am trying, Sir!" Leif grinned. "You are a help, to be sure."

Nicolas ruffled his hair. "I think a stiff North Sea breeze would still knock you from a deck."

Leif hopped off the wall and stretched his neck as tall as he could. "I've grown, Sir!"

Nicolas stood next to him. "I believe you have, Leif. I believe you have."

Stefan stomped up. "Are there any more?"

Leif nodded. "The fifth and sixth stalls. Then we are done."

"Should I get them?"

"If you want." Leif shrugged. Stefan trotted to the stable.

"I have a task for you boys, if you are interested." Nicolas packed away the accoutrements of the lunch. "Do you like to draw?"

"I don't know. I never tried."

Nicolas hid his surprise. "Well, I have been meeting with the *Storting*. Do you know what that is?" Leif shook his head. "It is the group of men who make decisions about Norway."

"What kind of decisions?"

"Things like laws. And citizens' rights. And trade agreements."

"Oh."

Nicolas was fairly certain Leif had no idea what he was talking about. No matter. "Here is what I need from you boys. We are looking for a design for a flag."

Leif screwed up his face. "What kind of flag?"

"A country flag. For Norway."

Leif's eyes rounded. "And you want us to draw it?"

"Yes. At least, I would like you to try. Come up with some ideas. Do you want to do that?"

Leif nodded. "Can I tell Stefan?"

Nicolas grabbed his shoulder to keep him from bolting. "Can you come to his room when you finish here?"

"Am I allowed?"

"You are if I invite you. I will have paper and pastels there for you boys to experiment with."

"Yes, Sir!" Leif vibrated with excitement.

"Go on, then." Leif ran off, all elbows and feet. "And you'll have supper with Stefan as well!" Nicolas called after him. Leif waved over his shoulder.

March 15, 1821

Nicolas set a package by Sydney's breakfast plate.

"What's that?"

"A present."

Sydney shook her head. "You don't need to give me presents, Nicolas. I don't expect it."

"Today is your thirty-second birthday and I wanted to mark it." He stroked her cheek. "It pleases me to give you things. I put quite a lot of thought into it."

Sydney lifted her mouth and Nicolas kissed her. "I suppose this is one hardship of marriage that I shall have to learn to bear," she teased.

"Go on, open it." Nicolas pulled a chair close and sat. Sydney undid the ribbon and the paper fell away. She lifted the lid of the revealed wooden box. Nestled in a bed of purple velvet was a golden circle, half-a-foot in diameter.

"What is it?" Sydney picked it up. "A crown?"

"It is. It was my grandmother's. She left it behind when she moved to America."

Sydney turned the circlet around and examined it from all angles. Made of solid gold, the front rose to a point, and tapered to a narrow back. A large oval ruby was centered in front, and surrounded by marquis-cut diamonds which radiated outward like rays of a sun. Fountains of sapphires and diamonds flowed out on either side and entwined with raised gold braid. A row of garnet baguettes lined the bottom edge.

"I had the garnets added, to go with your wedding ring." Nicolas pointed at the stones.

"It's beautiful, Nicolas. How old is it?"

"I would guess three or four hundred years. I'm not really sure. Put it on."

Sydney's eyes widened. "What?"

"I want to see how it looks on you."

"Why?"

Nicolas sighed his impatience. "Because if I am king, then you are queen. You will need a crown."

Sydney hesitated, then placed it on her head and fiddled until it felt secure. "Like this?"

"Yes." Nicolas adjusted it slightly. "Like that. Come look in the mirror!"

He pulled Sydney to her feet and led her to the dressing table. What Sydney saw in the mirror was hardly royal. The woman staring back at her had the look of a trapped animal.

"It suits you," Nicolas whispered. "You are beautiful, *min presang*." He kissed her ear.

"Thank you."

Nicolas continued to stare at her.

"Might I take it off?"

Nicolas scowled. "Do you not like it?"

Sydney turned to face him. "Of course I like it, Nicolas. It is a beautiful piece of your family's history. I am deeply honored that you want me to have it. And, that you added something of mine to it." She lifted the crown from her head. "Someday, it will be Kirstie's."

"I want you to wear it to dinner tonight."

"Oh, no. I don't believe that is necessary." Sydney placed the circlet in its velvet bed.

"I do."

Something in his tone warned her that this was not negotiable. Even so, she tried. "Why? What point are you trying to make?"

"I want to show that we are in agreement."

"Agreement?"

There was that sigh again. "About my candidacy."

"Do you think that my wearing this crown to dinner will show that?" Even as she asked, her stomach clenched; she knew it would.

"Yes." Nicolas spread his feet and clasped his hands behind his back. "I need to let Anders, and everyone else, know that if I am to be king, I will have a supportive queen by my side."

₨℄

Sydney felt ridiculous as she descended the stairs on her husband's arm. She was an American. Americans did not have kings or queens! She lifted her chin and forced herself to meet the palpably inquisitive looks launched from the hall below. There was nothing she could do but resolve to make the best of the evening.

"And here she is!" Anders turned to her. "Happy birthday, Lady Hansen!"

Sydney curtsied, her smile endearing, her silk dress rustling, and was careful not to lower her head so far that the crown fell off.

"You look absolutely beautiful, my dear." Erling took her hand and kissed it. "The coronet suits you."

"Thank you. It belonged to my husband's grandmother."

Erling smiled. "Anders told me. He said our father held it in the hope that Marit might return someday."

"What is this?" Sigrid's acid tone carried over their

conversation. "Have we a pretender to the throne?"

Nicolas rested his hand in the small of Sydney's back and pressed it reassuringly. "Only if the pretender is the American."

"Hm." Sigrid squinted at the crown. "Needs polishing." Then she patted Nicolas on the chest and sashayed into the Great Hall. Sydney's jaw tightened.

"Let's go in and enjoy your night, shall we?" Nicolas's smile strongly suggested her cooperation.

"Yes, Your Highness. Whatever you wish." Sydney imitated Sigrid's sway as she walked to her seat at the front of the room. Nicolas pressed his lips in a grim line, and followed.

Karl frowned as Nicolas held Sydney's chair.

"What is this?" He approached them with a stiff stride. "Was there an announcement that I missed?" Sydney felt her face warming.

"I beg your pardon?" Nicolas's tone was smooth.

Karl waved at the crown pressing its increasing weight into Sydney's skull. "You know well to what I refer, cousin."

"It's merely a family heirloom, Karl. A birthday gift to my wife."

Karl glared at Nicolas, and dropped his gaze to Sydney. He bowed slightly. "I hope your birthday has been pleasant, my Lady." Before Sydney could respond, he whirled and stomped to the opposite side of the room.

Sydney pulled Nicolas into the chair next to her. "May I take it off?"

"No. Not yet."

Sydney closed her eyes and tried to smother her embarrassment. "Please?" she whispered.

Nicolas pressed his lips to her ear; his warm breath condensed in its folds. "I desire to make a point and it is important that you to submit to my will in this matter." He lifted her hand to his lips and lingered over it. Any observer would interpret his actions as the ministrations of a devoted husband.

Sydney bit her lip, eyes lowered. Nicolas leaned back as the soup was served.

∽∾⊂∝

Nicolas opened his eyes and sucked a quick breath. Why was he in the window seat? *Oh, right. Hiding.*

He escaped to the empty sitting room, crawled behind the drapes, and fell asleep after a long dinner and uncounted cups of akevitt and beer. Sydney was quite irritated with him. Sigrid flirted with him in public and pressed for increasing intimacy. Avoiding both women tonight seemed a good idea.

He recognized the voices that woke him. The door closed and the lock clicked. He watched through a gap in the drapery, leaning back so he would not be seen.

Espen rested his hands on the back of the settle, the planes of his face limned in orange by the dying fire. "You must stop doing that in front of my father!" he growled.

"Forgive me, Espen. It's only because I love you so much." Dagmar stepped behind him and rested her head against his shoulder.

"But you embarrass me, Dag. Don't you see that?" Espen turned to face her.

Her hands slid up his back. "Then marry me, Espen."

"Dag— "

Her lips stopped him from speaking further. She pulled him close and opened her mouth to his tongue. Espen's hands slowly lifted to cradle her head as they kissed. Nicolas blushed and looked away until the kiss ended.

"Marry me, Espen," Dagmar said again. "Please, just marry me."

Espen shook his head and walked around the settle. "You know that's impossible."

"Why, Espen?"

He shot her an annoyed look.

"Do you love me?" Her simple question hung in the air.

Espen's shoulders slumped. "You know I do. And you know that doesn't change the matter!"

"We can make this work, Espen."

Espen threw his hands up. "And when there is no heir? What then?"

Dagmar stepped around the settle and grasped his hands. "There can be an heir! It's simple, really. I will merely develop some exotic condition that requires me to be treated in Paris. When I return, I will bring the infant with me."

"You have considered this, have you?"

"Only every time you touch me." She fiddled with the buttons of his flies.

"Dag, don't."

"The door is locked."

Espen's eyes darted that direction.

"Let me love you, Espen. Please let me love you." Her eyes met his.

He hesitated, then succumbed. He kissed her hungrily. Her fingers loosened his breeches and she pushed him onto the settle. Her head dropped to his lap.

Nicolas leaned back and held his breath without realizing it. His legs were cramping in the small space, but he could not give himself away. He waited, and tried not to listen to Espen's grunts of pleasure.

"Oh my Lord, Dag. You are amazing," he moaned.

"Will you love me?" Dagmar draped herself on the settle.

Espen's hand reached up her skirt. "Of course, darling. Of course."

Dagmar panted and mewed. Her swift finish was, apparently, not diminished in intensity.

Nicolas winced and prayed they would leave the room soon. His full bladder magnified his discomfort.

"You are the love of my life, Espen," Dagmar gasped. "If you do not marry me, I shan't be responsible for my actions."

Espen sat up straight. "What do you mean?"

"Nothing." Dagmar straightened her skirt. "Only that I ache for you. I must have you."

"You have me now."

Dagmar pushed to her feet. "Now is not enough."

Espen stood and buttoned his breeches. "Do not threaten me, Dag. I'll not have it. I have told you that before."

She shook her head and looked as though she might cry. "Don't be angry, Espen. Please?"

Espen wrapped his arms around her and kissed her. "I do love you."

"I know."

They left the room arm in arm.

Nicolas rolled out of the window seat and fell to his knees. He stretched one cramped leg, then the other, and bent them under his hips. He pulled himself up by the drapes, stumbled on pins and needles to the fireplace, and unbuttoned his flies.

He pissed into the fireplace. Pungent steam wafted through the room.

I am going to sleep in my own bed this night, he resolved. *I don't care how angry Sydney is.*

When he got to his room, she was not there.

Chapter Twenty Five

March 23, 1821

*L*ook, *Pappa*. Flags." Stefan spread the drawings on the table. "I did four, and Leif did six."

Nicolas flipped two of them over. "I don't see any names on them."

"That's so you don't know who drew it!" Leif grinned.

"Ah. Good thinking." Nicolas looked over the selection. "This is interesting…" The drawing of sailors on a Viking ship shooting flaming arrows at a sea monster screamed Stefan's name. "While it is excellent artwork, it might not fit a flag."

"I told you it looks too much like your map!" Leif pointed a the journey map pinned to the wall by Stefan's bed.

Stefan glanced at the drawing and his shoulders slumped. he punched Leif's arm.

"Now this one, this is more like a flag." Dark blue across the bottom third, and light blue on the top third, both a white crescent moon and yellow sun hung in the sky.

"That's the North Sea!" Leif pointed at the dark blue.

"This is yours?"

Leif blushed and nodded. Nicolas laid it to the side and picked up another, similar, drawing. This one had the dark blue bottom, and waves of color in the sky, much like the northern lights.

"And this is yours as well?"

"Yes."

Nicolas laid it on top of the other one. He picked up a red, white and blue design. Five vertical red and white stripes were crossed by a blue horizontal band across the middle.

"Hmm. Stefan, can you fetch the pastels?" Stefan did, and Nicolas colored one vertical white stripe, blue. "What do you think?"

"I like it, *Pappa.*"

Leif nodded his agreement.

Nicolas asked Stefan for a sheet of paper. He drew a Danish flag: red background with a white off-center cross. Then he drew a Swedish flag; same design with a yellow cross on a light blue background. He laid the red, white and blue one beside them.

"This one seems to go well, don't you think?"

Stefan and Leif nodded.

"What will you do, Sir?" Leif asked.

Nicolas smiled at the boys. "I believe that we three shall present these designs to the *Storting* together."

"Are we to go as well?" Leif's eyes were open so wide, Nicolas thought the brown orbs might actually fall out of their sockets.

"Of course. These are your designs. You should present them."

Stefan hopped up and down. "When, *Pappa*?"

"Tomorrow."

Leif looked down at his clothes. "What will I wear?"

Nicolas considered the boy and his over-sized handed-down clothes from the grooms. He was half-a-foot taller than Stefan, so that was no help.

"Let's go to town." He rolled up the designs and tied them with a leather thong. "I have other business to attend to, and then I shall make sure that you, Leif, are suitably attired to meet the members of the *Storting*!"

છાંછ

The next morning, Stefan and Nicolas emerged from their rooms, dressed in their best. Leif sat in the hallway in his new nankeen breeches, white shirt and black coat.

His leg bounced as he waited.

"Ready, Leif?" Nicolas handed him the roll of drawings.

The boy scrambled to his feet. "Yes, Sir!"

Nicolas and the boys took a carriage to the Cathedral School of Christiania. In the auditorium, he introduced them to Lord Wilhelm Christie, and to several of the members. He also explained why they were there.

"So these boys have been working on a flag, have they?" Wilhelm nodded his approval. "Let's take a look."

Leif handed him the rolled drawings. Wilhelm untied and flattened them. He gazed at each one with a furrowed brow and pursed lips. Then he looked at the boys.

"These are very interesting. I particularly like this one." He held up the red, white and blue one. "But I shall show them all to the assembly."

"Yes, my lord," Leif breathed.

Nicolas herded the boys to seats in the front corner. "You can watch everything from here, but you must be very quiet if you wish to stay. I'll take you back to the castle when we break for lunch."

"All right, *Pappa.*"

"Yes, Sir."

The *Storting* was called to order and attended to regular business. Through it all, Nicolas was glad to see the boys behave respectfully and quietly enduring their boredom. It wasn't until right before lunch that they began to consider the flags, though no decision was made.

Lord Wilhelm concluded the session by announcing, "I would like to publicly thank these fine young men and their efforts at creating a uniquely Norwegian flag." Stefan and Leif stood to accept their applause.

When Nicolas walked them back to the castle, he doubted either boy's feet were even close to touching the pavers.

March 31, 1821

Anders stood with his feet planted and his hands behind his back. He was not smiling. "I have received some very distressing information, Nicolas."

"Sir?"

"Your wife."

Nicolas frowned. "Sir?"

Anders paced in front of him. "Did we not have a discussion concerning her activities?"

"We spoke of her learning to be a midwife, as I recall."

Anders stopped and glared at Nicolas. "Yes. And what conclusion did we reach?"

Nicolas shifted in his chair. "We did not reach a conclusion. You suggested that I tell her to stop."

"It was more than a suggestion, Nicolas." Anders leaned on a chair back. "Did you speak with her?"

"I did."

"Did you tell her to stop?"

"I did."

"And did she stop?" .

Nicolas knew by the way he asked that Anders knew Sydney had not, in fact, stopped. "I believed that she did."

Anders straightened. "She did not." He began to pace again. "She did not stop, Nicolas."

"How can you know?"

Anders turned to face him. "She was seen following that girl—Agnes is it?—from the castle."

Nicolas jutted his jaw. "When?"

"She goes out at night. Friday, Saturday and Sunday."

"Why do *I* not know this?" Nicolas challenged.

One eyebrow lifted. "You are sleeping elsewhere, are you not?"

Nicolas felt his face flush. "Am I being followed?"

Anders snorted. "Of course."

Nicolas leaned on his knees, his eyes on the floor. "What do you wish me to do?"

"Send her back to Missouri."

Nicolas's head jerked up, incredulous. "What?"

Anders spoke slowly, as if to a child, "Send her back to Missouri."

"For what purpose?"

"Tell her that you are staying here, and you need her to, I don't know…" Anders waved impatiently. "Close out your interests there. Some such thing."

Nicolas's eyes narrowed. "And if I do not?"

Anders pulled a chair close and sat in front of Nicolas.

"You. Nicolas. You could be king! Do you comprehend what that means? To you? To your country?"

Nicolas winced. Anders grasped his hands.

"You are our best hope. And your son, Prince Stefan? He can reign one day as well! Think of it, Nicolas. Think of all that you could accomplish!"

Nicolas struggled to pull a steady breath. "I cannot send my wife away."

"It is temporary! Only until your estate there is settled!" Anders pushed.

"I am sorry, Anders. I cannot."

Anders threw Nicolas's hands aside and waved a finger under his nose. "Then get control of her, Nick! Or the consequences will be dire!"

"Yes, sir." Nicolas stood.

Anders stood as well. "This is not a game, Nicolas, not at all. It is very serious business. An entire country hangs on your actions."

"I understand, sir."

"Do you?" Anders' eyes bore into his. "I pray that you do, son. I pray that you do."

April 8, 1821

A hysterical scream jolted Sydney awake and shot Nicolas from their bed. He grabbed his breeches and hopped into them one-footed across the floor. Sydney slid out of bed and wrapped her dressing gown around her as Nicolas opened their door. Dagmar's maid stood in the hallway, hands over her eyes, screaming lungful after lungful.

Nicolas leaned into her open door and staggered back. "*Å min Gud…*"

Sydney grabbed the maid and shook her. She dropped her hands and babbled at Sydney in rapid, hysterical French. Sydney looked into the room.

Dagmar sprawled naked on the bed, throat slit, blood everywhere. Her pale, slender body was completely hairless. And it had a penis.

Sydney spun around to face Nicolas, hand at her throat. "Oh my God! Does Espen know?"

Nicolas stared at Sydney in shock, the scar outlining his clenched jaw. He grabbed her elbow and shoved her back toward their room. She had to run to keep up with him. He shut the bedroom door and fell back against it. Then he slid down the door until he sat on the floor, his head resting on his bent knees, his face in his splayed hands.

"Nicolas?"

His shoulders began to shake. Sydney knelt beside him. "Nick?" she whispered.

He was breathing too fast. Hoarse, incoherent sounds rumbled from his open mouth.

"Nick, please?"

Dilated eyes appeared over his hands. "Ah, Sydney. Sydney. Do you know what this means?"

"Maybe Espen didn't know she was a he."

"Oh, no. He knew." Nicolas pushed the heels of his hands against his eyes. "He most definitely knew."

"How can you be so sure?"

"Because I saw them together." In a ragged voice, Nicolas told Sydney about his evening in the window seat. "And… I heard him warn her, *him*, not to threaten him. Espen."

Sydney sat back on her heels. "They fought last night after dinner."

Nicolas frowned. "Where?"

"In the hallway outside the Great Hall. When I went to use the privy, they were there."

"What were they arguing about?"

"As best I could tell, Dagmar wanted Espen to make their relationship… 'official' was the word she, *he*, used."

"And Espen refused, of course?"

"Yes."

"Did Dagmar say anything else?"

"She, *he*, said that Espen could not hide forever." Sydney laid her hand on Nicolas's arm. "Do you think he did it?"

Nicolas jerked his head sideways. "No. He loved Dagmar. He truly did."

Sydney pulled her dressing gown close as if to protect herself from that thought.

"*Gud i himmel!* That man has to be Didrik!" Nicolas ran his hand through his hair. "It was Didrick passing as his own dead sister!"

Sydney wagged her head in disbelief. "Are you saying that it was Dagmar who died in Paris? And then Didrik took her identity? To live as a woman?"

"That seems the way of it." Nicolas stretched his legs in front of him and sighed heavily. "Oh, Espen... Espen. Cousin. Friend!"

Sydney rested her hand on his arm. Nicolas stared at her, his expression overwhelmed with pain and confusion.

"He was a sodomite, Sydney!"

"Both of them were," she whispered. "Him and Dag—*Didrik*."

"Espen!" He shook his head. "How could I not have known?"

"How could I not have known about Devin? My own husband?" she countered. "It isn't always obvious."

Nicolas stared at his hands. "He's not a killer."

"No."

"*Skitt!*" Nicolas slammed his fists on the floor. "So who did him in, if not Espen? Who was last seen with him?"

Sydney tapped her lips, considering the question. "At dinner he was flirting with that businessman from Stavanger. The one with the fleet of fishing boats."

"Ah, yes. Yes. He was well into his cups, as I recall."

"And his hands were all over—*Dagmar*—when they danced."

Nicolas nodded, frowning. "I remember. Espen was in a fit." He snorted. "Now we know why."

"Dagmar seemed to be taunting him—" Sydney's voice caught on the realization. "She, *he,* must have been trying to push Espen to... oh, dear."

"Did Dag leave the Hall with that man?"

Sydney paused, recalling the scene. "Yes. I think so."

Nicolas's jaw rippled. "It would seem, then, that the man from Stavanger was none too pleased to discover the truth of whom he invited to his bed."

"You believe he killed her, *him*, when he discovered he was a man?"

"It would make sense." His cheerless voice was barely audible. "I'd be tempted. The humiliation would..."

Sydney squeezed Nicolas's arm consolingly. The unsettling ramifications of the murder and the search for a king flitted through her mind.

Nicolas shuddered and wiped his eyes. He spoke her thoughts aloud, unaware.

"This is the end of Espen."

April 10, 1821

The businessman with the fleet of boats was gone. Anders ordered a search of Christiania and the port, but nothing turned up. He declared the murder the work of the fleet owner and sent a letter to Stavanger, though he told Nicolas that he doubted anything would come of it.

It was, as Anders put it, "hard to drum up outrage over the killing of a pervert."

Canute took to his bed and would not see anyone.

"Is he eating?" Nicolas asked Eirik.

"What?" Eirik looked confused. "Who?"

"Your father. It has been said that he has locked himself in his room."

Eirik shrugged. "I don't know. I've been otherwise occupied."

"Oh?"

"We have been packing. Linnet says we must leave as soon as possible." Eirik poured a glass of beer from a pitcher on the table. "She is quite distraught."

Nicolas patted his cousin's shoulder. "As are you, I would imagine."

"Me? Why me?"

Nicolas paused. "Because of Espen."

"Espen? What does this have to do with Espen? He did not commit the murder!" Eirik downed the beer and poured another.

"But, he had a relationship with Dagmar. Or perhaps, I should say, Didrik?"

"Lies!" Eirik shouted. "All Espen heard was lies! He had no idea!"

"Is that what he told you?"

"And why would he tell me anything else?" Eirik's face flushed and his chin jutted. "A brother tells his brother the truth!"

Nicolas lowered his voice. "Of course he does."

"Yes. That's the way of it." Eirik gulped the second beer. "I must go help Linnet. Thank you for your concern, Cousin. As you can see, you have nothing to worry about." Eirik stomped from the room.

Nicolas poured himself a glass of beer and took a healthy gulp. He felt numb in his grief. All he believed to be true about his cousin had been challenged the moment he saw the corpse.

He knew he needed to talk to Espen. Maybe no one else suspected that his relationship with Dagmar was physical. Maybe they believed he was deceived. Maybe his reputation was not completely ruined.

Maybe only Nicolas knew the truth.

His first two knocks on Espen's door did not elicit any response. At the third knock, a voice from within asked who was there.

"It's Nicolas, Espen. Might I come in?"

Silence.

"Please, Espen. I need to speak with you."

More silence.

"Espen, I have something to tell you."

The door cracked open, emitting no light. "What?"

Nicolas pushed on the door. "You do not want me to state it in the hallway."

Espen stepped back and let Nicolas into a room that stank of urine and vomit. He shut the door and turned the lock. Nicolas counted three empty bottles of akevitt and five or six beer pitchers. There were plates of uneaten food on a table. The drapes were closed and the only light in the room came from a weak fire.

Even so, Nicolas could see the red that rimmed Espen's puffy eyes. He was half dressed, wearing a nightshirt over loose breeches. But no hose or shoes. He was unsteady in his stance.

"Sit down, Cousin." Nicolas pressed him into a chair. He brushed off the seat of another chair and pulled it next to Espen.

"What did you want to tell me?" Espen's raw voice betrayed hours of sobbed grief.

Nicolas swallowed the bile that crept up his gullet. "I know. About you and Dagmar. Or Didrik."

Espen's eyes rounded and he jumped up. He tipped over the chair as he scrambled to put distance between him and Nicolas. "What do you know? Or think you know?"

"I saw you together once. I was sleeping in a window seat one night, when you both came into the room."

"Oh... God, no... You saw?"

Nicolas nodded.

"Everything?" Espen moaned.

"Yes." Nicolas looked away.

"So you knew she was a man?"

"Not at the time, no. I had no idea. But you had your hand on her, pleasuring her."

Espen groaned and grabbed his temples. He folded in on himself.

Nicolas continued, "When I saw the body, then I realized. You were aware Dagmar was a man, and even so, you fell in love with her. Him."

"I am ruined..."

Nicolas remained seated and spoke in a low, determined voice. "I'll not betray you, Espen. That is not my point in coming here."

Espen's shoulders slumped, but his dull, bloodshot eyes lifted. "So it's to be blackmail then?"

Nicolas shook his head. "No. Honestly, I doubt that's even possible."

"Why?" Espen's eyes darted around the room. "Am I in danger?"

"Espen, look at me."

His frantic gaze lit on Nicolas's face.

"Eirik insists that you were deceived. Some will choose to believe him. Others?" Nicolas shook his head. "Others have already decided as to your predilections."

Espen blanched. "So what is it, Nick?"

"I only wanted you to know that—" His voice caught. He ran his hands through his hair. "I cannot believe I am about to say these things to you!"

"What things?"

Nicolas swallowed again. "Espen, I cannot understand why you—why any man for that matter—it's not in any manner normal..."

Espen's lids drooped. "That is what you came to say? For God's sake, Nick!"

"No, that's not it."

Nicolas stood and paced around the room. He longed to open a window and let fresh air into the fetid chamber; he wished it could wash away all that had transpired as simply as it could wash away the stench. His hands went through his hair again and he drew a deep breath through his mouth.

"Espen, I pray that you will find a woman to satisfy you that way. If you cannot, it is probably best that you remain alone," he said.

Espen nodded, hands muffling his exhausted sobs.

"But, because of our friendship, I wanted to tell you that I understand your loss, I truly do. No one else here can tell you that."

After a pace, Espen reached out one shaking and tear-dampened hand and, though he hesitated, Nicolas clasped it.

"Thank you, Nick."

They sat for a while without speaking. The fire hissed and popped its death.

"What will you do now?" Nicolas finally asked.

Espen straightened and wiped his eyes and nose on the sleeve of his already rank shirt. "I expect I shall go to Paris. Dag had friends there. They deserve to hear of her passing from someone who cared about her."

"Will you return to Christiania?"

He shook his head slowly. "No. Never."

Chapter Twenty Six

April 14, 1821

*A*nders summoned Karl and Nicolas. He sat the two men down in his private chamber, offered each a drink, and settled into a chair facing them. Nicolas saw his hand tremble. They waited in silence for Anders to gather himself.

"We have a narrowed field." His eyes did not lift from his glass.

"Yes, Your Grace," Nicolas ventured. He glanced at Karl; Karl stared at Anders.

"A narrowed field..." Anders downed his drink and poured another. "I summoned you two to talk of the throne. What is happening in the *Storting*?"

"Well..." Nicolas gestured to Karl. "We have been hearing attestations concerning the nobility in Norway."

"There is a general feeling that all titles should be abolished," Karl expounded.

"All titles?" Anders straightened.

Nicolas shook his head. "Well, they have no quarrel with the idea of a king."

"What, then?" Anders turned to Karl.

"The titled elite. It seems the notion of equality amongst the king's subjects is a popular concept," Karl answered.

"And the sense of patriotism, which propels your own search for a Norse ruler, is very strong as well," Nicolas added.

"Patriotism? What about the flag?" Anders asked.

"We are to be presented with three options in a fortnight. We will vote at that time." Nicolas smiled in spite of himself. "My son, Stefan, and the stable boy, Leif, contributed some of their own designs."

"Did they?" Anders glanced around the room, dismissing that information. "How will you men vote on the subject of the nobility?"

Karl leaned back in his chair. "I will vote for no new titles to be awarded. I will vote to allow those who have a title to keep it throughout the remainder of their own life. But the titles will no longer be passed on."

Anders stared at Karl; his impassive expression gave no clue of his thoughts. Karl shifted in his chair.

Anders slid his narrowed gaze sideways. "Nicolas?"

Nicolas cleared his throat. "I support the same position that Karl supports."

"Is that not a mite lazy?" Anders smirked.

"No, sir not at all. It's because Karl is right." Karl smiled a little at Nicolas, and nodded his head in thanks.

"Fine." Anders stood. "Thank you both for coming. I believe we will need to select our candidate soon. Karl, if you don't mind, I need a word with Nicolas."

Karl's jaw clenched, but he bowed politely and smiled. Once he was gone, Anders threw his punch. "Has your wife ceased practicing her avocation?"

"I believe so."

Anders cocked one eyebrow, "And have you mentioned the possibility of her returning to Missouri without you?"

"No, sir."

Anders clasped his hands behind his back and rocked on his heels. "I need to make my choice, son."

Nicolas nodded somberly.

"You are aware that I sought you out?"

"I am."

"You are also aware that I have considered you the brightest hope?"

"Yes, sir."

Anders swung one hand onto Nicolas's shoulder. "You do not carry the madness, Nicolas. Do you understand the magnitude of that?"

"I had not truly considered it," Nicolas confessed, surprised.

"Consider it now, son. If we claim the throne, we cannot risk it being lost, once again, by a raving lunatic!" Anders' eyes held a spark of that very lunacy as they bore into Nicolas's. "I believe you remember my eldest brother?"

"I remember him well, sir." Nicolas hoped Anders did not detect his shudder.

Anders leaned closer. "We need a king of clean lineage."

"Yes, Your Grace."

His voice lowered. "Norway needs you, Nicolas Reidar Hansen."

"I am honored that you think so, sir."

Anders put his lips to Nicolas's ear. "Your wife is a liability."

A jolt went through Nicolas. His heart pounded and he felt a trickle of sweat roll down the groove of his back. He forced himself to breathe slowly. "I understand."

"Will you send her soon?" the snake's whisper hissed.

Nicolas shook his head. "I—I will consider it."

Anders pulled away. "The candidate must be presented quickly, before nobility is abolished."

April 18, 1821

"Narfi rode up, with his shield and sword, and carried on strangely, rolling his eyes about like a hunted beast. Some men were up on the wall with Cormac when he came, and his horse sheed at them."

Sydney leaned over and looked at the page Stefan read from. "Shied."

"*Shied* at them. 'Thou hast never a word but ill,' said Cormac, and leapt upon him and struck at the shiled."

Sydney looked again. "Shield."

Stefan dropped the book on his lap. "That's stupid."

Sydney laughed. "No one ever said English made sense! Would you rather read Norse?"

Stefan shrugged. "How much more?"

Sydney took the book, *The Life and Death of Cormac the Skald*, and turned the page. "Only to here. That is the end of chapter nine."

"Then I can go to the stable?"

"Yes."

Stefan sighed and settled into his chair, book propped on his stomach. Sydney's mind wandered to Nicolas's question this morning, "Are you still bleeding?"

The onset of her courses was always irregular, but this time over two months had passed. It came with such severity that Sydney was forced to her bed for two days, and bled for eleven days afterward. Nicolas was kind, expressing sympathy, and eager to massage her temples or knead her lower back, if either would give her ease. But he was no actor, and he could not conceal his immense relief that they had not made another child.

The long wait for her cycle had given Sydney pause. She had not felt sick, albeit with her first two pregnancies she had not been nauseous, either. But both her sons were born too early and never breathed. When she conceived Kirstie with Nicolas, she was ill within a month. Sydney glanced at the napping fifteen month-old's light brown curls and smiled.

That boot to his balls last year most likely rendered Nicolas sterile at any rate.

"So Cormac set his feet against the hilts, and pulled until he tore the pouch off, at which Skofnung creaked and groaned, but never came out of the scabbard." Stefan clapped the book shut. "Now?"

"Why did the sword not come out of the scabbard?"

"I don't know."

"Do you wonder?" Sydney was beginning to wonder about Stefan's concentration.

Stefan slapped his forehead, a precursory habit that Sydney assumed would morph into his father's hand-through-his-hair. "It's because of the warlock! But I don't know *why* it won't come out!"

Sydney smiled. "Go to yon horses, O Knight of Norway!" She waved her hand toward the door. "You have proven worthy."

Stefan hopped from the chair, gave her a perfunctory hug, and ran out the door. Sydney picked up the discarded book. The clock on the mantle chimed a soft three-fourths of a tune. Sydney glanced at it; it was nearly four.

Tomas stepped into the room, arms weighed down with two ewers of steaming water. He hefted them onto the dressing table. Sydney paused in curiosity. "Tomas?"

"Mister Hansen requested these," he explained.

"What is the occasion?" Sydney chuckled. "Has he landed in the manure pile again?"

Tomas rubbed the smile away. "I do not believe so. He seemed in quite good spirits."

Nicolas blew into the room. "Thank you, Tomas! You are dismissed until seven." He crossed to the children's door, spoke briefly to Maribeth, then pulled the door shut and locked it. He crossed back and locked the bedroom door behind Tomas. Sydney watched, her head following her husband back and forth.

Nicolas faced her and clapped his hands together. "Your course has finally ended. We have three hours, wife."

As realization dawned, Sydney stretched and sighed. "I do love the way you think at times!"

Nicolas came to her, took her face in his calloused hands, and kissed her well. He smelled of spring leaves and fresh wind, and tasted of beer.

As he undressed her, he rinsed a cloth in the rose-scented hot water and helped her wash. She did the same for him. Bit by bit, they shed both their clothing, and winter's stale patina. Their unshrouded skin, fresh and vibrant from their ministrations, rivaled the bright spring day. Clean and naked, Nicolas lifted Sydney and carried her to their bed.

Nicolas's hands were deliberately slow. Sydney's skin raised in gooseflesh as he traced her shape. His tongue tasted every part of her. She squirmed beneath his touch and begged him to enter her. She reached for him, hard and standing against his belly, but he moved away. She could not hold back any longer, and she arched against him, her fingers pressed into his flesh. Her gasps echoed in the room. Waves of indescribable pleasure flowed to her extremities, and she fell limp.

"That was not fair," she rasped, not truly complaining.

Nicolas's tongue tickled her ear, his hot breath revived her gooseflesh. "That was only the beginning," he promised. Then he climbed over her, spread her legs with his knees and nudged his way in.

"Å *min Gud!*" Sydney gasped again, and tightened on him.

"Å *min Gud...*" Nicolas echoed. He began to move. "I have missed you sorely these last two weeks," he rumbled. His first climax was swift and loud.

When the clock struck seven, both wore their dressing gowns and looked quite respectable. Sydney had brushed her wildly disheveled hair, but there was not much she could do about her lips; their flushed color smudged outside their boundaries. Nicolas eased himself into the chair in front of the dressing table, knees wide. His reflection grinned at her.

"You are quite the wanton, Lady Hansen."

"And you, Lord Hansen, are quite the performer. Three times in two hours, was it?"

Tomas knocked and entered the room. He crossed to the wardrobe without a word and pulled out Nicolas's dinner jacket. Haldis followed and curtsied to Sydney.

"I will wear the green tonight," Sydney stated. "It is the perfect color for such a beautiful spring evening. Don't you agree, Nicolas?"

"Anything you say, my love." He winked, his navy blue eyes shining.

Chapter Twenty Seven

April 18, 1821

Nicolas sat next to Sydney at dinner, not across from her or down a seat or two, as was the custom. He kept a hand on her, as if he wished to continue their afternoon's play. He spoke into her ear often; his deep voice vibrated her soul. She rested her hand on his thigh under the table, and felt exceedingly content for the first time in months. Even Anders' scowl from the head table did not disturb her mood. She lifted her chin and smiled at him.

Anders motioned for one of the butlers. He spoke in the man's ear, and then leaned back in his chair. He rubbed his forefinger under his nose while eyes that missed nothing swept the room. When the butler returned, Anders nodded and stood.

Sydney watched him from under lowered lashes while he walked to the end of the Great Hall. She was surprised to see Haldis waiting in the doorway for him. Anders bent his head to the maid's, turned his back to the Hall, nodded, then walked back toward the front of the Hall.

Sydney turned to ask Nicolas what he thought was happening when she realized Anders had not returned to his seat. He was nowhere in sight. She tugged at Nicolas's sleeve.

"Yes?"

"Something is afoot," Sydney whispered.

Nicolas leaned close and whispered in her ear, "Something is always afoot."

Sydney gave him a look. "This time, I believe it involves us."

Nicolas glanced around. "Whom should I be concerned about?"

"Anders."

"Oh." Nicolas adjusted his stance in the chair so he could see his uncle. The man sat in his seat once again, looking as calm as a tortoise. "Why?"

"He was speaking to Haldis."

Nicolas shifted his gaze back to Sydney. "Do you think she informed him of our afternoon activities?" He grinned. "It's so decadent, is it not? So unsuitable for a king!"

Nicolas planted a long, solid kiss on Sydney's upturned mouth. Sydney saw a shadow pass over Anders' face. He turned away.

"Be careful, husband," she whispered. "The game is dangerous."

Dinner was served. Nicolas and Sydney conversed with an older couple from northern Norway, who had traveled south to meet the candidates now that the weather allowed. Fresh bread and pickled herrings started the meal, followed by a delicious lentil and fish chowder. The meat dishes were brought out next, lamb and pork roast primarily, with a small platter of liver and kidneys.

Sydney noticed Nicolas's face grow alarmingly red. He began to pull at his stock and squinted at her through dilated pupils. "Is it hot in here?"

"No. What is amiss?"

"Can't—can't breath..." Nicolas pushed to his feet, swaying. He grabbed the back of his chair and took two steps before falling sideways to the floor.

"NICOLAS!" Sydney screamed. Her mind flashed to Vegard's death. Reflexively she turned and caught Sigrid's eye. The woman's face was gaunt and pale, her sunken eyes glazed over. Sydney knelt by her husband.

"Nick! Nick! Look at me!"

Nicolas blinked at her, but his eyes kept moving from hers. "Where are they going?" his voice rasped.

"Who?" Sydney looked over her shoulder. A crowd had gathered, but all stood rooted in place so as not to miss a thing.

"Those Indians!" He shook his head, his voice husky and dry.

"Make sure they don't get the horses."

"I will." Sydney's tears dripped on Nicolas's cheeks.

"Water..." he croaked.

"Bring him some water!" she shrieked. A glass was thrust at her. She tried to lift his head, but could not. Karl appeared at her side, and he lifted Nicolas's head and shoulders. Sydney poured some of the water into his mouth, but most of it onto his chest.

"Thank you," she sobbed.

Karl nodded, his face was so white it looked blue.

"Nicolas?" Sydney leaned her face in front of his. "Do you want more water?"

Nicolas's eyes rolled around and finally landed on hers. "What?"

"Water?"

"Water?" he repeated. His voice was so pinched, Sydney tried to pour the last drops from the glass between his lips. He coughed and gagged.

"Where am I?"

"Akershus Castle. In Christiania," she answered and accepted another glass of water from someone's hand. "Drink this."

Nicolas obliged for a moment, then began to writhe. "Get it off my chest!" he growled.

"Get what off?"

"I cannot breathe! It's crushing me! Get it off!" Nicolas began to bat at the air. Karl tried to hold him down, but had to let go of the furious man. "God damn it all to hell, get it OFF!"

Nicolas rolled to his knees and tried to stand. He fell backward into the crowd. Women screamed and men lowered him again to the floor.

Sydney looked around for help and saw Anders. At a distance from the crowd, his expression was unreadable. His eyes bore into hers. She lifted her chin in defiance and called out to him, "Has anyone summoned a doctor?"

He paused. "Yes."

Sydney knelt again and poured water into Nicolas. She untied his stock and opened the neck of his shirt while she kept talking to him. "Nicolas! Look at me!"

He squinted as though he could not quite make her out. His pupils were fully dilated; large black holes in the whites of his eyes.

"Where am I?" he asked over and over.

"Akershus Castle. In Christiania, Norway," she replied every time. "Do you know me?"

"*Min presang?*" his thin voice sounded childlike.

"Yes. Drink this."

"I cannot breathe." He panicked again and tried to stand. He fell sideways and was again lowered to the ground. "Where am I?"

The doctor pushed his way through the crowd. "What are the symptoms?" he asked without preamble.

"He turned red. He lost his balance. His voice sounds dry and rough. His pupils are dilated. He is confused. He has hallucinations. He feels like he cannot breathe," Sydney reeled off what she observed, her midwife's training making her aware.

"Belladonna." The doctor pushed Nicolas's sleeve up and rested his arm on a metal basin. He produced a steel fleam, centered it over a likely vein, and tapped it. Burgundy blood began to run over Nicolas's arm into the basin. The doctor nodded, satisfied. "Good cut."

"Belladonna? Deadly Nightshade?" Sydney fought rising panic. That was what killed Vegard. "Will he—" She could not say it. "Will he live?" she asked instead.

The doctor shrugged. "Some do."

Nicolas began to panic again. It took six men to hold him down until the bleeding was complete. The doctor wrapped a bandage around the wound.

"Give him plenty of water. More than he wants. Was he healthy before the poison?"

That afternoon's lovemaking seemed a century past. "Yes," Sydney managed.

"Then he might recover. But I cannot promise anything." He packed his instruments. "I shall return tomorrow morning. If he lives through the night, he has a chance."

The six men struggled to carry a faint, though uncooperative, Nicolas to the bedroom. Tomas helped Sydney undress him as he coughed and wheezed and asked where he was. Sydney saw a tear drip down Tomas's cheek.

"Don't you dare do that!" she admonished. "I cannot hold myself together if you fall apart."

"I beg your pardon, Lady." Tomas brushed away the offending

moisture.

"The doctor said to give him water, even if he fights it."

"I shall do so." Tomas turned to Haldis. "Bring pitchers of water. And one of beer."

Haldis looked at Sydney. "Please do as he asked," she confirmed.

"Very good, Madam."

Sydney cocked her head. "Beer?"

"To flavor the water. It may make him more amenable."

Sydney smiled for the first time in hours. "Good thinking, Tomas."

A moan from the bed drew their attention. Nicolas began to thrash against the covers. "I cannot breathe!" he squawked.

Sydney and Tomas held their vigil over Nicolas. They poured countless glasses of beer-flavored water into him. When he tried to climb out of the bed, Tomas pushed him back. When he claimed he could not breathe, Sydney fanned his face. When he spoke nonsense, they responded with reality. And when he asked where he was?

"Akershus Castle. In Christiania, Norway. Do you know me?"

"Min presang..." he whispered.

Sydney held the lamp over Nicolas and peered into his eyes. They rolled back, still dilated, but now dark purple circles underlined them. His skin was clammy and pale. She could tell by how hard Tomas had to push to keep him on the bed, that Nicolas was growing weaker.

"Maybe he is only tired," Tomas said softly.

Sydney set the lamp on the table. "Did I speak out loud?"

"No. But I believed our thoughts were on the same path." Tomas threw a towel over a growing wet spot on the sheet. "Ah! I waited too long."

Sydney pulled the sheet off the bed and handed it to Haldis. Tomas dried Nicolas's urine, then packed a clean towel under the semi-comatose man. "At the least we know he is swallowing the water."

"Ma'am?" Maribeth stood in the doorway. "I brought you some supper."

Sydney's stomach growled as the scent of the food drifted toward her. She looked at the clock, it was nearly one in the morning.

"Thank you, Maribeth." Sydney pointed to the table.

Maribeth glanced at Tomas. "I brought food for two."

"Thank you." His smile held something that Sydney was surprised to see.

Maribeth pulled her eyes from Tomas's. "Might I help while you eat?"

"See if he will drink any water." Sydney sat down gratefully to her meal. Tomas covered Nicolas's naked lower half with a clean sheet, then he joined Sydney.

Nicolas sat up. "Where am I?"

Sydney spoke with her mouth full, "Akershus Castle. In Christiania, Norway."

Nicolas looked at Maribeth and gasped for breath. "I cannot breathe."

"Fan his face." Tomas left his meal to assist Maribeth. He pushed Nicolas back onto the bed.

Maribeth stared at her employer, fear dominating her features. "Is he—is he going to be all right?"

Tomas nodded determinedly. "Of course. He is strong and healthy."

"But he looks—" Her glance flitted briefly to Sydney then shot back to Tomas. "Do you truly believe so?"

Tomas pushed sweaty strands of blond hair from Nicolas's face. "I must. We must."

Haldis carried off the tray of dirty dishes. When there came a knock on the door, Sydney assumed it was the returning maid. Her stomach turned over when she faced Sigrid. She looked very small and older than her years.

"What do you want?" Sydney did not invite her in.

Sigrid's eyes went past her to the bed, then refocused. "How is he?"

Sydney shrugged.

"Might I see him?"

"Why?"

Sigrid swallowed thickly. "I have known him for a long time. I want a chance to say—I mean, I don't want him to—I just want to talk to him."

Sydney drew a deep breath. "He is not going to die," she stated with authority.

"No. He is not. Please, Sydney." Sigrid laid a thin, shaky hand on Sydney's arm. Sydney's eyes dropped to the floor, and she stepped aside. Sigrid moved past her.

She stood by the bed and stared at Nicolas. He opened his eyes and looked at her; Sydney saw black holes that seemed to hold nothing. Sigrid turned away.

"Where am I?" he croaked.

"Akershus Castle. In Christiania, Norway," Sydney answered, exhausted to the breaking point. Being polite to Sigrid was beyond her limit. She approached the bed. "You have seen him. Now will you leave?"

Sigrid glanced over her shoulder at her erstwhile lover. "Do you know why he was poisoned?"

Sydney's heart jumped at hearing the words said aloud. Feeling a little faint, she grasped her wedding ring as an anchor, turning it around and around, and shook her head. Sigrid pulled her narrow frame as straight as she could and looked down her nose at Sydney.

"Because of you."

Maribeth gasped. Tomas stepped between the women.

"May I show you out, Duchess?" He placed one hand on Sigrid's back and pushed her.

"Unhand me if you wish to hold your job!" Sigrid barked. She moved toward the door, turning back to glare at Sydney. "Think about it."

Tomas shut the door solidly behind her. Sydney sank to the floor in a heap of crumpled clothing and began to sob. Maribeth knelt next to her and laid a tentative hand on her back. Sydney rocked to the side and rested her head in Maribeth's lap. Her wracking sobs echoed off the stone walls of the room. Maribeth stroked her hair.

Sydney cried until she hadn't the strength to continue. Maribeth and Haldis pulled her to her feet and helped her undress. They wrapped her in her dressing gown and sat her in a chair next to the bed. They propped her feet on an ottoman. Haldis went to get her some tea.

"We will stay with you," Maribeth promised. "Don't be concerned if you sleep."

"I want to keep watch," Sydney yawned. As if to punctuate her statement, Nicolas began to snore.

"That is good, Madam," Tomas assured Sydney.

"Is it?" She looked bleary-eyed at her husband.

"He is not struggling any more. And dying men don't snore," Tomas pointed out. Sydney nodded and accepted the tea from Haldis.

The three adults spoke little throughout the remainder of the night. Sydney dozed, but was not completely comfortable sitting up in the chair; precisely the reason she stayed in it. As the room grayed, then pinkened with the dawn, Nicolas croaked, "Sydney?"

She was at his side in a blink. "Yes?"

He turned his head slowly, as if moving a boulder of great size. He winced and squinted. "Sydney…"

"I am here, Nicolas."

He moved his mouth and tried to swallow. Tomas lifted his head and gave him a sip of water. Nicolas nodded his thanks. "Poison?" he rasped.

"Yes."

Nicolas closed his eyes and wobbled his arm toward Sydney's hand. She grasped his and pressed it to her lips.

"I'll live?"

"Yes," she whispered and brushed away tears with her free hand.

"Who's here?"

Sydney cleared her throat. "Maribeth, Tomas and Haldis."

Nicolas laid still, his breathing deep and steady. He turned toward Sydney and opened his eyes. They were blue again. "Go home, Sydney. *Dra hjem.*"

She frowned, confused. "What?"

"I need you to go home." Nicolas closed his eyes.

Sydney's heart began to pound. "Nick?"

He opened his eyes again, the effort of speaking obvious. "*Jeg sender deg…* I am sending you… to Missouri." Deep breath. "To take care of things." Deep breath. "Go home."

"Without you?" Sydney felt panic rising. Blood roared in her ears.

"Take Kirstie. Maribeth."

"What about Stefan?"

"Stays with me. *Han blir her.*" Nicolas began to cough. Tomas gave him more water, careful not to look at Sydney. Maribeth approached the bed, but Haldis held back.

"Nick?"

He opened his eyes, bright blue in the dawn light. He gazed steadily at her.

"Do you want me to leave Norway and return to Missouri without you?" Her voice was clear in spite of her shattering heart.

"Yes."

"Will I ever see you again?"

Nicolas swallowed with effort. "When things here are settled."

"You *will* send for me?" Her voice broke under the weight of what her question suggested.

Nicolas closed his eyes. "Of course."

Chapter Twenty Eight

April 20, 1821

*N*icolas sat by the fire while Haldis served his breakfast. Tomas hovered nearby. Sydney was in the next room with the children. She had not spoken much to him in the last twenty-four hours since he told her to return to Missouri.

"Thank you, Haldis." Nicolas looked askance at the bland offering. "This is it, then?" He called after the disappearing maid, "Might I have honey?" She shook her head and shut the chamber door.

"Tomorrow you can have anything you want," Tomas interjected. "Doctor's orders."

"Keep that bastard and his knife away from me, and I shall eat whatever I am served!" Nicolas picked up his spoon.

Tomas smiled. "After you frightened him out of his skin yesterday, I don't think you need to worry!"

"Did you not think that was amusing? Pretending to rise from the dead?" Nicolas chuckled.

"I shan't forget it. Neither will he, nor his valet, I'll wager!"

Nicolas spooned his bland boiled wheat into his mouth and watched his own valet putter incessantly around the room. "Did I thank you for your assistance, Tomas, when I was 'indisposed'?"

Tomas shook his head. "There is no need sir."

"Well, I thank you just the same."

"You are quite welcome." Tomas continued to fidget, moving things that did not require moving, then restoring them to their original situation.

There was no help for it, but to ask outright. "What is on your mind, Tomas?"

Tomas stilled. Slowly he turned to face Nicolas. "Is it obvious, my lord?"

"It is. Just come out with it." Nicolas waved his spoon in dispensation.

Tomas approached him. "May I sit, sir?"

"Please."

Tomas pulled the ottoman close. He rested his elbows on his knees. He pulled a deep breath.

"I realize that you are not, actually, the gentleman I should speak to in this matter. But, in this circumstance, you are the only gentleman I am able to speak to. So, I hope you do not misunderstand me. I know that what I am asking is a bit unorthodox. And still, I hope you may assist me?"

Nicolas stared at the younger man.

"Tomas?"

"Yes?"

"Are you planning to tell me what this matter might be?"

Tomas flushed deep red. "Oh. Yes. Of course."

Pause. "Tomas."

Another deep breath, then a whoosh of words. "In-leiu-of-her-father-who-resides-in-Missouri-I-am-asking-you-for-Maribeth's-hand-in-marriage."

A laugh exploded from Nicolas. Tomas wilted.

"Is that it?" Nicolas grinned. Tomas nodded, his glum gaze dropped to the floor. "Have you spoken to Maribeth? Is she amenable?"

Tomas nodded again, eyes still stuck to the carpet.

"And have you the means to support her and your future children?"

At that, he looked up. "I have land outside Christiania. Enough for a decent farm."

Nicolas slapped his shoulder. "Then sit up and look happy, man! You are about to be married!"

"What?"

"Yes, Tomas. If Maribeth wants to marry you and stay in Norway, I give my permission."

Tomas jumped to his feet. "Might I go tell her?"

"Of course."

Tomas ran to the connecting door to the children's room, jerked it open, and rushed through. Nicolas heard Maribeth's uncharacteristic whoop. The couple returned to stand before him, beaming.

"Thank you, sir." Maribeth dropped a small curtsy. "I thank you from the bottom of my heart."

Sydney appeared in the doorway, Kirstie on her hip. Nicolas glanced at her, and she at Haldis.

Then Sydney met his gaze, unsmiling. "I suppose the wedding should be soon. Before I leave, since I'm her chaperone."

"In that case, Tomas, I release you from my service for the day. Go and prepare for your nuptials." Nicolas waved his spoon again, this time in benediction.

"Thank you, my lord!" The couple disappeared into the other room.

Sydney glanced toward Haldis again, then stared angrily at Nicolas. She spoke in slow Norse, "So only Kirstie and I are leaving. Fine. We shall be gone in a fortnight."

❧☙

"Did he tell her to leave?"

"Yes, sir. As soon as he was lucid from the poisoning."

"Has he fully recovered then? No lasting effects?"

"Yes, sir."

"Excellent."

"There is one other thing, perhaps not so important."

"We shall judge that, Haldis."

She dipped her chin in acknowledgement. "The maid is staying. She is betrothed to Tomas."

"Nicolas's valet?"

"Yes, sir."

"How did this come about?"

"He asked Lord Hansen for her hand."

"And he agreed?"

"Yes, sir."

"Interesting." He tapped his chin. "She knows about the maid's betrothal?"

"Yes."

"And?"

"She said she and the little girl would be gone in two weeks."

"The boy stays with his father?"

"Yes, sir."

"And you are certain that you heard this correctly?"

"Yes, sir."

"Thank you, Haldis. You will be very well rewarded for your loyalty."

She gave a deep bow on the other side of the screen and murmured, "Thank you for allowing me to serve."

When the maid had quit the room, Erling turned to Anders, lifting his hand in salute. "You have done it!"

Anders gave a sly grin. "Did you ever doubt me?"

April 21, 1821

Nicolas stepped around the trunks in the bedroom. Sydney and Haldis were discussing which items she wanted in each trunk, and which items she would not take with her.

"Don't forget the statues."

Sydney stopped and turned to him, hands gripping her hips. "Are you serious?"

"Completely."

"Nicolas, how am I to handle them? They are huge! And heavier than one man can carry!"

"One of them goes to Gunnar, remember?" Nicolas took Sydney's hand and pulled her to a chair. She sat and regarded him, expectant and unsmiling.

"I have thought about the best way for you to travel. You should go by water the whole way, nothing overland. That way you can care for Kirstie without having to worry about meals or lodging."

Sydney nodded somberly. "Even so."

"You will go from Christiania to London, to Baltimore, and to

New Orleans by ship. Then take a paddleboat to St. Louis. When you are in Baltimore, send word to Gunnar to come get the gift."

"I have my doubts as to his gratitude," Sydney muttered.

Nicolas smiled. "I know my brother. Do not have a worry."

"Will they be restored in time?" Her tone clearly indicated she hoped the answer was no.

"I am just returned from checking on their welfare. They will be delivered to the dock the day you sail."

"Oh, perfect," she grunted.

"Do you need my trunks?" Nicolas twisted in the chair. "Or have you enough room?"

Sydney shrugged. "I shall make do."

Nicolas kissed her forehead. "I need to go. I shall see you at dinner?"

She held her breath and twirled the antique garnet ring, not trusting herself to give a civil response. He stood before she could summon an answer and left the room.

℠℞

Sigrid wore black. Custom dictated a year, but Nicolas doubted she would go that long. In the meantime, her choice of styles bordered on indecent. Laced into a low-cut gown which impelled all soft tissue, bosom or no, to swell above her décolletage, Nicolas wondered if it was an unfortunate shadow, or if there was actual areole peeking over the fabric. He dragged his gaze higher as she slipped into the seat next to him.

"Where is your wife?" she inquired, accepting a glass of wine.

Nicolas accepted wine as well. "She will not be joining us."

"Tonight, only?" Sigrid watched him over the rim of her wine goblet.

"Well, no. I expect she will take her meals in our room for the remainder of her stay."

Sigrid straightened and twisted to face Nicolas. He lifted his chin and blocked his view of her breast with his wine glass.

"What do you mean, 'the remainder of her stay'?" she squeaked.

Nicolas snorted. "The rumor mill must be grinding to a halt. Have you not heard?"

Sigrid shook her head.

"I have requested my wife to return to Missouri and deal with my holdings there. I plan to summon her back when the question of the throne is settled."

Sigrid gulped her wine and held her glass to be refilled. "When is she leaving?"

"In less than two weeks." Nicolas's glass was refilled as well.

"She is taking the baby, of course."

"Of course."

"What about the boy?"

Nicolas frowned a bit at that. Certainly she knew his son's name? "Stefan will remain here, with me."

"Stefan, yes." Sigrid leaned back in her chair. "This is certainly interesting news, Nick."

He waved his hand dismissively. "It is necessary."

"She will be gone a year."

Nicolas nodded and spooned lutefisk onto a piece of toast. He popped it in his mouth.

"What about that mousy little maid of hers?" Sigrid's lips were red from the wine. It looked well with the black dress she was almost wearing.

"Now that is interesting news as well..." Nicolas smiled crookedly. "She will marry Tomas, my valet, and remain in Norway."

Sigrid laughed harshly. "Are you quite serious?"

"That I am. Sydney is helping her plan the wedding for Friday."

"What is the rush? Is she *enceinte*?" Sigrid lifted one brow and drained her cup.

"No! It's because she is losing her chaperone."

"Chaperone?"

Nicolas ate another piece of toast and lutefisk. "Sydney."

"Oh." Sigrid motioned for more wine. Her other hand dropped to Nicolas's thigh. He covered it with his hand to keep it from moving closer to his groin. Sigrid gazed at him with a soft smile and half-closed eyes.

By the end of dinner, Sigrid leaned heavily against Nicolas's arm. When she turned to speak to him, he could not keep from noticing the rise and fall of her elevated bosom, her wine-stained mouth, and the invitation in her eyes.

"Would you escort me to my room, Nick? I believe I had more wine than I realized."

Nicolas declined comment; Sigrid always drank more than he thought prudent. Since Vegard's death, she seemed to have thrown all temperance to the wind. He stood and helped her to her feet.

Nicolas wrapped Sigrid's arm around his and led the wobbling widow out of the Hall. They climbed the stairs to the private rooms and turned down the wing where Sigrid stayed. When they reached her rooms, she tugged at Nicolas.

"Stay with me, Nick?" She looped her arms around his neck.

"No, Sigrid. I cannot." When Nicolas pulled her arms down, the shoulder of her dress slipped revealing her right breast.

"I need to go," he said. He turned to go but she reached for him again.

"I have always loved you, Nicky."

He deflected her grasp and backed away from her door.

"Nick? When she's gone?" Sigrid pleaded.

Nicolas nodded. "When she's gone."

April 27, 1821

Tomas rocked on his heels at the front of Akershus Fortress's chapel. He wore a new waistcoat and frock coat, both wedding gifts from Nicolas. His hair was trimmed and he shaved that morning.

Sydney helped Maribeth with her finishing touches, and Nicolas waited to escort her down the aisle. A trio of string players began to play.

"Are you ready yet?" Nicolas stage-whispered. "Tomas is rocking a groove into the floor!"

"Will I do, ma'am?" Maribeth's wide eyes flickered her concern as she smoothed the skirt of the gown Sydney had given her.

Sydney smiled. "You will more than do, Maribeth. You are radiant!"

Nicolas offered his arm.

"Wait! Her flowers!" Sydney scooped the bouquet of daffodils and tulips and laid it in Maribeth's free arm.

"Now?" Nicolas arched a brow.

"Now."

Sydney watched her tall, handsome husband walk slowly down the aisle. Her gaze traced his broad shoulders, curved buttocks, and long legs, their shape enhanced by his breeches and hose. When he turned to smile at Maribeth, Sydney's breath caught. He was so beautiful.

Sydney brushed her tears, relieved that the ceremony would be assumed their cause. Her heart was an anchor, holding her under waves of unyielding emotion.

It was obvious to the residents of Akershus that there were but seven days left in her own marriage. She forced a trembling smile for Maribeth's sake, and prayed to God her nightmares would not become reality.

May 3, 1821

A thin lavender line trimmed the eastern edge of the sky. Leif opened the castle's kitchen door, slow and silent. He grabbed any food he could find and stuffed it in a saddlebag. Then he crept into the Great Hall. He paced the room, silent bare feet leaving no mark on the polished floor. He reached a sideboard and opened a drawer filled with silver.

Leif stood over the drawer, trembling. The patina of the polished silver was visible in the dim light of the banked fire. His fingers twitched. He lifted a fork. The cold, heavy metal felt good in his hand. So smooth. He put the fork in his mouth, and imagined that a chunk of roast beef with gravy slid off the tines onto his tongue. He paused.

He thought of Nicolas, and he could not do it.

Wiping the fork on his trousers, he set it carefully back in place. He closed the drawer with a resigned sigh. He padded around the room, eyes evaluating everything he saw. He leaned over another sideboard to get a better look at a candlestick. Then he saw it.

On the floor, under the sideboard and next to the wall, a metallic glint. Leif dropped on his knees, bottom in the air, cheek pressed to the boards. He stretched one thin arm under the furniture, then flattened on his belly to reach farther. His fingers brushed the object.

"Ouch! *Skitt!*" He retracted his hand and sucked on his bleeding finger. Leif climbed to his feet and crossed to the fireplace.

He hefted the iron poker, and returned to the sideboard. Back on his stomach, he stuck the poker underneath and fished it out.

"O-o-oh," he blew through rounded lips.

The dagger was a lady's. Shorter than a man's, the cut on his finger proved it was no less sharp. The stainless steel blade shone as new. The grip was crusted in jewels: sapphires, rubies and emeralds. The guard was of braided gold with rows of small round diamonds. Leif had never seen anything so elegant in all his years.

The scuff of a footstep jolted Leif to action. He jammed the dagger into the saddlebag, tripped across the floor to replace the poker, then tiptoed toward the kitchen door. He rested his ear against it, heard nothing, and pushed through it.

Outside, he sat on the stone stoop and put on the shoes he left waiting there. Head high, he walked around to the front of the castle and out the front gate. Once on the awakening streets of Christiania, he never looked back.

Chapter Twenty Nine

May 4, 1821
Christiania

*S*ydney stood on the pier and looked up. The mast of the ship stood over the dock like a shepherd's staff, keeping the scurrying sailors and longshoremen herded in place. Unnerved by the thought of traveling halfway around the world alone, she held Kirstie on her hip and surreptitiously observed the other passengers. For the most part, they seemed pleasant enough.

There was just the one that gave her pause, hunched under his threadbare hooded cloak and using a crutch, he had a peg below the knee on his right leg. It was not his deformity that unnerved her, it was his stench. Somewhere between urine and rancid grease. It was obvious by wrinkled brows and kerchief-covered noses that the other passengers shared her reservations. She hoped his lodgings were not anywhere near hers.

Sydney's heart thumped powerfully, causing her to wonder if Tomas could hear it. She attempted to appear unconcerned, yet her gaze roved without pause, searching for a blond head rising above the pulsating humanity at the dock. Everyone heard him tell her to leave, to go back to Missouri without him, but of course he would come to the ship. Why would he not?

She turned to Tomas. "Will you escort me to my cabin?"

"Yes, ma'am. I had planned to." Tomas stood beside a smaller trunk, the one she would have with her in the stateroom.

"There they are!" Stefan pointed at the antique Viking statues tied to a wagon.

A team of draft horses strained to pull the load to the end of the pier. Six men followed and began to untie the ropes. Sydney watched in fascination as they lifted the poles the first statue rested on, three men to a side, and carried the lifeless monstrosity like pallbearers. When they carried it as far as the ship, the dockworkers tied it to a hoist. It was lifted onto the ship, and lowered through a hatch to the hold below.

"Did you see that?" Stefan bounced. The men trudged back to the wagon to repeat the process.

Sydney shook her head. "I don't understand your father," she said, meaning much more than the figureheads.

"Is he not coming, ma'am?" Maribeth turned her head toward town.

The weight of the statues pressed against Sydney's chest. She lifted her chin and forced her lungs to inflate.

"Of course he will," she whispered, unable to muster the will that full voice required.

"Shall we have you settled in?" Tomas's kind expression nearly stripped away her tentative composure. "Come on then, Stefan. Let's help your *mamma* and sister."

Stefan walked up the gangway, followed by the newly wedded couple. Sydney followed, deliberately putting one foot in front of the other and reminding herself to breathe, as the edges of her vision blurred and spotted.

Why wasn't he here?

Her cabin was like the ones they sailed in to Norway: a built-in bed on top of a chest of drawers, diminutive desk, one chair. A small round window opened for ventilation. Tomas set the trunk by the desk. Stefan climbed on the bed to look out the window.

"I wish I was going, too!" he said, his nose against the glass.

Tomas glanced at Sydney and cleared his throat. "You are."

His statement prompted a trio of exclamations, and questions through three pairs of startled eyes. "Lord Hansen instructed that I was not to tell you until you were on the ship. But it is his intention that Stefan travel with you back to Missouri."

Sydney dropped onto the chair, her legs suddenly unable to support her. Blood roared in her ears. "But—we didn't—what about his things?"

"I packed them last night and sent them to the ship."

"Which trunks?"

"Lord Hansen purchased new ones. They should be in the cabin next to this one."

Sydney handed Kirstie to Maribeth and pulled Stefan to her. "Tomas, I don't understand."

"Mister Hansen feels that the situation in Christiania, after he was poisoned, has grown too dangerous for Stefan. He wanted to remove the boy from harm's way. But he did not want Sir Anders to know, in the event that the gentleman might try to retain the boy."

"Oh," was all she could manage.

Sydney's mind juggled all the implications of Tomas's revelation. Yes, it was good to remove Stefan from danger. And Nicolas would never abandon his son.

True, he had all but ignored the boy for the first six years of his life. But he had changed in the last year and a half. Nicolas was becoming a true father.

So why was he not *here?*

Sydney tucked Stefan's auburn waves behind his ears. "So, he does plan to send for us after all?"

Tomas nodded. "I do believe he will."

Maribeth's gaze bounced from Tomas to Sydney, Stefan, and Kirstie. Her eyes welled with tears and ruddy splotches mottled her cheeks.

"You didn't know about this?" Sydney asked.

Maribeth shook her head, and the tears spilled their dam.

Sydney stood and hugged the maid. "Thank you for everything, Maribeth. You have been such a blessing to me."

"Thank you, ma'am," she sniffed. "I have so much because of your kindness."

"You have a husband who loves you, a new home in a new country, and soon you will have children of your own to care for." Sydney wiped her eyes. Her emotions floated on the surface and she could not submerge a one of them. "You'll not have time to miss us!"

Maribeth dabbed her nose with her embroidered wedding

handkerchief.

An impudent bell warned all extraneous persons to exit the ship. After another round of hugs, Tomas and Maribeth made their way down the plank. Sydney and the children stood on the deck and waved to them. Sydney wore a brave face, but all she could think of was locking herself in her cabin and drowning in her grief.

Where *was* he?

Why hadn't he come?

When the ship nudged away from the dock, Stefan began to scream.

"No! Wait! *Pappa!* What about *Pappa?*" His stricken face turned to Sydney's. She suddenly realized that he had not had a chance to say goodbye to his father because of the secrecy of his departure.

And Nicolas was not at the pier.

"*PAPPA!*" he screamed. He jumped up and down, red-faced. "Stop the ship!"

Sydney knelt in front of him, her face grim, her fear consuming her. "We c-cannot stop it, Stefan."

"We have to stop! We forgot *Pappa!*" His lip quivered and tears pooled in his bright blue eyes.

Could it be possible? That all of their secret planning and dangerous political games had brought her to this? Brought *them* to this?

Sydney took a deep breath, hating that she needed to be the one to tell him, and hating Nicolas even more for putting it on her. "It seems… that *Pappa* is staying here."

"No!" His head jerked and his voice wailed over the sympathetic cries of the dock's gulls. "He needs to come with us!"

Sydney's chest tightened and her throat closed up. She felt light-headed; her scalp prickled and her field of vision narrowed. She leaned one hand on the deck, concentrating on the rough, damp wood to keep her senses intact.

"No, Stefan. He needs to decide about being a king." Sydney drew a shaky breath and tightened her arm around Kirstie. The girl stared somberly at her mother and brother, lip quivering. "I believed he would come to the ship. But he did not."

"But—but why are *we* going?"

"We are going back to Missouri to take care of things there."

Sydney prayed that what she said to her stepson was not a lie. "*Pappa* will either send for us when he is King, or he will come home to Cheltenham if he is not."

"When?" Tears streamed unheeded down Stefan's narrowing cheeks. By the chill against her skin, she knew they ran down hers as well.

"I—I don't know." Sydney tried to give him a comforting smile and failed miserably. Her arms and legs were numb. Reality seemed to exist elsewhere, and she was living squarely in a nightmare.

"I want my *Pappa!*" Stefan wailed and crumpled to the deck planks. "I want my *Pappa...*"

Sydney rolled her hips sideways and crossed her legs, cradling Kirstie. She patted and rubbed Stefan's back while he poured out a heartbreak that only began to mirror hers.

Why, oh why, hadn't Nicolas come?

The salt-laden wind freshened as the mountains of Norway sank inexorably into the North Sea.

After an eternity Stefan quieted, exhausted by his grief. Hers would have to wait, for the sake of Nicolas's children.

Sydney pulled Stefan close. She felt his ribs twitch with spastic gasps and her tears dampened his hair. He wrapped his arms around her waist and held her, very tightly.

"Let's go find your cabin, shall we?" Sydney suggested, though her words seemed to come from somewhere outside her body.

Stefan ran his sleeve under his nose, his eyes bloodshot and swollen. He allowed Sydney to pull him to his feet. They climbed down the ladder to the stateroom level, Stefan lowering his sister into Sydney's arms, before following his *mamma* down the slippery rungs.

They walked through the dining room to the corridor.

"Tomas said yours is the one next to mine..."

Sydney stood in the narrow passage. The door to the left of her cabin opened, and a middle-aged couple stepped out. They smiled a greeting and patted Kirstie's curls before continuing down the hall.

"So it must be that one." Sydney grasped the handle on the cabin door to the right of hers, and pushed.

She froze. Her mouth opened to scream, but she was unable to draw the necessary breath. The misshapen one-legged cripple, still in the rancid cloak and his crutch tossed aside, was pawing through

Stefan's trunk.

Sydney stumbled back against the wall of the corridor. Her hand waved convulsively for Stefan's.

"Get out!" she coughed, her voice failing. "I—I shall call the captain!"

She turned to make good on her threat, but was stopped by a massive hand on her shoulder. It pulled her backward into the cabin. Sydney pushed Kirstie into Stefan's arms and drew a breath to shout for help, when another hand clamped over her mouth.

Fear shot through her, giving her strength she didn't possess. She fought like one gone berserk. She kicked her heels backward, searching for shin. She connected and the miscreant grunted. She bit down and tasted blood, but his hand pressed her mouth so hard, she was not sure whose.

Stefan stood rooted, mouth open. His shoulders jerked as he gasped in indecision, unsure of what to do. Kirstie began to squirm and cry, caught in the vise of his panicked grip.

"Oof—!" One of Sydney's elbows sank into the beast's belly. She slammed her heel into his instep and he yelped. She tried to hook her foot around his peg and knock him off balance. His arm became a band of steel, pinning her against him. He pressed his mouth to her ear.

"*Min presang.*"

Sydney's efforts changed flavor instantly. She twisted to see her captor. Navy blue eyes peeked out from under the hood. "Have a care, eh?"

"Nicolas?" Relief buckled her knees and left her faint. When she sagged in his arms, he hobbled sideways and lowered her into the cabin's tiny chair.

"*Pappa?*" Stefan crept forward. "Are you my *Pappa?*"

Nicolas threw back the hood. His blond hair stuck out everywhere. "I am indeed, son." He shrugged the hideous cloak to the floor.

Kirstie stopped crying when she saw her father and stretched her arms toward him. Stefan set her down and squinted at Nicolas, still not sure. "What happened to your leg?"

Nicolas grinned and pulled his dirk from his belt. He cut the leather strap that held his lower right leg bent out of sight. Then he unstrapped the peg from his knee.

He straightened and stretched the abused member. "Ouch... Remind me never to become a cripple..."

He held his arms out to Stefan. The boy ran into them and Nicolas pulled him close.

"I thought we forgot you!" Stefan scolded loudly. He sniffed. "I thought you were still in the castle!"

"I'm sorry about that, son. It had to be a secret. Can you forgive me?" His words were for Stefan, but his eyes were on Sydney.

Her breath came in uneven spasms. She was furious beyond reason and relieved beyond description.

Stefan nodded and looped his arms around his father, his face tucked securely in Nicolas's neck. Kirstie toddled to him and held up her hands. He scooped her to his shoulder and kissed her soundly.

"Are we safe?" Sydney whispered. She was shaking and felt light-headed, shattered by the whirlwind of events and the subsequent swamp of emotions.

Nicolas shook his head and gazed at her from behind his children. "Not yet. After London."

৪১৩৪

"How did you ever find such an awful garment?" Sydney waved the air in front of her nose.

"It was in the stable," Nicolas rolled it up. "What shall I do with it?"

There was no reason for him to remain disguised. Tomas would cover his absence with the story that Nicolas was indisposed with the flux. Fear of catching the disorder would keep Anders away for two to three days. Tomas assured Nicolas that he would uphold the illusion by carrying trays of tea and dry toast into the room, and dirty dishes away. By the time the truth was out, the Hansens would be more than halfway to London.

"Get it out of this cabin before it lends its stench to everything we own. Please!"

Nicolas opened their tiny window and pushed the cloak overboard. "Better?"

She nodded. "Yes! But leave the window open for a bit, would you?"

Dinner was served at seven bells. With no maid, Sydney and Nicolas were forced to bring Kirstie with them to the table. Thankfully, her sun-kissed curls and intent blue-gray eyes charmed the women, who in turn fought over the chance to hold the cheerful toddler. She ate anything they offered her, though at times her face scrunched into a comic critique of a particular dish.

"Do I know you?" one man blurted, drawing everyone's attention, particularly Nicolas's. "I've seen you before!"

"Perhaps," Nicolas said casually.

"What is your name, sir, if I might be so bold?" The man's face took on a suspicious tint.

"Nick Reidar," he answered without a pause, exaggerating his American accent. "And this is my wife, Siobhan."

Sydney leaned over and whispered to Stefan, aborting any comments forthcoming from the boy. His eyes twinkled at her words. He was eager to play along with the adults' game.

The man continued to stare at Nicolas, who met his perusal with calm disinterest. "And you are?"

"Donovan Jansen."

"I'm pleased to meet you."

"You are not from Norway."

"No, Mister Jansen. We are returning home to America."

"Lord Jansen."

Nicolas tipped his head. "I beg your pardon, sir. Might you pass the potatoes?"

When the meal was complete, Nicolas leaned back in his chair and scratched his chest. "I believe I will join these gentlemen on the deck for cigars."

Sydney stood. "And I shall see the children to bed." She lifted a sleepy Kirstie from her neighbor's lap. "Come along, Stefan."

Stefan's chin was an inch from the tabletop, his cheeks propped between two fists. Drooping eyelids lifted at his spoken name, and his eyes rolled a little. "But I'm not sleepy," he protested.

"I know, but I need your help with your sister." Sydney held out one hand. "Come, please."

Stefan submitted to a face wash and hair comb before slumping on the edge of the bed. Sydney tucked Kirstie next to the wall.

"Lie here, Stefan, so she doesn't roll off the bed." Sydney patted his pillow. "I'll come back in a few minutes and check on

Kirstie."

She kissed the children, lowered the wick on a hanging lamp, and closed the door behind her. After going to the privy at the head of the ship, she returned to the cabin. Both children were soundly asleep, unmoved from where she left them.

଼ଠ

In his desperation to hold onto her, Nicolas curled himself over her. Lying on her back, Sydney rolled into a ball; her knees brushed her shoulders and her arms circled his ribs. She rested her forehead against his throat. He owned every part of her. And she loved him for it.

Their joining was energetic, silent. Sydney pressed her lips hard; the only sounds escaping were rhythmic breaths through flared nostrils as Nicolas drove home, deep inside her. She ground herself against him as blessed spasms twisted her body without mercy.

He pressed his face into her hair and quaked. The temblor of his release shook them both. Panting, he did not move, but stayed over her, resting on elbows and knees.

His breath warmed her scalp. "I could not have lived if I lost you."

"We played a dangerous game," Sydney whispered.

"That we did."

"Do you believe we have won out?" She thrummed her fingertips over his skin.

He rolled onto his back, his long legs protruding off the end of the bunk. "I... do."

"Why did you hesitate?" Sydney propped on her elbow. "Is aught amiss?"

Nicolas shrugged. "I felt I was being followed. It's probably my imagination, especially after *Lord* Jansen thought he knew me."

"Was it when you came to the dock?"

"No. Here."

"On the ship?"

He nodded; she felt it, more than saw it, in the dark cabin. "Who would follow you? And why?"

"There are reasons."

"Nick?"

He reached for her. She rested her cheek on the coarse, curly pillow of his chest. He tangled his fingers in her hair. "Trust me, *min presang.*"

"Do you not trust me?"

"Of course I do. But I don't have anything specific to tell you. Yet."

Sydney sighed heavily and closed her eyes, adjusting her position. She faintly heard the snort and blow of Nicolas's first snore as her own body succumbed to satiated exhaustion.

Chapter Thirty

May 7, 1821
Shipboard
Christiania to London

*T*he hair on the back of his neck prickled.

Nicolas stood at the bow of the ship and stared at the clouds lurking over Scotland. He could not see Scotland, the curve of the earth hid her from view. But he knew she was there.

Just as he knew he was being watched.

Nicolas shaded his eyes with his palm and slid them to the side, looking past his elbow. Crewmen went about their business and paid him no heed.

He strolled over to a coil of rope and lowered himself onto it. He stretched his arms and crossed them behind his head. From his recumbent position, he feigned sleep and watched for unexpected movement through slitted lids.

The seasoned hunter was patient. It took the better part of an hour, but his prey made a fatal move. A dark head appeared around the edge of a canon, then jerked back. Nicolas could not see the face, but he marked the hiding spot.

With a languorous stretch, Nicolas stood. He sauntered toward the canon.

No one was there.

No matter. He had the scent. Tracking was the easy part. Nicolas strolled amidships, and climbed down the ladder in search of lunch.

∽〇〇〇

"*Mamma*, are ghosts real?"

Sydney, folding a laundered diaper, turned and looked at Stefan. His blue eyes, under lowered brows, peered intently over the top of the book he held propped on the desk. "Some people believe so. Is that what you are reading about?"

He shook his head and laid the book down. "What do you believe, *Mamma?*"

"I'm not sure. I have never seen a ghost, so I don't feel qualified to pass judgment." Sydney tucked the folded diaper into a drawer and picked up another one. They spoke softly so as not to awaken Kirstie, napping soundly with her thumb dangling from her slack mouth.

Stefan crumpled his lips and rested his forehead in his hand. "Well, if ghosts are real, could they be on a ship?"

Sydney paused, then resumed her movements, hoping Stefan did not notice. "Why do you ask? Have you seen a ghost?"

"No." He sounded disappointed. "But when we go eat and come back, my stuff is moved."

"Moved?" Sydney tried to sound casual, though her heart stepped up its cadence. Her glance flitted through the cabin. "Is anything missing?"

Stefan shrugged. "I don't know." The cabin door swung open.

"There you are! Anyone hungry?" Nicolas's deep voice bounced off the walls.

"Shhh!" Sydney pressed her finger to her lips and nodded her head toward the bed. Kirstie stirred and sucked her thumb purposefully for a few seconds, then went slack again with a soft sigh. "Stefan, go with your father. I shall be along soon," she whispered.

Stefan nodded and closed his book. He followed his father out the door and as it closed she heard him ask, "*Pappa*, are ghosts real?"

ℰℭ

"What do you make of it?" Sydney asked Nicolas as they washed for dinner.

"Something is afoot and there is no question about it." Nicolas lowered his voice. "I am being watched, of that I am now quite certain."

"Has someone been in this cabin as well?" Sydney looked around and tried to memorize each item's position.

"I haven't noticed. But then, I wasn't sensible of the possibility."

"What will you do?"

"Lay a trap. As any decent hunter would do." Nicolas's eyes lit up at the thought. "Too bad I threw out that cloak."

Sydney shot him a look.

"Well, if not for the smell," he qualified. Nicolas tapped his knuckle on his chin. "So what then? Get him to follow me? Or lure him to Stefan's room."

"I would highly prefer that you get him to follow you," Sydney stated with authority. "I don't want to disrupt the children any more than we already have."

"You make a good point," Nicolas agreed. "After dinner tonight, I will go on deck to smoke a cigar. I shall spend some time in the head for good measure. I might as well kill two birds with the one pebble, eh?"

Sydney smiled.

"Then, when I stroll around in the dark, I shall see if my 'ghost' follows."

"Will you be armed?" Sydney's eyes fell to the hunting dirk on the desk.

"I always am." Nicolas tucked the weapon into his waistband under his frock coat. He offered his arm. "Are we ready?"

After dinner, Sydney took the children while Nicolas commented rather loudly that he would be on deck. He pulled a cigar from his waistcoat as his exclamation point. He lit it with one of the oil lamps and casually climbed to the upper deck.

The ship cleft through the waves, peeling back ragged white edges as they slipped silently through the darkening water. Pale orange faded to pink and bled into the purpling sky—as dark as it would get. Nicolas breathed deeply of the clean, salty air. He blew cigar smoke into the breeze. His every nerve was primed, waiting.

When he finished the cigar, he tossed the end into the water, watching the glowing ash arc gracefully until it disappeared into the North Sea. There was no sign of his ghost thus far. Nicolas opened the gate that led to the privy seat at the bow of the ship. Unfastening his flies, he pushed his breeches to his knees and settled on the wooden ledge. The wind that filled the sails and pushed the ship forward pushed any offensive odor forward as well.

After a suitable time, Nicolas stood and reassembled his clothing. A movement drew his surreptitious attention. He felt for his dirk and moved it forward. He climbed away from the bowsprit and through the privacy gate.

Thin silver feathers tickled the rising moon as they passed her on the wind. Nicolas welcomed the added light, his eyes adjusting and roving. There was no sign of any human occupation at the moment, so he ambled along the port side of the ship, the side the moon illuminated.

He stopped and turned suddenly. Nothing. He continued his walk. He turned again, this time catching a shadow. Ahead of him was a shed-like structure housing one of the ship's wheels. He walked past it, paused, turned, and walked to the other side.

The shadow followed. Nicolas pressed against the painted clapboard and held his breath. A thin figure ventured around the corner. Nicolas's meat-hook of a hand shot out and looped around the culprit's neck.

"A-H-H-H-H-H!" his captive screamed. He squirmed like a dervish, all elbows and knees and over-large clothing. "Let me GO!" he screamed in Norse, his voice cracking under the weight of puberty.

"Leif?" Nicolas loosened his grasp, incredulous. "Is that you?"

"L-let g-go of m-me!" his Norse sputtered as he tried to contain his sobs.

"I shall let go of you, son, if you will calm down and tell me what the devil you are doing on this ship!" Nicolas growled.

Leif stilled then, panting and trembling. The whites of his eyes glowed in the moonlight, making his thin cheeks look even more gaunt. He hitched up his pants and crossed his arms in an attempt to look forbidding.

"I won't go back."

Nicolas snorted. "Before we discuss that, how did you get *here?*"

Leif shrugged, his voice challenging. "It was not so hard."

"Perhaps I should be asking you *why* you are here."

At that, what little composure Leif feigned, abandoned him. His lower lip scrunched and jerked down at the corners, his brow compressed and balls of saltwater splashed down his cheeks. He gasped. Grunting sobs, which should have emanated from a much stouter body, were startlingly loud in the night. Leif's shoulders shook with such force that Nicolas thought the boy's bony body might sustain damage. He gathered the adolescent boy in his arms and held him tight against his chest.

"There you go, son. Just let it out. You are safe here." Nicolas had no idea if what he said was in any way appropriate for the moment, but felt Leif's skinny arms wrap around his waist in response. He patted Leif's back and let him cry.

Eventually, only spastic gasps and sniffles were left of the torrent.

"Can we talk now, son?" Nicolas loosened his grasp.

Leif nodded and stepped back. He wiped his cheeks on one sleeve, his nose on the other. Nicolas led him to a corner of the deck and they sat on the coil of rope. Nicolas regarded the young stable boy, trying to discern what prompted him to stowaway.

"You snuck onto the ship."

"Yes, Sir."

"Why?"

Leif stared at his own feet as they curled and tucked under his trousers. "Tomas told me you were leaving."

"Yes, I asked him to," Nicolas said.

"Tomas said no one else in the castle knew."

"They didn't. It was a secret. But I didn't feel right about taking Stefan away without letting you know. You and he are such good friends."

Nicolas had to strain to hear Leif's next words. "I did not follow Stefan, Sir."

"No?"

Leif shook his head, eyes still on his feet. "I followed you."

"Me?" Nicolas startled.

"Don't be angry, Sir." Leif's lean face lifted and his eyes—black as tar in the moonlight—burned into Nicolas's.

Nicolas recognized the boy's desperation. "I'm not angry, Leif. But I still don't know why."

Leif's struggle for composure resurfaced. "I wanted to leave... The grooms, they..." He sniffed and wiped again with the sleeve. "Well, since my mother died, no one has paid me much mind."

Nicolas's stomach clenched.

Leif shook his head, awestruck eyes never leaving Nicolas's. "But you, Sir, you treated me like somebody. You talked to me. You taught me things and gave me a sword. You took me to the *Storting*. You gave them my drawings!" His visage darkened. "I never... well, I just couldn't think of how, I mean, what it would be like if you left."

He paused. "I believed you would be king, and everything would turn out."

"I see."

"So when Tomas told me you were leaving, I decided to follow you."

Nicolas rubbed his mouth. "You know you took quite a risk? Do you know what they do with stowaways if they are caught?"

Leif jumped to his feet. One finger curled out from his fist, and he jabbed it at Nicolas. "I will throw myself overboard before I let them send me back! I swear it on my mother's grave!"

Nicolas spread open palms in front of his chest. "No one will send you back. I promise." Leif dropped his fist and his shoulders relaxed. "But had you given any thought to where you will live? Or how?"

Leif jammed his fists into his trousers, suddenly shy. He nodded.

"Can you tell me, son?" Nicolas prodded.

"I expect I could stay in London. I am not afraid to work. I know horses pretty well. Unless, maybe..." His voice trailed off and he faced the deck planks.

"Leif?"

He drew a deep breath, held it, and then loosed his dream in an avalanche.

"Unless-I-could-go-with-you-all-the-way-to-Missouri-in-America-and-work-for-you-there." Face down, he ventured a look at Nicolas from under his brows.

Nicolas leaned back and folded his arms across his chest. He narrowed his eyes and considered what to do next.

"Have you any money to make your way in London?" he asked, curious.

Leif nodded and lifted one pant leg. Tied to his calf was a jeweled dagger. Nicolas sucked a surprised breath. Even in the moonlight, it glinted with inner fire.

"Might I have a closer look?"

Leif hesitated, and then untied the weapon. He handed it to Nicolas with caution. "It's sharp."

Nicolas turned it over in his hand. He recognized it. "Where did you get this?"

"I found it behind a sideboard in the Great Hall. Early in the morning on the day you left. We left." Leif grimaced. "Are you going to keep it?"

"I am for now. But you will get it back."

"When?" Leif looked as though he was going to throw up.

"When you need it." Nicolas wrapped the blade in his handkerchief.

"When we get to London?"

"What will you do with it there?" Nicolas stood and tucked the dagger by his dirk.

"Pry the jewels out and sell them." Leif's eyes were on Nicolas's waistband. "Or sell the whole thing."

Nicolas laid his hand on Leif's shoulder. "I don't believe that will be necessary."

Leif lifted his chin and looked into Nicolas's eyes with such longing and desperation, that Nicolas had to swallow hard before he could speak. "When you work for me in Missouri, I will see you housed, fed and decently clothed."

For a space, Leif just stared at him. "Sir?"

"But you will have to learn English."

Leif nodded, stunned.

"And I expect you to go to school. You can do your chores in the early mornings and late afternoons. And your schoolwork after dinner." The corner of Nicolas's mouth curved. "Will you accept my terms?"

Leif straightened and stuck out a shaking, knobby hand. "Um, yes. Sir. I do."

Nicolas took it and shook it. "Then we are agreed."

"Th-thank you, Sir."

"So, where have you been sleeping?"

"Down in the bottom of the ship. By your statues."

"Really?" Nicolas looked at him with interest. "Is it quiet down there?"

"Like a tomb." Leif shuddered. "A tomb with rats."

Nicolas laughed. "Then I believe our cabins will not be too uncomfortable for you. Have you anything down there now?"

Leif nodded. "My saddlebag."

"Go on down and get it, then come to my cabin. I shall explain to Lady Hansen that we are now a party of five." Nicolas waved his dismissal.

"Yes, Sir. Thank you, Sir." Leif backed away. "I'll be right there, Sir." Then he turned and ran full tilt across the deck, disappearing down the steps of the ladder.

Chapter Thirty One

May 7, 1821
Shipboard
Christiania to London

*I*t was Dagmar's dagger.

"I don't expect 'she' will have need of it." Sydney handed the knife back to Nicolas, who rewrapped it in the handkerchief.

"And Espen is gone, not to return." He tucked it in the bottom of Sydney's trunk.

"What do you believe it to be worth?"

Nicolas rested fists on his hips. "Enough to buy a bit of land. Or start a business. I'll hold onto it until Leif becomes of age, then he can decide. At the least, he shan't be penniless."

"And he will receive some recompense for what he has been put through." Sydney regarded Nicolas, head cocked, "Are you taking him on as an employee? Or as family?"

Nicolas thought a moment. "Family. But as a cousin, not a son. He will never supplant Stefan. Or Kirstie, for that matter."

"You are related to his father, are you not?" Sydney pointed out.

"If his father was truly Sebastian Fredericksen, he was my mother's first cousin."

Sydney tapped her chin and continued her regard. "So will you call him Leif Fredericksen? Or Leif Sebastiansen?"

Nicolas's brow dipped. "I cannot say. Perhaps I should let him choose, eh?"

"There lies the one advantage to being a bastard." Sydney chuckled.

Nicolas twisted to look at the small clock on the desk. "I wonder what's taking him so long. He should be here by this time."

He took the two steps necessary to cross the small cabin and reached for the door handle. It pushed from outside as he pulled it open, and Leif tumbled in. He righted himself and grinned up at Nicolas through a split lip and swelling eye.

"*Trist jeg er sen!*" Sorry I am late.

Sydney gasped. Nicolas lifted Leif's chin with a knuckle. "*Hva skjedde til du?*" What happened to you?

Leif shrugged off the saddlebag and dropped his rolled blanket in the floor. "*En av «rottene» tok friheter.*" One of the 'rats' took liberties.

The corner of Nicolas's mouth twitched. "*Og hvilken staten er denne «rotta» i nå?*" And what state is this 'rat' in now?

"*Han pissed seg og passerte ut.*" He pissed himself and passed out.

"With your help, I imagine," Nicolas muttered.

Leif nodded. His grin didn't fade.

Nicolas sighed. "I best go talk to the captain. I shall need to pay your passage, in any case. Wash up here, then. Lady Hansen will see you safe in the next cabin, with Stefan and Kirstie. Is the floor all right for tonight?"

"I am used to it."

"*Du trenger enda et teppe?*" Sydney asked. Do you need another blanket?

"No, ma'am," Leif answered in English, and grinned.

May 8, 1821

The light in the small window was the color of polished pewter. Indigo-bottomed clouds with silver crests hung low in the sky. Dawn struggled to make headway, as the ship rocked forward in the same quest. Nicolas opened the window. A spray of salt air moistened his cheeks.

"Looks to be a rough day ahead," he grumbled.

A series of shouts from the children's cabin catapulted him from the bed. He flung his door open and collided with Stefan in the corridor.

"LEIF IS HERE! He's in my room!" he squealed, hopping and pointing.

Nicolas smacked his palm against his chest and leaned on the wall as relief buckled his knees. "Yes, son, I know," he gasped and wiped sweat from his brow. "You gave me quite a start, do you realize that?"

"How did he *get* here?" Stefan shouted, his father's near-apoplexy unnoticed. Another cabin door cracked open and a vulgar *shhhh!* emanated before it slammed shut.

Nicolas pushed Stefan back into his cabin and followed, closing the door. Leif bounced a tearful Kirstie, the little girl frightened by her rude awakening. She reached for her father as soon as she saw him. Nicolas took her from Leif and she wrapped her chubby arms around his neck and tried to walk up his chest. He succeeded in settling her, then sat on the small desk.

Stefan rocked next to Leif and poked him repeatedly. Leif laughed and fended off the good-natured attack. Stefan giggled with unrestrained joy.

"It seems, son, that Leif was so distraught at losing his friend, that he snuck onto the ship before it sailed," Nicolas spoke Norse for Leif's benefit.

"You did?" Stefan's eyes widened.

"He did. And that was against the law, was it not?" Nicolas addressed Leif. Leif nodded and blushed.

Stefan panicked. "Is he going to jail?" he asked in Norse.

"No," Nicolas hastened to assure his son. "I have paid his passage to London. And after that..." He paused to enjoy the coming announcement, frowning to throw Stefan off. "After that, I will pay his passage right back."

"Back?" Stefan's shoulder drooped. Leif's mouth began to twitch.

"Yes, back. Back to Missouri."

"But, *Pappa!* Why can't he—what?" Stefan's mouth hung open.

"Back to Missouri. Leif is coming to work for me."

Stefan spun to face his friend. "Are you going to live with me?"
"Yes."

"Forever?" It was such a wondrous thought, Stefan needed to make sure.

Leif shrugged. "Maybe."

"He needs to learn English, Stefan. Can you help him with that?" Nicolas laid his hand heavily on his son's shoulder. He shook it a little to make sure he had Stefan's attention. "And he will go to school with you when he is not working."

"*Ja.* Yes. You. Learn. English," he pointed and spoke slowly to Leif.

"Yes. Learn. English." He grinned and messed up Stefan's hair.

May 10, 1821
London

Nicolas stood on the dock and oversaw the unloading of their things. He pointed to the largest trunks. "They can be stored here until we sail next. Put the smaller ones over there." A cab waited, the driver ready to load the luggage. Then came the statues.

Nicolas motioned to the head longshoreman. "A word, sir?"

The bowlegged crew chief waddled his portly frame toward Nicolas. "Aye?"

Nicolas draped his arm over the shorter man's shoulder and turned him away from the crew. He glanced backward for effect. "There is a delicate issue with these particular items."

"Oh?" the veteran grumbled. "Such as?"

"Well." Nicolas lowered his voice. "These carvings have been in my family for eight hundred years. Long before God-fearing men came to the outer corners of Scandinavia, you see."

"Aye. So?"

"So... they carry a tiny, little—*curse*—if you will."

The man jerked back. "What sort o' curse?"

Nicolas waved his hand dismissively and glanced at the man's private area. "It's nothing really. I just wouldn't want any of your men to find their members, um, diminished."

"Diminished?" The longshoreman clapped his hands over his crotch. "And how might tha' happen, exactly?"

Nicolas glanced at the crew behind them, drawn by the words

'curse' and their chief's protective stance. "It seems Thor was a bit of a vindictive god. He didn't care for men messing with things he considered his."

"Are them statues his?" The chief's eyes darted to the offending carvings.

"They were," Nicolas clarified. "He made them a gift."

"Whose are they now?" One of the longshoremen's voices floated above the din of the dock. Nicolas turned, his eyes pinned every man who faced him.

"Mine," he growled.

Someone scoffed, "Ye don't go believin' that line o' hooey, do ye?" A few men shuffled their feet, eyes darting to discern who stood on which side of the curse story. And then they sized up the huge Norwegian.

Nicolas's long hair was loose in the wind and he had not shaved in a week. His hunting dirk was at his side, clearly in view. He clenched his jaw, knowing the scar would become visible. He pulled to his full height, expanded his chest and clenched his fists. The chief took another step back.

Nicolas cocked one eyebrow. "You are free to challenge the curse, if you so choose."

The men stared at him, unmoving.

He pointed at their trousers. "But I will not be held responsible, should your pricks shrink to the size of your pinkies. Mark my words!" He held his little finger high over his head.

The chief cleared his throat. "I am not s'sure we're willin' to hold these blasted things. How long did ye say?"

Nicolas turned slowly to face him. "One week. But, I understand your reluctance, sir. It is a considerable risk." He paused and slid his hand into his greatcoat pocket. "So I shall pay you double the regular rate."

The longshoreman brightened at that. Nicolas held out the coins and the man reached to claim them.

"There is one week's storage in advance. If, when I return, the statues are unmolested, and your men intact, then I shall pay you the same amount again. Are we agreed?"

"Well, I s'pose we can bide. One week only?" He hefted the coins and counted them with his fingers.

"If my family and I can book passage within that time, as I

expect, yes."

He narrowed his eyes up at Nicolas. "And if not?"

"You will be paid double again. And," he glanced at the man who spoke the challenge with an Irish lilt, "I will even pay for a priest to pray for your protection, so long at the statues are left absolutely alone."

"Yes, sir! Rest assured, your property will be well cared for, it will." The chief slapped him on the back. "Hop to it, ye worthless scrubs!" he bellowed.

"Thank you, sir." Nicolas dipped his chin. "You are clearly a gentleman of honor. It is a pleasure doing business with you."

೮ഠ൮౩

Sydney and her three charges waited in the comfort of a teahouse three blocks from the dock. Sipping sweet tea and munching scones, they watched hordes of busy Londoners rush through the streets.

"*Det er mye folk her,*" Leif's eyes followed them.

"There are lots of people here," Stefan said in English.

"Dere are loats of pipple here?" Leif repeated. Stefan nodded.

Nicolas joined them, pulling up a chair and motioning to the waiter. He circled a pointed finger over the refreshments, and the waiter nodded.

"Is everything taken care of?" Sydney pushed the last scone toward him.

Nicolas ran a knuckle under his nose, smiling. "It is. I will tell you about it in the cab."

Leif pointed out the window. "Dere are loats of pipple here!"

Nicolas looked at him, eyebrows arched in surprise. "Yes there are."

When they finished, Nicolas gave the cabbie instructions, then climbed in with his expanded family.

At the open window, Stefan's hair blew around his face. "Where are we going, *Pappa*?"

"I thought we might take a drive through the city. We will go past the Tower and end up at Buckingham Palace."

Leif's eyes bounced from lips to lips as he struggled to follow the conversation. Kirstie pointed at him, twisting to look at her mother.

"Leif," Sydney answered. "Can you say Leif?"

"Lay!" she grinned at him. "Lay!" He smiled back. That, he understood.

At the palace, Nicolas herded everyone out of the cab. He asked the cabbie to unload the trunks.

"Right 'ere?" the man frowned.

"Yes. We are being met." Nicolas paid the confused cabbie and sent him on his way. Sydney withheld comment until the man drove off.

"What are you doing, Nicolas?" she asked, standing in front of Buckingham Palace with an adolescent, a boy and a toddler, and three traveling trunks. Nicolas waved down another cab.

"I want to confuse any followers who may have decided I should not have left Christiania as I did." Leif's head swiveled at the city name.

"Christiania?" he asked. *"Du tenker på å dra tilbake?"*

"No," Nicolas shook his head and spoke slowly, "I am not thinking of going back."

"Note t'inking of going bach," Leif repeated and heaved a relieved sigh.

They rode the second cab until they were about five miles from the docks. Nicolas pounded the roof and the cabbie stopped in front of an inn. Nicolas went inside and reappeared a moment later, shaking his head. He spoke to the driver, and then climbed back inside. They rode for another half mile, and stopped in front of a hotel. Nicolas climbed out again, and this time emerged smiling.

"We shall stay here," he stated. The cabbie unloaded the trunks and carried them inside.

While Sydney began the task of settling everyone in, Nicolas eyed Leif's too-large clothing. He realized suddenly the boy had not changed his trousers since Nicolas had found him out.

"Have you any other clothing?" he asked Leif in Norse. Leif bit his lips and shook his head. "Well, we shall have to remedy that. Stefan!"

He turned away from the window. "Yes, *Pappa*?"

"Come along. We're going to buy Leif some respectable attire. And teach him some more English, in the process."

Nicolas slipped his arm around Sydney's waist. He glanced toward the open door of their bedchamber. A large bed dominated the room. "I will enjoy your company this evening, wife, and make up for my absence this afternoon."

"I look forward to it." Her smile was slow and soft.

෨෨ඏ

Nicolas sat at the tailor's shop and watched in disbelief as Leif undressed. Nicolas knew the boy was skinny, but he did not realize how skinny. His abdomen was a concave space between sharp hipbones. His chest sunk under his collar bones and his ribs were countable. He also sported a variety of scars on his back and buttocks.

Nicolas pulled his attention aside and instructed the tailor, "Smallclothes first." The man nodded and pulled out some pre-made short pants and a sleeveless shirt. Leif stepped behind a curtain and changed into them.

"Do they fit?" Nicolas called out in Norse.

"*Ja.* Um, yes."

"Good. Come back out, son." Leif stepped around the curtain. The tailor stepped forward and began to take measurements while he made suggestions. Leif tried not to squirm or laugh, but Stefan had no such compunction. He giggled freely. It was not helpful. Nicolas shot him a sobering look.

"He'll need four breeches and six shirts at the least." The tailor looked at Leif over his spectacles. "How old are you?"

"He is thirteen," Nicolas answered.

The tailor's eyes shifted. "Is he a dummy?"

"He doesn't speak English. Yet. He's from... Sweden."

Stefan frowned but Nicolas shook his head.

The tailor continued his task. "Ah. Well. At his age, he probably should have a waistcoat or two, and frock coat." He looked to Nicolas for confirmation. "When do you need them?"

"In five days. We will sail in six days for France." Nicolas frowned at Stefan to be quiet.

Stefan snapped his mouth shut and swallowed his objection. Nicolas glanced at Leif, relieved that the adolescent did not understand him.

The tailor stroked his chin. "I can do it. At the end of the business day, in five days?"

Nicolas paid the tailor half his fee while Leif got dressed. "Have you anything we might take with us today?"

"*Pappa?*" Stefan whispered.

"Yes, the smallclothes. And I have two white linen shirts that will fit him." The tailor set the items on his counter and began to wrap the apparel.

"*Pappa?*" Stefan pulled on his sleeve.

"*Ingen vi ikke drar etter Frankrike.*" No, we are not going to France.

"Oh."

The tailor glanced from father to son and cleared his throat. Leif emerged from the curtain, dressed once again in the grooms' hand-me-downs. The tailor tsked. Nicolas accepted the package and handed it to Leif.

Once on the street, Stefan looked up at his father. "Why did you say Leif is from Sweden and we are going to France?"

Nicolas debated whether to tell the truth. He ruffled his son's hair. "Not everyone needs to know our business, eh?"

Chapter *Thirty Two*

May 15, 1821
London

$\mathcal{N}$icolas burst into the hotel room waving a newspaper. Sydney and Leif looked up from their English lesson.

"They did it!" He looked incredulous. "They actually did it!"

"Did what?" Sydney pulled the paper from Nicolas's hand. It was folded to the third page. The headline read: *Norway's Storting Abolishes Nobility*. She read the article out loud.

"By an easy margin the *Storting*, Norway's parliament, voted on May the 4th to abolish all future titles of nobility. Those holding titles may retain them until their death, at which time the titles will not be passed on to their heirs."

Sydney looked up at Nicolas. "Did you expect this?"

"I did. They were quite taken with the American idea of equality."

Sydney returned to the article. "A plan to remove the Swedish king, and restore the throne of Norway to a nobleman of Norse descent, was quashed by the vote and is no longer under consideration."

Nicolas sank into a chair. "I left just in time."

Sydney read silently, then turned the page. "Look at this!" she exclaimed. "They did select a flag!"

Stefan dropped his book and jumped off the window seat. "Let me see!" Sydney laid the paper on the table and four heads peered at the drawing.

"Stefan, can you bring your pastels?" Nicolas asked. Stefan was back in a moment. Nicolas read the description of colors and Sydney colored the newspaper. The final choice was a blue sideways cross outlined in white on a red background.

"That is almost like your drawing, boys!" Nicolas exclaimed. Stefan punched Leif's arm, and Leif mussed Stefan's hair, grinning.

Nicolas handed Stefan the pastels to put away. "Is the lesson done? We need to pick up Leif's clothes." Sydney nodded to Leif, encouraging him to speak.

"I am learn English. My name is Leif. I work for Nicolas Hansen." His smile split his face. Nicolas smiled back and realized with a start that they had not discussed his surname.

"Very good, Leif."

"Thank you, sir."

"Are you ready to come with me?" he tried.

Leif frowned, concentrating, "I come with you. Sir." His eyebrows lifted in question.

"Yes! Good. Let's go," Nicolas motioned toward the door. "To get your clothes. *Fao din klær.*"

"Oh! Yes, sir." Leif crossed the room and Nicolas followed him into the hall.

As they walked the quiet London side street, Nicolas broached the surname subject. He spoke in Norse to assure himself that Leif understood.

"Have you ever been called anything besides Leif?" he began.

"What do you mean?" The young teenager matched his stride with Nicolas's. Nicolas took smaller steps so the boy didn't hurt himself.

"Have you a surname that I am not aware of?"

Leif shook his head. "When Sebastian Fredericksen married my mother, I was to be Leif Sebastiansen. But he died before he got around to it." Leif shrugged. "I guess he was a real busy man."

"Hm," Nicolas hummed his empathy. "If you could choose today, what surname would you choose?"

"Can I?" Leif stopped walking. His pubescent voice hopped octaves in excitement. "Choose, I mean?"

Nicolas swung around to face him. "I believe so."

Leif's brows dipped. He chewed the inside of one cheek. He looked up at Nicolas, his head tilted to the side. "What is your whole name?"

"Nicolas Reidar Hansen."

"Where did you get Reidar?"

"It was my father's name."

Leif rested his hands on his hips, confused. "Why aren't you Nicolas Reidarsen?"

"Ah! Because in America, we don't do that. The father's surname became the whole family's surname. My mother and father were both born in America, and followed the new tradition."

"Oh," Leif sighed and chewed the opposite cheek. "So I can be Leif Sebastian, like you are Nicolas Reidar?"

"The names do fit well together," Nicolas spoke slowly. "But you still need a surname."

Leif's face turned bright red. "I thought—" He tangled his fingers.

"Thought what?"

"That I could be, I mean, if I can choose anything? Like you said, Sir? I really can?"

Nicolas nodded. "Yes. Within reason. What is on your mind?"

Leif whispered, "Hansen."

Nicolas leaned back. "Hansen? You want to be Leif Sebastian Hansen?"

Leif nodded, staring at the ground. Nicolas had to strain to hear him. "More than anything, Sir."

Nicolas's eyes stung and he swallowed a very large lump that threatened to choke him. He rested a huge hand on the boy's doorknob of a shoulder. "Then it shall be so. From this day forward, you shall be known as Leif Sebastian Hansen."

One brown eye appeared under a flop of ash-blond hair. "Truly?"

"Truly. You are, after all, my relation. My mother and your father were first cousins, were they not? When I introduce you in America as my cousin, no one will question the name!" Nicolas grinned.

Leif threw his arms around Nicolas and pressed his face against his chest. Nicolas felt his shirt moisten as he patted the boy's back.

"Thank you, Sir." His muffled voice hopped octaves again. "I swear you will never regret this. I will bring honor to the Hansen name, Sir, or die trying!"

"Well, let's hope it doesn't come to that!" Nicolas laughed and unwrapped the boy. "Let's begin that process by seeing you dressed respectably, eh?"

Leif nodded and fell into step with Nicolas once again. And he never stopped smiling.

> June 17, 1821
> Shipboard
> London to Baltimore

Four weeks passed and the ship strove forward at a steady pace for most of that time. For the second day, however, she stood still, her sails limp.

Sydney blotted her neck with a damp cloth while Stefan and Leif took turns reading out loud. They sat on deck, in the shade of an otherwise unoccupied sail. Nicolas carried Kirstie on his shoulders and wandered the deck in fruitless search of a breeze. Sydney sighed and looked at the hazy horizon. It was impossible to tell where the silvery blue water ended and the pale blue sky began. She had the sensation of being trapped inside a glass globe, waiting until a curious hand shook them from their lethargy.

Sydney turned back to her pupils and realized they had, at some point, stopped reading. They faced her, bodies drooping.

"Can we be done, Mamma?" Stefan pleaded.

Sydney's wry smile was enough of an answer. The boys closed their books.

"Put them away in your cabins," she admonished. "We shall try again after supper."

She watched them amble off, struck by how different they were. Stefan was tall and solid, like his six-four, two hundred and fifty-pound father. Five years older, Leif was slight, though he was finally putting on some weight, and only half-a-foot taller. Sydney wondered if he would grow more, now that he was getting regular meals.

"What are you thinking about?" Nicolas sat next to her and set Kirstie on the deck. "You seem as far away as the wind."

"Those boys." She pointed with her chin at their disappearing backs. "They are so different."

"That they are." Nicolas played pat-a-cake with Kirstie. "How is their schooling coming?"

"Stefan is Stefan. Bright but lazy. I expect it's good that he needs to help Leif, because it forces him to know the lessons."

"And Leif?"

"Leif is doing well with his English. His writing is illegible thus far. But the boy is brilliant in arithmetic."

"Really?" Nicolas looked at her then. His navy blue eyes were cool pools. Sydney wished she could swim in them.

"He memorized his facts in less than a week, and understands and solves every problem I can conceive."

"Would you like me to take over that portion of his tutoring?" Nicolas offered. "I did study engineering, you might recall."

"Would you? That would be very helpful." Sydney rested her head against Nicolas's shoulder. "How much longer will we be stalled, do you think?"

"It's impossible to know."

Kirstie dropped to her bottom on the deck and yawned, rubbing her eyes.

Sydney lifted her daughter, who dropped her head on Sydney's shoulder and stuck her thumb in her mouth. Sydney patted Kirstie's back. "I'll go put her down for her nap."

Once Kirstie was settled, Sydney returned to the deck. She found a likely spot and sat down to read. Nicolas stretched out and rested his head in her lap. She combed her fingers absently through his hair and smiled when he began to snore.

Was that a breeze? Sydney lifted her chin and sniffed. There was a difference in the air. She noticed the horizon had solidified.

Nicolas wiggled his head, and his chest expanded with a huge sigh. He snored again.

Sydney brushed a dancing strand of hair behind her ear; that was a breeze! She heard the crack of canvas and looked up. The sail bulged, drooped, then bulged again. She felt the ship shift under her, like a tethered horse eager to run.

"Nicolas?" she shook his shoulder.

"Hmm?"

"I think we have some wind."

The water looked strange. Around them it was pale silk, but a dark, scudded shadow approached, though the sky was cloudless.

Nicolas sat up and ran his hands through his hair. "What?"

"Wind! Feel it?" Sydney stood. Her shirt flattened against her chest. She threw her arms wide as the shadow reached them.

The sails snapped to attention and the ship rocked forward. Crewman began shouting and scaling the masts. Sails raised, lowered and swung to new angles as the ship nosed south of the afternoon sun. The ship strained against the freshened waves, slapping them away and jumping over them.

Leif rounded the corner. "Sir! Ma'am! We move!" He did a little jig. Stefan followed. Laughing, he imitated Leif's dance. Nicolas pulled to his feet and joined them. Sydney clapped her hands as the three males wiggled and kicked in a spontaneous celebration.

"It shouldn't be long now!" Nicolas shouted. "America, here we come!"

Chapter Thirty Three

June 24, 1821
Baltimore

*T*he first thing Nicolas did when they reached Baltimore was send a messenger to Gunnar stating they had returned from Norway, and would be in Philadelphia three days hence.

The second thing he did, was ask Sydney to pick a statue.

She cast a jaundiced eye at the carved pieces, now garishly re-painted.

"Truthfully, I have no preference. They both are hideous."

"Can we have the dragon?" Stefan hopped on one foot. "Please, *Pappa?*"

"And give Gunnar the mermaid?" Nicolas looked at Sydney for confirmation.

"And ask his forgiveness afterwards?" Sydney chuckled and shook her head. "If Stefan wants the dragon, then the dragon it is!"

Stefan punched Leif and grinned.

"You keep sea dragon from longship?" Leif asked, eyes hopeful.

"Yes!" Stefan giggled. "We can fight it and practice with our swords!" He mimed several thrusts.

Leif's eyes twinkled. "Dragon win."

Stefan froze and his jaw dropped. "What'd you say?"

"I say 'dragon win'!" Leif curled against Stefan's raining fists, belly laughs punctuating the ineffectual blows.

"Boys!" Nicolas barked. "Lend a hand, eh?"

June 27, 1821
Philadelphia

Gunnar was outside the house, pacing in the shade of the portico when Nicolas turned into the long drive. He waved both arms and trotted toward them. Nicolas stopped the wagon and jumped down, and embraced his brother in one smooth move. The men pounded each other's backs, laughing. Leif's eyes widened when he saw Gunnar, even taller than Nicolas.

"Marriage suits you." Nicolas smacked Gunnar's belly with the back of his hand. "You are growing yet."

Gunnar blushed, and sideswiped Nick's head.

"More than you know," he teased. "I have news."

"As have I!" Nicolas rested his fists on his hips; his smile could not get bigger.

Sydney joined the men. "I believe I have guessed your news, Gunnar." She nodded toward the house.

Brigid stood in the doorway, one hand on the jamb and one on the small of her back. She was hugely pregnant.

Nicolas smacked Gunnar again.

"You are to be a father!" he bellowed. "I cannot believe it!"

"Believe it!" Gunnar laughed. "And the babe is overdue."

"Sydney is a midwife, now." Nicolas's pride was evident. "She gained that skill in Christiania!"

"I believe that I am safe in saying, that Brigid would be pleased to make use of your skills this very day." Gunnar grinned at his wife.

She smiled and waved. Gunnar waved back.

Stefan climbed down from the wagon, but Leif hung back, suddenly shy in the boisterous company of these big men.

Gunnar shook his nephew's shoulder.

"Surely this cannot be Stefan! Why I believe you have grown a foot since I saw you last!"

Stefan looked down, then squinted up at his uncle. "I didn't grow any more feet. Uncle Gunnar, you're funny!"

Gunnar's explosion of mirth was deafening.

"And who might this be?" He nodded toward Leif.

"This," Nicolas turned and motioned for Leif to join them, "is our cousin, Leif Sebastian. He has come from Christiania to work on my estate."

Leif came to stand by Nicolas.

"And," Nicolas continued, "I have given him use of the name Hansen to ease his transition."

Gunnar held out his hand. "Hello, cousin."

"Hello." Leif shook it. "Mister Hansen."

"Call me Gunnar, seeing as how we are related, and you a man of the world. How old are you?"

"I am thirteen."

"Nearly grown!" Gunnar nodded. "Welcome to America."

"Thank you." Leif bobbed his head.

"Leif has been learning English on our journey." Nicolas patted his shoulder. "And he is doing very well."

"Well, come in and have something to eat! How long will you bide?" Gunnar led them up the steps to his very patient and swollen bride.

"Only a day or two." Nicolas looked to Sydney. "We are eager to get home."

"I can understand that, but perhaps we can persuade you to extend your visit a bit." Gunnar slid his hand around Brigid's non-existent waist.

"Well, I do have much to tell you." Nicolas glanced at the wagon. "And I brought you a gift."

"Did you then?" Gunnar's eyes twinkled. "We shall have to see about that presently!"

"Not until they have had a chance to wash up and have supper!" Brigid stated. "Show everyone to their rooms and I will check on the meal."

"Aye-aye, Cap'n!" Gunnar saluted his wife, and then kissed her soundly. She turned to the hall and swayed in the direction of the kitchen.

Sydney winked at Gunnar. "She looks as though the babe is about to fall out."

"Your mouth to God's ears!" he grunted, lifting a trunk.

၈၁၃

Nicolas pushed back from the dinner table and scratched his belly, "That was the best roasted beef that I have had in—well, I cannot recall!"

"Thank you." Brigid blushed.

He clapped his palms together. "Now, then. Would you care to finally see what we brought you from Norway?"

The four adults went out to the portico where the wagon still stood. Nicolas pulled back a tarp, revealing the antique mermaid, lying on her side.

"Oh, Nicolas. You should not have. *Really*." Brigid looked puzzled. "What is it, exactly?"

"It is a figurehead from a Viking longship. It's hundreds of years old!" Nicolas beamed.

"Is it, then?" Gunnar walked around the wagon. "And you lugged it all the way from Norway? Just for us?"

"That I did!"

Gunnar paused and stared at his brother. "Why?"

"Why?"

"Yes, why. It's the ugliest thing I've ever seen!" Gunnar began to snicker.

"And heavy, too!" Nicolas's mouth curved at the corners. "Enough to break a man!"

Gunnar shook his head. "Whatever possessed you?"

"I asked him that myself, many times!" Sydney interjected.

"Did you receive an answer?" Brigid grinned in spite of herself.

"No!"

Nicolas looked like a cat that had feasted on a flock of canaries. "Have you an axe, Gunn?"

"An axe? Yes, of course."

"Fetch it."

"Nicolas, don't tell me that after all this time and effort, you plan to destroy this thing?" Sydney cried, incredulous.

Nicolas gave nothing away. He waited in silence, rocking on his heels, until Gunnar returned with the requested implement.

Nicolas hefted the axe. "Now, all of you, be prepared to rescind every one of your uncharitable thoughts!"

He swung it at the base of the statue. He jerked it out of the cleft and swung it again. On the third swing, the base gave way, caving inward. He flipped the axe over and used the other end of the blade to pry the bottom off the carving.

The glint of gold caught everyone's eye.

"No!" Sydney stared at Nicolas. "There isn't—*is* there?"

Nicolas cackled as he reached inside and pulled out a handful of gold coins. "Brother, have I got a story to tell you!"

Gunnar turned pale and sat down, hard, on the steps to the house. "Where did you—how much is—oh, Lord!"

Sydney pushed his head down between his knees. "Are you all right?"

Gunnar lifted his head and narrowed his eyes at Nicolas. "How much?"

"Just shy of twenty-six thousand dollars."

Gunnar grew white as rice. "I believe I may lose my supper."

Sydney grabbed Nicolas's arm, realization dawning. "And the dragon?"

"The same." Nicolas could not contain his glee. "I sold the family lands in Rollag."

Gunnar stared at his older sibling. "Why did you do that?"

"You spoke the truth, Gunn. I did nothing to deserve this. It was the luck of my birth." Nicolas shook his brother's shoulder. "It's yours as much as mine."

Sydney wasn't sure if she was more angry or thrilled. "But why didn't you tell *me?*"

Nicolas waved his hands. "I'll tell you all everything from the beginning. But first, let's put this in a safer place, shall we?"

The gold was retrieved from the statue, packed into two heavy satchels and stowed under Gunnar's bed. Once the children were settled in for the night, Nicolas began his tale.

"When we arrived in Christiania, I went to see my land. It was as it always had been: beautiful, but underutilized. So I instructed the land agent to re-draw the plots and doubled the number of leases."

"Thereby doubling the value!" Gunnar slapped his thigh.

Nicolas bounced a nod. "Once all the leases were signed, I visited with the brother of an old friend. Matias Ivarsen."

"Nelson's *brother?*" Sydney asked, surprised.

"And who are these Nelson brothers?" Brigid shifted her

position on the settle.

"Lawyers. Nelson lives in St. Louis and has worked for our family for more years than I know. He referred me to Matias, who is the spit of his brother, by the by."

"Why did you need a lawyer?" Brigid shifted again.

"To sell the land, of course! All ten thousand acres."

Brigid's eyes rounded. "Ten thousand? Ten thousand!" She looked at Gunnar. "Did you know that?"

"That's why you bought the statues? You planned this from the start!" Sydney huffed.

Nicolas grinned at everyone like a delirious hyena. "Well, I saw to that possibility fairly early on."

"But—what about being king?" Gunnar asked. "Was that not the purpose in the summons?"

"It was. And I strongly considered it." Nicolas took Sydney's hand in his. He raised it to his lips and kissed it. "This amazing woman and I played a game of duplicity throughout. At times, I feared it might be too dangerous, and I would lose her."

Sydney's gaze dropped to her lap.

"I assumed, and correctly," he continued, "that my valet and Sydney's maid were asked to spy on us."

"Maid!" Gunnar smacked his forehead, "Where is that quiet girl you had with you? I forgot her name."

Sydney smiled then. "Maribeth. She married Nicolas's valet and remains in Norway."

"The one who was a spy?" Brigid's brows puckered.

"He reversed his loyalties, after a bit." Nicolas chuckled.

Sydney cocked one brow. "It was good that we trusted each other, because at times it seemed as though our marriage was doomed. Especially when we didn't see Nicolas board the ship to leave with us."

"How did you become a midwife?" Gunnar draped his arm around Brigid.

Sydney laughed and told them about the Lady Linnet and her unorthodox demands. "But I loved it so much, that I apprenticed with the midwife."

"Much to Anders' displeasure, I assure you!" Nicolas added. "Royal family members do not spend their time delivering the peasants' brats, you see."

"So I had to sneak out to keep apprenticing…"

"And I had to pretend I didn't know…"

"And Nicolas had to be seen going to Sigrid's room late at night…"

"Because Anders strongly wanted me to be king, but he wanted his daughter Sigrid to replace Sydney as my queen…"

"So badly that her husband was poisoned…"

Gunnar and Brigid's jaws fell in perfect unison.

"Did he die?" Brigid squeaked.

"He did," Nicolas answered quietly.

Sydney continued, "We had to make it look as though our marriage was failing. Even so, they poisoned Nicolas as well. "

Two pair of eyes shifted to Nicolas in shock.

"As a warning," he qualified. "They didn't kill *me*."

Gunnar snorted. "Obviously. You are too stubborn to die."

Nicolas flashed a wry smile and shook his head.

"What did you do?" Brigid squeaked.

Sydney pulled a steadying breath. "In front of witnesses, Nicolas ordered me to leave Norway with only Kirstie, and leave Stefan behind."

"I had them convinced that I would take the throne," he explained. "And as I said, I did strongly consider it. Until I saw they were willing to do murder, that is. I feared for Sydney, then."

"When it came time for me to leave, Tomas brought Stefan to the dock, but Nicolas was nowhere to be seen. I must admit, I was more than a mite worried!" Sydney turned to her husband.

"I had to come in disguise of course. And I saw the statues loaded onto the ship myself before I boarded," he explained.

"Ah, yes. The statues." Sydney punched Nicolas playfully. "I never understood why they were so blasted important!"

Nicolas kissed her loudly. "And now, you do."

Chapter Thirty Four

June 28, 1821
Philadelphia

Sydney opened her eyes and didn't know where she was. Jolted—just as when she woke up alone and in Nicolas's house over two years ago—she sat straight up, eyes wide.

"All is fine, *min presang*." Nicolas rested his hand on her hip. "We are in Philadelphia. At Gunnar's." He had seen her awaken this way before. "Are you well?"

Sydney's body eased as she woke fully and she nodded, rubbing her eyes. "What time is it?" she croaked.

"The clock chimed three just now. That may have been what woke you."

Sydney stretched, stiff from curling on the settle. "It has been more than an hour. Have you heard aught?"

The bedroom door slammed open. "Sydney! Sydney, are you there?" Gunnar's deep voice charged through the quiet house.

Nicolas heaved himself off the settle. "She'll be right up."

"What's happened?" Sydney asked as she climbed the stairs.

"She's all wet of a sudden." Gunnar rocked from foot to foot.

Sydney reached him and put her hand on his arm. "This is what I hoped would happen."

Brigid breathed through the contraction. "That hurt more than the others," she said when it passed.

Sydney helped her get more comfortable. "Maybe now we'll see that baby of yours!"

Hours later, Sydney pulled the boy from his mother's exhausted body. He blinked, drew a breath and screamed his indignation. Once mother and son were presentable, Nicolas came to see his nephew and brought the children.

Stefan leaned in for a close look. Leif held back, unsure of his place in the gathering. Nicolas waved him over. "Come see what all the fuss is about."

"He is so little," Leif whispered.

Nicolas faced Gunnar. "And does he have a name?"

Brigid smiled. "I believe that 'Rory' will be a fit."

"Roar-y? Because he roars?" Stefan squinted in confusion.

Brigid laughed. "No! It's Irish. It means red king and his hair is red."

Gunnar nodded his agreement. "Rory Magnus Hansen."

The clock chimed eight in benediction.

"It is time to leave them alone." Sydney yawned. "And time for me to get some sleep."

Once behind closed doors, Sydney untied her skirt and stepped out of it, and pulled her blouse over her head. She quickly washed her face and arms with the cold water in the ewer. Nicolas peeled back the sheets and she melted into the mattress.

"Well done, *min presang*," he whispered.

"Hm," she answered, eyes closed.

"I love you," he kissed her.

"Hmm hm."

She did not hear him leave the room.

July 12, 1821
Shipboard
Baltimore to New Orleans

Nicolas stepped onto the deck. The first mate stood amidships and held a spyglass to one eye.

"Do you see anything Mister Browning?" he called to the sailor high in the crow's nest.

"Not yet, sir!"

Four small cannons lined the railing, aimed in the direction of the offending vessel. Crewmen stood ready at each. As the tall ship approached, no one spoke.

"Be ready with a warning shot," the first mate ordered, spyglass still pressed in place.

"Aye, sir." One of the crews seemed to know that was their job. A man lifted a smooth black ball to the mouth of the canon. The ship sailed toward them.

"Canon ready, sir."

"On my count."

"Yes, sir."

"Ready... Aim..."

"Sir! She's hoistin' colors!" Mister Browning's urgent voice floated down from his precarious perch.

"What are they?" The mate dropped his spyglass, squinted, then refocused.

"British, sir."

"My arse," the mate muttered. Nicolas glanced at him, but he was unmoved. "What is their trajectory?"

Mister Browning was quiet for a pace. "It appears they will pass behind us, sir."

The mate lowered his glass. Every man on deck and in the rigging watched in silence as the ship passed about three hundred yards portside.

"She's a slaver, sir."

Mister Browning's grim proclamation was soon unnecessary. As the ship crossed behind them, the sounds of misery rode to them on the breeze. Wails of mourning, expressed by chants in unfamiliar tongues, wafted to them in a cacophony of hopeless supplication.

And then came the smell.

Nicolas had smelled death. Animals left too long un-scavenged by man or beast. Bodies in the homes of sick or lonely settlers that no one knew had passed. The refuse heaps outside Newgate prison in London, where the unclaimed dead were too much work to bury.

But none of that matched this. The sweat of over-crowded and unwashed bodies. The stench of shit and piss. The rot of human carcasses.

Nicolas felt his gorge rise. He turned away and crossed the deck to the opposite rail. Three crewmen heaved their lunches into the water below.

"Stand down, men!" the first mate ordered. He blew the 'all clear' on his tiny whistle, then spun on his heel. "I shall tell the captain to press on as quickly as possible."

Sydney held a handkerchief to her nose as she waited in the corridor. "What is that horrid smell, Nicolas?"

"It will diminish, soon." He entered their cabin and splashed cold water on his face. "We'll press on at full sail."

"Thank the Lord." Sydney followed and sat on the bed. "What was it?"

"A slave ship."

Sydney stared at him in stunned silence. She slowly shook her head. "The smell…"

"Sweat, shit, piss and dead bodies." He stuffed his handkerchief back into his pocket.

"I had heard stories," Sydney whispered.

Nicolas looked into her sorrowful gray-green eyes. "I doubt they were exaggerated."

Sydney shook her head.

"I wish Rickard could smell that." Nicolas ran his hands through his hair. "Maybe then…" his voice trailed off.

"It wouldn't change anything."

She sounded as hopeless as the slaves.

July 27, 1821
Riverboat
New Orleans to St. Louis

Leif stood by the huge paddle and squinted in disbelief. "What moves this?"

"Steam. From hot water."

He looked at Nicolas. "How water get hot?"

Nicolas pointed below deck. "Coal. Black rocks? They are burned down there. The fire heats the water."

"No wind?"

"No wind." Nicolas waved his hand above them. "No sails!"

Leif shook his head and raised one eyebrow. "I will see."

After three days in New Orleans, Nicolas was eager to get going. He mailed a letter to John at his estate, and one to Rickard as well, telling both men that they hoped to dock in St. Louis by Thursday, August 16th. He would send a messenger as soon as they docked, though he did wonder whether the boat or the letters would arrive first.

"Are you eager to be home?" Sydney joined them, Kirstie on her hip. The girl reached for her *pappa.*

"I am." Nicolas lifted his daughter and sat her on his arm. Her curly dark-blond hair blew into her face and she shook her head. "I reckon Addie will be astounded by how much this one has grown, eh, *liten datter?*" He bounced Kirstie and she giggled.

"I've grown, too!" Stefan straightened and stretched his neck. "See?"

"Yes, you have!" Sydney placed the edge of her hand against her chest. "When we left Cheltenham you came to here on me. Now you come to here!" She moved her hand up three inches.

"Really?" Stefan turned to Leif. "I am going to be taller than you!"

Leif laughed and curled his arms up over his shoulders. "I am stronger, Stefan. You know I am!"

Stefan poised to leap at the older boy when a shout of warning caused them all to step away from the paddle housing. The boat shivered and belched. She shivered again. Her creaking voice, determined and strained, manifested her efforts to move the wheel. Slowly, it began to turn. The boat eased forward in the water, shivering less as the wheel rotated faster.

Leif's face was split by a wide grin.

"Boat is moving! No wind!" He laughed and slapped his thigh. "Sir, I not believe you, but you say the truth!" He laughed again.

August 16, 1821
St. Louis

They stood at the railing, watching St. Louis take shape out of the morning mist rising from the Mississippi River. The sun held back modestly, clothing herself in wisps of gray. Sydney could feel Nicolas vibrating with excitement.

"*Å min Gud!*" He shook his arms. "It will be good to sleep in my own bed again!"

"I wonder if Sessa or Fyrste will remember me?" Sydney

sighed.

"Wolf will know me," Stefan stated with authority, referring to his pet lamb.

"And the cat will know me!" Leif added. Three pair of eyes shifted to him. "After I feed it once." They all laughed at his joke and he added, "Then there is a cat, yes?"

"Yes!" Stefan giggled. "A white one. And she eats a lot!"

"I don't believe it is possible for this boat to move any slower. If indeed, it is moving at all!" Nicolas leaned over the edge. A telltale ripple flowed outward from the bow.

"What time are we expected to dock?" Sydney asked.

"Ten o'clock."

"And what time is it now?"

"We finished breakfast at nine." Nicolas squinted ahead. "I do believe I see the pier!"

Everyone leaned over to look.

"Could that be Rickard?" Sydney shaded her eyes against the silver glare from the cloudy sky.

A smile spread over Nicolas's face. "It sure is! *I Guds navn!* It sure is! RICK!"

Rickard had been facing the boat and at Nicolas's shout, waved both hands.

"*Gud forbanner det* but I have missed him!" Nicolas laughed.

Leif looked at Nicolas, his confusion clear. "*Hvorfor du taler Norse?*"

Nicolas dropped his gaze to the boy. "Oh, it's an old habit of mine. I swear in Norse because people here don't understand."

"Oh." Leif grinned. "*Forbannet fin ide.*" Damned fine idea.

As soon as the plank was lowered, Nicolas bounded down its length and into Rickard's embrace. The men slapped each other's backs and laughed like schoolboys, so great was their joy at being reunited.

"I see you didn't miss any meals on your journey!" Rickard grabbed a handful of Nicolas's side.

"And you?" Nicolas stepped back, "What is different about you? I cannot name it."

Rickard blushed. "I'm married."

"Married!" Nicolas bellowed. "To whom?"

Sydney stepped next to Nicolas. "I expect to the lovely Bronnie

Price."

"Sydney!" Rickard swept her up and spun her in a riotous circle. He set her down and smacked a loud kiss on her lips. "You look as beautiful as ever! But where is my niece?"

"Right there." She pointed to Kirstie in Stefan's arms.

"Good Lord! That cannot be the infant I last saw!" He reached for the girl who warily allowed him to lift her from her brother's arms. "Hello, little beauty. I am your *Onkel* Rick. Can you say *Onkel* Rick?"

Kirstie looked at Rickard solemnly, then at her smiling parents. She reached for her *pappa*. Nicolas took his daughter.

"So." Rickard rested his fists on his hips and looked around. "Where is Stefan? Did you leave him in Norway?"

"Here, *Onkel* Rick!" Stefan hopped in front of Rickard.

"Young man, will you kindly step aside? I am looking for my nephew." Rickard looked over Stefan's head.

"*Onkel* Rick! It's me!" Stefan waved his hands in Rickard's face.

"You cannot be Stefan. Stefan is a little boy with auburn hair like yours, and blue eyes like yours, but... Wait a minute!" Rickard looked shocked. "Stefan?"

"Yes!" Stefan's giggle rippled the air. "You are funny *Onkel* Rick!"

Rickard grabbed Stefan up in a bear hug. He ruffled Stefan's hair.

"And this," Nicolas waved Leif forward, "is Leif Hansen, my cousin. He has come to work for me."

Leif stuck out his hand and Rickard grasped it, his smile the picture of decorum. "Welcome to Missouri. I hope you find it to your liking."

"Yes. Thank you." Leif bobbed his head.

"How old are you?"

"Thirteen. And half. Almost."

Rickard's glance went to Nicolas, but Nicolas shook his head. before Rick spoke. "Orphan."

Sydney looked around the pier. "Where is Bronnie?"

"She is at the hotel." Rickard waved over his shoulder.

"I cannot wait to see her! When were you married?"

"September, last." Rickard pinched back a smile.

Sydney's intuition shifted gears. "Have you other news?"

"Our first child is due in about two months or so."

"You old conniver!" Nicolas pounded his friend's back. "When were you planning to tell us?"

"As soon as you arrived." Rickard laughed. "And so I have!"

"Sydney's a midwife now! She delivered Gunnar's son in June!"

Rickard was momentarily stunned by the all information contained in those statements. "Gunnar married?"

"While we were with him last year, on our way to Norway!"

"And you happened to be there when his child was born this year?"

Nicolas spread his hands. "We have impeccable timing, so it seems."

Rickard turned to Sydney. "Why did you become a midwife?"

"It's a long story to be savored, along with many other stories, over a fried catfish dinner!" she suggested.

Rickard picked up on it. "Excellent idea! We shall retrieve Bronnie at the hotel."

"We will stay there tonight as well, until John can come collect us." Nicolas frowned at Rickard. "Have you been waiting for us long in St. Louis?"

"Waiting? No! We have been celebrating here."

"Celebrating? What is the occasion?"

Rickard looked at Nicolas as though he was feeble-minded. "Have you not heard?"

"Heard what?"

Rickard savored his upper hand. "You truly do not know?"

"It seems we do not, Rickard. What has occurred?" Sydney tugged his sleeve.

"Well, then." Rickard straightened and extended his hands. "Allow me to be the first to welcome you all..."

Nicolas and Sydney exchanged anticipatory glances.

"...to the newly created..."

Rickard paused.

"...twenty-fourth state of these United States of America!"

Jaws dropped.

"Missouri is a *state?* As of when?"

"Friday last; August the tenth!"

"Six days ago?" Nicolas slapped his forehead. "We just missed it?"

"That you did!" Rickard jerked his thumb toward a large carriage. "Would you care for me to drive you to the hotel? The livery can bring your trunks."

Nicolas held up a finger. "First I have a very important piece to safely stow."

Rickard arched a brow. "That sounds interesting."

Nicolas talked to the longshoreman as the dragon emerged from the bottom of the paddleboat, leashed on a winch. A wagon master adjusted the position of his wagon and the dragon was laid to rest in its bed.

"That?" Rickard's incredulous look made Sydney laugh.

"It's part of the story," she explained and patted Rickard's back.

He looked at her like he doubted Nick's sanity. "I cannot wait."

༄ལༀ

"I cannot eat another bite," Nicolas laid his napkin over his fourth plate of catfish.

"That is a great relief." Rickard's eyes twinkled. "I shall alert the newspapers that the Mississippi shall not be stripped of her catfish population after all!"

"Not for lack of effort, mind you!" Nicolas laughed and belched. "Best catfish in all of Missouri!"

Bronnie touched Sydney's hand. "Now that we know all about your deceptions, and your escape, can you tell me about being a midwife? Have you been present at a number of births?"

"Yes, and I have delivered a number of babies as well. I would say maybe seventy-five…"

"Really?" Bronnie's eyes widened. Her hands pressed her restless belly.

"Really?" Nicolas and Rickard echoed.

Sydney looked at Nicolas, exasperated. "It was nine months, so at the least, thirty-six weeks! Two babies a week would put me at seventy two. Some weeks were less, but some weeks were much busier than that!"

"I had no idea." Nicolas sounded impressed. He signaled for another pitcher of beer, and then addressed Rickard. "Tell me about statehood. Are we slave or free?"

"Slave." Rickard's voice remained level. "Maine came in as a free state under the Missouri Compromise of 1820. That keeps the number of slave and non-slave states equal at twelve each."

"We have a compromise named after us? Who wrote it?" Sydney refilled everyone's glasses.

"A man by the name of Henry Clay."

"He's from Lexington! In Kentucky!" Sydney bit her lower lip. "I believe that I might have met him once."

"So that is the way of it then?" Nicolas lifted his glass. "One free state for every slave state added?" He drained the cup, then plunked it on the table. "Did I tell you, Rick, about the slave ship we passed?"

"Nicolas." Sydney's soft voice carried its warning effortlessly. "Not now, please."

Nicolas's navy eyes darkened, but he said no more.

"Where have they put the capitol?" Sydney turned to Rickard.

He dragged his somber gaze from Nicolas to her. "Governor McNair made St. Charles the temporary capitol. The first legislators met there on June 4th of this year."

"That's not far from St. Louis, is it?"

Nicolas shook his head as if to shake off his mood. "About twelve miles to the northwest. Give or take. But what do you mean by temporary?"

"There is to be a new city built—Jefferson City—right in the center of the state. But nothing is there now." With a wry chuckle Rickard added, "Nothing but land, which has just increased a hundredfold in value!"

Chapter Thirty Five

August 17, 1821

*T*he first thing Nicolas saw at his estate was new wood siding on the top half of the stable. The new roof was not yet completed. Jeremy McCain, the young man Nicolas hired more than a year ago, was hammering shingles over the lathes.

"Our luck with twisters must have run out," Nicolas said. "I wonder if aught else was damaged?"

John stopped the carriage in front of the house and gave a loud whistle. The front door disappeared and Addie's welcoming bulk filled the frame. She hustled across the porch, her arms hitching as she carefully took the steps one at a time.

"Oh, my Lord! There you are! I have never seen such a sight in all my days, as welcome as you all!" She dabbed her eyes with her ever-present white apron. "Come on down and let me give you a hug!" She stretched her arms out.

Stefan was the first to reach her. "Addie! Look! I grew!" he exclaimed, his last two words muffled by her ample bosom.

"So you did! I almost didn't recognize you! I swear, you'll be taller than me by tomorrow morning!"

Stefan laughed and turned to Leif. "Did you hear that?"

"I hear," Leif growled. He stood by the carriage.

Nicolas lifted Kirstie, awakening her, and stepped out of the carriage. He held out a hand for Sydney.

"Is that my baby girl?" Addie gasped. "She's gotten so big!" She wiped another tear.

Sydney flew into the older woman's arms. "Lord knows, I have missed you, Addie!"

When Sydney took Kirstie, Nicolas picked up his erstwhile nanny and spun her around before setting her back on her feet. Addie grabbed him for support.

"Lord, have mercy!" Addie gasped and shaded her eyes. "Who is this young man?"

"This is Leif Sebastian Hansen, my young cousin. He has come to America to work for me. He is particularly good with horses."

Addie stuck out her hand and Leif stepped forward to shake it. "Welcome to the Hansen manor, Mister Leif."

"Thank you." Leif dipped his chin.

All heads turned at the sound of the livery pulling into the yard. Addie stared at the statue reclining in the bed of that wagon.

She turned to Nicolas, her jaw dropped in surprise. "I know I called you 'Sir Nicky' most of your life, but I never expected you to slay a real dragon! What in God's good name have you got there?"

"It's an antique oak carving from a Viking longship." Nicolas waved the wagon closer. "We shall set it here!" he called to the driver.

Sydney faced the house. Anne stood in the doorway, gripping the doorjamb, her lower lip firmly in her teeth. Before she could call out to the girl, Jeremy trotted around the corner.

"Mister Hansen! Welcome home, sir!" He offered Nicolas his hand. Nicolas shook it heartily.

Jeremy turned to Sydney, his smile blinding. "And you, Madam!"

"Thank you, Jeremy." Sydney waved to Anne. "Come out and join us!" Anne left the sanctuary of the doorway and edged toward them.

"Come on, men! Help me slide this off the wagon and set it up!" Nicolas instructed. Between John, Jeremy, Nicolas and the livery driver, the dragon was placed upright in front of the house. Nicolas wiped his brow on his sleeve and tipped the driver handsomely.

Stefan hopped around it. "I can practice my sword on it, can't I

Pappa?"

"Sword?" Addie's eyes rounded. "Certainly you don't mean—"

"He does," Sydney confirmed.

Stefan parried and lunged with an imaginary weapon.

Nicolas clapped his hands and addressed the small crowd. "We are so glad to be home! Let us get our things unloaded, and we shall, all of us, have dinner together. We have so much to tell you!"

Everyone picked up something and headed into the house, but Sydney held back. She turned to look at her favorite tree, the red maple. Two small, white, stone crosses were barely visible over the tall grass of the front yard. She sighed, warmed by the sight of them.

She climbed the porch steps and entered the manor, closed her eyes, and inhaled. The essences of leather and tobacco reached her from Nicolas's study on her left. She turned to the drawing room on her right, and breathed in the scents of the wool carpet, beeswax polish, and the idle fireplace.

She trailed her fingers along the wall of the hallway to the kitchen, and peeked into the dining room. She smelled silver polish and pepper. Warm aromas of baking bread and roasting meat wafted from the kitchen.

It smelled like home.

Sydney doubled back to the staircase. As she climbed the stairs, she paused in front of the portraits. She clearly saw Anders in his father Frederick's face. She touched the smile, suddenly knowing that these people were very real.

With a deeply contented sigh, Sydney continued up the stairs. She entered her bedroom; the trunks waited there for her. They could wait a bit longer.

But a stack of letters from her mother sat—neatly tied with ribbon—on her dressing table. Sydney grabbed them up and put them to her nose. *Lavender.* Sailing up the Mississippi prevented a return visit to her parents' home, so these would have to do.

A pang of regret threatened to prompt tears. She sniffed, swallowed, and tucked the letters under her arm, loathe to let go of them. Instead, she opened the door to the adjoining nursery.

"Bless Addie's heart!" she breathed. The room was transformed from a baby's room to a toddler's room, with plenty of pink.

"This is your room, Kirstie! Do you like it?" Sydney tickled her daughter, who rewarded her with a delighted giggle.

She walked through her daughter's brightened room and back into the hall. Nicolas was coming out of the opposite room, the room she first woke up in over two years ago.

"I shall put Leif in here." He looked back over his shoulder. He seemed distracted.

"Nicolas?"

He turned back to face her.

"Is aught amiss?"

He raked his fingers through his hair. "Might I ask you a question, *min presang?*"

"Of course."

He rested his hands on his hips and shook his head. His voice was so low she had to lean forward to hear him. "Were John and Addie this old when we left?"

Sydney rested her hand on his arm. "Yes."

"Why did I not see it?" he wondered.

"You saw them everyday. I would wager they looked the same to you as they did when you were a boy."

Nicolas nodded, and a wry smile curved his lips. "I shall talk to John and Jeremy. Perhaps we will keep the young ones on and allow John and Addie to retire from their duties."

"That might be a good idea," Sydney agreed.

"I shall have to add on to the house, of course. I don't believe they would be willing to go far."

"No, I do not imagine they would."

ഇറ

Sydney entered the kitchen, tying an apron over her skirt. She was taken back to see Addie sitting at the table, snapping peas, and Anne bustling around preparing dinner. In *Addie's* kitchen?

"How might I help?" Sydney asked Addie.

It was Anne who answered. "Could you stir this gravy so it doesn't burn?"

"Of course."

As she stirred the sauce, Sydney watched the camaraderie between Addie and Anne. Anne deferred to Addie's suggestions, but it seemed to be out of politeness. Anne was clearly in charge.

The dining room was just large enough to hold the expanded Hansen household. Once all the food was set out, Nicolas said the blessing.

"Thank you, Father, for bringing us all together here this day. Your bounty is plentiful, and we are exceedingly grateful."

Sydney crossed herself. A chorus of 'amens' preceded the dismantling of that very bounty.

"I miss Maribeth," Addie wiped yet another tear as she contemplated her plate. "Are you certain she is happy?"

"She was positively glowing on her wedding day, Addie. She wanted me to tell you every detail!" Sydney assured her. "She was a beautiful bride."

"She was that!" Nicolas nodded. "I never realized she had it in her."

"Lots of people got married," Stefan added.

"Oh?" Addie smiled at him. "Who else got married then?"

"Maribeth... *Onkel* Rick..." Stefan ticked off his fingers. "...and *Onkel* Gunnar."

"What? What!" Addie shrieked. "Nicolas Reidar Hansen! Why didn't you say anything? Gunnar, married? How do you know? Did you see him? Where is he? Is he still in the navy?"

Nicolas's grin widened. "I intended to tell you when I had your undivided attention. We saw him in Philadelphia. He left the navy and moved into the estate house there. He married a local girl."

"Oh! Isn't that just the most wonderful news? Do you suppose they might come out to Missouri soon? It's hard to travel with children. Maybe they will come before they have a baby?" Addie's earnest hopefulness rang in her voice.

"Too late." Stefan spooned mashed potatoes into his mouth.

"What's that?" Addie's head swiveled so quickly Sydney thought it might twist off. "What's too late?"

Sydney laid a hand on Addie's arm. "I delivered their son, Rory Magnus Hansen, when we saw them in June."

"Oh! Oh, my!" Addie fanned herself with her napkin.

John nodded. "A son. Good for Gunnar." And he returned to his roasted chicken.

৪০৫৪

After dinner, Nicolas retrieved his brandy flask.

"John, will you walk with me to the stable?" He grabbed two glasses.

John followed him outside. They strolled toward the stable under a darkening purple sky. Specks of light brightened as black swallowed the last traces of sunset. In the stable Nicolas lit a lamp and spoke to his stallion, Fyrste.

"*Du hus meg, gammel mann?*" Do you remember me, old man? "*Jeg har vært borte en lang tid.*" I have been away a long time.

Fyrste's head bobbed at Nicolas's voice and he sniffed the proffered knuckles. His tail began to twitch and he shook his mane in greeting, prancing in the stall.

"Well, look at that! I believe he is happy to see me!" Nicolas opened the stall and stepped in. He ran his hands over the quivering stallion. "He's in good condition."

John nodded. "Jeremy rode him every other day. Him and Anne kept the horses in shape."

"Really?" Nicolas was pleasantly surprised by that news. "What about Sessa?"

"She's broke real good now. Jeremy's got her takin' jumps like she was a hunter." There was a note of pride in John's voice.

Nicolas patted Fyrste. "I am glad to hear it, John." He pointed at the new beams overhead, "Were we hit by a twister finally?"

John shook his head, his mouth a grim line. "Uh, no. We had some troubles."

"Troubles? What particular sort of troubles?"

"Some of those in the Territory did not take kindly to havin' a half-breed woman married to a white man. They let us know."

Nicolas exited the stall and shut the door. "How?"

John pointed at the stable walls. Nicolas lifted the lantern. He could now see the blackened stones of the bottom half.

"They set it aflame, did they? *Skitt!*" He spat on the ground. "Is aught else amiss?"

"Jeremy and Anne, they only went to church the one Sunday because of it."

Nicolas wagged his head and spat again. He handed John the lantern and climbed up to inspect the new construction. It was correctly designed and solidly built.

"Did Jeremy do this?" he called down to John.

"He did."

Nicolas nodded his satisfaction. He climbed back down and sat on a hay bale. John sat on another. Nicolas poured brandy into the two glasses and handed one to John, then took a healthy swallow of the amber fire.

"I have been thinking." Nicolas cleared his throat. "You and Addie have served the estate for a good long time. Longer than I have lived!"

John nodded and waited.

"I believe it's time for you two to retire and enjoy what you have earned." Nicolas looked hard at John. Under the drooped awnings of gray-fringed lids, his brown irises were ringed with clouds. Why didn't he see that before? "I hope I might keep Jeremy and Anne here in your stead."

John nodded again, and Nicolas waited.

Finally, "Yes."

"Yes?" Nicolas prompted.

"Them two. Good choice." John sipped his brandy. "Addie won't go far. You know that."

Nicolas snorted his agreement and offered John a refill. "I have been thinking about expanding the manor. Adding two rooms off the south wall along the kitchen." Nicolas capped the flask. "A bedroom, and a parlor with two doors; one that opens to the back hallway, and one that goes directly outside."

John's eyebrows lifted. "Oh?"

"That way, the two of you might have your privacy, should you desire it." Nicolas downed the last of his brandy. "What do you think?"

John smiled broadly for the first time since Nicolas returned to the estate. "I believe Addie will reckon she's died and gone to Heaven."

August 18, 1821

Nicolas waved Jeremy to a seat in his study and closed the door. He shifted his leather chair, and lowered himself into the creaking hide, facing the younger man.

"I had a talk with John last night. I asked him how you have fared here in the year."

"I expected that."

"I am pleased to report that he was favorable in his evaluation."

Jeremy blushed and his mouth twitched. "Thank you. That's good to hear."

"And has the work here suited you?"

"Very much."

"And your wife?" Nicolas prodded.

"She has been content as well."

Nicolas clapped his hands together. "Good! And have you made plans for your future?"

"Um, no. Not yet." His brows dipped.

"Might you consider staying on here?"

Jeremy shifted in his seat. "You heard about the troubles, sir. It was because of Anne. I expect you'll need to consider that before you make me an offer of employment."

Nicolas pushed up from his chair and grabbed the brandy flask from the drawer. He poured himself a glass and held the flask out to Jeremy in silent question. Jeremy shook his head.

"Was it just the one incident with the fire?" Nicolas stared at the pewter flask, his thumb rubbing the smooth metal.

"There were words now and again." Jeremy shrugged. "There always are."

Nicolas lifted his chin. "Do you and Anne wish to stay?"

Jeremy blinked. "I, uh, well we," he stammered. "That is… yes."

"Then consider it done." Nicolas dropped the heavy pewter flask into the drawer with a resounding *thunk*.

Jeremy stood to face Nicolas. "I don't wish to put your family in danger."

Nicolas rested his hand on Jeremy's shoulder and shook it gently. "Anyone who lives in my house, lives under my protection. I don't wish *your* family to be in danger."

"Are you certain of this?"

Nicolas allowed one corner of his mouth to lift. "I could have been the king of Norway, son! But I chose to return to this place. Rest assured I'll guard it, and *all* of its inhabitants, with my very life."

"Thank you, Mister Hansen."

"There is another matter I wish to discuss." Nicolas dropped back into his leather chair. He motioned for Jeremy to sit as well. "I have decided it's time for John and Addie to retire."

Jeremy nodded. "All right, sir."

"Anne will take over Addie's responsibilities and you will take over John's. Your salary will be doubled."

"Yes—what?" Jeremy cocked his head, disbelieving. "Did you say 'doubled'?"

"I did. And Anne will be paid as well, of course."

Jeremy sat back, stunned. "Room, board and a salary for each of us?"

Nicolas waved his hand. "It's what I did for the Spencers. It is only fitting that I do the same for you, is it not?"

"Yes, sir. I mean, if you say so." Jeremy reddened. "God bless you, Mister Hansen!"

Nicolas lifted the brandy glass in toast. "He has, Mr. McCain. He most certainly has!"

Chapter Thirty Six

September 5, 1821

*N*icolas rode into the yard as the day's last rays snuck through a bank of clouds, piercing the western sky. He slid out of the saddle and popped his head in the back door.

"Anne? I am returned!"

"Yes, Mister Hansen. Dinner will be ready in half an hour."

Addie shuffled to the door. "Will Rick be joining us tonight?" she called after Nicolas.

He stopped and turned around, Fyrste's reins in his hand. "Rick? Not that I know of. Why do you ask?"

Addie waved her hand. "Oh, it's not important." She returned to her seat at the kitchen table. Nicolas shrugged and continued to the stable.

"Did you leave your plans with the mason?" Sydney asked as Nicolas held her chair for dinner.

Nicolas walked around and sat across from her. "I did. He expects to begin in three weeks. He'll order the stone tomorrow." Nicolas picked a piece of meat from the platter and dropped it in his mouth. "Mm-mm! That's delicious!" He forked several slices onto his plate. "Did you meet the new teacher?"

"We did. The boys and I walked to the school."

"And how is she?" Nicolas paused in the spooning of potatoes.

"He. And he seems quite capable. His name is Michael O'Grady. He appears to be in his forties. His wife was there, helping to prepare the classroom. They have three grown daughters, none of whom are married, and all of whom are teachers in southern Illinois, which is where they hail from." Sydney lifted her wineglass in a toast. "Mr. O'Grady's wife, Winnie, is from St. Louis originally and that is what drew them back to this side of the Mississippi."

"You did not happen to discover his shoe size in the inquisition, did you?"

Sydney laughed. "No, but I did warn him that he is the fourth Cheltenham teacher in as many years. So he may have a bit of catching-up to do!"

Nicolas leaned back. "How did Leif take to him?"

"He seemed somewhat overwhelmed, but Mr. O'Grady sat him down in a desk, and showed him where his books and slate go. I believe he'll do fine."

"At the least, his English is much improved. And he seems to be gaining weight, finally."

Sydney forked her beans. "Is his work here satisfactory?"

"Yes. I have no complaints." Nicolas tore a chunk of bread to sop up his gravy.

Sydney glanced over her shoulder. She leaned toward Nicolas and lowered her voice. "Did you get Stefan's gift?"

Nicolas nodded. "I hid it in the stable. I'll bring it inside after he is in bed."

Sydney giggled.

Nicolas slapped his forehead. "That's it! I should have thought of it!"

"What?"

"Addie asked me if Rick was joining us tonight because tomorrow is Stefan's birthday!" Nicolas grinned at her. "She'll be mighty pleased with the end of *that* particular tradition, I'll wager."

September 27, 1821

A train of three wagons lumbered into the Hansen yard, laden with quarried limestone blocks. Nicolas had already dug out and leveled a trough for the foundation, so the mason and his two Negro slaves unloaded the stones and set them along the edge. It took them until dark to do so.

The men set up camp next to the paddock where their six Clydesdales grazed. They cooked over a fire and slept in the wagons. St. Louis was too far away to travel back and forth, and money spent for lodging in Cheltenham was "as foolish as tossin' it in a half-full privy!" the mason explained. "This'll do."

Nicolas hadn't paid much attention to the men that first day; he was busy finishing the cover over the safe-hole he built under the floor in the dining room. Covered by the polished floor planks and a wool Turkish carpet, no one would find it on their own. The gold from Norway was now tucked securely inside, though the dragon still stood guard over the front yard and took regular thrashings from Stefan and Leif's swords.

On the second morning, he met with the mason and offered him a cup of coffee. The man readily accepted. They sat on the back porch and confirmed the building plans while one of the slaves tied guide strings to posts at each end of the foundation. The other mixed the mortar.

The slave mixing the mortar, Nicolas noticed, always seemed to be swinging his back in Nicolas's direction. That was odd, but there wasn't any reason he could think of that it mattered. The man meant nothing to him, and as long as he did his job there was no problem.

The base of the wall and the first layer of stone were done by the end of the day. Nicolas inspected the job and complimented the mason.

"Thank ye, sir." He turned to the slaves. "Git that fire goin' now! I'm hungry enough to eat that chicken raw!"

"Have you enough food?" Nicolas waved toward the chicken coop.

"Yeah, I can't even eat the whole chicken myself!" the mason declared.

"What about them?"

"Who? Them darkies?"

"Um, yes."

"Aw, they get all the innards. Darkies love the innards!"

Nicolas thought he saw one of the men straighten and start to turn around. But he stilled and pulled a deep breath that lifted his broad shoulders. It occurred to Nicolas that the man might be hungry. Splitting the guts of one chicken between two hardworking men would make a puny meal. But he sensed that if he interfered, the mason might take his irritation out on the men.

And yet, Missouri was a still slave state. Nicolas had no right to meddle.

The next day Nicolas began to knock out the granite blocks for the doorway to the new rooms. He put Leif and Stefan in charge of hauling them out of the way when they returned from school that afternoon. Jeremy helped him to finish the edges before dark.

The sun lowered in the early autumn sky and the air chilled. Nicolas jumped down through the new doorway into the new room to take measurements for the floorboards they would cut the next day. Hurrying his task, he stepped backward and collided with one of the slaves.

"Oh! Sorry!" Nicolas turned to face him. Their eyes met.

A ripple of recognition passed through the other man's eyes before his lids lowered and he turned away. He climbed out of the stone enclosure and trotted off toward the wagons.

Nicolas watched him go, puzzled and unable to put his finger on why.

The third day was unseasonably warm for the last day of September. The walls were getting taller more quickly, now that they reached the level where doors and windows left open spaces. Jeremy framed the windows, and Nicolas, the doorways. The five men worked in near silence, sweating through the hot afternoon. One slave climbed a ladder to replenish the bucket of mortar when his grip, wet with sweat, slipped. The bucket tipped and dumped mortar onto the other Negro.

"*Le condamner de dieu vous, vous le noir stupide!*" he exploded. He pulled off his ruined shirt and threw it on the ground. Without looking back, he stomped to the pump and helped himself to water.

Nicolas froze, his heart pounding.

The man's back was a web of scars. Could it be? *Jack?*

Nicolas went back to his task, though he was too distracted to see what he was looking at. Jack and his wife—what was her name? Sarah.

Runaway slaves. He caught them stealing a chicken from his coop just over a year ago as the couple made their way north. Sydney shamed him by giving them her iron skillet and a quilt before he gave them two chickens.

So they had not made it to safety.

"*Skitt,*" Nicolas muttered and pretended to re-measure the door frame.

Sarah was pregnant. They had already walked an ungodly number of miles by the time they reached Cheltenham. What happened to her? And the child?

Nicolas turned to look at the other side of the door frame and stared past it to the Negro rinsing himself under the pump. Nicolas was sure it was him, now. The man had been educated and carried himself well. Yes, that was him.

Now what should he do?

September 30, 1821

Sydney lay across Nicolas, her back against his chest and his hands exploring her body. She got gooseflesh from his touch. He loved to do that to her.

"*Min presang*, you take my breath away," he sighed.

She hummed a wordless response. One hand reached behind her and stroked his scalp, giving him gooseflesh in return. "Can you close the window some?" she purred. "The breeze is a little chilly."

"Whatever you wish, wife," he whispered in her ear and proceeded to tickle it with the tip of his tongue.

With a chuckle, Sydney rolled off him. "You wear me out, husband!"

Nicolas sat on the edge of the mattress, his feet dropping firmly to the wood floor. From the bedroom window he could see the red glow of the campfire coals across the yard. He turned back to Sydney.

"Do you remember those runaway slaves?"

She lay on the bed, unmoving in the aftermath of her satisfaction. "The pregnant girl and the man with the whipped back? Of course. Why?"

Nicolas gazed out the window again. "Jack is here."

She sat up. "Jack?" She scrambled off the bed crossed to the window, though there wasn't anything discernable to see. "Is he with the mason?"

"Yes."

"Did you speak to him?"

Nicolas shook his head and shrugged. "For what purpose?"

"Don't you wonder what happened to them? To Sarah? And the baby?"

Nicolas's jaw flexed. He didn't respond.

Sydney's gaze shifted up to him. "Nicolas?"

"Of course I wonder!" he snapped. "I have not thought of aught else all evening."

Sydney crossed her arms and raised one dark and delicate brow. "All evening, is it?"

Nicolas had to laugh at that; his tension lightened some. "Well except for the one passionate interlude, that is."

Sydney walked back to the bed. "What will you do?"

Nicolas followed and leaned on the footboard. "Nothing, I suppose."

"Nothing?" she prodded.

He snorted. "Or try to talk to the man and see what information I may get."

"For what purpose?" Sydney whispered his words. "Merely to satisfy our curiosity?"

Nicolas pulled a deep breath and hissed it out slowly between his teeth.

"That I cannot say."

Chapter Thirty Seven

October 1, 1821

*N*icolas brought the mason a plate of fresh apple muffins and a cup of coffee.

"Mind if I offer these to your boys?" he asked. "Might encourage them to work harder."

"A whippin'll do that!" the mason scoffed, then waved in their general direction. "I don't care. Just don't get 'em used to it."

Nicolas sauntered over to where the Negroes sat. He held out the plate. The one man took two, but Jack only stared at the ground.

"Here, take this to the house," Nicolas ordered the first man. He grabbed the last two muffins and handed the man the empty plate. "Go on, now!" The man bobbed his head and hurried off.

Nicolas stood in front of Jack and pretended to look at the sky. "Where is Sarah?" he murmured.

Jack startled and looked up. Nicolas repeated the question still examining the few clouds on the horizon.

"St. Charles," he rasped.

"Where were you caught?"

"St. Louis." Jack cleared his throat and stood. He spoke in a louder voice, "No, sir, I don' think it's gonna rain. No sir."

The other slave stopped next to them. Nicolas handed the muffins to Jack and strode back to the house.

He wasn't able to find another chance to speak privately to Jack until the late afternoon. By that time, it clearly was going to rain. Lightning hissed and thunder shouted. Drops the size of cherries bounced off the dry ground. Nicolas helped the three men move their camp supplies into the stable.

"You might sleep up there tonight." He pointed at the hayloft. "And if the weather doesn't slow, please have dinner at the house."

"Thank ye, sir." The mason nodded. "I believe I will."

œ’ℂβ

Under cover of a trip to the privy, Nicolas ran to the stable. The mason hadn't thought to allow the Negroes to eat, so he made sure Jeremy took them a basket of food. He stepped inside and shook water from his hair. The two slaves sat on hay bales in front of the stalls, the basket of food between them. They gazed at him by the light of a single lamp.

"Are you finished?" He could not think of aught else to say.

"No," Jack answered. "No, we are not."

The other man turned to him. "Jack," he warned.

"Hush, Silas! I'll give the man his basket when I am good and ready!" Jack snapped.

Silas's eyes rounded. He ducked his head.

"What did you say to me?" Nicolas growled, taking the bait.

"I spoke English. Did you not understand me?"

"Insolent nigger! You!" He pointed at Silas. "You take that basket to the house. Don't come back until I come get you!" Nicolas rolled up his sleeves and clenched his fists. Silas was out the door so fast, he left a wake.

"I'll teach you to talk to your betters that way!" Nicolas shouted. He slammed his palm against the wall. Jack stood up and threw a bale of hay at the door. Then another.

The men stopped and listened. They only heard the rain.

"We haven't much time," Nicolas began. "Tell me what happened."

Jack paused, as if deciding how honest to be. "We got to St. Louis, but the man we were to meet never showed up. We were caught when we tried to buy food."

"You were sold?"

"Yes, to the mason. Ignorant jackass." Jack spat on the ground.

"Sarah?"

Jack turned away. "She was sold to a brothel."

"The child?"

Jack shrugged.

"Was it a live birth?"

Jack shrugged again. "I have not seen or spoken to her since that day."

"*Å min Gud.*"

"*Mon Dieu.*" Jack echoed.

The only sound in the stable was the rain beating the new roof. Fyrste nickered to his master. Nicolas crossed over and stroked the stallion's muzzle while he pondered what to do next.

"You better hit me." Jack pointed to his cheek. "It won't hurt so bad here."

Nicolas nodded. He reluctantly grasped Jack's chin with his left hand, and planted his right fist perfectly on the younger man's cheekbone. He shook out his hand to relieve the sting. "Sorry."

The Negro nodded while his fingers explored the swelling. "That will do. I'll pretend to have a cracked rib as well."

Nicolas offered his hand. Jack hesitated, then shook it with a warm, firm grip. Nicolas walked back to the house, glad the rain disguised the tears of anger and frustration he couldn't hold back.

October 3, 1821

The walls were nearly completed. The men would be leaving soon.

Nicolas stood in his bedroom and looked down at the addition beneath him. He toyed with the crown he had given Sydney on her birthday. Sunlight tipped into the window and played through the stones; captured lightning. The gold grew warm in his hand. He didn't hear her come in.

"What are you pondering so soberly, husband?" Sydney wrapped her arms around his waist and leaned against his back.

"My life," he began. "At the age of seventeen, I moved to Philadelphia and studied at a college there. At nineteen, I went to Norway as a prince. At twenty, I returned to America and attended university in Boston for two years. I was twenty-three when I returned to Cheltenham, twenty-four when I married, and at twenty-six I became a widower with a son."

He twirled the crown.

"For nearly six years, until you fell in my creek, I stopped living. Then within a year of our marriage, we were off to Christiania."

"Why are you considering your life's path now?"

"You might have been a queen," he whispered.

He felt her arms tighten around him. "But I did not desire to be."

Nicolas spun the crown in his hand, feeling the smoothness of the gold. "Do you believe that kings can change the world?"

"I know they can. They have."

"But do they ever do good? I mean, truly do good things?" Nicolas twisted and looked down at her. "Might they actually change the world and make it better?"

"I'm sure that's possible."

Nicolas turned back to the window. "Perhaps I should have been king after all."

Sydney let go of Nicolas and walked around in front of him. She leaned against the windowsill, arms crossed. "King Nicolas? What wilt thou change?"

He thought she was mocking him. But the intensity of her gray-green gaze held no mirth. He swallowed hard. The crossroad he had reached—while sipping brandy on his porch during the wee hours last night—was tearing him apart.

"Nick?"

"Jack." It was all he could manage.

Sydney gasped. "Will you?" All color drained from her face.

"I feel that I must. No matter how opposed I am, I still cannot, in all good conscience…" He let the statement trail off. He was too horrified to put it in words.

"Sarah, too." It was not a question. It was a condition.

He nodded. "If we can find her."

"Oh, Nicolas! Oh my Lord." Sydney sank to the floor.

He knelt beside her and pulled her to him.

"Can you change the world from Missouri?" Her voice was muffled against his chest.

"I must try. The gold does no good otherwise."

They held each other, the forgotten crown on the floor, still sparkling in the sun.

October 4, 1821

Nicolas replaced the Turkish carpet and crawled out from under the dining room table. "Rickard will never let me live this one down," he muttered. The gold coins clinked in his pocket as he fingered them. He squared his shoulders and strode out the back door.

The mason and the Negroes were assembling their tools, the job completed. The Clydesdales were harnessed to the wagons and their huge hooves churned up the grass. If he didn't act now, it would be too late.

"I want to purchase one of your men," Nicolas began.

The mason squinted up at him. "What men?"

Nicolas pointed to the Negroes. "Those men."

Silas appeared confused. Jack straightened and his eyes shot arrows at Nicolas.

The mason scratched his head and considered the pair of slaves."You want to buy one of my darkies? What am I s'posed to do then?"

"Buy another." Nicolas's tone was offhand. "That's of no concern to me."

The mason, still stunned, turned back to Nicolas. "Well, which one were you thinkin' of?"

"I don't know." Nicolas strolled around them, avoiding Jack's gaze. "Which one gives you the most trouble?"

Sensing a trick question, the mason shifted his pointed finger from Jack to Silas. "That one there."

"I see." Nicolas stood in front of Jack, considering him from several angles. Ripples moved through ebony cheeks as his jaw flexed. Nicolas saw his fingers twitch.

"This one seems a bit jumpy. How much did you pay for him?" Nicolas leaned to the side and focused on the mason.

"F-f—eighty-five."

"Eighty-five dollars?" Nicolas sounded incredulous. "Why so much?"

"He's young. And strong. But not too strong, you see." The

mason's forehead was sweating.

Nicolas looked at Silas. "And this one? How much?"

"He ain't for sale."

Nicolas spun on his heel. "No?"

"Uh, no. Only the other'n."

"Hm." Nicolas shrugged and walked a couple steps away as if he had changed his mind.

"Were you satisfied with my work?" The mason blurted and waved at the completed stone walls.

"Yes! Very much so!" Nicolas returned and extended his hand. "It was a pleasure doing business with you sir."

The mason shook it. "Thank ye, as well."

After an awkward pause, the mason turned back to the wagons. "Let's go, then!"

The mason, Jack and Silas climbed into the benches of the three wagons. With a baleful glance at Nicolas, the mason slapped the reins and clicked his Clydesdales into motion.

"I will give you one hundred dollars." Nicolas's deep voice carried over the creaks of wheels, hooves and leather.

The mason pulled back on the reins. "What?" He wanted to make sure he heard right.

"One hundred. Take it or leave it."

"Get off the wagon, Jack!" the mason shouted.

He jumped down and started pulling the reins forward to tie the team to another wagon. "You're stayin' here. This man owns you now."

Nicolas swallowed the bile creeping up his gullet. *This man owns you* were words that he never in his life thought would apply to him. He clamped his jaws together. There was no other way, in a slave state.

Skitt.

Jack climbed down slowly. He stood beside the wagon, stiff, eyes on the ground. Nicolas reached into his pocket and pulled out the gold coins. He dropped two into the mason's outstretched hand.

"Thank ye again, sir." The mason tipped his hat. Without even a glance at Jack, he climbed back onto the wagon. He slapped the reins again, whistled, and drove the team off the Hansen property. Silas followed with the tethered wagon rumbling behind him.

Neither Jack nor Nicolas moved until they could no longer see or hear the wagons. Nicolas turned to Jack. "I cannot free you, though that would be my choice. But you would only be caught again," he said. Resignation colored his tone.

Jack nodded, silent.

"I will do this for you…" Nicolas waited until Jack's eyes rose to meet his. "I will pay you a salary, as I do every one of my staff. Someday you can take that money and go wherever you wish."

"You will pay me?" Jack repeated. "A Negro?"

"I will."

Jack faced Nicolas and stood straight. He extended his hand. "You, sir, are a man of honor."

Nicolas shook his hand. "I try."

Sydney opened the front door. Nicolas beckoned to Jack to follow him and he climbed the porch steps. "I believe you remember my wife, Sydney?"

"Yes, ma'am. You were exceedingly generous as I recall." Jack bowed.

Sydney considered Nicolas. "Is your business completed, then?"

"This part is." He drew a deep breath and blew it out through rounded lips. Nicolas rested his hands on his hips, and shook his head, his own words repulsive to himself. "Now that I own the husband, I will search out and buy the wife."

Jack's jaw dropped. "You will?"

"And then?" Sydney prompted.

"And then," Nicolas lifted his eyes to hers, "I will change the world."

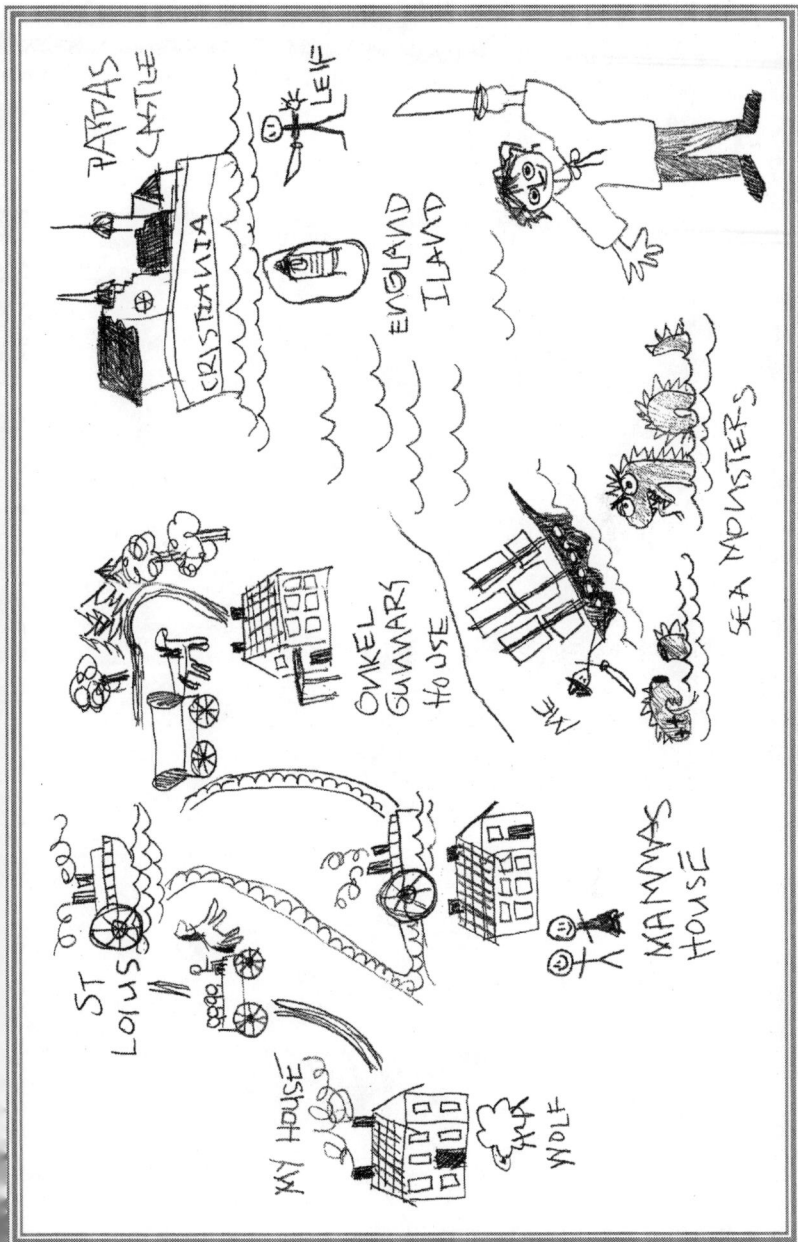

Following is an excerpt from:

A Matter of Principle

by Kris Tualla

Coming in January 2011
from Goodnight Publishing

*I*t doesn't look too bad, as whore-houses go."

Nicolas Hansen had a wide-brimmed leather hat jammed on his head to hide his blond hair. Nothing could be done about his size. At six-foot four, and over two hundred and fifty pounds, he was noticeable. "I'll go in, then. You know what to do."

Jaqriel nodded. In spite of the chill in the autumn air, nervous perspiration gave his dark skin the patina of polished walnut. He took Rusten's reins from Nicolas, his conspicuous gray stallion Fyrste stabled elsewhere for the duration, and sat on the edge of the wooden sidewalk. Jaqriel leaned against a lamp post; it would be a long chilly night.

Nicolas climbed the steps and knocked on the door. A woman dressed in violet satin, nearly obscured in an eye-stinging cloud of perfume, ushered him in.

"What might a fine, strapping specimen such as yourself be wanting this fine evening?" she cooed.

"I should like to enjoy a brandy by the fire, Madam. Perhaps you might put some of my choices on display?" He fingered the coins in his pocket so that they clinked together.

"Why, of course, sir! Do you have any particular tastes that I might satisfy?"

"Dark." He looked meaningfully at his hostess. "I prefer dark."

She smiled and pressed him into a chair. "I'll see whom I can find." Turning to a sideboard, she selected a cut-crystal goblet and poured a generous serving of brandy. He accepted the drink and asked about food.

"A slice of beef? A wedge of cheese? Something to sustain me throughout the evening?"

"Absolutely!" She disappeared through a swinging door.

Nicolas considered his surroundings. A brocade factory must have exploded in the room, covering every surface. But, at the least the room was clean.

The swinging door pushed open and a slender Negress, skin the color of caramel, carried a tray of food into the room. Nicolas pulled the brim of his hat down to the bridge of his nose and grunted his thanks. She set the tray on the low table in front of his chair. She didn't look at him.

The hostess breezed into the room. "Ah, good! You are sustained!" she trilled. "The girls will be down presently. Is there any other wish I may fulfill?" Her hand brushed across the back of Nicolas's neck. He held out his empty brandy glass. It was promptly refilled.

As he ate from the tray, Nicolas endured the parade of willing prostitutes. Tall, short, thin, plump, some more bold than others. He played along for a bit, as much as he could tolerate, then motioned the madam to his side.

"Yes, darling?" she breathed in his ear.

"The girl who brought the food."

"Her?" Penciled brows pulled together above purpled lids. "But she's a Negro."

"I believe I told you that I prefer dark, did I not?"

"Yes, but she's a serving girl. A scullery maid!" The woman's voice took on an important tone. "She's never been used in that way. She will most likely not be as—pliant—as my other girls." She waved her hand toward the women draped in various stages of dress over the colorful furniture. "Surely one of these girls will suit you?"

Nicolas pulled a gold coin from his pocket. "Shall I take my business elsewhere?"

"I, uh…"

He shrugged and moved to stand. She quickly linked her arm through his. "Might I show you to our best room? She will be up presently, I assure you!"

Nicolas dropped the coin into the woman's décolletage. "I shall stay the night. Send a bottle of brandy up with her."

Nicolas pulled the sheets back; they were clean and exuded lavender. Rosie was right, this was a decent sort of brothel. He marveled again at the society of whores, which allowed her to find this establishment on his behalf. Nicolas moved to the window. Off to the right he could see Jaqriel under the lamp, sitting at Rusten's feet.

Good.

A quick knock on the door preceded the shoving of the Negress into his presence. The door shut behind her before she could escape. Her quickly downcast eyes were red-rimmed and her breath came in gasps. The brandy bottle slid from her hand and hit the carpet with a muted thud.

"Don't cry, Sarah. Things are not as they seem," Nicolas assured her. A flicker of confusion rippled her brow. He pulled off the wide leather hat and combed his fingers through his long, thick hair. "Do you know me?"

Eyes the color of rust met his in a sullen, iron gaze.

"It was a year and a half ago, now. I found Jack in my hen house. My wife gave you a skillet and a quilt."

The Negress' eyes widened. "And a shirt." Sarah's soft voice was spiced with Cajun flavor.

Nicolas nodded. "I forgot about the shirt."

Sarah's eyes swept the room, then passed over Nicolas. She paid particular attention to the state of his breeches, making him feel distinctly disrobed. "Wh-why are you here?" she asked, stuttering her fear. "Will you use me, then?"

"No!" Nicolas pulled back. "No, nothing like that. I brought Jack. We've come for you."

Sarah straightened and took a step forward. "Jack is here?"

"He's outside with my horse." Nicolas waved toward the window.

Sarah walked unevenly across the room and looked outside. When she saw Jaqriel, she backed away from the window.

"No-o-o!" she wailed and collapsed to the floor. She wrapped her arms around her waist as loud sobs ricocheted through her. "No, no, no, no. I can't see him. He won't want to see me!"

Nicolas's jaw dropped. What now?

"Sarah, please don't cry." He waved his hands in awkward circles, not knowing how to comfort her.

"He will hate me, now!" Sarah's words were muffled against the elaborate carpet. "I can't see him!"

A sharp rap at the door startled them both. Nicolas backed away and pulled the door open. It was Madam Purple.

"Is aught amiss, sir?" She leaned to the side to see around his bulk. "I heard distressing sounds."

Nicolas glanced over his shoulder and was relieved to see Sarah sitting on her knees, under tenuous control for the moment. "Nothing's amiss, Madam, I assure you. I fear our game was louder than we intended." He flashed his most congenial smile.

"Game?" Madam Purple leaned farther and Nicolas obliged by opening the door wider. Sarah smiled tremulously.

"Yes, um, plantation overseer and the, uh, reluctant—dairy maid." Nicolas made it up as he spoke. "I'm sure you understand these sort of peculiarities?"

"Yes, well, in my business? Of course!" Her eyes undressed Nicolas, pausing long on his groin. This was the second time in five minutes. He resisted the urge to cup himself protectively.

Nicolas smiled again and bowed. "I promise to be quieter."

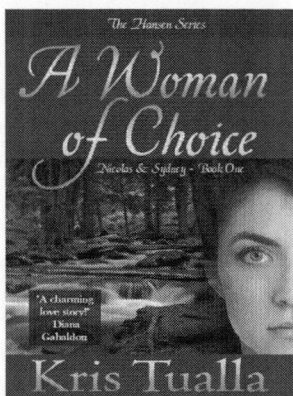

A Woman of Choice

The Hansen Series:
Nicolas & Sydney
Book One

Available now!

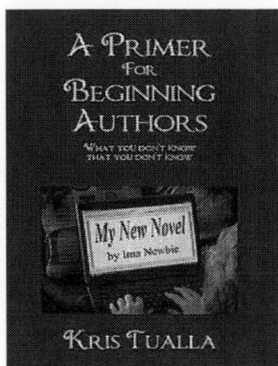

A Matter of Principle

The Hansen Series:
Nicolas & Sydney
Book Three

January 2011

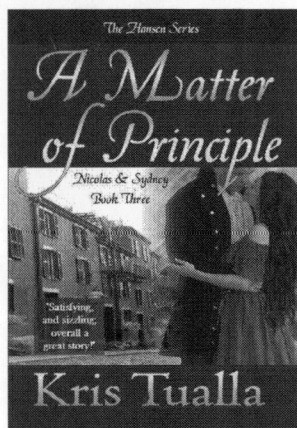

A Primer for Beginning Authors

What you don't know that you don't know.

Available now!

From Goodnight Publishing

Kris Tualla is pursuing her dream of becoming a multi-published author of historical fiction. She started in 2006 with nothing but a nugget of a character in mind and absolutely no idea where to go from there. She has created a dynasty - The Hansen Series - with six novels currently in line for publication.

For more information and release dates visit:
www.GoodnightPublishing.com

For inquiries about publication, contact:
info@GoodnightPublishing.com

Kris Tualla is an amusing, enthusiastic presenter and available for workshops and speaking engagements. Please contact her at any site listed below.

http://www.KrisTualla.com
http://kristualla.wordpress.com
http://www.facebook.com/KrisTualla
http://www.youtube.com/user/ktualla
http://twitter.com/ktualla

14770103R00193

Made in the USA
Lexington, KY
18 April 2012